PENGUIN CLASSICS

COMEDIES AND SATIRES

Edgar Allan Poe was born in Boston in 1809, the son of itinerant actors. Both his parents died within two years of his birth. Edgar was taken into the home of a Richmond merchant, John Allan, although he was never legally adopted. Poe's relationship with his foster-father was not good and was further strained when he was forced to withdraw from the University of Virginia because Allan refused to finance him. After a reconciliation, Poe entered the Military Academy at West Point in 1830; he was dishonourably discharged in January 1831. It was a deliberate action on Poe's part and again was largely due to Allan's tight-fistedness. His early work as a writer went unrecognized and he was forced to earn his living on newspapers, working as an editor in Richmond, Philadelphia and New York. He achieved respect as a literary critic but it was not until the publication of *The Raven and Other Poems* in 1845 that he gained success as a writer. And, despite his increasing fame, Poe remained in the same poverty which characterized most of his life. In 1836 he married his cousin, Virginia, who was then fourteen; she died eleven years later of tuberculosis.

Poe's life and personality have attracted almost as much attention as his writing, and he has been variously pictured as a sado-masochist, dipsomaniac, drug addict and manic depressive. There can be little doubt that Poe was a disturbed and tormented man, and like so many of his characters, often driven to the brink of madness. Writing of the effect of Virginia's death, Poe said: 'I became insane, with long intervals of horrible sanity. During these fits of absolute unconsciousness, I drank . . . my enemies referred the insanity to the drink, rather than the drink to the insanity.' Poe died a few years later in 1849 and was buried in Baltimore beside his wife.

•

David Galloway is Ordinarius Professor for American Studies at the Ruhr University in Bochum, Germany. His critical works include *The Absurd Hero*, *Henry James: The Portrait of a Lady*, and *Edward Lewis Wallant*; he is also the author of four novels – *Melody Jones*, *A Family Album*, *Lamaar Ransom: Private Eye* and *Lake Tahoe*. He has also edited the *Selected Writings of Edgar Allan Poe* for the Penguin Classics.

D1079782

Comedies and Satires

Edgar Allan Poe

*Edited with an introduction
by David Galloway*

PENGUIN BOOKS

PENGUIN BOOKS

Published by the Penguin Group
27 Wrights Lane, London w8 5tz, England
Viking Penguin Inc., 40 West 23rd Street, New York, New York 10010, USA
Penguin Books Australia Ltd, Ringwood, Victoria, Australia
Penguin Books Canada Ltd, 2801 John Street, Markham, Ontario, Canada l3r 1b4
Penguin Books (NZ) Ltd, 182–190 Wairau Road, Auckland 10, New Zealand

Penguin Books Ltd, Registered Offices: Harmondsworth, Middlesex, England

This collection first published as *The Other Poe* 1983
Reprinted in Penguin Classics as *Comedies and Satires* 1987
Reprinted 1988

Printed and bound in Great Britain by
Cox & Wyman Ltd, Reading
Filmset in Monophoto Photina by
Northumberland Press Ltd, Gateshead

Contents

Introduction

ON 15 June 1833 the proprietors of the *Baltimore Sunday Visitor*, 'feeling desirous of encouraging literature', announced prizes of $50 for the best tale and $25 for the best poem submitted to them before 1 October. Though the judges had appealed to 'writers throughout the country who are desirous of entering the lists', both prizes went to Baltimore residents: to John H. Hewitt's 'Song of the Winds' and Edgar A. Poe's gripping fantasy, 'MS. Found in a Bottle'. Later Poe would insist that the poetry award had been denied him only because the judges were unwilling to give a single writer first place in both categories; since the *Visitor* lost no time in publishing 'The Coliseum', his entry for the poetry competition, the claim may well have been justified.

'MS. Found in a Bottle' was not Poe's first published fiction; five tales had already appeared in a Philadelphia newspaper, but after a common practice of the time, all were printed anonymously. These, like the six stories submitted to the *Baltimore Sunday Visitor*, formed part of a larger, somewhat amorphous collection of burlesques entitled *Tales of the Folio Club*, in which the author spoofed the reigning literary fashions of his time. To the modern reader, Poe's name has become synonymous with the tale of terror and suspense, but even those classics acquire new dimensions when placed in the remarkably versatile context of his other writings. In mocking the formulas of popular periodicals, the young writer learned much about the craft of fiction – just as, with a more serious and 'elevated' tone, his early poetry made extensive use of romantic models. Inadvertently, Poe was also learning much about the expectations of contemporary audiences, and the lessons would serve him well in his career as an editor. But the

7

comic mode was not merely a phase in Poe's exuberant apprenticeship: comedies, satires and hoaxes account for more than half his total output of short stories, and the last of them, 'X-ing a Paragrab', appeared only a few months before the author's obscure death in 1849. Today, only the hoaxes are likely to be anthologized and collected; for that reason they are omitted from this volume, whose aim is to introduce the reader to 'the other Poe' – a writer whose comic vision was informed by a keen sense of pretence and 'puffery'. In tone, the best of his comic tales look back to the writings of Washington Irving, another pioneer of the American short story; and they often anticipate the achievements of Mark Twain, the greatest of all American humorists.

Viewed in this context, Poe appears far less exotic than in the dark, doomed, decadent image handed down by literary mythology and embraced with apostolic fervor by Rimbaud and Baudelaire. In these lesser-known writings we are repeatedly reminded that Edgar Allan Poe was a professional man of letters with an astute sense of the contemporary market. Whether he transformed Gothic conventions into slapstick or into symbolic explorations of the mind and soul of his agonized protagonists, his writings testify to an intense day-to-day involvement with the American literary scene. That scene was essentially provincial, and Poe was not immune to the petty quarrels of its self-proclaimed literati; imported models, like those canonized by *Blackwood's Edinburgh Magazine*, were accepted (and imitated) with pious seriousness. In letters, editorials, and such revenge tales as 'The Cask of Amontillado' and 'Hop-Frog', Poe grimly challenged the complacency of this establishment, but comedy also provided a useful weapon: with techniques that are sometimes reminiscent of Swift and Rabelais, social and literary vanities were turned topsy-turvy. Even the formulas of his own serious fiction – premature burial, detection, the ubiquitous plague – would be subjected to the corrective force of parody.

The passage of time has inevitably blunted the thrust of many of these works; their topical allusions are now archly obscure, and the stories fail to rise above them to silhouette more universal foibles. Furthermore, we can no longer treat seriously many of the modes which Poe burlesqued; indeed, the originals themselves often read like self-parodies. The first of Poe's published stories, 'Metzengerstein', lost the *Philadelphia Saturday Courier* fiction competition to a work entitled 'Love's Martyr', by Delia C. Bacon. Understandably, the fledgling author was offended at being bested by such sentimental melodrama, and satirizing the excesses of 'the tribe of female scribblers' seems a logical and understandable response; but where we are unable to treat the original seriously, the persiflage loses much of its sting. Similarly, attacks on the benighted editorial policies of particular (and often short-lived) magazines of the day can hardly bring sympathetic chuckles from later generations of readers – even those armed with copious footnotes. 'The Literary Life of Thingum Bob, Esq.' is perhaps an exception, for its real subject is the process by which the cultural establishment creates fashions, inflating some reputations and ruthlessly tomahawking others. Today, however, the story's involuted technique seems unnecessarily longwinded, and the vendettas of the literary world are more succinctly anatomized in 'Lionizing' and 'X-ing a Paragrab'. In the former story a colossal nose is sufficient to make the obscure Robert Jones a salon favorite; Poe borrowed the device for his preposterous fable from Laurence Sterne's *Tristram Shandy*, and may have recognized the implied bawdiness of the original, in which the nose as a sign of manly superiority is a euphemism for the penis. But it was above all the monstrously exaggerated literary reputation that provoked Poe's satiric reflex, together with the exaggerated show of erudition which he frequently parodied, but was all too prone to use for dressing up his own prose.

Poe came to speak of his early comedies as 'grotesques', thereby stressing the exaggerations of Gothic convention and elevated Yankee language on which most depended – though he once, somewhat confusingly, described them as 'arabesques'. Despite the author's persistent efforts to find a publisher, the tales never appeared in the single volume Poe had begun planning as early as 1833. His letters give the total number variously as eleven, sixteen, and seventeen, but the proposed frame narrative describes only eleven charter members of the Folio Club. Like Chaucer's pilgrims, each is to present a tale which reflects his own character, and presumably a prize would have been awarded for the most entertaining. The descriptions of the 'remarkable men' who compose this 'Junto of *Dunderheadism*' are worth quoting for what they reveal of the concept of this unpublished work:

> There was, first of all, Mr Snap, the President, who is a very lank man with a hawk nose, and was formerly in the service of the *Down-East Review*.
> Then there was Mr Convolvulus Gondola, a young gentleman who had travelled a good deal.
> Then there was De Rerum Naturâ, Esqr., who wore a very singular pair of green spectacles.
> Then there was a very little man in a black coat with very black eyes.
> Then there was Mr Solomon Seadrift who had every appearance of a fish.
> Then there was Mr Horribile Dictu, with white eyelashes, who had graduated at Göttingen.
> Then there was Mr Blackwood who had written certain articles for foreign magazines.
> Then there was the host, Mr Rouge-et-Noir, who admired Lady Morgan.
> Then there was a stout gentleman who admired Sir Walter Scott.
> Then there was Chronologos Chronology who admired Horace Smith, and had a very big nose which had been in Asia Minor . . .

Had a publisher been willing to sponsor the project, Poe might have modified somewhat the prankishness of this brief outline; certainly, the concept of a club of windy literary gentlemen belaboring the literary fashions of the day was not without promise, and the frame narrative might have provided *Tales of the Folio Club* with a substance that is lacking in many of the individual narrations.

Even where we have lost all direct awareness of Poe's allusions, his sheer exuberance of language and bizarre inventiveness can sometimes pull an old chestnut entertainingly from the fire – as in 'How to Write a *Blackwood* Article' and its accompanying cautionary tale, 'A Predicament'. Here Poe drew literally on 'The Man in the Bell', published by *Blackwood's* in 1830, which relates how a man climbs the belfry of a cathedral and is caught with his head in a narrow window of the clockface, until the minute hand decapitates him. 'A Predicament' gains its comic force, however, not from any specific knowledge of the original, and not even from the ludicrous poetics spelled out in the preceding essay, but from the bewitchingly addle-brained voice of the literary lady who narrates it. Accompanied by her faithful companions, Diana the poodle and Pompey the slave, she embarks on a quest for

the *very* disturbing influence of the serene, and godlike, and heavenly, and exalting, and elevated, and purifying effect of what may be rightly termed the most enviable, the most *truly* enviable – nay! the most benignly beautiful, the most deliciously ethereal, and, as it were, the most *pretty* (if I may use so bold an expression) *thing* (pardon me, gentle reader!) in the world . . .

At the end of her outing in Edinburgh, where *Blackwood's* was published, Senora Psyche Zenobia finds herself 'Dogless, niggerless, headless'. The poetic heroine refers to the clock hand relentlessly pressing against her neck as the *Scythe of Time* (a phrase which provided the title for the story's first publication in 1838), and despite the absurdity of her predicament, Poe's fans will recognize an immediate parallel to a tale published four years later – namely, 'The Pit and the Pendulum'. As the clock hand descends, Zenobia notes, 'I threw up my hands and endeavored, with all my strength, to force upward the ponderous iron bar.' The nameless narrator of 'The Pit and the Pendulum' relates, 'I grew frantically mad, and struggled to force myself upward against the sweep of the fearful scimitar.' The parallels in language, the repetitions which build toward hysterical effect, underscore the cousinage of the two tales. 'Down, down, down it came,' Zenobia thrills, 'closer and yet closer . . . Down and still down it came.' The victim of the fiendish tortures of the Inquisition borrows her breathless tone: 'Down – steadily down it crept . . . Down – certainly, relentlessly down . . . Down – still unceasingly – still inevitably down.' And when these improbably parallel narrators realize the hopelessness of their positions, both experience brief but transcendent moments of euphoria in the face of death.

'A Predicament' and 'The Pit and the Pendulum' offer an important clue to Poe's method: starting with a pre-existent pattern borrowed from a contemporary periodical, he first makes it his own through the inversions of comedy, calculatedly exaggerating the superficial elements of narrative; later, when his own mastery of the pattern is established, the transformation is achieved by concentrating on the interior, psychological implications of plot. In 'King Pest', for example, Poe composed a grotesque farce based on an episode entitled 'The Palace of Wines' from Benjamin Disraeli's *Vivian Grey*. In Poe's version, a pair of sailors carouse through the waterfront pubs of fourteenth-century London; unwittingly, they cross a barrier that cordons off the diseased area of the city and there, in an undertaker's establishment, encounter King Pest and the royal family drinking wine from human skulls. Though the seamen eventually best their murderous host and escape with two ladies of the court, the story's darker elements cannot be overlooked. The vivid descriptions of pestilence certainly owed a debt to the observations Poe made during the cholera epidemic that ravaged Baltimore in 1831, and they anticipate his later treatment of physical disease and mortal decay as an indication of man's spiritual condition. Crossing the barrier between the known and the unknown, between sanity and madness, the waking life and the dream, would also become a powerful physical symbol in the serious writings, as it is in the apocalyptic vision of *The Narrative of Arthur Gordon Pym*. The closest and most telling parallel to 'King Pest', however, is 'The Masque of the Red Death', which Poe published eight years later; here a nobleman barricades himself and his friends in a magnificent, castellated abbey to escape the plague, only to find the sinister figure of the Red Death awaiting them there.

Such transformations and re-transformations of narrative premises are typical of Poe; individual stories, too, were reworked for subsequent publication, occasionally retitled, and some were fundamentally altered in tone. Collections (and proposed collections) of both verse and prose were continuously reshuffled, recycled and revised. As his own confidence and his reputation grew, he would even mock his own most cherished fictional devices. In 'The Unparalleled Adventure of One Hans Pfall' (1835) Poe had spoofed the sensationalist, pseudo-scientific accounts of space travel then so much in vogue, but his imaginative descriptions of a bankrupt's voyage to the moon were so plausible that they inevitably gave the vogue new impetus. In 1844 Poe trumped his competitors with 'The Balloon Hoax', whose appearance in New York's first penny newspaper as an historic 'Extra' caused the offices of the *Sun* to be mobbed by curiosity-seekers. Having established his own mastery of the form, he once more inverted it in the punning parody of 'Mellonta Tauta' (1849).

Similarly, with 'The Murders in the Rue Morgue' (1841) Edgar Allan Poe staked his claim as originator of the modern detective story; numerous authors, including Voltaire, had written crime-solving stories, but it was Poe who created the figure of the eccentric, ratiocinative private detective who perceives the pattern in a series of apparently unrelated facts and events. Poe borrowed the name of his master detective, C. Auguste Dupin, from the heroine, Marie Dupin, of an episode in the 'Unpublished Passages in the Life of Vidocq, the French Minister of Police'. In this fictionalized memoir of a real detective (who is casually referred to in 'The Murders in the Rue Morgue'), the narrator remains outside the main events, and his solution of a crime is likely to be a matter of *felix culpa*. After ingeniously transforming the suggestions he found in Vidocq, Poe applied Dupin's skills to the solution of an actual murder in 'The Mystery of Marie Rogêt' (1842), then burlesqued his own creation in 'Thou Art the Man' (1844). The latter is not only a detective story without a detective, but one in which both the crime and its solution are treated farcically. For aficionados of detective fiction, to be sure, another classic device emerges here: the prime suspect, saved from the gallows at the last minute, is a scoundrel, while the true murderer is a man of seemingly unimpeachable probity. The total effect, however, remains one of broad and rather vulgar burlesque.

Though the numerous tales dealing with that subject have led some critics to label Poe as morbid, the fear of being buried alive was commonplace in his time; charnel houses were equipped with alarm systems so that the 'dead' could signal for help, and luxury coffins were fitted with ventilators and speaking tubes. Both factual and fictional accounts of premature burial were a journalistic staple of the nineteenth century, and Poe incorporated the motif in numerous short stories, of which 'The

Fall of the House of Usher' (1839) proved the most celebrated and influential. He had, however, first used the motif in one of the projected *Tales of the Folio Club*. Under the original title of 'A Decided Loss', the story related the misadventures of a man who, soon after his wedding, literally loses his breath while vilifying his wife (the sort of perverse quarrel that leads to murder in 'The Black Cat'). Searching for his lost breath, the narrator, Mr Lackobreath, discovers love-letters to his wife from their neighbor, Mr Windenough; this, together with his 'pulmonary incapacity', persuades him to seek the refuge of a 'foreign climate'. After being crushed by a fat fellow-traveler, he is taken for dead and flung from the coach, breaking his arms and his skull; the surgeon and the apothecary who attend him pronounce him dead in spite of his guttural protests, rob him and remove various parts of his body for their experiments. Trussed and gagged and stored in an attic, the narrator is so alarmed when two cats begin eating his nose that he springs from the window and into a hangman's cart on its way to the gallows. The convicted man escapes, and Mr Lackobreath is hanged in his stead, but later leaves his coffin and retrieves his breath from the neighbor who had accidentally caught it. Poe subtitled his caprice 'A Tale Neither In Nor Out of *Blackwood*', and the Scottish publication had, indeed, specified the requisite pattern: 'the record of a gentleman's sensations when entombed before the *breath* was out of his body'. Poe subsequently revised the story, adding a long description of the sensations of a man being hanged, and generously peppering the whole with obscure literary allusions; he also changed the title to 'Loss of Breath'.

Five years after the publication of 'The Fall of the House of Usher', Poe once more spoofed the motif of 'The Premature Burial', in a story of that title which appeared in the *Philadelphia Dollar Newspaper* in 1844. Beginning with a series of allegedly factual accounts intended to establish the credibility of his own experience, the cataleptic narrator describes awakening in a coffin, his jaws bound shut, feeling the wooden lid a few inches above his head and smelling freshly turned earth. His screams bring to his bedside the gruff crew of the sloop on which he is sailing: the coffin is a wooden berth, the cerements binding his jaws a silk scarf, the smell of moist earth comes from the ship's cargo. What begins as a tale of terror ends as a comedy of errors, and both elements will figure prominently in Poe's next treatment of the theme – 'The Cask of Amontillado'.

The problem of identity is another motif which threads through Poe's classic tales, in which dead wives take possession of their husbands' brides, brothers and sisters share a single spirit, and sinister *Doppelgänger* warn of the consequences of dividing moral and physical existence. We know that the concept of the multiple nature of self was one of intense personal concern to Poe: he endowed the tormented hero of 'William Wilson' (1840) not only with his own birthdate, but with numerous details of his own childhood and youth. A comic equivalent to the crisis of identity is the story of mistaken identity, which provided the central mechanism for 'The Spectacles' (1843), where a near-sighted young man falls hopelessly in love with his own great-great-grandmother. In a fragment of song ('Ninon, Ninon, Ninon, à bas ...'), Poe alludes to his source in the remarkable life of Ninon de l'Enclos (1615–1705); celebrated for her extraordinary beauty, intelligence and wit, even at the age of seventy she was said to have a numerous entourage of lovers. Her son by the Marquis de Gersai was never told of his mother's identity, and she was over sixty when he was presented to her salon and instantly fell in love with his brilliant hostess. Intrigued and no doubt flattered by the remarkable coincidence, Ninon delayed telling the young man about his origin, but her rejection of his amorous advances drove him to suicide. To exaggerate the comic effect, and perhaps to distance somewhat the problem of incestuous love touching his own life, Poe made his heroine the narrator's great-great-grandmother. Eugénie Lalande is a bald, wrinkled, toothless woman of eighty-two who retains her brilliant air through the 'art' of make-up and pretends to accept her suitor's proposal of marriage in order to punish him for his refusal to wear spectacles. Vanity is thus the central target of Poe's story; the fashionable ruses of wigs and make-up, false teeth and flounces are another; the romantic fantasy of 'love at first sight' sets the plot in motion, and it climaxes in a burlesque of the complex inter-relationships of Europe's noble families. Nonetheless, the familiar problem of identity is central to the tale – as it is to 'The Man that was Used Up', in which wigs and prosthetic devices also play a crucial role in establishing a 'counterfeit' identity.

'The Man that was Used Up' is one of the most complex and intriguing of Poe's comic ventures; we know from its publishing history how highly the author himself regarded it. The story appeared first in *Burton's Gentleman's Magazine* in 1839, soon after Poe assumed an editorial position with the influential periodical. In 1842 he outlined a new, two-volume edition of his tales to be entitled *Phantasy Pieces*, with 'The Murders in the Rue Morgue' and 'The Man that was Used Up' heading the table of contents. Lee and Blanchard, publishers of *Tales of the Grotesque and Arabesque*, promptly rejected the proposal, but Poe stuck by the concept, and in 1843 a Philadelphia publishing house released a slender pamphlet entitled *The Prose Romances of Edgar A. Poe*, with a title page hopefully proclaiming it the first of a 'Uniform Serial Edition'. The two stories included, both substantially revised, were 'The Murders in the Rue Morgue' and 'The Man that was Used Up'; to the latter Poe had added a motto from Corneille. Despite the relatively modest price of $12\frac{1}{2}$ cents, the pamphlet was not a success, and the uniform serial edition went no farther. Later, as editor of the *Broadway Journal*, when Poe was particularly anxious to establish his literary image in New York, he again reprinted the tale; interestingly, of the nineteen stories appearing there in 1845, twelve were comedies.

With this black farce of military hero-worship, Poe literally offers us a man used up in the service of his country, though the splendid public image of Brevet Brigadier-General A. B. C. Smith is unimpaired:

His head of hair would have done honor to a Brutus; nothing could be more richly flowing, or possess a brighter gloss. It was of a jetty black; – which was also the color ... of his unimaginable whiskers. You perceive I cannot speak of these latter without enthusiasm; it is not too much to say that they were the handsomest pair of whiskers under the sun. At all events, they encircled, and at times partially overshadowed, a mouth utterly unequalled. Here were the most entirely even, and the most brilliantly white of all conceivable teeth. From between them, upon every proper occasion, issued a voice of surpassing clearness, melody and strength. In the matter of eyes, also, my acquaintance was pre-eminently endowed. Either one of such a pair was worth a couple of the ordinary ocular organs. They were of a deep hazel, exceedingly large and lustrous; and there was perceptible about them, ever and anon, just that amount of interesting obliquity which gives pregnancy to expression.

Poe's narrator goes on to extol the General's dignified manner and his 'luminous' conversation, rich with praise for the marvels of the modern age: ' "Parachutes and railroads – man-traps and spring-guns!" ' But attempts to learn from his acquaintances the sources of General Smith's fame are greeted only with rapturous clichés: celebrity is its own excuse for being. The curious narrator thus determines to interview the great man himself, and when he pays his call is ushered into the bedroom by an ancient Negro valet. There he finds 'a large and exceedingly odd-looking bundle of something' lying at his feet; when he gives it an irritable kick, the bundle responds 'in one of the smallest, and altogether the funniest little voices, between a squeak and a whistle, that I ever heard in all the days of my existence'. This grotesque lump is the General himself, and the narrator watches in speechless astonishment as his valet assembles the dashing military figure – with the aid of a cork leg and arm, false bosom and shoulders, a wig, false teeth and palate and a glass eye.

In the story's subtitle, 'A Tale of the Late Bugaboo and Kickapoo Campaign', Poe was perhaps playing on General William Henry Harrison's presidential campaign slogan: 'Tippecanoe and Tyler Too'. He was sympathetic to Harrison's candidacy, but distrustful of America's unquestioning reverence for military heroes. Similarly, though intrigued by scientific and technical progress, Poe presented military technology in an absurd light – together with the General's incessant chauvinistic claims for the superiority of American-made prosthetic devices. The grotesque elements of the story establish an important antecedent for the darker, more perverse humor of Mark Twain – as in the macabre sketch of 'Those Extraordinary Twins' which provided the germ for *Puddin'head Wilson*; and Twain would come to share Poe's skepticism about technological progress. 'The Man that was Used Up' also has links with the writings of Stephen Crane and Frank Norris; with 'The Book of the Grotesque' which prefaces Sherwood Anderson's *Winesburg, Ohio*; with the cripples who people the novels of Nathanael West; with such mechanized figures as Popeye in William Faulkner's *Sanctuary*; with the hospital episodes in Joseph Heller's *Catch-22*; and with the savage anatomical passages in Thomas Pynchon's *V*.

The story succeeds because it rises above topical allusions and concerns to stress their more universal dimensions: the nature of fame, the relationship between man and the machine, the vagaries of appearance and reality. Quite separate and apart from the reference of the subtitle, which Poe added later, 'The Man that was Used Up' is pre-eminently a political cautionary tale. As such, it is far more persuasive than the elaborate historical parody of 'Mellonta Tauta', in which another of Poe's scribbling heroines takes a futuristic balloon flight over the 'Amriccan' continent and comments on the obscure history of its former inhabitants. Poe repeatedly made clear his distrust of the democratic mob, underscored man's inability to learn from the lessons of history, and deplored the conformity of his fellow-citizens. 'Mellonta Tauta' reiterates those points in a cumbersome, self-conscious fashion that is brightened only by the comic voice of the voyaging Pundita, with its ebullient mixture of trivia, fractured history and malapropisms. As a political parable with the central, punning metaphor of 'revolution', 'The Devil in the Belfry' is more successful, despite its allegorical mannerisms.

Poe's acute sense for the grotesque and the perverse, which informed some of his most chilling narratives, suggested a virtually limitless range of comic themes: the sentimental rituals of courtship in 'Why the Little Frenchman Wears his Arm in a Sling' and 'The Spectacles'; the free-wheeling, self-made entrepreneur in 'The Business Man' and 'Diddling Considered as One of the Exact Sciences'; biblical history and religious bigotry in 'A Tale of Jerusalem'; supernatural visitations in 'The Devil in the Belfry', 'Never Bet the Devil Your Head', and 'The Angel of the Odd'. But his most recurrent themes were politics and philosophy, literary fashions and foibles, science and pseudo-science. All were drawn together in 'The System of Doctor Tarr and Professor Fether', where the inmates of a French asylum take advantage of the liberties permitted by the new 'soothing system' to overpower and confine their keepers. When the narrator, intrigued by the humanistic advances of modern medicine, visits the establishment, the roles of the director and his family are played by the inmates. They have, they claim, found the soothing method impracticable, and have once more caused their patients to be locked away. During a drunken, tumultuous dinner, their descriptions of the patients' maladies grow increasingly animated, until it becomes clear the eccentricities they describe are their own. Allusions to the excesses of the French Revolution are frequent, as are those to the slavocracy of the Southern states. The new, permissive 'system of soothing', which provides the dramatic impulse for the story, was personally familiar to Poe: he had met Dr Pliny Earle, who served as resident physician for institutions in Frankford, Pennsylvania, and Bloomington, New York, that promoted a so-called 'Moral Treatment' of the insane. The results had so favorably impressed Charles Dickens on his American tour of 1842 that it may well have provided a topic of conversation when he met with Poe in Philadelphia. In that case, even if Poe was unfamiliar with the euphoric description of such treatments in Dickens's *American Notes*, he may well have been parodying Dickensian heartiness. At the core of the tale, however, rest sober and sobering reflections on the fine line dividing madness and sanity, and the speed with which the roles can be interchanged in a world governed by appearances. It is a lunatic who delivers the story's most disturbing moral:

There is no accounting for the caprices of madmen; and, in my opinion, as well as in that of Doctor Tarr and Professor Fether, it is *never* safe to permit them to run at large unattended. A lunatic may be 'soothed', as it is called, for a time, but, in the end, he is very apt to become obstreperous. His cunning, too, is proverbial, and great. If he has a project in view, he conceals his design with a marvellous wisdom; and the dexterity with which he counterfeits sanity presents, to the metaphysician, one of the most singular problems in the study of mind. When a madman appears *thoroughly* sane, indeed, it is high time to put him in a strait-jacket.

Even if we radically discount (as we must) the sensationalist legends of Poe's own mental instability, it is clear that the subject treated in 'The System of Doctor Tarr and Professor Fether' was of intense personal concern to its author. In a remarkably candid letter written to an admirer in 1848, he sought to analyze the sources of his own instability, citing as a primary cause the recurrent illnesses preceding the death of his young wife Virginia Clemm. With each of her painful collapses, he wrote.

I felt all the agonies of her death – and at each accession of the disorder I loved her more dearly and clung to her life with desperate pertinacity. But I am constitutionally sensitive – nervous in a very unusual degree. I became insane, with long intervals of horrible sanity. During these fits of absolute unconsciousness, I drank – God only knows how often or how much. As a matter of course, my enemies referred the insanity to the drink, rather than the drink to the insanity.

Even a man of hardier temperament might well have been plunged into depressions by the illnesses and deaths, frustrations and reversals that punctuated Edgar Allan Poe's brief life. Numerous commentators have suggested that art itself was the therapy with which Poe held absolute insanity at bay; some claim he invented the detective story in order to keep from going mad. Such arguments often seem inspired by the glamorous and tragic image of Poe given such lustrous patina by the Decadents, though it is unimpeachably true that many of the recurrent themes of Poe's art sprang directly from his own private agonies. Yet it is not merely in his tales of doomed brides, sinister chambers and obsessive geniuses that he struggled to come to terms with subjective griefs and fears; the cleansing, distancing power of laughter also frequently came to his aid. Alcoholism and insanity, the subjects of the letter quoted above, are frequent elements in the comedies, and the raucous fantasies of 'The Angel of the Odd' deal with delirium tremens. Incest, too, is a theme of the grotesques: the hero of 'The Spectacles' is deflected from marrying his great-great-grandmother, but does marry his own distant, youthful cousin.

The potential therapeutic function of the comic writings becomes clear when we consider the period of Poe's life when he began to compose them – in the early 1830s, when he had sabotaged his West Point commission and gone to live with his impoverished aunt in Baltimore. He was then twenty-two years of age and had published three volumes of poetry; though he declared himself 'irrecoverably a poet', it was clear to him that he could not make a living at his craft. That awareness may well account for the intensity with which he sought a reconciliation with his wealthy foster father, John Allan. The young man's letters are in turn abject, pleading, and accusing; one of the last concludes with the lines,

... I am perishing – absolutely perishing for want of aid. And yet I am not idle – nor addicted to any vice – nor have I committed any offence against society which would render me deserving of so hard a fate. For God's sake pity me, and save me from destruction.

Even when Allan responded to Poe's most urgent and humiliating appeal for financial assistance, he did so after more than a month's delay. That the poet began to write prose in this period is certainly no coincidence; then, as now, the writer of fiction stood a better chance of supporting himself, and Poe could not have been insensible to the implications of the announcement in the *Baltimore Sunday Visitor* offering 'a premium of 50 dollars for the best Tale and 25 dollars for the best Poem'.

There were better days to come, yet Poe never distanced himself for long from the demons of poverty. Even as an indefatigable and highly successful magazine editor, he was rarely free from financial worries, for the considerable profits he turned went to his employers. During the two years he edited the *Southern Literary Messenger* its circulation increased from 500 to 3,500, while his salary scarcely inched beyond the ten dollars a week, plus occasional extras, at which he had been hired. Poe's work for *Graham's* produced even more dramatic results: the magazine's profits during the first year of his editorship were $25,000, but Poe never received more than $800 a year. It is hardly surprising that the editor often clashed with the publisher, or that in 'The Business Man' a boy is fired for including a two-cent paper dickey on his expense account when he might have cut four from a single sheet of foolscap. Still, Poe's accounts of the fiddling and diddling of the business world are remarkably good-humored, and the real scamps are the Huck-Finnish narrators themselves.

If Poe's 'youthful *dadas*', as Baudelaire indulgently termed them, were a kind of therapy, these first ventures in prose also marked the beginnings of an intensive fictional apprenticeship: through it he not only mastered popular idioms but developed such devices as the unreliable narrator. Yet even the author's greatest devotees have frequently ignored these accomplishments. Arthur Hobson Quinn's definitive critical biography disposes of most of the comic works with a single phrase; of the revisions to 'The Man that was Used Up' he notes, 'It has fifteen corrections of the 1840 text, but the trivial nature of the story makes any comparison superfluous.' The reader who ignores these works, comprising more than half of Poe's fictional efforts, not only risks a distorted view of the author's achievements; he loses important insights into some of Poe's most 'classic' tales. Sometimes with venom, sometimes with burlesque, and sometimes with libel actions, Edgar Allan Poe dueled with contemporary critics, and the celebrated revenge thriller, 'The Cask of Amontillado', is often thought to encapsulate his sense of literary injury. Wearing jester's motley and bells, the foolish victim is lured to his death by his lust for wine, then walled up alive by the vengeful Fortunato; the figure of the clown, alcoholism and premature burial had all been extensively examined in the comic tales that precede 'The Cask of Amontillado', and it too is a kind of savage comedy in which the victim dies laughing at the 'excellent jest' his host has played, and the host is never apprehended for his crime. The story was a turning-point for Poe, a reversal of the murder-will-out premise of 'The Tell-Tale Heart' and 'The Black Cat'. The triumph of revenge is also the theme of Poe's last published story, 'Hop-Frog', in which a dwarf in motley and bells repays a monarch's cruelty with a joke that costs the king and his ministers their lives. In such stories the comic is established as an integral part of Poe's fictional achievement; it is one too long neglected as a major aspect of his remarkable, multi-valenced talent.

David Galloway

Note on the Text

During his lifetime Poe continuously revised and reprinted individual works, and even what are usually taken for definitive versions are heavily amended with marginal notes. This edition does not attempt to collate the numerous textual variations in the comic tales, but the notes at the end of the volume indicate the important stages of their publishing history. With a single exception, I have relied on the Scribner's edition of *The Works of Edgar Allan Poe* (New York, 1914); the text of 'The Man that was Used Up' is taken from *The Complete Tales and Poems of Edgar Allan Poe* (Random House, New York, 1938). The tales are arranged in the chronology of their first publication.

D.G.

Lionizing

... all people went
Upon their ten toes in wild wonderment.[1]
BISHOP HALL, *Satires*

I AM – that is to say, I *was* – a great man; but I am neither
the author of Junius[2] nor the man in the mask;[3] for my name,
I believe, is Robert Jones, and I was born somewhere in the
city of Fum-Fudge.

The first action of my life was the taking hold of my nose
with both hands. My mother saw this and called me a genius;
my father wept for joy and presented me with a treatise on
Nosology.[4] This I mastered before I was breeched.

I now began to feel my way in the science, and soon came
to understand that, provided a man had a nose sufficiently conspicuous, he might, by merely following it, arrive at a Lionship.
But my attention was not confined to theories alone. Every morning I gave my proboscis a couple of pulls and swallowed a
half-dozen of drams.

When I came of age my father asked me, one day, if I would
step with him into his study.

'My son,' said he, when we were seated, 'what is the chief
end of your existence?'

'My father,' I answered, 'it is the study of Nosology.'

'And what, Robert,' he inquired, 'is Nosology?'

'Sir,' I said, 'it is the Science of Noses.'

'And can you tell me,' he demanded, 'what is the meaning
of a nose?'

'A nose, my father,' I replied, greatly softened, 'has been
variously defined by about a thousand different authors.' (Here
I pulled out my watch.) 'It is now noon or thereabouts –
we shall have time enough to get through with them all
before midnight. To commence then: – the nose, according to

Bartholinus,[5] is that protuberance – that bump – that excrescence – that –'

'Will do, Robert,' interrupted the good old gentleman. 'I am thunderstruck at the extent of your information – I am positively – upon my soul.' (Here he closed his eyes and placed his hand upon his heart.) 'Come here!' (Here he took me by the arm.) 'Your education may now be considered as finished – it is high time you should scuffle for yourself – and you cannot do a better thing than merely follow your nose – so – so – so –' (here he kicked me downstairs and out of the door) – 'so get out of my house, and God bless you!'

As I felt within me the divine *afflatus*, I considered this accident rather fortunate than otherwise. I resolved to be guided by the paternal advice. I determined to follow my nose. I gave it a pull or two upon the spot, and wrote a pamphlet on Nosology forthwith.

All Fum-Fudge was in an uproar.

'Wonderful genius!' said the *Quarterly*.[6]

'Superb physiologist!' said the *Westminster*.

'Clever fellow!' said the *Foreign*.

'Fine writer!' said the *Edinburgh*.

'Profound thinker!' said the *Dublin*.

'Great man!' said Bentley.

'Divine soul!' said Fraser.

'One of us!' said Blackwood.

'Who can he be?' said Mrs Bas-Bleu.

'What can he be?' said big Miss Bas-Bleu.

'Where can he be?' said little Miss Bas-Bleu. – But I paid these people no attention whatever – I just stepped into the shop of an artist.

The Duchess of Bless-my-Soul was sitting for her portrait; the Marquis of So-and-So was holding the Duchess's poodle; the Earl of This-and-That was flirting with her salts; and His Royal Highness of Touch-me-Not was leaning upon the back of her chair.

I approached the artist and turned up my nose.

'Oh, beautiful!' sighed her Grace.

'Oh my!' lisped the Marquis.

'Oh, shocking!' groaned the Earl.

'Oh, abominable!' growled His Royal Highness.

'What will you take for it?' asked the artist.

'For his *nose*!' shouted her Grace.

'A thousand pounds,' said I, sitting down.

'A thousand pounds?' inquired the artist, musingly.

'A thousand pounds,' said I.

'Beautiful!' said he, entranced.

'A thousand pounds,' said I.

'Do you warrant it?' he asked, turning the nose to the light.

'I do,' said I, blowing it well.

'Is it *quite* original?' he inquired, touching it with reverence.

'Humph!' said I, twisting it to one side.

'Has *no* copy been taken?' he demanded, surveying it through a microscope.

'None,' said I, turning it up.

'*Admirable!*' he ejaculated, thrown quite off his guard by the beauty of the manoeuvre.

'A thousand pounds,' said I.

'A *thousand* pounds,' said he.

'Precisely,' said I.

'A thousand *pounds?*' said he.

'Just so,' said I.

'You shall have them,' said he. 'What a piece of *virtù!*' So he drew me a check upon the spot, and took a sketch of my nose. I engaged rooms in Jermyn Street,[7] and sent Her Majesty[8] the ninety-ninth edition of the 'Nosology', with a portrait of the proboscis.

That sad little rake, the Prince of Wales,[9] invited me to dinner.

We were all lions and *recherchés*.

There was a modern Platonist.[10] He quoted Porphyry, Iamblichus, Plotinus, Proclus, Hierocles, Maximus Tyrius, and Syrianus.

There was a human-perfectibility man. He quoted Turgot, Price, Priestley, Condorcet, De Staël,[11] and the 'Ambitious Student in Ill Health'.

There was Sir Positive Paradox. He observed that all fools were philosophers, and that all philosophers were fools.

There was Aestheticus Ethix. He spoke of fire, unity, and atoms;

bi-part and pre-existent soul; affinity and discord; primitive intelligence and homoömeria.[12]

There was Theologos Theology. He talked of Eusebius and Arius; heresy and the Council of Nice; Puseyism[13] and consubstantialism; Homoousion and Homooiousion.[14]

There was Fricassée from the Rocher de Cancale.[15] He mentioned Muriton of red tongue; cauliflowers with *velouté* sauce; veal *à la St Menehoult*; marinade *à la St Florentin*; and orange jellies *en mosaïque*.

There was Bibulus O'Bumper. He touched upon Latour and Marcobrünnen; upon Mousseux and Chambertin; upon Richebourg and St George; upon Haubrion, Léonville, and Médoc; upon Barac and Preignac; upon Graves, upon Sauterne, upon Lafitte, and upon St Peray. He shook his head at Clos de Vougeot, and told, with his eyes shut, the difference between Sherry and Amontillado.

There was Signor Tintontintino from Florence. He discoursed of Cimabue, Arpino, Carpaccio, and Agostino – of the gloom of Caravaggio, of the amenity of Albani, of the colors of Titian, of the vrouws of Rubens, and of the waggeries of Jan Steen.

There was the President of the Fum-Fudge University. He was of opinion that the moon was called Bendis in Thrace, Bubastis in Egypt, Dian in Rome, and Artemis in Greece.

There was a Grand Turk from Stamboul. He could not help thinking that the angels were horses, cocks, and bulls; that somebody in the sixth heaven had seventy thousand heads; and that the earth was supported by a sky-blue cow with an incalculable number of green horns.

There was Delphinus Polyglott. He told us what had become of the eighty-three lost tragedies of Aeschylus; of the fifty-four orations of Isaeus; of the three hundred and ninety-one speeches of Lysias; of the hundred and eighty treatises of Theophrastus; of the eighth book of the conic sections of Apollonius; of Pindar's hymns and dithyrambics; and of the five and forty tragedies of Homer Junior.[16]

There was Ferdinand Fitz-Fossillus Feldspar. He informed us all about internal fires and tertiary formations; about aeriforms, fluidforms, and solidiforms; about quartz and marl; about schist and schorl; about gypsum and trap; about talc and calc; about blende and hornblende; about mica-slate and pudding-stone; about cyanite and lepidolite; about haematite and tremolite; about antimony and chalcedony; about manganese and whatever you please.

There was myself. I spoke of myself; – of myself, of myself, of myself; – of Nosology, of my pamphlet, and of myself. I turned up my nose, and spoke of myself.

'Marvellous clever man!' said the Prince.

'Superb!' said his guests; and next morning her Grace of Bless-my-Soul paid me a visit.

'Will you go to Almack's,[17] pretty creature?' she said, tapping me under the chin.

'Upon honor,' said I.

'Nose and all?' she asked.

'As I live,' I replied.

'Here then is a card, my life. Shall I say you *will* be there?'

'Dear Duchess, with all my heart.'

'Pshaw, no! – but with all your nose?'

'Every bit of it, my love,' said I; so I gave it a twist or two, and found myself at Almack's.

The rooms were crowded to suffocation.

'He is coming!' said somebody on the staircase.

'He is coming!' said somebody farther up.

'He is coming!' said somebody farther still.

'He is come!' exclaimed the Duchess. 'He is come, the little love!' – and, seizing me firmly by both hands, she kissed me thrice upon the nose.

A marked sensation immediately ensued.

'*Diavolo!*' cried Count Capricornutti.

'*Dios guarda!*' muttered Don Stiletto.

'*Mille tonnerres!*' ejaculated the Prince de Grenouille.

'*Tausend Teufel!*' growled the Elector of Bluddennuff.

It was not to be borne. I grew angry. I turned short upon Bluddennuff.

'Sir!' said I to him, 'you are a baboon.'

'Sir,' he replied, after a pause, '*Donner und Blitzen!*'

This was all that could be desired. We exchanged cards. At

Chalk Farm,[18] the next morning, I shot off his nose – and then called upon my friends.

'*Bête!*' said the first.

'Fool!' said the second.

'Dolt!' said the third.

'Ass!' said the fourth.

'Ninny!' said the fifth.

'Noodle!' said the sixth.

'Be off!' said the seventh.

At all this I felt mortified, and so called upon my father.

'Father,' I asked, 'what is the chief end of my existence?'

'My son,' he replied, 'it is still the study of Nosology; but in hitting the Elector upon the nose you have overshot your mark. You have a fine nose, it is true; but then Bluddennuff has none. You are damned, and he has become the hero of the day. I grant you that in Fum-Fudge the greatness of a lion is in proportion to the size of his proboscis – but, good heavens! there is no competing with a lion who has no proboscis at all.'

Loss of Breath

A Tale Neither In Nor Out of *Blackwood*

Oh, breathe not, etc. –
MOORE. *Melodies*[1]

THE most notorious ill-fortune must in the end yield to the untiring courage of philosophy, as the most stubborn city to the ceaseless vigilance of an enemy. Salmanezer, as we have it in the holy writings, lay three years before Samaria; yet it fell. Sardanapalus – see Diodorus – maintained himself seven in Nineveh; but to no purpose. Troy expired at the close of the second lustrum; and Azotus, as Aristaeus declares upon his honor as a gentleman, opened at last her gates to Psammitichus, after having barred them for the fifth part of a century.[2]

'Thou wretch! – thou vixen! – thou shrew!' said I to my wife on the morning after our wedding, 'thou witch! – thou hag! – thou whipper-snapper! – thou sink of iniquity! – thou fiery-faced quintessence of all that is abominable! – thou – thou –' here standing upon tiptoe, seizing her by the throat, and placing my mouth close to her ear, I. was preparing to launch forth a new and more decided epithet of opprobrium, which should not fail, if ejaculated, to convince her of her insignificance, when, to my extreme horror and astonishment, I discovered that *I had lost my breath.*

The phrases 'I am out of breath', 'I have lost my breath', etc., are often enough repeated in common conversation; but it had never occurred to me that the terrible accident of which I speak could *bona fide* and actually happen! Imagine – that is if you have a fanciful turn – imagine, I say, my wonder, my consternation, my despair!

There is a good genius, however, which has never entirely deserted me. In my most ungovernable moods I still retain a sense of propriety, *et le chemin des passions me conduit* – as Lord

Edouard in the *Julie* says it did him – *à la philosophie véritable.*[3]

Although I could not at first precisely ascertain to what degree the occurrence had affected me, I determined at all events to conceal the matter from my wife, until further experience should discover to me the extent of this my unheard of calamity. Altering my countenance, therefore, in a moment, from its bepuffed and distorted appearance to an expression of arch and coquettish benignity, I gave my lady a pat on the cheek, and a kiss on the other, and without saying one syllable (Furies! I could not), left her astonished at my drollery, as I pirouetted out of the room in a *pas de zéphyr.*

Behold me then safely ensconced in my private boudoir, a fearful instance of the ill consequences attending upon irascibility; alive, with the qualifications of the dead; dead, with the propensities of the living; an anomaly on the face of the earth – being very calm, yet breathless.

Yes! breathless. I am serious in asserting that my breath was entirely gone. I could not have stirred with it a feather if my life had been at issue, or sullied even the delicacy of a mirror. Hard fate! – yet there was some alleviation to the first overwhelming paroxysm of my sorrow. I found, upon trial, that the powers of utterance, which, upon my inability to proceed in the conversation with my wife, I then concluded to be totally destroyed, were in fact only partially impeded, and I discovered that, had I at that interesting crisis dropped my voice to a singularly deep guttural,[4] I might still have continued to her the communication of my sentiments; this pitch of voice (the guttural) depending, I find, not upon the current of the breath, but upon a certain spasmodic action of the muscles of the throat.[5]

Throwing myself upon a chair, I remained for some time absorbed in meditation. My reflections, be sure, were of no consolatory kind. A thousand vague and lachrymatory fancies took possession of my soul, and even the idea of suicide flitted across my brain; but it is a trait in the perversity of human nature to reject the obvious and the ready for the far-distant and equivocal. Thus I shuddered at self-murder as the most decided of atrocities, while the tabby cat purred strenuously upon the rug, and the very water-dog wheezed assiduously under the table; each taking to itself much merit for the strength of its lungs, and all obviously done in derision of my own pulmonary incapacity.

Oppressed with a tumult of vague hopes and fears, I at length heard the footsteps of my wife descending the staircase. Being now assured of her absence, I returned with a palpitating heart to the scene of my disaster.

Carefully locking the door on the inside, I commenced a vigorous search. It was possible, I thought, that, concealed in some obscure corner, or lurking in some closet or drawer, might be found the lost object of my inquiry. It might have a vapory – it might even have a tangible form. Most philosophers, upon many points of philosophy, are still very unphilosophical. William Godwin, however, says in his *Mandeville* that 'invisible things are the only realities', and this all will allow is a case in point.[6] I would have the judicious reader pause before accusing such asseverations of an undue quantum of absurdity. Anaxagoras, it will be remembered, maintained that snow is black,[7] and this I have since found to be the case.

Long and earnestly did I continue the investigation; but the contemptible reward of my industry and perseverance proved to be only a set of false teeth, two pairs of hips, an eye, and a bundle of *billets-doux* from Mr Windenough to my wife. I might as well here observe that this confirmation of my lady's partiality for Mr W— occasioned me little uneasiness. That Mrs Lackobreath should admire anything so dissimilar to myself was a natural and necessary evil. I am, it is well known, of a robust and corpulent appearance, and at the same time somewhat diminutive in stature. What wonder, then, that the lath-like tenuity of my acquaintance, and his altitude, which has grown into a proverb, should have met with all due estimation in the eyes of Mrs Lackobreath. But to return.

My exertions, as I have before said, proved fruitless. Closet after closet – drawer after drawer – corner after corner – were scrutinized to no purpose. At one time, however, I thought myself sure of my prize, having in rummaging a dressing-case accidentally demolished a bottle of Grandjean's Oil of Archangels – which, as an agreeable perfume, I here take the liberty of recommending.

With a heavy heart I returned to my boudoir – there to ponder upon some method of eluding my wife's penetration, until I could make arrangements prior to my leaving the country, for to this I had already made up my mind. In a foreign climate, being unknown, I might, with some probability of success, endeavor to conceal my unhappy calamity – a calamity calculated even more than beggary to estrange the affections of the multitude, and to draw down upon the wretch the well-merited indignation of the virtuous and the happy. I was not long in hesitation. Being naturally quick, I committed to memory the entire tragedy of *Metamora*.[8] I had the good fortune to recollect that in the accentuation of this drama, or at least of such portion of it as is allotted to the hero, the tones of voice in which I found myself deficient were altogether unnecessary, and that the deep guttural was expected to reign monotonously throughout.

I practised for some time by the borders of a well-frequented marsh; herein, however, having no reference to a similar proceeding of Demosthenes, but from a design peculiarly and conscientiously my own. Thus armed at all points, I determined to make my wife believe that I was suddenly smitten with a passion for the stage. In this I succeeded to a miracle; and to every question or suggestion found myself at liberty to reply in my most frog-like and sepulchral tones with some passage from the tragedy; any portion of which, as I soon took great pleasure in observing, would apply equally well to any particular subject. It is not to be supposed, however, that in the delivery of such passages I was found at all deficient in the looking asquint, the showing my teeth, the working my knees, the shuffling my feet, or in any of those unmentionable graces which are now justly considered the characteristics of a popular performer. To be sure, they spoke of confining me in a strait-jacket; but good God! they never suspected me of having lost my breath.

Having at length put my affairs in order, I took my seat very early one morning in the mail stage for —, giving it to be understood, among my acquaintances, that business of the last importance required my immediate personal attendance in that city.

The coach was crammed to repletion; but in the uncertain twilight the features of my companions could not be distinguished. Without making any effectual resistance, I suffered myself to be placed between two gentlemen of colossal dimensions; while a third, of a size larger, requesting pardon for the liberty he was about to take, threw himself upon my body at full length, and, falling asleep in an instant, drowned all my guttural ejaculations for relief in a snore which would have put to blush the roarings of the bull of Phalaris.[9] Happily the state of my respiratory faculties rendered suffocation an accident entirely out of the question.

As, however, the day broke more distinctly, in our approach to the outskirts of the city, my tormentor, arising and adjusting his shirt-collar, thanked me in a very friendly manner for my civility. Seeing that I remained motionless (all my limbs were dislocated and my head twisted on one side), his apprehensions began to be excited; and, arousing the rest of the passengers, he communicated in a very decided manner his opinion that a dead man had been palmed upon them during the night for a living and responsible fellow-traveller; here giving me a thump on the right eye, by way of demonstrating the truth of his suggestion.

Hereupon all, one after another (there were nine in company), believed it their duty to pull me by the ear. A young practising physician, too, having applied a pocket-mirror to my mouth, and found me without breath, the assertion of my persecutor was pronounced a true bill; and the whole party expressed a determination to endure lamely no such impositions for the future, and to proceed no farther with any such carcasses for the present.

I was here, accordingly, thrown out at the sign of the Crow (by which tavern the coach happened to be passing) without meeting with any farther accident than the breaking of both my arms, under the left hind wheel of the vehicle. I must, besides, do the driver the justice to state that he did not forget to throw after me the largest of my trunks, which, unfortunately falling on my head, fractured my skull in a manner at once interesting and extraordinary.

The landlord of the Crow, who is a hospitable man, finding that my trunk contained sufficient to indemnify him for any little trouble he might take in my behalf, sent forthwith for a surgeon of his acquaintance, and delivered me to his care with a bill and receipt for ten dollars.

The purchaser took me to his apartments and commenced operations immediately. Having cut off my ears, however, he discovered signs of animation. He now rang the bell, and sent for a neighboring apothecary with whom to consult in the emergency. In case of his suspicions with regard to my existence proving ultimately correct, he, in the mean time, made an incision in my stomach, and removed several of my viscera for private dissection.

The apothecary had an idea that I was actually dead. This idea I endeavored to confute, kicking and plunging with all my might, and making the most furious contortions – for the operations of the surgeon had, in a measure, restored me to the possession of my faculties. All, however, was attributed to the effects of a new galvanic battery, wherewith the apothecary, who is really a man of information, performed several curious experiments, in which, from my personal share in their fulfilment, I could not help feeling deeply interested. It was a source of mortification to me, nevertheless, that, although I made several attempts at conversation, my powers of speech were so entirely in abeyance that I could not even open my mouth; much less then make reply to some ingenious but fanciful theories of which, under other circumstances, my minute acquaintance with the Hippocratian pathology would have afforded me a ready confutation.

Not being able to arrive at a conclusion, the practitioners remanded me for farther examination. I was taken up into a garret; and, the surgeon's lady having accommodated me with drawers and stockings, the surgeon himself fastened my hands, and tied up my jaws with a pocket handkerchief – then bolted the door on the outside as he hurried to his dinner, leaving me alone to silence and to meditation.

I now discovered to my extreme delight that I could have spoken had not my mouth been tied up by the pocket handkerchief. Consoling myself with this reflection, I was mentally repeating some passages of the *Omnipresence of the Deity*, as is my custom before resigning myself to sleep, when two cats, of a greedy and vituperative turn, entering at a hole in the wall, leaped up with a flourish, *à la Catalani*,[10] and, alighting opposite one another on my visage, betook themselves to indecorous contention for the paltry consideration of my nose.

But, as the loss of his ears proved the means of elevating, to the throne of Cyrus, the Magian, or Mige-Gush, of Persia,[11] and as the cutting off his nose gave Zopyrus possession of Babylon, so the loss of a few ounces of my countenance proved the salvation of my body. Aroused by the pain, and burning with indignation, I burst at a single effort the fastenings and the bandage. Stalking across the room, I cast a glance of contempt at the belligerents, and, throwing open the sash, to their extreme horror and disappointment, precipitated myself very dexterously from the window.

The mail-robber, W—, to whom I bore a singular resemblance, was at this moment passing from the city jail to the scaffold erected for his execution in the suburbs. His extreme infirmity, and long-continued ill health, had obtained him the privilege of remaining unmanacled; and, habited in his gallows costume – one very similar to my own – he lay at full length in the bottom of the hangman's cart (which happened to be under the windows of the surgeon at the moment of my precipitation) without any other guard than the driver, who was asleep, and two recruits of the sixth infantry, who were drunk.

As ill-luck would have it, I alit upon my feet within the vehicle. W—, who was an acute fellow, perceived his opportunity. Leaping up immediately, he bolted out behind, and, turning down an alley, was out of sight in the twinkling of an eye. The recruits, aroused by the bustle, could not exactly comprehend the merits of the transaction. Seeing, however, a man, the precise counterpart of the felon, standing upright in the cart before their eyes, they were of opinion that the rascal (meaning W—) was after making his escape (so they expressed themselves), and, having communicated this opinion to one another, they took each a dram, and then knocked me down with the butt-ends of their muskets.

It was not long ere we arrived at the place of destination. Of course, nothing could be said in my defence. Hanging was my inevitable fate. I resigned myself thereto with a feeling half stupid, half acrimonious. Being little of a cynic, I had all the sentiments of a dog.[12] The hangman, however, adjusted the noose about my neck. The drop fell.

I forbear to depict my sensations upon the gallows; although here, undoubtedly, I could speak to the point, and it is a topic upon which nothing has been well said. In fact, to write upon such a theme, it is necessary to have been hanged. Every author should confine himself to matters of experience.[13] Thus Mark Antony composed a treatise upon getting drunk.[14]

I may just mention, however, that die I did not. My body *was*, but I had no breath *to be*, suspended; and, but for the knot under my left ear (which had the feel of a military stock), I dare say that I should have experienced very little inconvenience. As for the jerk given to my neck upon the falling of the drop, it merely proved a corrective to the twist afforded me by the fat gentleman in the coach.

For good reasons, however, I did my best to give the crowd the worth of their trouble. My convulsions were said to be extraordinary. My spasms it would have been difficult to beat. The populace *encored*. Several gentlemen swooned; and a multitude of ladies were carried home in hysterics. Pinxit availed himself of the opportunity to retouch, from a sketch taken upon the spot, his admirable painting of the 'Marsyas Flayed Alive'.[15]

When I had afforded sufficient amusement, it was thought proper to remove my body from the gallows; this the more especially as the real culprit had in the mean time been retaken and recognized; a fact which I was so unlucky as not to know.

Much sympathy was, of course, exercised in my behalf, and, as no one made claim to my corpse, it was ordered that I should be interred in a public vault.[16]

Here, after due interval, I was deposited. The sexton departed, and I was left alone. A line of Marston's *Malcontent* –

> Death's a good fellow, and keeps open house –[17]

struck me at that moment as a palpable lie.

I knocked off, however, the lid of my coffin, and stepped out. The place was dreadfully dreary and damp, and I became troubled with ennui. By way of amusement, I felt my way among the numerous coffins ranged in order around. I lifted them down, one by one, and, breaking open their lids, busied myself in speculations about the mortality within.

'This,' I soliloquized, tumbling over a carcass, puffy, bloated, and rotund – 'this has been, no doubt, in every sense of the word, an unhappy – an unfortunate man. It has been his terrible lot not to walk, but to waddle – to pass through life not like a human being, but like an elephant – not like a man, but like a rhinoceros.

'His attempts at getting on have been mere abortions, and his circumgyratory proceedings a palpable failure. Taking a step forward, it has been his misfortune to take two towards the right, and three towards the left. His studies have been confined to the poetry of Crabbe.[18] He can have had no idea of the wonder of a *pirouette*. To him a *pas de papillon* has been an abstract conception. He has never ascended the summit of a hill. He has never viewed from any steeple the glories of a metropolis. Heat has been his mortal enemy. In the dog-days, his days have been the days of a dog. Therein, he has dreamed of flames and suffocation, of mountains upon mountains, of Pelion upon Ossa.[19] He was short of breath; to say all in a word, he was short of breath. He thought it extravagant to play upon wind instruments. He was the inventor of self-moving fans, wind-sails, and ventilators. He patronized Du Pont, the bellows-maker, and died miserably in attempting to smoke a cigar. His was a case in which I feel deep interest – a lot in which I sincerely sympathize.

'But here,' – said I – 'here' – and I dragged spitefully from its receptacle a gaunt, tall, and peculiar-looking form, whose remarkable appearance struck me with a sense of unwelcome familiarity – 'here is a wretch entitled to no earthly commiseration.' Thus saying, in order to obtain a more distinct view of my subject, I applied my thumb and forefinger to its nose, and, causing it to assume a sitting position upon the ground, held it thus, at the length of my arm, while I continued my soliloquy.

– 'Entitled,' I repeated, 'to no earthly commiseration. Who

indeed would think of compassionating a shadow? Besides, has he not had his full share of the blessings of mortality? He was the originator of tall monuments – shot-towers – lightning rods – Lombardy poplars. His treatise upon "Shades and Shadows" has immortalized him. He edited with distinguished ability the last edition of *South on the Bones*.[20] He went early to college, and studied pneumatics. He then came home, talked eternally, and played upon the French-horn. He patronized the bagpipes. Captain Barclay, who walked against Time, would not walk against *him*. Windham and Allbreath were his favorite writers, – his favorite artist, Phiz. He died gloriously while inhaling gas – *levique flatu corrumpitur*, like the *fama pudicitae* in Hieronymus.* He was indubitably a —'

'How *can* you? – how – *can* – you?' – interrupted the object of my animadversions, gasping for breath, and tearing off, with a desperate exertion, the bandage around its jaws – 'how *can* you, Mr Lackobreath, be so infernally cruel as to pinch me in that manner by the nose? Did you not see how they had fastened up my mouth? and you *must* know, if you know anything, how vast a superfluity of breath I have to dispose of! If you do *not* know, however, sit down and you shall see. In my situation it is really a great relief to be able to open one's mouth – to be able to expatiate – to be able to communicate with a person like yourself, who do not think yourself called upon at every period to interrupt the thread of a gentleman's discourse. Interruptions are annoying and should undoubtedly be abolished – don't you think so? – no reply, I beg you, – one person is enough to be speaking at a time. I shall be done by-and-by, and then you may begin. How the devil, sir, did you get into this place? – not a word I beseech you – been here some time myself – terrible accident! – heard of it, I suppose – awful calamity! – walking under your windows – some short while ago – about the time you were stage-struck – horrible occurrence! – heard of "catching one's breath," eh? – hold your tongue I tell you! – I caught somebody else's! – had always

---

* *'Tenera res in feminis fama pudicitae est; et quasi flos pulcherrimus, cito ad levem marcessit auram, levique flatu corrumpitur, maxime, etc.'* – S. Hieron, Epist. LXXXV, 'Ad Salvinam'

too much of my own – met Blab at the corner of the street – wouldn't give me a chance for a word – couldn't get in a syllable edgeways – attacked, consequently, with epilepsis – Blab made his escape – damn all fools! – they took me up for dead, and put me in this place – pretty doings all of them! – heard all you said about me – every word a lie – horrible! – wonderful! – outrageous! – hideous! – incomprehensible! – et cetera – et cetera – et cetera – et cetera –'

It is impossible to conceive my astonishment at so unexpected a discourse; or the joy with which I became gradually convinced that the breath so fortunately caught by the gentleman (whom I soon recognized as my neighbor, Windenough) was, in fact, the identical expiration mislaid by myself in the conversation with my wife. Time, place, and circumstance rendered it a matter beyond question. I did not, however, immediately release my hold upon Mr W—'s proboscis; not at least during the long period in which the inventor of Lombardy poplars continued to favor me with his explanations.

In this respect I was actuated by that habitual prudence which was ever my predominating trait. I reflected that many difficulties might still lie in the path of my preservation, which only extreme exertion on my part would be able to surmount. Many persons, I considered, are prone to estimate commodities in their possession – however valueless to the then proprietor – however trouble-some, or distressing – in direct ratio with advantages to be derived by others from their attainment, or by themselves from their abandonment. Might not this be the case with Mr Windenough? In displaying anxiety for the breath of which he was at present so willing to get rid, might I not lay myself open to the exactions of his avarice? There are scoundrels in this world, I remembered with a sigh, who will not scruple to take unfair opportunities with even a next-door neighbor, and (this remark is from Epictetus) it is precisely at that time when men are most anxious to throw off the burden of their own calamities that they feel the least desirous of relieving them in others.

Upon considerations similar to these, and still retaining my grasp upon the nose of Mr W—, I accordingly thought proper to model my reply.

'Monster!' I began in a tone of the deepest indignation, 'monster; and double-winded idiot! – dost *thou*, whom, for thine iniquities, it has pleased heaven to accurse with a twofold respiration – dost *thou*, I say, presume to address me in the familiar language of an old acquaintance? – "I lie", forsooth! and "hold my tongue", to be sure! – pretty conversation indeed, to a gentleman with a single breath! – all this, too, when I have it in my power to relieve the calamity under which thou dost so justly suffer, to curtail the superfluities of thine unhappy respiration.'

Like Brutus, I paused for a reply – with which, like a tornado, Mr Windenough immediately overwhelmed me. Protestation followed upon protestation, and apology upon apology. There were no terms with which he was unwilling to comply, and there were none of which I failed to take the fullest advantage.

Preliminaries being at length arranged, my acquaintance delivered me the respiration; for which (having carefully examined it) I gave him afterwards a receipt.

I am aware that by many I shall be held to blame for speaking, in a manner so cursory, of a transaction so impalpable. It will be thought that I should have entered more minutely into the details of an occurrence by which – and this is very true – much new light might be thrown upon a highly interesting branch of physical philosophy.

To all this I am sorry that I cannot reply. A hint is the only answer which I am permitted to make. There were *circumstances* – but I think it much safer upon consideration to say as little as possible about an affair so delicate – *so delicate*, I repeat, and at the time involving the interests of a third party whose sulphurous resentment I have not the least desire, at this moment, of incurring.

We were not long after this necessary arrangement in effecting an escape from the dungeons of the sepulchre. The united strength of our resuscitated voices was soon sufficiently apparent. Scissors, the Whig Editor, republished a treatise upon 'the nature and origin of subterranean noises'. A reply – rejoinder – confutation – and justification – followed in the columns of a Democratic Gazette. It was not until the opening of the vault, to decide the controversy, that the appearance of Mr Windenough and myself proved both parties to have been decidedly in the wrong.

I cannot conclude these details of some very singular passages in a life at all times sufficiently eventful, without again recalling to the attention of the reader the merits of that indiscriminate philosophy which is a sure and ready shield against those shafts of calamity which can neither be seen, felt, nor fully understood. It was in the spirit of this wisdom that, among the ancient Hebrews, it was believed the gates of Heaven would be inevitably opened to that sinner, or saint, who, with good lungs and implicit confidence, should vociferate the word '*Amen!*' It was in the spirit of this wisdom that, when a great plague raged at Athens, and every means had been in vain attempted for its removal, Epimenides, as Laertius relates in his second book of that philosopher, advised the erection of a shrine and temple 'to the proper God'.[21]

King Pest

A Tale Containing an Allegory

The goddes do beare and well allow in kinges
The thinges that they abhorre in rascall routes.
BUCKHURST, *Ferrex and Porrex*, II. i[1]

ABOUT twelve o'clock, one night in the month of October, and during the chivalrous reign of the third Edward,[2] two seamen belonging to the crew of the *Free and Easy*, a trading schooner plying between Sluys and the Thames, and then at anchor in that river, were much astonished to find themselves seated in the tap-room of an ale-house in the parish of St Andrews, London – which ale-house bore for sign the portraiture of a Jolly Tar.

The room, although ill-contrived, smoke-blackened, low-pitched, and in every other respect agreeing with the general character of such places at the period, was, nevertheless, in the opinion of the grotesque groups scattered here and there within it, sufficiently well adapted to its purpose.

Of these groups our two seamen formed, I think, the most interesting, if not the most conspicuous.

The one who appeared to be the elder, and whom his companion addressed by the characteristic appellation of 'Legs', was at the same time much the taller of the two. He might have measured six feet and a half, and an habitual stoop in the shoulders seemed to have been the necessary consequence of an altitude so enormous. Superfluities in height were, however, more than accounted for by deficiencies in other respects. He was exceedingly thin; and might, as his associates asserted, have answered, when drunk, for a pennant at the mast head, or, when sober, have served for a jib-boom. But these jests, and others of a similar nature, had evidently produced, at no time, any effect upon the cachinnatory muscles of the tar. With high cheek-bones, a large hawk-nose, retreating chin, fallen under-jaw, and huge

44

protruding white eyes, the expression of his countenance, although tinged with a species of dogged indifference to matters and things in general, was not the less utterly solemn and serious beyond all attempts at imitation or description.

The younger seaman was, in all outward appearance, the converse of his companion. His stature could not have exceeded four feet. A pair of stumpy bow-legs supported his squat, unwieldy figure, while his unusually short and thick arms, with no ordinary fists at their extremities, swung off dangling from his sides like the fins of a sea-turtle. Small eyes, of no particular color, twinkled far back in his head. His nose remained buried in the mass of flesh which enveloped his round, full, and purple face; and his thick upper lip rested upon the still thicker one beneath with an air of complacent self-satisfaction, much heightened by the owner's habit of licking them at intervals. He evidently regarded his tall shipmate with a feeling half wondrous, half quizzical; and stared up occasionally in his face as the red setting sun stares up at the crags of Ben Nevis.[3]

Various and eventful, however, had been the peregrinations of the worthy couple in and about the different tap-houses of the neighborhood during the earlier hours of the night. Funds even the most ample are not always everlasting; and it was with empty pockets our friends had ventured upon the present hostelry.

At the precise period, then, when this history properly commences, Legs, and his fellow, Hugh Tarpaulin, sat, each with both elbows resting upon the large oaken table in the middle of the floor, and with a hand upon either cheek. They were eyeing, from behind a huge flagon of unpaid-for 'humming-stuff', the portentous words, 'No Chalk', which to their indignation and astonishment were scored over the doorway by means of that very mineral whose presence they purported to deny. Not that the gift of deciphering written characters – a gift among the commonalty of that day considered little less cabalistical than the art of inditing – could, in strict justice, have been laid to the charge of either disciple of the sea; but there was, to say the truth, a certain twist in the formation of the letters, an indescribable lee-lurch about the whole, which foreboded in the opinion of both seamen a long run of dirty weather; and determined them at once, in the allegorical words of Legs himself, to 'pump ship, clew up all sail, and scud before the wind'.

Having accordingly disposed of what remained of the ale, and looped up the points of their short doublets, they finally made a bolt for the street. Although Tarpaulin rolled twice into the fireplace, mistaking it for the door, yet their escape was at length happily effected; and half after twelve o'clock found our heroes ripe for mischief, and running for life down a dark alley in the direction of St Andrew's Stair, hotly pursued by the landlady of the Jolly Tar.

At the epoch of this eventful tale, and periodically for many years before and after, all England, but more especially the metropolis, resounded with the fearful cry of 'Plague!'[4] The city was in a great measure depopulated; and in those horrible regions, in the vicinity of the Thames, where amid the dark, narrow, and filthy lanes and alleys the Demon of Disease was supposed to have had his nativity, Awe, Terror, and Superstition were alone to be found stalking abroad.

By authority of the king such districts were placed *under ban*, and all persons forbidden, under pain of death, to intrude upon their dismal solitude.[5] Yet neither the mandate of the monarch, nor the huge barriers erected at the entrances of the streets, nor the prospect of that loathsome death which, with almost absolute certainty, overwhelmed the wretch whom no peril could deter from the adventure, prevented the unfurnished and un-tenanted dwellings from being stripped, by the hand of nightly rapine, of every article, such as iron, brass, or lead-work, which could in any manner be turned to a profitable account.

Above all, it was usually found, upon the annual winter open-ing of the barriers, that locks, bolts, and secret cellars had proved but slender protection to those rich stores of wines and liquors which, in consideration of the risk and trouble of removal, many of the numerous dealers having shops in the neighborhood had consented to trust, during the period of exile, to so insufficient a security.

But there were very few of the terror-stricken people who

attributed these doings to the agency of human hands.[6] Pest-spirits, plague-goblins, and fever-demons were the popular imps of mischief; and tales so blood-chilling were hourly told that the whole mass of forbidden buildings was, at length, enveloped in terror as in a shroud, and the plunderer himself was often scared away by the horrors his own depredations had created; leaving the entire vast circuit of prohibited district to gloom, silence, pestilence, and death.

It was by one of the terrific barriers already mentioned, and which indicated the region beyond to be under the Pest-ban, that, in scrambling down an alley, Legs and the worthy Hugh Tarpaulin found their progress suddenly impeded. To return was out of the question, and no time was to be lost, as their pursuers were close upon their heels. With thorough-bred seamen, to clamber up the roughly fashioned plank-work was a trifle; and, maddened with the two-fold excitement of exercise and liquor, they leaped unhesitatingly down within the enclosure, and, holding on their drunken course with shouts and yellings, were soon bewildered in its noisome and intricate recesses.

Had they not, indeed, been intoxicated beyond moral sense, their reeling footsteps must have been palsied by the horrors of their situation. The air was cold and misty. The paving-stones, loosened from their beds, lay in wild disorder amid the tall, rank grass, which sprang up around the feet and ankles. Fallen houses choked up the streets. The most fetid and poisonous smells everywhere prevailed; and by the aid of that ghastly light which, even at midnight, never fails to emanate from a vapory and pestilential atmosphere, might be discerned lying in the by-paths and alleys, or rotting in the windowless habitations, the carcass of many a nocturnal plunderer arrested by the hand of the plague in the very perpetration of his robbery.

But it lay not in the power of images, or sensations, or impediments such as these, to stay the course of men who, naturally brave, and, at that time especially, brimful of courage and of 'humming stuff', would have reeled, as straight as their condition might have permitted, undauntedly into the very jaws of Death. Onward – still onward stalked the grim Legs, making the desolate solemnity echo and re-echo with yells like the terrific war-whoop of the Indian; and onward, still onward rolled the dumpy Tarpaulin, hanging on to the doublet of his more active companion, and far surpassing the latter's most strenuous exertions in the way of vocal music, by bull-roarings *in basso*, from the profundity of his stentorian lungs.

They had now evidently reached the stronghold of the pestilence. Their way at every step or plunge grew more noisome and more horrible – the paths more narrow and more intricate. Huge stones and beams, falling momently from the decaying roofs above them, gave evidence, by their sullen and heavy descent, of the vast height of the surrounding houses; and while actual exertion became necessary to force a passage through frequent heaps of rubbish, it was by no means seldom that the hand fell upon a skeleton or rested upon a more fleshy corpse.

Suddenly, as the seamen stumbled against the entrance of a tall and ghastly-looking building, a yell more than usually shrill from the throat of the excited Legs was replied to from within, in a rapid succession of wild, laughter-like, and fiendish shrieks. Nothing daunted at sounds which, of such a nature, at such a time, and in such a place, might have curdled the very blood in hearts less irrevocably on fire, the drunken couple rushed headlong against the door, burst it open, and staggered into the midst of things with a volley of curses.

The room within which they found themselves proved to be the shop of an undertaker; but an open trap-door, in a corner of the floor near the entrance, looked down upon a long range of wine-cellars, whose depths the occasional sound of bursting bottles proclaimed to be well stored with their appropriate contents.[7] In the middle of the room stood a table, in the centre of which, again, arose a huge tub of what appeared to be punch. Bottles of various wines and cordials, together with jugs, pitchers, and flagons of every shape and quality, were scattered profusely upon the board. Around it, upon coffin-tressels, was seated a company of six. This company I will endeavor to delineate, one by one.

Fronting the entrance, and elevated a little above his companions, sat a personage who appeared to be the president of the table. His stature was gaunt and tall, and Legs was confounded to behold in him a figure more emaciated than himself. His face was as yellow as saffron[8] – but no feature, excepting one alone, was sufficiently marked to merit a particular description. This one consisted in a forehead so unusually and hideously lofty as to have the appearance of a bonnet or crown of flesh super-added upon the natural head. His mouth was puckered and dimpled into an expression of ghastly affability, and his eyes, as indeed the eyes of all at table, were glazed over with the fumes of intoxication. This gentleman was clothed from head to foot in a richly embroidered black silk-velvet pall, wrapped negligently around his form after the fashion of a Spanish cloak. His head was stuck full of sable hearse-plumes, which he nodded to and fro with a jaunty and knowing air; and in his right hand he held a huge human thigh-bone, with which he appeared to have been just knocking down some member of the company for a song.

Opposite him, and with her back to the door, was a lady of no whit the less extraordinary character. Although quite as tall as the person just described, she had no right to complain of his unnatural emaciation. She was evidently in the last stage of a dropsy; and her figure resembled nearly that of the huge puncheon of October beer which stood, with the head driven in, close by her side in a corner of the chamber. Her face was exceedingly round, red, and full; and the same peculiarity, or rather want of peculiarity, attached itself to her countenance, which I before mentioned in the case of the president – that is to say, only one feature of her face was sufficiently distinguished to need a separate characterization; indeed, the acute Tarpaulin immediately observed that the same remark might have applied to each individual person of the party, every one of whom seemed to possess a monopoly of some particular portion of physiognomy. With the lady in question this portion proved to be the mouth. Commencing at the right ear, it swept with a terrific chasm to the left – the short pendants which she wore in either auricle continually bobbing into the aperture. She made, however, every exertion to keep her mouth closed and look dignified, in a dress consisting of a newly starched and ironed shroud coming up

49

close under her chin, with a crimpled ruffle of cambric muslin.

At her right hand sat a diminutive young lady whom she appeared to patronize. This delicate little creature, in the trembling of her wasted fingers, in the livid hue of her lips, and in the slight hectic spot which tinged her otherwise leaden complexion, gave evident indications of a galloping consumption. An air of extreme *haut ton*, however, pervaded her whole appearance; she wore in a graceful and *dégagé* manner a large and beautiful winding-sheet of the finest India lawn; her hair hung in ringlets over her neck; a soft smile played about her mouth; but her nose, extremely long, thin, sinuous, flexible, and pimpled, hung down far below her under lip, and in spite of the delicate manner in which she now and then moved it to one side or the other with her tongue, gave to her countenance a somewhat equivocal expression.

Over against her, and upon the left of the dropsical lady, was seated a little puffy, wheezing, and gouty old man, whose cheeks reposed upon the shoulders of their owner, like two huge bladders of Oporto wine. With his arms folded, and with one bandaged leg deposited upon the table, he seemed to think himself entitled to some consideration. He evidently prided himself much upon every inch of his personal appearance, but took more especial delight in calling attention to his gaudy-colored surtout. This, to say the truth, must have cost him no little money, and was made to fit him exceedingly well – being fashioned from one of the curiously embroidered silken covers appertaining to those glorious escutcheons which, in England and elsewhere, are customarily hung up, in some conspicuous place, upon the dwellings of departed aristocracy.

Next to him, and at the right hand of the president, was a gentleman in long white hose and cotton drawers. His frame shook, in a ridiculous manner, with a fit of what Tarpaulin called 'the horrors'. His jaws, which had been newly shaved, were tightly tied up by a bandage of muslin; and his arms, being fastened in a similar way at the wrists, prevented him from helping himself too freely to the liquors upon the table; a precaution rendered necessary, in the opinion of Legs, by the peculiarly sottish and wine-bibbing cast of his visage. A pair of prodigious ears, nevertheless, which it was no doubt found impossible to confine, towered away into the atmosphere of the apartment, and were occasionally pricked up in a spasm, at the sound of the drawing of a cork.

Fronting him, sixthly and lastly, was situated a singularly stiff-looking personage, who, being afflicted with paralysis, must, to speak seriously, have felt very ill at ease in his unaccommodating habiliments. He was habited, somewhat uniquely, in a new and handsome mahogany coffin. Its top or head-piece pressed upon the skull of the wearer, and extended over it in the fashion of a hood, giving to the entire face an air of indescribable interest. Armholes had been cut in the sides, for the sake not more of elegance than of convenience; but the dress, nevertheless, prevented its proprietor from sitting as erect as his associates; and as he lay reclining against his tressel, at an angle of forty-five degrees, a pair of huge goggle eyes rolled up their awful whites towards the ceiling in absolute amazement at their own enormity.

Before each of the party lay a portion of a skull, which was used as a drinking-cup. Overhead was suspended a human skeleton, by means of a rope tied round one of the legs and fastened to a ring in the ceiling. The other limb, confined by no such fetter, stuck off from the body at right angles, causing the whole loose and rattling frame to dangle and twirl about at the caprice of every occasional puff of wind which found its way into the apartment. In the cranium of this hideous thing lay a quantity of ignited charcoal, which threw a fitful but vivid light over the entire scene; while coffins, and other wares appertaining to the shop of an undertaker, were piled high up around the room, and against the windows, preventing any ray from escaping into the street.

At sight of this extraordinary assembly, and of their still more extraordinary paraphernalia, our two seamen did not conduct themselves with that degree of decorum which might have been expected. Legs, leaning against the wall near which he happened to be standing, dropped his lower jaw still lower than usual, and spread open his eyes to their fullest extent; while Hugh Tarpaulin, stooping down so as to bring his nose upon a level with the table, and spreading out a palm upon either knee, burst into a long, loud, and obstreperous roar of very ill-timed and immoderate laughter.

Without, however, taking offence at behavior so excessively rude, the tall president smiled very graciously upon the intruders – nodded to them in a dignified manner with his head of sable plumes – and, arising, took each by an arm, and led him to a seat which some others of the company had placed in the mean time for his accommodation. Legs to all this offered not the slightest resistance, but sat down as he was directed; while the gallant Hugh, removing his coffin-tressel from its station, near the head of the table, to the vicinity of the little consumptive lady in the winding-sheet, plumped down by her side in high glee, and, pouring out a skull of red wine, quaffed it to their better acquaintance. But at this presumption the stiff gentleman in the coffin seemed exceedingly nettled; and serious consequences might have ensued, had not the president, rapping upon the table with his truncheon, diverted the attention of all present to the following speech:–

'It becomes our duty upon the present happy occasion –'

'Avast there!' interrupted Legs, looking very serious, 'avast there a bit, I say, and tell us who the devil ye all are, and what business ye have here, rigged off like the foul fiends, and swilling the snug blue ruin stowed away for the winter by my honest shipmate, Will Wimble, the undertaker!'

At this unpardonable piece of ill-breeding, all the original company half started to their feet, and uttered the same rapid succession of wild fiendish shrieks which had before caught the attention of the seamen. The president, however, was the first to recover his composure, and at length, turning to Legs with great dignity, recommenced:–

'Most willingly will we gratify any reasonable curiosity on the part of guests so illustrious, unbidden though they be. Know then that in these dominions I am monarch, and here rule with undivided empire under the title of "King Pest, the First".

'This apartment, which you no doubt profanely supposed to be the shop of Will Wimble, the undertaker – a man whom we know not, and whose plebeian appellation has never before this night thwarted our royal ears – this apartment, I say, is the Dais-Chamber of our Palace, devoted to the councils of our kingdom, and to other sacred and lofty purposes.

'The noble lady who sits opposite is Queen Pest, our Serene Consort. The other exalted personages whom you behold are all of our family, and wear the insignia of the blood royal under the respective titles of "His Grace, the Arch Duke Pest-Iferous", "His Grace, the Duke Pest-Ilential", "His Grace, the Duke Tem-Pest", and "Her Serene Highness, the Arch Duchess Ana-Pest".

'As regards,' continued he, 'your demand of the business upon which we sit here in council, we might be pardoned for replying that it concerns, and concerns *alone*, our own private and regal interest, and is in no manner important to any other than ourself. But, in consideration of those rights to which as guests and strangers you may feel yourselves entitled, we will furthermore explain that we are here this night, prepared by deep research and accurate investigation, to examine, analyze, and thoroughly determine the indefinable spirit – the incomprehensible qualities and nature – of those inestimable treasures of the palate, the wines, ales, and liquors of this goodly metropolis;[9] by so doing to advance not more our own designs than the true welfare of that unearthly sovereign whose reign is over us all, whose dominions are unlimited, and whose name is "Death".'

'Whose name is Davy Jones!'[10] ejaculated Tarpaulin, helping the lady by his side to a skull of liquor, and pouring out a second for himself.

'Profane varlet!' said the president, now turning his attention to the worthy Hugh, 'profane and execrable wretch! – we have said that, in consideration of those rights which, even in thy filthy person, we feel no inclination to violate, we have condescended to make reply to thy rude and unseasonable inquiries. We, nevertheless, for your unhallowed intrusion upon our councils, believe it our duty to mulct thee and thy companion in each a gallon of Black Strap[11] – having imbibed which to the prosperity of our kingdom, at a single draught, and upon your bended knees, ye shall be forthwith free either to proceed upon your way, or remain and be admitted to the privileges of our table, according to your respective and individual pleasures.'

'It would be a matter of utter unpossibility,' replied Legs, whom the assumptions and dignity of King Pest, the First, had evidently inspired with some feelings of respect, and who arose and steadied himself by the table as he spoke – 'it would, please your Majesty, be a matter of utter unpossibility to stow away in my hold even one fourth part of that same liquor which your Majesty has just mentioned. To say nothing of the stuffs placed on board in the forenoon by way of ballast, and not to mention the various ales and liquors shipped this evening at various seaports, I have, at present, a full cargo of "humming stuff" taken in and duly paid for at the sign of the Jolly Tar. You will, therefore, please your Majesty, be so good as to take the will for the deed; for by no manner of means either can I or will I swallow another drop; least of all a drop of that villanous bilge-water that answers to the hail of "Black Strap".'

'Belay that!' interrupted Tarpaulin – astonished not more at the length of his companion's speech than at the nature of his refusal – 'Belay that, you lubber! – and I say, Legs, none of your palaver! *My* hull is still light, although I confess you yourself seem to be a little top-heavy; and as for the matter of your share of the cargo, why rather than raise a squall I would find stowage-room for it myself, but –'

'This proceeding,' interposed the president, 'is by no means in accordance with the terms of the mulct or sentence, which is in its nature Median,[12] and not to be altered or recalled. The conditions we have imposed must be fulfilled to the letter, and that without a moment's hesitation; in failure of which fulfilment we decree that you do here be tied neck and heels together, and duly drowned as rebels in yon hogshead of October beer!'

'A sentence! – a sentence! – a righteous and just sentence! – a glorious decree! – a most worthy and upright, and holy condemnation!' shouted the Pest family altogether. The king elevated his forehead into innumerable wrinkles; the gouty little old man puffed like a pair of bellows; the lady of the winding-sheet waved her nose to and fro; the gentleman in the cotton drawers pricked up his ears; she of the shroud gasped like a dying fish; and he of the coffin looked stiff and rolled up his eyes.

'Ugh! ugh! ugh!' chuckled Tarpaulin, without heeding the general excitation, 'ugh! ugh! ugh! – ugh! ugh! ugh! ugh! – ugh! ugh! ugh – I was saying,' said he, 'I was saying when Mr King Pest poked in his marlin-spike, that as for the matter of two or three gallons more or less of Black Strap, it was a trifle to a tight sea-boat like myself not overstowed; but when it comes to drinking the health of the Devil (whom God assoilzie) and going down upon my marrowbones to His ill-favored Majesty there, whom I know, as well as I know myself to be a sinner, to be nobody in the whole world but Tim Hurlygurly,[13] the stage-player! – why! it's quite another guess sort of a thing, and utterly and altogether past my comprehension.'

He was not allowed to finish this speech in tranquillity. At the name of Tim Hurlygurly the whole assembly leaped from their seats.

'Treason!' shouted His Majesty, King Pest, the First.

'Treason!' said the little man with the gout.

'Treason!' screamed the Arch Duchess Ana-Pest.

'Treason!' muttered the gentleman with his jaws tied up.

'Treason!' growled he of the coffin.

'Treason! treason!' shrieked Her Majesty of the mouth; and, seizing by the hinder part of his breeches the unfortunate Tarpaulin, who had just commenced pouring out for himself a skull of liquor, she lifted him high into the air, and let him fall without ceremony into the huge open puncheon of his beloved ale. Bobbing up and down, for a few seconds, like an apple in a bowl of toddy, he, at length, finally disappeared amid the whirlpool of foam which, in the already effervescent liquor, his struggles easily succeeded in creating.

Not tamely, however, did the tall seaman behold the discomfiture of his companion. Jostling King Pest through the open trap, the valiant Legs slammed the door down upon him with an oath, and strode towards the centre of the room. Here tearing down the skeleton which swung over the table, he laid it about him with so much energy and good-will, that, as the last glimpses of light died away within the apartment, he succeeded in knocking out the brains of the little gentleman with the gout. Rushing then with all his force against the fatal hogshead full of October ale and Hugh Tarpaulin, he rolled it over and over in an instant. Out burst a deluge of liquor so fierce – so impetuous – so overwhelming – that the room was flooded from wall to wall – the loaded table was overturned – the tressels were thrown upon their backs – the tub of punch into the fireplace – and the ladies into hysterics. Piles of death-furniture floundered about. Jugs, pitchers, and carboys mingled promiscuously in the *mêlée*, and wicker flagons encountered desperately with bottles of junk. The man with the horrors was drowned upon the spot – the little stiff gentleman floated off in his coffin – and the victorious Legs, seizing by the waist the fat lady in the shroud, rushed out with her into the street, and made a bee-line for the *Free and Easy*, followed under easy sail by the redoubtable Hugh Tarpaulin, who, having sneezed three or four times, panted and puffed after him with the Arch Duchess Ana-Pest.

A Tale of Jerusalem

Intonsos rigidam in frontem descendere canos
Passus erat.
LUCAN, *Pharsalia*, ii. 375–61

... a bristly *bore*.
(Translation)

'LET us hurry to the walls,' said Abel-Phittim to Buzi-Ben-Levi
and Simeon the Pharisee, on the tenth day of the month
Thammuz, in the year of the world three thousand nine hundred
and forty-one[2] – 'let us hasten to the ramparts adjoining the
gates of Benjamin, which is in the city of David, and overlooking
the camp of the uncircumcised; for it is the last hour of the
fourth watch, being sunrise; and the idolaters, in fulfilment of
the promise of Pompey, should be awaiting us with the lambs
for the sacrifices.'

Simeon, Abel-Phittim, and Buzi-Ben-Levi, were the Gizbarim,
or sub-collectors of the offering,[3] in the holy city of Jerusalem.

'Verily,' replied the Pharisee, 'let us hasten, for this generosity
in the heathen is unwonted; and fickle-mindedness has ever
been an attribute of the worshippers of Baal.'

'That they are fickle-minded and treacherous is as true as the
Pentateuch,' said Buzi-Ben-Levi, 'but that is only towards the
people of Adonai.[4] When was it ever known that the Ammonites
proved wanting to their own interests? Methinks it is no great
stretch of generosity to allow us lambs for the altar of the Lord,
receiving in lieu thereof thirty silver shekels per head!'

'Thou forgettest, however, Ben-Levi,' replied Abel-Phittim,
'that the Roman Pompey who is now impiously besieging the
city of the Most High, has no assurity that we apply not the
lambs thus purchased for the altar to the sustenance of the
body rather than of the spirit.'

'Now, by the five corners of my beard,' shouted the Pharisee,
who belonged to the sect called 'The Dashers' (that little knot

57

of saints whose manner of *dashing* and lacerating the feet against the pavement was long a thorn and a reproach to less zealous devotees – a stumbling block to less gifted perambulators) – 'by the five corners of that beard which as a priest I am forbidden to shave! – have we lived to see the day when a blaspheming and idolatrous upstart of Rome shall accuse us of appropriating to the appetites of the flesh the most holy and consecrated elements? Have we lived to see the day when –'

'Let us not question the motives of the Philistine,' interrupted Abel-Phittim, 'for to-day we profit for the first time by his avarice or by his generosity; but rather let us hurry to the ramparts, lest offerings should be wanting for that altar whose fire the rains of heaven cannot extinguish, and whose pillars of smoke no tempest can turn aside.'

That part of the city to which our worthy Gizbarim now hastened, and which bore the name of its architect King David, was esteemed the most strongly ‘fortified district of Jerusalem, being situated upon the steep and lofty hill of Zion. Here a broad, deep circumvallatory trench, hewn from the solid rock, was defended by a wall of great strength erected upon its inner edge. This wall was adorned, at regular interspaces, by square towers of white marble; the lowest sixty, and the highest one hundred and twenty cubits in height. But, in the vicinity of the gate of Benjamin, the wall arose by no means from the margin of the fosse. On the contrary, between the level of the ditch and the basement of the rampart, sprang up a perpendicular cliff of two hundred and fifty cubits, forming part of the precipitous Mount Moriah. So that when Simeon and his associates arrived on the summit of the tower called Adoni-Bezek – the loftiest of all the turrets around about Jerusalem, and the usual place of conference with the besieging army – they looked down upon the camp of the enemy from an eminence excelling, by many feet, that of the Pyramid of Cheops,[5] and, by several, that of the temple of Belus.

'Verily,' sighed the Pharisee, as he peered dizzily over the precipice, 'the uncircumcised are as the sands by the sea-shore – as the locusts in the wilderness! The valley of The King hath become the valley of Adommin.'[6]

'And yet,' added Ben-Levi, 'thou canst not point me out a Philistine – no, not one – from Aleph to Tau – from the wilderness to the battlements – who seemeth any bigger than the letter Jod!'

'Lower away the basket with the shekels of silver!' here shouted a Roman soldier in a hoarse, rough voice, which appeared to issue from the regions of Pluto – 'lower away the basket with the accursed coin which it has broken the jaw of a noble Roman to pronounce! Is it thus you evince your gratitude to our master Pompeius, who, in his condescension, has thought fit to listen to your idolatrous importunities? The god Phoebus, who is a true god,[7] has been charioted for an hour – and were you not to be on the ramparts by sunrise? Aedepol! do you think that we, the conquerors of the world, have nothing better to do than stand waiting by the walls of every kennel, to traffic with the dogs of the earth? Lower away! I say – and see that your trumpery be bright in color, and just in weight!'

'El Elohim!'[8] ejaculated the Pharisee, as the discordant tones of the centurion rattled up the crags of the precipice, and fainted away against the temple – 'El Elohim! *who* is the god Phoebus? *whom* doth the blasphemer invoke? Thou, Buzi-Ben-Levi, who art read in the laws of the Gentiles, and hast sojourned among them who dabble with the Teraphim! – is it Nergal of whom the idolater speaketh? – or Ashimah? – or Nibhaz? – or Tartak? – or Adramalech? – or Anamalech? – or Succoth-Benith? – or Dagon? – or Belial? – or Baal-Perith? – or Baal-Peor? – or Baal-Zebub?'[9]

'Verily it is neither – but beware how thou lettest the rope slip too rapidly through thy fingers; for, should the wicker-work chance to hang on the projection of yonder crag, there will be a woeful outpouring of the holy things of the sanctuary.'

By the assistance of some rudely constructed machinery, the heavily laden basket was now carefully lowered down among the multitude; and, from the giddy pinnacle, the Romans were seen gathering confusedly round it; but, owing to the vast height and the prevalence of a fog, no distinct view of their operations could be obtained.

Half an hour had already elapsed.

'We shall be too late,' sighed the Pharisee, as at the expiration of this period, he looked over into the abyss – 'we shall be too late! we shall be turned out of office by the Katholim.'

'No more,' responded Abel-Phittim, 'no more shall we feast upon the fat of the land; no longer shall our beards be odorous with frankincense – our loins girded up with fine linen from the Temple.'

'Raca!' swore Ben-Levi, 'Raca! do they mean to defraud us of the purchase-money? or, Holy Moses!· are they weighing the shekels of the tabernacle?'.

'They have given the signal at last,' cried the Pharisee, 'they have given the signal at last – pull away, Abel-Phittim! – and thou, Buzi-Ben-Levi, pull away! – for verily the Philistines have either still hold upon the basket, or the Lord hath softened their hearts to place therein a beast of good weight!' And the Gizbarim pulled away, while their burden swung heavily upwards through the still increasing mist.

'Booshoh he!' – as, at the conclusion of an hour, some object at the extremity of the rope became indistinctly visible – 'Booshoh he!' was the exclamation which burst from the lips of Ben-Levi.

'Booshoh he! – for shame! – it is a ram from the thickets of Engedi, and as rugged as the valley of Jehoshaphat!'

'It is a firstling of the flock,' said Abel-Phittim,. 'I know him by the bleating of his lips, and the innocent folding of his limbs. His eyes are more beautiful than the jewels of the Pectoral,[10] and his flesh is like the honey of Hebron.'

'It is a fatted calf from the pastures of Bashan,' said the Pharisee, 'the heathen have dealt wonderfully with us! let us raise up our voices in a psalm! let us give thanks on the shawm and on the psaltery – on the harp and on the huggab – on the cythern and on the sackbut!'

It was not until the basket had arrived within a few feet of the Gizbarim, that a low grunt betrayed to their perception a *hog* of no common size.

'Now El Emanu!' slowly, and with upturned eyes, ejaculated the trio, as, letting go their hold, the emancipated porker tumbled headlong among the philistines, 'El Emanu! – God be with us – *it is the unutterable flesh!*'[11]

How to Write a *Blackwood* Article

In the name of the Prophet – figs![1]
Cry of Turkish Fig-pedlar

I PRESUME everybody has heard of me. My name is the Signora Psyche Zenobia. This I know to be a fact. Nobody but my enemies ever calls me Suky Snobbs. I have been assured that Suky is but a vulgar corruption of Psyche, which is good Greek, and means 'the soul' (that's me, I'm *all* soul), and sometimes 'a butterfly', which latter meaning undoubtedly alludes to my appearance in my new crimson satin dress, with the sky-blue Arabian *mantelet*, and the trimmings of green *agraffas*, and the seven flounces of orange-colored *auriculas*. As for Snobbs – any person who should look at me would be instantly aware that my name wasn't Snobbs. Miss Tabitha Turnip propagated that report through sheer envy. Tabitha Turnip indeed! Oh, the little wretch! But what can we expect from a turnip? Wonder if she remembers the old adage about 'blood out of a turnip, etc.' (Mem.: put her in mind of it the first opportunity.) (Mem. again – pull her nose.) Where was I? Ah! I have been assured that Snobbs is a mere corruption of Zenobia,[2] and that Zenobia was a queen (so am I. Dr Moneypenny always calls me the Queen of Hearts), and that Zenobia, as well as Psyche, is good Greek, and that my father was 'a Greek', and that consequently I have a right to our patronymic, which is Zenobia, and not by any means Snobbs. Nobody but Tabitha Turnip calls me Suky Snobbs. I am the Signora Psyche Zenobia.

As I said before, everybody has heard of me. I am that very Signora Psyche Zenobia so justly celebrated as corresponding secretary to the 'Philadelphia, Regular, Exchange, Tea, Total, Young, Belles, Lettres, Universal, Experimental, Bibliographical, Association, To, Civilize, Humanity'. Dr Moneypenny made the title for us, and says he chose it because it sounded big, like an empty rum-puncheon. (A vulgar man that sometimes, but he's deep.) We all sign the initials of the society after our names, in the fashion of the R.S.A., Royal Society of Arts – the S.D.U.K., Society for the Diffusion of Useful Knowledge, etc. etc. Dr Moneypenny says that S stands for *stale*, and that D.U.K. spells duck (but it don't), and that S.D.U.K. stands for Stale Duck, and not for Lord Brougham's[3] Society; but then Dr Moneypenny is such a queer man that I am never sure when he is telling me the truth. At any rate we always add to our names the initials P.R.E.T.T.Y.B.L.U.E.B.A.T.C.H. – that is to say, Philadelphia, Regular, Exchange, Tea, Total, Young, Belles, Lettres, Universal, Experimental, Bibliographical, Association, To, Civilize, Human-ity – one letter for each word, which is a decided improvement upon Lord Brougham. Dr Moneypenny will have it that our initials give our true character, but for my life I can't see what he means.[4]

Notwithstanding the good offices of the Doctor, and the strenuous exertions of the Association to get itself into notice, it met with no very great success until I joined it. The truth is, members indulged in too flippant a tone of discussion. The papers read every Saturday evening were characterized less by depth than buffoonery. They were all whipped syllabub. There was no investigation of first causes, first principles. There was no investigation of anything at all. There was no attention paid to that great point, the 'fitness of things'. In short, there was no fine writing like this. It was all low – very! No profundity, no reading, no metaphysics, nothing which the learned call spirituality and which the unlearned choose to stigmatize as cant. (Dr M. says I ought to spell 'cant' with a capital K – but I know better.)

When I joined the Society it was my endeavor to intro-duce a better style of thinking and writing, and all the world knows how well I have succeeded. We get up as good papers now in the P.R.E.T.T.Y.B.L.U.E.B.A.T.C.H. as any to be found even in *Blackwood*. I say *Blackwood*, because I have been assured that the finest writing, upon every subject, is to be discovered in the pages of that justly celebrated magazine. We now take it for our model upon all themes, and are getting into rapid notice accordingly.

And, after all, it's not so very difficult a matter to compose an
article of the genuine *Blackwood* stamp, if one only goes properly
about it. Of course I don't speak of the political articles. Everybody knows how *they* are managed, since Dr Moneypenny explained it. Mr Blackwood has a pair of tailor's shears, and three
apprentices who stand by him for orders. One hands him *The
Times*,[5] another the *Examiner*, and a third a Gulley's *New Com-
pendium of Slang-Whang*. Mr B— merely cuts out and intersperses.
It is soon done: nothing but *Examiner*, *Slang-Whang*, and *Times*;
then *Times*, *Slang-Whang*, and *Examiner*; and then *Times*, *Examiner*, and *Slang-Whang*.

But the chief merit of the magazine lies in its miscellaneous
articles; and the best of these come under the head of what Dr
Moneypenny calls the *bizarreries* (whatever that may mean) and
what everybody else calls the *intensities*. This is a species of
writing which I have long known how to appreciate, although
it is only since my late visit to Mr Blackwood (deputed by the
Society) that I have been made aware of the exact method of
composition. This method is very simple, but not so much so as
the politics. Upon my calling at Mr B—'s, and making known to
him the wishes of the Society, he received me with great civility,
took me into his study, and gave me a clear explanation of the
whole process.

'My dear madam,' said he, evidently struck with my majestic
appearance, for I had on the crimson satin, with the green *agraffas*,
and orange-colored *auriculas*, 'my *dear* madam,' said he, 'sit down.
The matter stands thus. In the first place, your writer of intensities
must have very black ink, and a very big pen, with a very blunt
nib. And, mark me, Miss Psyche Zenobia!' he continued, after a
pause, with the most impressive energy and solemnity of manner,
'mark me! – *that pen – must – never be mended!* Herein, madam, lies
the secret, the soul, of intensity. I assume upon myself to say, that
no individual, of however great genius, ever wrote with a good pen
– understand me – a good article. You may take it for granted that
when manuscript can be read it is never worth reading. This is a
leading principle in our faith, to which if you cannot readily
assent, our conference is at an end.'

He paused. But, of course, as I had no wish to put an end

The Other Poe

to the conference, I assented to a proposition so very obvious, and one, too, of whose truth I had all along been sufficiently aware. He seemed pleased, and went on with his instructions.

'It may appear invidious in me, Miss Psyche Zenobia, to refer you to any article, or set of articles, in the way of model or study; yet perhaps I may as well call your attention to a few cases. Let me see. There was "The Dead Alive",[6] a capital thing! the record of a gentleman's sensations when entombed before the breath was out of his body; full of taste, terror, sentiment, metaphysics, and erudition. You would have sworn that the writer had been born and brought up in a coffin. Then we had the *Confessions of an Opium Eater*[7] – fine, very fine! – glorious imagination – deep philosophy – acute speculation – plenty of fire and fury, and a good spicing of the decidedly unintelligible. That was a nice bit of flummery, and went down the throats of the people delightfully. They would have it that Coleridge wrote the paper – but not so. It was composed by my pet baboon, Juniper, over a rummer of Hollands and water, "hot without sugar".' (This I could scarcely have believed had it been anybody but Mr Blackwood, who assured me of it.) 'Then there was "The Involuntary Experimentalist",[8] all about a gentleman who got baked in an oven, and came out alive and well, although certainly done to a turn. And then there was *The Diary of a Late Physician*,[9] where the merit lay in good rant, and indifferent Greek – both of them taking things with the public. And then there was "The Man in the Bell",[10] a paper, by the bye, Miss Zenobia, which I cannot sufficiently recommend to your attention. It is the history of a young person who goes to sleep under the clapper of a church bell, and is awakened by its tolling for a funeral. The sound drives him mad, and, accordingly, pulling out his tablets, he gives a record of his sensations. Sensations are the great things, after all. Should you ever be drowned or hung, be sure and make a note of your sensations; they will be worth ten guineas a sheet. If you wish to write forcibly, Miss Zenobia, pay minute attention to the sensations.'

'That I certainly will, Mr Blackwood,' said I.

'Good!' he replied. 'I see you are a pupil after my own heart. But I must put you *au fait* to the details necessary in composing what may be denominated a genuine *Blackwood* article of the sensation stamp, the kind which you will understand me to say I consider the best for all purposes.

'The first thing requisite is to get yourself into such a scrape as no one ever got into before. The oven, for instance, – that was a good hit. But if you have no oven or big bell at hand, and if you cannot conveniently tumble out of a balloon, or be swallowed up in an earthquake, or get stuck fast in a chimney, you will have to be contented with simply imagining some similar misadventure. I should prefer, however, that you have the actual fact to bear you out. Nothing so well assists the fancy as an experimental knowledge of the matter in hand. "Truth is strange," you know, "stranger than fiction" – besides being more to the purpose.'

Here I assured him I had an excellent pair of garters, and would go and hang myself forthwith.

'Good!' he replied, 'do so; although hanging is somewhat hackneyed. Perhaps you might do better. Take a dose of Brandreth's pills, and then give us your sensations. However, my instructions will apply equally well to any variety of misadventure, and in your way home you may easily get knocked in the head, or run over by an omnibus, or bitten by a mad dog, or drowned in a gutter. But to proceed.

'Having determined upon your subject, you must next consider the tone, or manner, of your narration. There is the tone didactic, the tone enthusiastic, the tone natural – all commonplace enough. But then there is the tone laconic, or curt, which has lately come much into use. It consists in short sentences. Somehow thus: Can't be too brief. Can't be too snappish. Always a full stop. And never a paragraph.

'Then there is the tone elevated, diffusive, and interjectional. Some of our best novelists patronize this tone. The words must be all in a whirl, like a humming-top, and make a noise very similar, which answers remarkably well instead of meaning. This is the best of all possible styles where the writer is in too great a hurry to think.

'The tone metaphysical is also a good one. If you know any big words this is your chance for them. Talk of the Ionic and Eleatic schools – of Archytas, Gorgias, and Alcmaeon. Say something about objectivity and subjectivity. Be sure and abuse a man, named Locke. Turn up your nose at things in general, and when you let slip anything a little *too* absurd, you need not be at the trouble of scratching it out, but just add a foot-note, and say that you are indebted for the above profound observation to the *Kritik der reinen Vernunft*, or to the *Metaphysische Anfangsgrunde der Naturwissenschaft*.[11] This will look erudite and – and – and frank.

'There are various other tones of equal celebrity, but I shall mention only two more, the tone transcendental and the tone heterogeneous. In the former the merit consists in seeing into the nature of affairs a very great deal farther than anybody else. This second sight is very efficient when properly managed. A little reading of the *Dial*[12] will carry you a great way. Eschew, in this case, big words; get them as small as possible, and write them upside down. Look over Channing's poems and quote what he says about a "fat little man with a delusive show of Can".[13] Put in something about the Supernal Oneness. Don't say a syllable about the Infernal Twoness. Above all, study innuendo. Hint everything – assert nothing. If you feel inclined to say "bread and butter", do not by any means say it outright. You may say anything and everything *approaching* to "bread and butter". You may hint at buckwheat cake, or you may even go so far as to insinuate oatmeal porridge, but if bread and butter be your real meaning, be cautious, my *dear* Miss Psyche, not on any account to say "bread and butter"!'

I assured him that I should never say it again as long as I lived. He kissed me, and continued:

'As for the tone heterogeneous, it is merely a judicious mixture, in equal proportions, of all the other tones in the world, and is consequently made up of everything deep, great, odd, piquant, pertinent, and pretty.

'Let us suppose now you have determined upon your incidents and tone. The most important portion – in fact, the soul of the whole business, is yet to be attended to; I allude to *the filling up*. It is not to be supposed that a lady, or gentleman either, has been leading the life of a bookworm. And yet above all things it is necessary that your article have an air of erudition, or at least afford evidence of extensive general reading. Now I'll put you in the way of accomplishing this point. See here!' (pulling down some three or four ordinary-looking volumes, and opening them at random). 'By casting your eye down almost any page of any book in the world, you will be able to perceive at once a host of little scraps of either learning of *bel-esprit-ism*, which are the very thing for the spicing of a *Blackwood* article. You might as well note down a few while I read them to you. I shall make two divisions: first, PIQUANT FACTS FOR THE MANUFACTURE OF SIMILES; and second, PIQUANT EXPRESSIONS TO BE INTRODUCED AS OCCASION MAY REQUIRE. Write now!' – and I wrote as he dictated.

'PIQUANT FACTS FOR SIMILES. "There were originally but three Muses – Melete, Mneme, Aoede – meditation, memory, and singing." You may make a great deal of that little fact if properly worked. You see it is not generally known, and looks *recherché*. You must be careful and give the thing with a downright improviso air.

'Again. "The river Alpheus passed beneath the sea, and emerged without injury to the purity of its waters." Rather stale that, to be sure, but, if properly dressed and dished up, will look quite as fresh as ever.

'Here is something better. "The Persian Iris appears to some persons to possess a sweet and very powerful perfume, while to others it is perfectly scentless." Fine that, and very delicate! Turn it about a little, and it will do wonders. We'll have something else in the botanical line. There's nothing goes down so well, especially with the help of a little Latin. Write!

' "The *Epidendrum Flos Aeris*, of Java, bears a very beautiful flower, and will live when pulled up by the roots. The natives suspend it by a cord from the ceiling, and enjoy its fragrance for years." That's capital! That will do for the Similes. Now for the Piquant Expressions.

'PIQUANT EXPRESSIONS. "The venerable Chinese novel *Ju-Kiao-Li*."[14] Good! By introducing these few words with dexterity you will evince your intimate acquaintance with the language and literature of the Chinese. With the aid of this you may possibly get along without either Arabic, or Sanscrit, or Chickasaw. There is no passing muster, however, without Spanish, Italian, German, Latin, and Greek. I must look you out a little specimen of each. Any scrap will answer, because you must depend upon your own ingenuity to make it fit into your article. Now write!

' "*Aussi tendre que Zaïre*" – as tender as Zaire – French. Alludes to the frequent repetition of the phrase, *la tendre Zaïre*, in the French tragedy of that name.[15] Properly introduced, will show not only your knowledge of the language, but your general reading and wit. You can say, for instance, that the chicken you were eating (write an article about being choked to death by a chicken-bone) was not altogether *aussi tendre que Zaïre*. Write!

> Ven muerte tan escondida,
>   Que no te sienta venir,
> Porque el plazer del morir,
>   No me torne à dar la vida.

That's Spanish, from Miguel de Cervantes.[16] "Come quickly, O death! but be sure and don't let me see you coming, lest the pleasure I shall feel at your appearance should unfortunately bring me back again to life." This you may slip in quite *à propos* when you are struggling in the last agonies with the chicken-bone. Write!

> Il pover' huomo che non sen' era accorto,
> Andava combattendo, ed era morto.

That's Italian, you perceive – from Ariosto.[17] It means that a great hero, in the heat of combat, not perceiving that he had been fairly killed, continued to fight valiantly, dead as he was. The application of this to your own case is obvious; for I trust, Miss Psyche, that you will not neglect to kick for at least an hour and a half after you have been choked to death by that chicken-bone. Please to write!

> Und sterb' ich doch, so sterb' ich denn
> Durch sie – durch sie!

That's German – from Schiller.[18] "And if I die, at least I die – for thee – for thee!" Here it is clear that you are apostrophizing the *cause* of your disaster, the chicken. Indeed, what gentleman (or lady either) of sense, *wouldn't* die, I should like to know, for a well-fattened capon of the right Molucca breed, stuffed with capers and mushrooms, and served up in a salad-bowl, with orange-jellies *en mosaïques*. Write! (You can get them that way at Tortoni's.) – Write, if you please!

'Here is a nice little Latin phrase, and rare too (one can't be too *recherché* or brief in one's Latin, it's getting so common) – *ignoratio elenchi*. He has committed an *ignoratio elenchi*; that is to say, he has understood the words of your proposition, but not the idea. The man was *a fool*, you see. Some poor fellow whom you addressed while choking with that chicken-bone, and who therefore didn't precisely understand what you were talking about. Throw the *ignoratio elenchi* in his teeth, and at once you have him annihilated. If he dare to reply, you can tell him from Lucan (here it is) that speeches are mere *anemonae. verborum*, anemone words. The anemone, with great brilliancy, has no smell. Or, if he begin to bluster, you may be down upon him with *insomnia Jovis*, reveries of Jupiter – a phrase which Silius Italicus (see here!) applies to thoughts pompous and inflated. This will be sure and cut him to the heart. He can do nothing but roll over and die. Will you be kind enough to write?

'In Greek we must have something pretty – from Demosthenes,[19] for example. Ἀνὴρ ὁ Φεύγων καὶ πάλιν μαχήσεται. (Aner o pheugon kai palin makesetai.) There is a tolerably good translation of it in *Hudibras* –

> For he that flies may fight again,
> Which he can never do that's slain.

In a *Blackwood* article nothing makes so fine a show as your Greek. The very letters have an air of profundity about them. Only observe, madam, the astute look of that Epsilon! That Phi ought certainly to be a bishop! Was ever there a smarter fellow than that Omicron? Just twig that Tau! In short, there is nothing like Greek for a genuine sensation-paper. In the present case your application is the most obvious thing in the world. Rap out the sentence, with a huge oath, and by way of ultimatum at the good-for-nothing dunder-headed villain who couldn't understand your plain English in relation to the chicken-bone. He'll take the hint and be off, you may depend upon it.'

These were all the instructions Mr B— could afford me upon the topic in question, but I felt they would be entirely sufficient. I was, at length, able to write a genuine *Blackwood* article, and determined to do it forthwith. In taking leave of me, Mr B— made a proposition for the purchase of the paper when written; but, as he could offer me only fifty guineas a sheet, I thought it better to let our society have it than sacrifice it for so paltry a sum. Notwithstanding this niggardly spirit, however, the gentleman showed his consideration for me in all other respects, and indeed treated me with the greatest civility. His parting words made a deep impression upon my heart, and I hope I shall always remember them with gratitude.

'My dear Miss Zenobia,' he said, while the tears stood in his eyes, 'is there *anything* else I can do to promote the success of your laudable undertaking? Let me reflect! It is just possible that you may not be able, so soon as convenient, to – to – get yourself drowned, or – choked with a chicken-bone, or – or hung, – or – bitten by a – but stay! Now I think me of it, there are a couple of very excellent bull-dogs in the yard – fine fellows, I assure you – savage, and all that – indeed just the thing for your money – they'll have you eaten up, *auriculas* and all, in less than five minutes (here's my watch!) – and then only think of the sensations! Here! I say – Tom! – Peter! – Dick, you villain! – let out those' – but as I was really in a great hurry, and had not another moment to spare, I was reluctantly forced to expedite my departure, and accordingly took leave *at once* – somewhat more abruptly, I admit, than strict courtesy would have otherwise allowed.

It was my primary object upon quitting Mr Blackwood to get into some immediate difficulty, pursuant to his advice, and with this view I spent the greater part of the day in wandering about Edinburgh, seeking for desperate adventures – adventures adequate to the intensity of my feelings, and adapted to the vast character of the article I intended to write. In this excursion I was attended by my negro servant Pompey, and my little lap-dog Diana, whom I had brought with me from Philadelphia. It was not, however, until late in the afternoon that I fully succeeded in my arduous undertaking. An important event then happened of which the following *Blackwood* article, in the tone heterogeneous, is the substance and result.

Article for *Blackwood*

A Predicament

What chance, good lady, hath bereft you thus?
MILTON, *Comus*[1]

IT was a quiet and still afternoon when I strolled forth in the goodly city of Edina.[2] The confusion and bustle in the streets were terrible. Men were talking. Women were screaming. Children were choking. Pigs were whistling. Carts, they rattled. Bulls, they bellowed. Cows, they lowed. Horses, they neighed. Cats, they caterwauled. Dogs, they danced. *Danced!* Could it then be possible? *Danced!* Alas, thought I, *my* dancing days are over! Thus it is ever. What a host of gloomy recollections will ever and anon be awakened in the mind of genius and imaginative contemplation, especially of a genius doomed to the everlasting, and eternal, and continual, and, as one might say, the – *continued* – yes, the *continued and continuous*, bitter, harassing, disturbing, and, if I may be allowed the expression, the *very* disturbing influence of the serene, and godlike, and heavenly, and exalting, and elevated, and purifying effect of what may be rightly termed the most enviable, the most *truly* enviable – nay! the most benignly beautiful, the most deliciously ethereal, and, as it were, the most *pretty* (if I may use so bold an expression) *thing* (pardon me, gentle reader!) in the world – but I am always led away by my feelings. In *such* a mind, I repeat, what a host of recollections are stirred up by a trifle! The dogs danced! *I* – I *could* not! They frisked – I wept. They capered – I sobbed aloud. Touching circumstances! which cannot fail to bring to the recollection of the classical reader that exquisite passage in relation to the fitness of things, which is to to be found in the commencement of the third volume of that admirable and venerable Chinese novel, the *Jo-Go-Slow*.

In my solitary walk through the city I had two humble but faithful companions. Diana, my poodle! sweetest of creatures!

She had a quantity of hair over one eye, and a blue riband tied fashionably around her neck. Diana was not more than five inches in height, but her head was somewhat bigger than her body, and her tail, being cut off exceedingly close, gave an air of injured innocence to the interesting animal which rendered her a favourite with all.

And Pompey, my negro! – sweet Pompey! how shall I ever forget thee? I had taken Pompey's arm. He was three feet in height (I like to be particular) and about seventy, or perhaps eighty, years of age. He had bow-legs and was corpulent. His mouth should not be called small, nor his ears short. His teeth, however, were like pearl, and his large full eyes were deliciously white. Nature had endowed him with no neck, and had placed his ankles (as usual with that race) in the middle of the upper portion of the feet. He was clad with a striking simplicity. His sole garments were a stock of nine inches in height, and a nearly new drab overcoat which had formerly been in the service of the tall, stately, and illustrious Dr Moneypenny. It was a good overcoat. It was well cut. It was well made. The coat was nearly new. Pompey held it up out of the dirt with both hands.

There were three persons in our party, and two of them have already been the subject of remark. There was a third – that third person was myself. I am the Signora Psyche Zenobia. I am *not* Suky Snobbs. My appearance is commanding. On the memorable occasion of which I speak I was habited in a crimson satin dress, with a sky-blue Arabian mantelet. And the dress had trimmings of green *agraffas*, and seven graceful flounces of the orange-colored *auriculas*. I thus formed the third of the party. There was the poodle. There was Pompey. There was myself. We were *three*. Thus it is said there were originally but three Furies – Melty, Nimmy, and Hetty – Meditation, Memory, and Fiddling.

Leaning upon the arm of the gallant Pompey, and attended at a respectful distance by Diana, I proceeded down one of the populous and very pleasant streets of the now deserted Edina. On a sudden, there presented itself to view a church – a Gothic cathedral – vast, venerable, and with a tall steeple, which towered into the sky. What madness now possessed me? Why did

I rush upon my fate? I was seized with an uncontrollable desire to ascend the giddy pinnacle, and thence survey the immense extent of the city. The door of the cathedral stood invitingly open. My destiny prevailed. I entered the ominous arch-way. Where then was my guardian angel? – if indeed such angels there be. *If!* Distressing monosyllable! what a world of mystery, and meaning, and doubt, and uncertainty is there involved in thy two letters! I entered the ominous archway! I entered; and, without injury to my orange-colored *auriculas*, I passed beneath the portal, and emerged within the vestibule. Thus it is said the immense river Alfred passed, unscathed, and unwetted, beneath the sea.

I thought the staircases would never have an end. *Round!* Yes, they went round and up, and round and up and round and up, until I could not help surmising, with the sagacious Pompey, upon whose supporting arm I leaned in all the confidence of early affection – I *could* not help surmising that the upper end of the continuous spiral ladder had been accidentally, or perhaps designedly, removed. I paused for breath; and, in the mean time, an incident occurred of too momentous a nature in a moral, and also in a metaphysical, point of view, to be passed over without notice. It appeared to me – indeed I was quite confident of the fact – I could not be mistaken – no! I had, for some moments, carefully and anxiously observed the motions of my Diana – I say that *I could not be* mistaken – Diana *smelt a rat!* At once I called Pompey's attention to the subject, and he – he agreed with me. There was then no longer any reasonable room for doubt. The rat had been smelled – and by Diana. Heavens! shall I ever forget the intense excitement of that moment? Alas! what is the boasted intellect of man? The rat! – it was there – that is to say, it was somewhere. Diana smelled the rat. I – I *could* not! Thus it is said the Prussian Isis has, for some persons, a sweet and very powerful perfume, while to others it is perfectly scentless.

The staircase had been surmounted, and there were now only three or four more upward steps intervening between us and the summit. We still ascended, and now only one step remained. One step! One little, little step! Upon one such little step in the great staircase of human life how vast a sum of human happiness or misery often depends! I thought of myself, then of Pompey, and then of the mysterious and inexplicable destiny which surrounded us. I thought of Pompey! – alas, I thought of love! I thought of the many false *steps* which have been taken, and may be taken again. I resolved to be more cautious, more reserved. I abandoned the arm of Pompey, and, without his assistance, surmounted the one remaining step and gained the chamber of the belfry. I was followed immediately afterwards by my poodle. Pompey alone remained behind. I stood at the head of the staircase, and encouraged him to ascend. He stretched forth to me his hand, and unfortunately in so doing was forced to abandon his firm hold upon the overcoat. Will the gods never cease their persecution? The overcoat is dropped, and, with one of his feet, Pompey stepped upon the long and trailing skirt of the overcoat. He stumbled and fell – this consequence was inevitable. He fell forwards, and, with his accursed head, striking me full in the – in the breast, precipitated me headlong, together with himself, upon the hard, filthy, and detestable floor of the belfry. But my revenge was sure, sudden, and complete. Seizing him furiously by the wool with both hands, I tore out a vast quantity of the black, and crisp, and curling material, and tossed it from me with every manifestation of disdain. It fell among the ropes of the belfry and remained. Pompey arose, and said no word. But he regarded me piteously with his large eyes and – sighed. Ye gods – that sigh! It sunk into my heart. And the hair – the wool! Could I have reached that wool I would have bathed it with my tears, in testimony of regret. But alas! it was now far beyond my grasp. As it dangled among the cordage of the bell, I fancied it still alive. I fancied that it stood on end with indignation. Thus the *happydandy Flos Aeris* of Java bears, it is said, a beautiful flower, which will live when pulled up by the roots. The natives suspend it by a cord from the ceiling and enjoy its fragrance for years.

Our quarrel was now made up, and we looked about the room for an aperture through which to survey the city of Edina. Windows there were none. The sole light admitted into the gloomy chamber proceeded from a square opening, about a foot in diameter, at a height of about seven feet from the floor. Yet what will the energy of true genius not effect? I resolved to clamber up to this hole. A vast quantity of wheels, pinions, and other cabalistic-looking machinery stood opposite the hole, close to it; and through the hole there passed an iron rod from the machinery. Between the wheels and the wall where the hole lay there was barely room for my body – yet I was desperate, and determined to persevere. I called Pompey to my side.

'You perceive that aperture, Pompey. I wish to look through it. You will stand here just beneath the hole – so. Now, hold out one of your hands, Pompey, and let me step upon it – thus. Now, the other hand, Pompey, and with its aid I will get upon your shoulders.'

He did everything I wished, and I found, upon getting up, that I could easily pass my head and neck through the aperture. The prospect was sublime. Nothing could be more magnificent. I merely paused a moment to bid Diana behave herself, and assure Pompey that I would be considerate and bear as lightly as possible upon his shoulders. I told him I would be tender of his feelings – *ossi tender que beef-steak*. Having done this justice to my faithful friend, I gave myself up with great zest and enthusiasm to the enjoyment of the scene which so obligingly spread itself out before my eyes.

Upon this subject, however, I shall forbear to dilate. I will not describe the city of Edinburgh. Every one has been to Edinburgh – the classic Edina. I will confine myself to the momentous details of my own lamentable adventure. Having in some measure satisfied my curiosity in regard to the extent, situation, and general appearance of the city, I had leisure to survey the church in which I was, and the delicate architecture of the steeple. I observed that the aperture through which I had thrust my head was an opening in the dial-plate of a gigantic clock, and must have appeared, from the street, as a large keyhole, such as we see in the face of French watches. No doubt the true object was to admit the arm of an attendant, to adjust, when necessary, the hands of the clock from within. I observed also, with surprise, the immense size of these hands, the longest of which could not have been less than ten feet in length, and, where broadest, eight or nine inches in breadth. They were of solid steel apparently, and their edges appeared to be sharp. Having noticed these particulars, and some others, I again turned my eyes upon the glorious prospect below, and soon became absorbed in contemplation.

From this, after some minutes, I was aroused by the voice of Pompey, who declared he could stand it no longer, and requested that I would be so kind as to come down. This was unreasonable, and I told him so in a speech of some length. He replied, but with an evident misunderstanding of my ideas upon the subject. I accordingly grew angry, and told him, in plain words, that he was a fool, that he had committed an *ignoramus e-clench-eye*, that his notions were mere *insommary Bovis*, and his words were little better than *an ennemywerrybor'em*. With this he appeared satisfied, and I resumed my contemplations.

It might have been half an hour after this altercation when, as I was deeply absorbed in the heavenly scenery beneath me, I was startled by something very cold which pressed with a gentle pressure upon the back of my neck. It is needless to say that I felt inexpressibly alarmed. I knew that Pompey was beneath my feet, and that Diana was sitting, according to my explicit directions, upon her hind legs in the farthest corner of the room. What could it be? Alas! I but too soon discovered. Turning my head gently to one side, I perceived, to my extreme horror, that the huge, glittering, cimeter-like minute-hand of the clock had, in the course of its hourly revolution, *descended upon my neck*. There was, I knew, not a second to be lost. I pulled back at once – but it was too late. There was no chance of forcing my head through the mouth of that terrible trap in which it was so fairly caught, and which grew narrower and narrower with a rapidity too horrible to be conceived. The agony of that moment is not to be imagined. I threw up my hands and endeavored with all my strength, to force upward the ponderous iron bar. I might as well have tried to lift the cathedral itself. Down, down, down it came, closer and yet closer. I screamed to Pompey for aid; but he said that I had hurt his feelings by calling him 'an ignorant old squint eye'. I yelled to Diana; but she only said 'bow-wow-wow', and that 'I had told her on no account to stir from the corner'. Thus I had no relief to expect from my associates.

Meantime the ponderous and terrific *Scythe of Time* (for I now discovered the literal import of that classical phrase) had not stopped, nor was it likely to stop, in its career. Down and still down, it came. It had already buried its sharp edge a full inch in my flesh, and my sensations grew indistinct and confused. At one time I fancied myself in Philadelphia with the stately Dr Moneypenny, at another in the back parlor of Mr Blackwood receiving his invaluable instructions. And then again the sweet recollection of better and earlier times came over me, and I thought of that happy period when the world was not all a desert, and Pompey not altogether cruel.

The ticking of the machinery amused me. *Amused me*, I say, for my sensations now bordered upon perfect happiness, and the most trifling circumstances afforded me pleasure. The eternal *click-clack, click-clack, click-clack,* of the clock was the most melodious of music in my ears, and occasionally even put me in mind of the grateful sermonic harangues of Dr Ollapod. Then there were the great figures upon the dial-plate – how intelligent, how intellectual, they all looked! And presently they took to dancing the Mazurka, and I think it was the figure V who performed the most to my satisfaction. She was evidently a lady of breeding. None of your swaggerers, and nothing at all indelicate in her motions. She did the pirouette to admiration – whirling round upon her apex. I made an endeavor to hand her a chair, for I saw that she appeared fatigued with her exertions, and it was not until then that I fully perceived my lamentable situation. Lamentable indeed! The bar had buried itself two inches in my neck. I was aroused to a sense of exquisite pain. I prayed for death, and, in the agony of the moment, could not help repeating those exquisite verses of the poet Miguel De Cervantes:–

> Vanny Buren, tan escondida
> Query no te senty venny
> Pork and pleasure, delly morry
> Nommy, torny, darry, widdy!

But now a new horror presented itself, and one indeed sufficient to startle the strongest nerves. My eyes, from the cruel pressure of the machine, were absolutely starting from their sockets. While I was thinking how I should possibly manage without them, one actually tumbled out of my head, and, rolling down the steep side of the steeple, lodged in the rain gutter which ran along the eaves of the main building. The loss of the eye was not so much as the insolent air of independence and contempt with which it regarded me after it was out. There it lay in the gutter just under my nose, and the airs it gave itself would have been ridiculous had they not been disgusting. Such a winking and blinking were never before seen. This behavior on the part of my eye in the gutter was not only irritating on account of its manifest insolence and shameful ingratitude, but was also exceedingly inconvenient on account of the sympathy which always exists between two eyes of the same head, however far apart. I was forced, in a manner, to wink and to blink, whether I would or not, in exact concert with the scoundrelly thing that lay just under my nose. I was presently relieved, however, by the dropping out of the other eye. In falling it took the same direction (possibly a concerted plot) as its fellow. Both rolled out of the gutter together, and in truth I was very glad to get rid of them.

The bar was now four inches and a half deep in my neck, and there was only a little bit of skin to cut through. My sensations were those of entire happiness, for I felt that in a few minutes, at farthest, I should be relieved from my disagreeable situation. And in this expectation I was not at all deceived. At twenty-five minutes past five in the afternoon precisely, the huge minute-hand had proceeded sufficiently far on its terrible revolution to sever the small remainder of my neck. I was not sorry to see the head which had occasioned me so much embarrassment at length make a final separation from my body. It first rolled down the side of the steeple, then lodged, for a few seconds, in the gutter, and then made its way, with a plunge, into the middle of the street.[3]

I will candidly confess that my feelings were now of the most singular – nay, of the most mysterious, the most perplexing and incomprehensible character. My senses were here and there at one and the same moment. With my head I imagined, at one time, that I, the head, was the real Signora Psyche Zenobia – at another I felt convinced that myself, the body, was the proper identity. To clear my ideas upon this topic I felt in my pocket for my snuff-box, but, upon getting it, and endeavoring to apply a pinch of its grateful contents in the ordinary manner, I became immediately aware of my peculiar deficiency, and threw the box at once down to my head. It took a pinch with great satisfaction, and smiled me an acknowledgment in return. Shortly afterwards it made me a speech, which I could hear but indistinctly without ears. I gathered enough, however, to know that it was astonished at my wishing to remain alive under such circumstances. In the concluding sentences it quoted the noble words of Ariosto –

> Il pover hommy che non sera corty
> And have a combat tenty erry morty;

thus comparing me to the hero who, in the heat of the combat, not perceiving that he was dead, continued to contest the battle with inextinguishable valor. There was nothing now to prevent my getting down from my elevation, and I did so. What it was that Pompey saw so *very* peculiar in my appearance I have never yet been able to find out. The fellow opened his mouth from ear to ear, and shut his two eyes as if he were endeavoring to crack nuts between the lids. Finally, throwing off his overcoat, he made one spring for the staircase and disappeared. I hurled after the scoundrel those vehement words of Demosthenes –

> Andrew O'Phlegethon, you really make haste to fly,

and then turned to the darling of my heart, to the one-eyed, the shaggy-haired Diana. Alas! what a horrible vision affronted my eyes! *Was* that a rat I saw skulking into his hole? *Are* these the picked bones of the little angel who has been cruelly devoured by the monster? Ye gods! and what *do* I behold – *is* that the departed spirit, the shade, the ghost of my beloved puppy, which I perceive sitting with a grace so melancholy in the corner? Hearken! for she speaks, and, heavens! it is in the German of Schiller –

> Unt stubby duk, so stubby dun
> Duk she! duk she!

Alas! and are not her words too true?

> And if I died at least I died
> For thee – for thee.

79

Sweet creature! she *too* has sacrificed herself in my behalf. Dogless, niggerless, headless, what *now* remains for the unhappy Signora Psyche Zenobia? Alas – *nothing!* I have done.

The Devil in the Belfry

What o'clock is it?
Old Saying

EVERYBODY knows, in a general way, that the finest place in the world is – or, alas, *was* – the Dutch borough of Vondervottei-mittiss.[1] Yet, as it lies some distance from any of the main roads, being in a somewhat out-of-the-way situation, there are, perhaps, very few of my readers who have ever paid it a visit. For the benefit of those who have not, therefore, it will be only proper that I should enter into some account of it. And this is, indeed, the more necessary, as, with the hope of enlisting public sympathy in behalf of the inhabitants, I design here to give a history of the calamitous events which have so lately occurred within its limits. No one who knows me will doubt that the duty thus self-imposed will be executed to the best of my ability, with all that rigid impartiality, all that cautious examination into facts, and diligent collation of authorities, which should ever distinguish him who aspires to the title of historian.

By the united aid of medals, manuscripts, and inscriptions, I am enabled to say, positively, that the borough of Vondervottei-mittiss has existed, from its origin, in precisely the same condition which it at present preserves. Of the date of this origin, however, I grieve that I can only speak with that species of indefinite definiteness which mathematicians are, at times, forced to put up with in certain algebraic formulae. The date, I may thus say, in regard to the remoteness of its antiquity, cannot be less than any assignable quantity whatsoever.

Touching the derivation of the name Vonderdotteimittiss, I confess myself, with sorrow, equally at fault. Among a multitude of opinions upon this delicate point – some acute, some learned, some sufficiently the reverse – I am able to select nothing which

81

ought to be considered satisfactory. Perhaps the idea of Grogs-wigg, nearly coincident with that of Kroutaplenttey, is to be cautiously preferred. It runs: – '*Vondervotteimittiss – Vonder, lege Donder – Votteimittiss, quasi und Bleitziz – Bleitziz obsol: pro Blitzen.*' This derivation, to say the truth, is still countenanced by some traces of the electric fluid evident on the summit of the steeple of the House of the Town Council. I do not choose, however, to commit myself on a theme of such importance, and must refer the reader desirous of information to the *Oratiunculae de Rebus Praeter-Veteris*, of Dundergutz. See, also, Blunderbuzzard, *De Derivationibus*, pp. 27 to 5010, Folio, Gothic edit., Red and Black character, Catch-word and No Cipher; wherein consult, also, marginal notes in the autograph of Stuffundpuff, with the Sub-Commentaries of Gruntundguzzell.

Notwithstanding the obscurity which thus envelops the date of the foundation of Vondervotteimittiss, and the derivation of its name, there can be no doubt, as I said before, that it has always existed as we find it at this epoch. The oldest man in the borough can remember not the slightest difference in the appearance of any portion of it; and, indeed, the very suggestion of such a possibility is considered an insult. The site of the village is in a perfectly circular valley, about a quarter of a mile in circumference, and entirely surrounded by gentle hills, over whose summit the people have never yet ventured to pass. For this they assign the very good reason that they do not believe there is anything at all on the other side.

Round the skirts of the valley (which is quite level, and paved throughout with flat tiles) extends a continuous row of sixty little houses. These, having their backs on the hills, must look, of course, to the centre of the plain, which is just sixty yards from the front door of each dwelling. Every house has a small garden before it, with a circular path, a sun-dial, and twenty-four cabbages. The buildings themselves are so precisely alike that one can in no manner be distinguished from the other. Owing to the vast antiquity, the style of architecture is somewhat odd, but it is not for that reason the less strikingly picturesque. They are fashioned of hard-burned little bricks, red, with black ends, so that the walls look like a chess-board upon a great scale.

The gables are turned to the front, and there are cornices, as big as all the rest of the house, over the eaves and over the main doors. The windows are narrow and deep, with very tiny panes and a great deal of sash. On the roof is a vast quantity of tiles with long curly ears. The woodwork, throughout, is of a dark hue, and there is much carving about it, with but a trifling variety of pattern; for, time out of mind, the carvers of Vondervotteimittiss have never been able to carve more than two objects – a timepiece and a cabbage. But these they do exceedingly well, and intersperse them with singular ingenuity, wherever they find room for the chisel.[2]

The dwellings are as much alike inside as out, and the furniture is all upon one plan. The floors are of square tiles, the chairs and tables of black-looking wood with thin crooked legs and puppy feet. The mantel-pieces are wide and high, and have not only timepieces and cabbages sculptured over the front, but a real timepiece, which makes a prodigious ticking, on the top in the middle, with a flower-pot containing a cabbage standing on each extremity by way of outrider. Between each cabbage and the timepiece, again, is a little china man having a large stomach with a great round hole in it, through which is seen the dialplate of a watch.

The fireplaces are large and deep, with fierce crooked-looking firedogs. There is constantly a rousing fire, and a huge pot over it, full of sauer-kraut and pork, to which the good woman of the house is always busy in attending. She is a little fat old lady, with blue eyes and a red face, and wears a huge cap like a sugar-loaf, ornamented with purple and yellow ribbons. Her dress is of orange-colored linsey-woolsey, made very full behind and very short in the waist – and indeed very short in other respects, not reaching below the middle of her leg. This is somewhat thick, and so are her ankles, but she has a fine pair of green stockings to cover them. Her shoes, of pink leather, are fastened each with a bunch of yellow ribbons puckered up in the shape of a cabbage. In her left hand she has a little heavy Dutch watch; in her right she wields a ladle for the sauer-kraut and pork. By her side there stands a fat tabby cat, with a gilt toy repeater tied to its tail, which 'the boys' have there fastened by way of a quiz.

The boys themselves are, all three of them, in the garden attending the pig. They are each two feet in height. They have three-cornered cocked hats, purple waistcoats reaching down to their thighs, buckskin knee-breeches, red woollen stockings, heavy shoes with big silver buckles, and long surtout coats with large buttons of mother-of-pearl. Each, too, has a pipe in his mouth, and a little dumpy watch in his right hand. He takes a puff and a look, and then a look and a puff. The pig – which is corpulent and lazy – is occupied now in picking up the stray leaves that fall from the cabbages, and now in giving a kick behind at the gilt repeater, which the urchins have also tied to *his* tail, in order to make him look as handsome as the cat.

Right at the front door, in a high-backed leather-bottomed arm-chair, with crooked legs and puppy feet like the tables, is seated the old man of the house himself. He is an exceedingly puffy little old gentleman, with big circular eyes and a huge double chin. His dress resembles that of the boys – and I need say nothing farther about it. All the difference is, that his pipe is somewhat bigger than theirs, and he can make a greater smoke. Like them, he has a watch, but he carries his watch in his pocket. To say the truth, he has something of more importance than a watch to attend to – and what that is I shall presently explain. He sits with his right leg upon his left knee, wears a grave countenance, and always keeps one of his eyes, at least, resolutely bent upon a certain remarkable object in the centre of the plain.

This object is situated in the steeple of the House of the Town Council. The Town Council are all very little, round, oily, intelligent men, with big saucer eyes and fat double chins, and have their coats much longer and their shoe-buckles much bigger than the ordinary inhabitants of Vondervotteimittiss. Since my sojourn in the borough, they have had several special meetings, and have adopted these three important resolutions:–

'That it is wrong to alter the good old course of things';

'That there is nothing tolerable out of Vondervotteimittiss'; and –

'That we will stick by our clocks and our cabbages'.

Above the session-room of the Council is the steeple, and in the steeple is the belfry, where exists, and has existed time out of mind, the pride and wonder of the village – the great clock of the borough of Vondervotteimittiss. And this is the object to which the eyes of the old gentlemen are turned who sit in the leather-bottomed arm-chairs.

The great clock has seven faces, one in each of the seven sides of the steeple, so that it can be readily seen from all quarters. Its faces are large and white, and its hands heavy and black. There is a belfry-man whose sole duty is to attend to it; but this duty is the most perfect of sinecures, for the clock of Vondervotteimittiss was never yet known to have anything the matter with it. Until lately, the bare supposition of such a thing was considered heretical. From the remotest period of antiquity to which the archives have reference, the hours have been regularly struck by the big bell. And, indeed, the case was just the same with all the other clocks and watches in the borough. Never was such a place for keeping the true time. When the large clapper thought proper to say 'Twelve o'clock!' all its obedient followers opened their throats simultaneously, and responded like a very echo. In short, the good burghers were fond of their sauer-kraut, but then they were proud of their clocks.

All people who hold sinecure offices are held in more or less respect, and, as the belfry-man of Vondervotteimittiss has the most perfect of sinecures, he is the most perfectly respected of any man in the world. He is the chief dignitary of the borough, and the very pigs look up to him with a sentiment of reverence. His coat-tail is *very* far longer – his pipe, his shoe-buckles, his eyes, and his stomach, *very* far bigger – than those of any other old gentleman in the village; and as to his chin, it is not only double, but triple.

I have thus painted the happy estate of Vondervotteimittiss: alas, that so fair a picture should ever experience a reverse!

There has been long a saying, among the wisest inhabitants, that 'no good can come from over the hills'; and it really seemed that the words had in them something of the spirit of prophecy. It wanted five minutes of noon, on the day before yesterday, when there appeared a very odd-looking object on the summit of the ridge to the eastward. Such an occurrence, of course, attracted universal attention, and every little old gentleman who sat in a leather-bottomed arm-chair turned one of his eyes with a stare of dismay upon the phenomenon, still keeping the other upon the clock in the steeple.

By the time that it wanted only three minutes to noon, the droll object in question was perceived to be a very diminutive foreign-looking young man. He descended the hills at a great rate, so that everybody had soon a good look at him. He was really the most finicky little personage that had ever been seen in Vondervotteimittiss. His countenance was of a dark snuff-color, and he had a long hooked nose, pea eyes, a wide mouth, and an excellent set of teeth, which latter he seemed anxious of displaying, as he was grinning from ear to ear. What with mustachios and whiskers, there was none of the rest of his face to be seen. His head was uncovered, and his hair neatly done up in *papillotes*. His dress was a tight-fitting swallow-tailed black coat (from one of whose pockets dangled a vast length of white handkerchief), black kerseymere knee-breeches, black stockings, and stumpy looking pumps, with huge bunches of black satin ribbon for bows. Under one arm he carried a huge *chapeau-de-bras*, and under the other a fiddle nearly five times as big as himself. In his left hand was a gold snuff-box, from which, as he capered down the hill, cutting all manner of fantastical steps, he took snuff incessantly with an air of the greatest possible self-satisfaction. God bless me! – here was a sight for the honest burghers of Vondervotteimittiss!

To speak plainly, the fellow had, in spite of his grinning, an audacious and sinister kind of face; and, as he curvetted right into the village, the odd stumpy appearance of his pumps excited no little suspicion; and many a burgher who beheld him that day would have given a trifle for a peep beneath the white cambric handkerchief which hung so obtrusively from the pocket of his swallow-tailed coat. But what mainly occasioned a righteous indignation was that the scoundrelly popinjay, while he cut a fandango here, and a whirligig there, did not seem to have the remotest idea in the world of such a thing as *keeping time* in his steps.

The good people of the borough had scarcely a chance, however, to get their eyes thoroughly open, when, just as it wanted half a minute of noon, the rascal bounced, as I say, right into the midst of them; gave a *chassez* here, and a *balancez* there; and then, after a *pirouette* and a *pas-de-zéphyr*, pigeon-winged himself right up into the belfry of the House of the Town Council, where the wonder-stricken belfry-man sat smoking in a state of dignity and dismay. But the little chap seized him at once by the nose; gave it a swing and a pull; clapped the big *chapeau-de-bras* upon his head; knocked it down over his eyes and mouth; and then, lifting up the big fiddle, beat him with it so long and so soundly that, what with the belfry-man being so fat, and the fiddle being so hollow, you would have sworn that there was a regiment of double-bass drummers all beating the devil's tattoo up in the belfry of the steeple of Vondervotteimittiss.

There is no knowing to what desperate act of vengeance this unprincipled attack might have aroused the inhabitants, but for the important fact that it now wanted only half a second of noon. The bell was about to strike, and it was a matter of absolute and pre-eminent necessity that everybody should look well at his watch. It was evident, however, that just at this moment the fellow in the steeple was doing something that he had no business to do with the clock. But as it now began to strike, nobody had any time to attend to his manoeuvres, for they had all to count the strokes of the bell as it sounded.

'One!' said the clock.

'Von!' echoed every little old gentleman in every leather-bottomed arm-chair in Vondervotteimittiss. 'Von!' said his watch also; 'von!' said the watch of his vrow, and 'von!' said the watches of the boys, and the little gilt repeaters on the tails of the cat and pig.

'Two!' continued the big bell; and

'Doo!' repeated all the repeaters.

'Three! Four! Five! Six! Seven! Eight! Nine! Ten!' said the bell.

'Dree! Vour! Fibe! Sax! Seben! Aight! Noin! Den!' answered the others.

'Eleven!' said the big one.

'Eleben!' assented the little fellows.

'Twelve!' said the bell.

'Dvelf!' they replied, perfectly satisfied, and dropping their voices.

'Und dvelf it iss!' said all the little old gentlemen, putting up their watches. But the big bell had not done with them yet.

'Thirteen!' said he.

'Der Teufel!' gasped the little old gentlemen, turning pale, dropping their pipes, and putting down all their right legs from over their left knees.

'Der Teufel!' groaned they, 'Dirteen! Dirteen!! – Mein Gott, it is Dirteen o'clock!!'

Why attempt to describe the terrible scene which ensued? All Vondervotteimittiss flew at once into a lamentable state of uproar.

'Vot is cum'd to mein pelly?' roared all the boys, – 'I've been ongry for dis hour!'

'Vot is cum'd to mein kraut?' screamed all the vrows. 'It has been done to rags for dis hour!'

'Vot is cum'd to mein pipe?' swore all the little old gentlemen. 'Donder and Blitzen! it has been smoked out for dis hour!' – and they filled them up again in a great rage, and, sinking back in their arm-chairs, puffed away so fast and so fiercely that the whole valley was immediately filled with impenetrable smoke.

Meantime the cabbages all turned very red in the face, and it seemed as if old Nick himself had taken possession of everything in the shape of a timepiece. The clocks carved upon the furniture took to dancing bewitched, while those upon the mantel-pieces could scarcely contain themselves for fury, and kept such a continual striking of thirteen, and such a frisking and wriggling of their pendulums as was really horrible to see. But, worse than all, neither the cats nor the pigs could put up any longer with the behaviour of the little repeaters tied to their tails, and resented it by scampering all over the place, scratching and poking, and squeaking and screeching, and caterwauling and squalling, and flying into the faces, and running under the petticoats, of the people, and creating altogether the most abominable din and confusion which it is possible for a reasonable person to conceive. And, to make matters still more distressing, the rascally little scapegrace in the steeple was evidently exerting himself to the utmost. Every now and then one might catch a glimpse of the scoundrel through the smoke. There he sat in the belfry upon the belfry-man, who was lying upon his back. In his teeth the villain held the bell-rope, which he kept jerking about with his head, raising such a clatter that my ears ring again even to think of it. On his lap lay the big fiddle at which he was scraping out of all time and tune, with both hands, making a great show, the nincompoop! of playing 'Judy O'Flannagan and Paddy O'Raferty'.

Affairs being thus miserably situated, I left the place in disgust, and now appeal for aid to all lovers of correct time and fine kraut. Let us proceed in a body to the borough, and restore the ancient order of things in Vondervotteimittiss by ejecting that little fellow from the steeple.

The Man that was Used Up

A Tale of the Late Bugaboo and Kickapoo Campaign

Pleurez, pleurez, mes yeux, et fondez-vous en eau!
La moitié de ma vie a mis l'autre au tombeau.
CORNEILLE, *Le Cid*. III. iii[1]

I CANNOT just now remember when or where I first made the acquaintance of that truly fine-looking fellow, Brevet Brigadier-General John A. B. C. Smith. Some one *did* introduce me to the gentleman, I am sure, – at some public meeting, I know very well – held about something of great importance, no doubt – at some place or other, I feel convinced – whose name I have unaccountably forgotten. The truth is that the introduction was attended, upon my part, with a degree of anxious embarrassment which operated to prevent any definite impressions of either time or place. I am constitutionally nervous; this, with me, is a family failing, and I can't help it. In especial, the slightest appearance of mystery – of any point I cannot exactly comprehend – puts me at once into a pitiable state of agitation.

There was something, as it were, remarkable – yes, *remarkable*, although this is but a feeble term to express my full meaning – about the entire individuality of the personage in question. He was, perhaps, six feet in height and of a presence singularly commanding. There was an *air distingué* pervading the whole man, which spoke of high breeding, and hinted at high birth. Upon this topic, the topic of Smith's personal appearance, I have a kind of melancholy satisfaction in being minute. His head of hair would have done honor to a Brutus; nothing could be more richly flowing, or possess a brighter gloss. It was of a jetty black; which was also the color, or more properly, the no color, of his unimaginable whiskers. You perceive I cannot speak of these latter without enthusiasm; it is not too much to say that they were the handsomest pair of whiskers under the sun. At all events, they encircled, and at times partially overshadowed, a mouth utterly unequalled. Here were the most entirely even and the most brilliantly white of all conceivable teeth. From between them, upon every proper occasion, issued a voice of surpassing clearness, melody, and strength. In the matter of eyes, also, my acquaintance was pre-eminently endowed. Either one of such a pair was worth a couple of the ordinary ocular organs. They were of a deep hazel, exceedingly large and lustrous; and there was perceptible about them, ever and anon, just that amount of interesting obliquity which gives pregnancy to expression.

The bust of the General was unquestionably the finest bust I ever saw. For your life you could not have found a fault with its wonderful proportion. This rare peculiarity set off to great advantage a pair of shoulders which would have called up a blush of conscious inferiority into the countenance of the marble Apollo. I have a passion for fine shoulders, and may say that I never beheld them in perfection before. The arms altogether were admirably modelled. Nor were the lower limbs less superb. These were, indeed, the *ne plus ultra* of good legs. Every connoisseur in such matters admitted the legs to be good. There was neither too much flesh nor too little, – neither rudeness nor fragility. I could not imagine a more graceful curve than that of the *os fermoris*, and there was just that due gentle prominence in the rear of the *fibula* which goes to the conformation of a properly proportioned calf. I wish to God my young and talented friend, Chiponchipino, the sculptor, had but seen the legs of Brevet Brigadier-General John A. B. C. Smith.

But although men so absolutely fine-looking are neither as plenty as reasons or blackberries, still I could not bring myself to believe that *the remarkable* something to which I alluded just now, – that the odd air of *je ne sais quoi* which hung about my new acquaintance, – lay altogether, or indeed at all, in the supreme excellence of his bodily endowments. Perhaps it might be traced to the *manner*; yet here again I could not pretend to be positive. There *was* a primness, not to say stiffness, in his carriage; a degree of measured, and, if I may so express it, of rectangular precision, attending his every movement, which, observed in a more diminutive figure, would have had the least little savor in the world of affectation, pomposity, or constraint, but which, noticed in a gentleman of his undoubted dimensions, was readily placed to the account of reserve, *hauteur* – of a commendable sense, in short, of what is due to the dignity of colossal proportion.

The kind friend who presented me to General Smith whispered in my ear some words of comment upon the man. He was a *remarkable* man – a *very* remarkable man – indeed one of the *most* remarkable men of the age. He was an especial favorite, too, with the ladies, chiefly on account of his high reputation for courage.

'In *that* point he is unrivalled; indeed, he is a perfect desperado – a downright fire-eater, and no mistake,' said my friend, here dropping his voice excessively low, and thrilling me with the mystery of his tone.

'A downright fire-eater, and *no* mistake. Showed *that*, I should say, to some purpose, in the late tremendous swamp-fight away down South, with the Bugaboo and Kickapoo Indians.' (Here my friend opened his eyes to some extent.) 'Bless my soul! – blood and thunder, and all that! – *prodigies* of valor! – heard of him of course? – you know he's the man –'

'Man alive, how *do* you do? why, how *are* ye? very glad to see ye, indeed!' here interrupted the General himself, seizing my companion by the hand as he drew near, and bowing stiffly but profoundly, as I was presented. I then thought (and I think so still) that I never heard a clearer nor a stronger voice nor beheld a finer set of teeth; but I *must* say that I was sorry for the interruption just at that moment, as, owing to the whispers and insinuations aforesaid, my interest had been greatly excited in the hero of the Bugaboo and Kickapoo campaign.

However, the delightfully luminous conversation of Brevet Brigadier-General John A. B. C. Smith soon completely dissipated this chagrin. My friend leaving us immediately, we had quite a long *tête-à-tête*, and I was not only pleased but *really* – instructed. I never heard a more fluent talker, or a man of greater general information. With becoming modesty, he forbore, nevertheless, to touch upon the theme I had just then most at heart: I mean the mysterious circumstances attending the Bugaboo War; and, on my own part, what I conceive to be a proper sense of delicacy forbade me to broach the subject; although, in truth, I was exceedingly tempted to do so. I perceived, too, that the gallant soldier preferred topics of philosophical interest, and that he delighted especially in commenting upon the rapid march of mechanical invention. Indeed, lead him where I would, this was a point to which he invariably came back.

'There is nothing at all like it,' he would say; 'we are a wonderful people, and live in a wonderful age. Parachutes and railroads – man-traps and spring-guns! Our steamboats are upon every sea, and the Nassau balloon packet is about to run regular trips (fare either way only twenty pounds sterling) between London and Timbuctoo. And who shall calculate the immense influence upon social life – upon arts – upon commerce – upon literature – which will be the immediate result of the great principles of electro-magnetics! Nor is this all, let me assure you! There is really no end to the march of invention. The most wonderful – the most ingenious – and let me add, Mr – Mr – Thompson, I believe, is your name – let me add, I say, the most *useful* – the most truly *useful* mechanical contrivances are daily springing up like mushrooms, if I may so express myself, or, more figuratively, like – ah – grasshoppers – like grasshoppers, Mr Thompson – about us and ah – ah – ah – around us!'

Thompson, to be sure, is not my name; but it is needless to say that I left General Smith with a heightened interest in the man, with an exalted opinion of his conversational powers, and a deep sense of the valuable privileges we enjoy in living in this age of mechanical inventions. My curiosity, however, had not been altogether satisfied, and I resolved to prosecute immediate inquiry among my acquaintances touching the Brevet Brigadier-General himself, and particularly respecting the tremendous events *quorum pars magna fuit*, during the Bugaboo and Kickapoo campaign.

The first opportunity which presented itself, and which (*horresco referens*) I did not in the least scruple to seize, occurred at the Church of the Reverend Doctor Drummummupp, where I found myself established, one Sunday, just at sermon time, not only in the pew, but by the side, of that worthy and communicative little friend of mine, Miss Tabitha T. Thus seated, I congratulated myself, and with much reason, upon the very flattering state of affairs. If any person knew anything about Brevet Brigadier-General John A. B. C. Smith, that person, it was clear to me, was Miss Tabitha T. We telegraphed a few signals, and then commenced, *sotto voce*, a brisk *tête-à-tête*.

'Smith!' said she, in reply to my very earnest inquiry; 'Smith! – why, not General John A. B. C.? Bless me, I thought you *knew* all about *him*! This is a wonderfully inventive age! Horrid affair that! – a bloody set of wretches, those Kickapoos! – fought like a hero – prodigies of valor – immortal renown. Smith! – Brevet Brigadier-General John A. B. C.! – why, you know he's the man –'

'Man,' here broke in Dr Drummummupp, at the top of his voice, and with a thump that came near knocking the pulpit about our ears; 'man that is born of a woman hath but a short time to live; he cometh up and is cut down like a flower!' I started to the extremity of the pew, and perceived by the animated looks of the divine that the wrath which had nearly proved fatal to the pulpit had been excited by the whispers of the lady and myself. There was no help for it; so I submitted with a good grace, and listened, in all the martyrdom of dignified silence, to the balance of that very capital discourse.

Next evening found me a somewhat late visitor at the Rantipole theatre, where I felt sure of satisfying my curiosity at once, by merely stepping into the box of those exquisite specimens of affability and omniscience, the Misses Arabella and Miranda Cognoscenti. That fine tragedian, Climax, was doing Iago to a very crowded house, and I experienced some little difficulty in making my wishes understood; especially as our box was next the slips, and completely overlooked the stage.

'Smith?' said Miss Arabella, as she at length comprehended the purport of my query; 'Smith? – why, not General John A. B. C.?'

'Smith?' inquired Miranda, musingly. 'God bless me, did you ever behold a finer figure?'

'Never, madam, but *do* tell me –'

'Or so inimitable grace?'

'Never, upon my word! – but pray inform me –'

'Or so just an appreciation of stage effect?'

'Madam!'

'Or a more delicate sense of the true beauties of Shakespeare? Be so good as to look at that leg!'

'The devil!' and I turned again to her sister.

'Smith?' said she, 'why, not General John A. B. C.? Horrid affair that, wasn't it? – great wretches, those Bugaboos – savage and so on – but we live in a wonderfully inventive age! – Smith! – Oh, yes! great man! – perfect desperado – immortal renown – prodigies of valor! *Never heard!*' (This was given in a scream.) 'Bless my soul! – why, he's the man –'

> '. . . mandragora
> Nor all the drowsy syrups of the world
> Shall ever medicine thee to that sweet sleep
> Which thou owedst yesterday!'

here roared out Climax just in my ear, and shaking his fist in my face all the time, in a way that I *couldn't* stand, and I *wouldn't*. I left the Misses Cognoscenti immediately, went behind the scenes forthwith, and gave the beggarly scoundrel such a thrashing as I trust he will remember to the day of his death.

At the *soirée* of the lovely widow, Mrs Kathleen O'Trump, I was confident that I should meet with no similar disappointment. Accordingly, I was no sooner seated at the card-table, with my pretty hostess for a *viv-à-vis*, than I propounded those questions the solution of which had become a matter so essential to my peace.

'Smith?' said my partner, 'why, not General John A. B. C.? Horrid affair that, wasn't it? – diamonds, did you say? – terrible wretches those Kickapoos! – we are playing *whist*, if you please, Mr Tattle – however, this is the age of invention, most certainly *the* age, one may say – *the age par excellence* – speak French? – oh, quite a hero – perfect desperado! – *no hearts*, Mr Tattle? I don't believe it! – Immortal renown and all that – prodigies of valor! *Never heard!!* – why, bless me, he's the man –'

'Mann? – *Captain* Mann?' here screamed some little feminine interloper from the farthest corner of the room. 'Are you talking about Captain Mann and the duel? – oh, I *must* hear – do tell – go on, Mrs O'Trump! – do now go on!' And go on Mrs O'Trump

95

did – all about a certain Captain Mann, who was either shot or hung, or should have been shot and hung. Yes! Mrs O'Trump, she went on, and I – I went off. There was no chance of hearing anything farther that evening in regard to Brevet Brigadier-General John A. B. C. Smith.

Still I consoled myself with the reflection that the tide of ill luck would not run against me forever, and so determined to make a bold push for information at the rout of that bewitching little angel, the graceful Mrs Pirouette.

'Smith?' said Mrs P— as we twirled about together in a *pas de zéphyr*, 'Smith? – why, not General John A. B. C.? Dreadful business that of the Bugaboos, wasn't it? – terrible creatures, those Indians! *do* turn out your toes! I really am ashamed of you – man of great courage, poor fellow! – but this is a wonderful age for invention – oh, dear me, I'm out of breath – quite a desperado – prodigies of valor – *never heard!!* – can't believe it – I shall have to sit down and enlighten you – Smith! why, he's the man –'

'Man-*Fred*, I tell you!' here bawled out Miss Bas-Bleu, as I led Mrs Pirouette to a seat. 'Did ever anybody hear the like? It's Man-*Fred*, I say, and not at all by any means Man-*Friday*.' Here Miss Bas-Bleu beckoned to me in a very peremptory manner; and I was obliged, will I nill I, to leave Mrs P— for the purpose of deciding a dispute touching the title of a certain poetical drama of Lord Byron's. Although I pronounced, with great promptness, that the true title was Man-*Friday*, and not by any means Man-*Fred*, yet when I returned to seek Mrs Pirouette she was not to be discovered, and I made my retreat from the house in a very bitter spirit of animosity against the whole race of the Bas-Bleus.

Matters had now assumed a really serious aspect, and I resolved to call at once upon my particular friend, Mr Theodore Sinivate; for I knew that here at least I should get something like definite information.

'Smith?' said he, in his well-known peculiar way of drawling out his syllables; 'Smith? – why, not General John A. B. C.? Savage affair that with the Kickapo-o-o-os, wasn't it? Say! don't you think so? – perfect despera-a-ado – great pity, 'pon my honor! – wonderfully inventive age! – pro-o-odigies of valor! By the bye, did you ever hear about Captain Ma-a-a-a-n?'

'Captain Mann be d—d!' said I, 'please to go on with your story.'

'Hem! – oh well! – quite *la même cho-o-ose*, as we say in France. Smith, eh? Brigadier-General John A – B – C.? I say' – (here Mr S— thought proper to put his finger to the side of his nose) – 'I say, you don't mean to insinuate now, really and truly, and conscientiously, that you don't know all about that affair of Smith's, as well as I do, eh? Smith? John A – B – C.? Why, bless me, he's the ma-a-an –'

'*Mr* Sinivate,' said I, imploringly, '*is* he the man in the mask?'

'No-o-o!' said he, looking wise, 'nor the man in the mo-o-on.'

This reply I considered a pointed and positive insult, and so left the house at once in high dudgeon, with a firm resolve to call my friend, Mr Sinivate, to a speedy account for his ungentlemanly conduct and ill-breeding.

In the mean time, however, I had no notion of being thwarted touching the information I desired. There was one resource left me yet. I would go to the fountain-head. I would call forthwith upon the General himself, and demand, in explicit terms, a solution of this abominable piece of mystery. Here, at least, there should be no chance for equivocation. I would be plain, positive, peremptory – as short as pie-crust – as concise as Tacitus or Montesquieu.

It was early when I called, and the General was dressing; but I pleaded urgent business, and was shown at once into his bedroom by an old negro valet, who remained in attendance during my visit. As I entered the chamber, I looked about, of course, for the occupant, but did not immediately perceive him. There was a large and exceedingly odd-looking bundle of some thing which lay close by my feet on the floor, and, as I was not in the best humor in the world, I gave it a kick out of the way.

'Hem! ahem! rather civil that, I should say!' said the bundle, in one of the smallest, and altogether the funniest little voices, between a squeak and a whistle, that I ever heard in all the days of my existence.

'Ahem! rather civil that, I should observe.'

I fairly shouted with terror, and made off, at a tangent, into the farthest extremity of the room.

'God bless me! my dear fellow,' here again whistled the bundle, 'what – what – what – why, what *is* the matter? I really believe you don't know me at all.'

What *could* I say to all this – what *could* I? I staggered into an arm-chair, and, with staring eyes and open mouth, awaited the solution of the wonder.

'Strange you shouldn't know me though, isn't it?' presently re-squeaked the nondescript, which I now perceived was performing, upon the floor, some inexplicable evolution, very analogous to the drawing on of a stocking. There was only a single leg, however, apparent.

'Strange you shouldn't know me, though, isn't it? Pompey, bring me that leg!' Here Pompey handed the bundle a very capital cork leg, already dressed, which it screwed on in a trice; and then it stood up before my eyes.

'And a bloody action it *was*,' continued the thing, as if in a soliloquy; 'but then one mustn't fight with the Bugaboos and Kickapoos, and think of coming off with a mere scratch. Pompey, I'll thank you now for that arm. Thomas' (turning to me) 'is decidedly the best hand at a cork leg; but if you should ever want an arm, my dear fellow, you must really let me recommend you to Bishop.' Here Pompey screwed on an arm.

'We had rather hot work of it, that you may say. Now, you dog, slip on my shoulders and bosom! Pettitt makes the best shoulders, but for a bosom you will have to go to Ducrow.'

'Bosom!' said I.

'Pompey, will you *never* be ready with that wig? Scalping is a rough process after all; but then you can procure such a capital scratch at De L'Orme's.'

'Scratch!'

'Now, you nigger, my teeth! For a *good* set of these you had better go to Parmly's at once; high prices, but excellent work. I swallowed some very capital articles, though, when the big Bugaboo rammed me down with the butt end of his rifle.'

'Butt end! ram down!! my eye!!'

'Oh, yes, by the bye, my eye – here, Pompey, you scamp, screw

98

it in! Those Kickapoos are not so very slow at a gouge; but he's a belied man, that Dr Williams, after all; you can't imagine how well I see with the eyes of his make.'

I now began very clearly to perceive that the object before me was nothing more nor less than my new acquaintance, Brevet Brigadier-General John A. B. C. Smith. The manipulations of Pompey had made, I must confess, a very striking difference in the appearance of the personal man. The voice, however, still puzzled me no little; but even this apparent mystery was speedily cleared up.

'Pompey, you black rascal,' squeaked the General, 'I really do believe you would let me go out without my palate.'

Hereupon the negro, grumbling out an apology, went up to his master, opened his mouth with the knowing air of a horse-jockey, and adjusted therein a somewhat singular-looking machine, in a very dextrous manner, that I could not altogether comprehend. The alteration, however, in the entire expression of the General's countenance was instantaneous and surprising. When he again spoke, his voice had resumed all that rich melody and strength which I had noticed upon our original introduction.

'D—n the vagabonds!' said he, in so clear a tone that I positively started at the change, 'D—n the vagabonds! they not only knocked in the roof of my mouth, but took the trouble to cut off at least seven-eighths of my tongue. There isn't Bonfanti's equal, however, in America, for really good articles of this description. I can recommend you to him with confidence' (here the General bowed), 'and assure you that I have the greatest pleasure in so doing.'

I acknowledged his kindness in my best manner, and took leave of him at once, with a perfect understanding of the true state of affairs – with a full comprehension of the mystery which had troubled me so long. It was evident. It was a clear case. Brevet Brigadier-General John A. B. C. Smith was the man – was *the man that was used up.*

The Business Man

Method is the soul of business.
Old Saying

I AM a business man. I am a methodical man. Method is *the* thing, after all. But there are no people I more heartily despise than your eccentric fools who prate about method without understanding it; attending strictly to its letter, and violating its spirit. These fellows are always doing the most out-of-the-way things in what they call an orderly manner. Now here, I conceive, is a positive paradox. True method appertains to the ordinary and the obvious alone, and cannot be applied to the *outré*. What definite idea can a body attach to such expressions as 'methodical Jack o' Dandy', or 'a systematical Will o' the Wisp'?

My notions upon this head might not have been so clear as they are but for a fortunate accident which happened to me when I was a very little boy. A good-hearted old Irish nurse (whom I shall not forget in my will) took me up one day by the heels, when I was making more noise than necessary, and, swinging me round two or three times, d—d my eyes for 'a skreeking little spalpeen', and then knocked my head into a cocked hat against the bedpost. This, I say, decided my fate and made my fortune. A bump arose at once on my sinciput, and turned out to be as pretty an organ of *order* as one shall see on a summer's day. Hence that positive appetite for system and regularity which has made me the distinguished man of business that I am.

If there is anything on earth I hate, it is a genius. Your geniuses are all arrant asses – the greater the genius the greater the ass – and to this rule there is no exception whatever. Especially, you cannot make a man of business out of a genius, any more than money out of a Jew or the best nutmegs out of pine-knots. The creatures are always going off at a tangent into some fantastic employment, or ridiculous speculation, entirely at variance with the 'fitness of things', and having no business whatever to be considered as a business at all. Thus you may tell these characters immediately by the nature of their occupations. If you ever perceive a man setting up as a merchant or a manufacturer; or going into the cotton or tobacco trade, or any of those eccentric pursuits; or getting to be a dry-goods dealer, or soap-boiler, or something of that kind; or pretending to be a lawyer, or a blacksmith, or a physician – anything out of the usual way – you may set him down at once as a genius, and then, according to the rule-of-three, he's an ass.

Now I am not in any respect a genius, but a regular business man. My Day-Book and Ledger will evince this in a minute. They are well kept, though I say it myself; and, in my general habits of accuracy and punctuality, I am not to be beat by a clock. Moreover, my occupations have been always made to chime in with the ordinary habitudes of my fellowmen. Not that I feel the least indebted, upon this score, to my exceedingly weak-minded parents, who, beyond doubt, would have made an arrant genius of me at last, if my guardian angel had not come in good time to the rescue. In biography the truth is everything, and in autobiography it is especially so, – yet I scarcely hope to be believed when I state, however solemnly, that my poor father put me, when I was about fifteen years of age, into the counting-house of what he termed 'a respectable hardware and commission merchant doing a capital bit of business!' A capital bit of fiddlestick! However, the consequence of this folly was that, in two or three days, I had to be sent home to my button-headed family in a high state of fever, and with a most violent and dangerous pain in the sinciput, all round about my organ of order. It was nearly a gone case with me then – just touch-and-go for six weeks – the physicians giving me up and all that sort of thing. But, although I suffered much, I was a thankful boy in the main. I was saved from being a 'respectable hardware and commission merchant doing a capital bit of business', and I felt grateful to the protuberance which had been the means of my salvation, as well as to the kind-hearted female who had originally put these means within my reach.

The most of boys run away from home at ten or twelve years of age, but I waited till I was sixteen. I don't know that I should have gone, even then, if I had not happened to hear my old mother talk about setting me up on my own hook in the grocery way. The *grocery* way! – only think of that! I resolved to be off forthwith, and try and establish myself in some decent occupation, without dancing attendance any longer upon the caprices of these eccentric old people, and running the risk of being made a genius of in the end. In this project I succeeded perfectly well at the first effort, and by the time I was fairly eighteen found myself doing an extensive and profitable business in the Tailor's Walking-Advertisement line.

I was enabled to discharge the onerous duties of this profession only by that rigid adherence to system which formed the leading feature of my mind. A scrupulous *method* characterized my actions as well as my accounts. In my case, it was method, not money, which made the man; at least all of him that was not made by the tailor[1] whom I served. At nine, every morning, I called upon that individual for the clothes of the day. Ten o'clock found me in some fashionable promenade or other place of public amusement. The precise regularity with which I turned my handsome person about, so as to bring successively into view every portion of the suit upon my back, was the admiration of all the knowing men in the trade. Noon never passed without my bringing home a customer to the house of my employers, Messrs Cut and Come-again. I say this proudly, but with tears in my eyes – for the firm proved themselves the basest of ingrates. The little account about which we quarreled and finally parted cannot, in any item, be thought overcharged, by gentlemen really conversant with the nature of the business. Upon this point, however, I feel a degree of proud satisfaction in permitting the reader to judge for himself. My bill ran thus: –

MESSRS CUT AND COMEAGAIN, MERCHANT TAILORS.
TO PETER PROFFIT, Walking Advertiser, Drs.

July 10.	To promenade, as usual, and customer brought home,	$00.25
July 11.	To promenade, as usual, and customer brought home,	25

July 12.	To one lie, second class; damaged black cloth sold for invisible green,	25
July 13.	To one lie, first class, extra quality and size; recommending milled satinet as broadcloth,	75
July 20.	To purchasing brand-new paper shirt-collar or dickey, to set off gray Petersham,	2
Aug. 15.	To wearing double-padded bobtail frock (thermometer 106 in the shade),	25
Aug. 16.	Standing on one leg three hours, to show off new-style strapped pants at 12½ cents per leg an hour,	37½
Aug. 17.	To promenade, as usual, and large customer brought (fat man),	50
Aug. 18.	To promenade, as usual, and large customer brought (medium size),	25
Aug. 19.	To promenade, as usual, and large customer brought (small man and bad pay),	6
		$2.95½

The item chiefly disputed in this bill was the very moderate charge of two pennies for the dickey. Upon my word of honor, this was not an unreasonable price for that dickey. It was one of the cleanest and prettiest little dickeys I ever saw; and I have good reason to believe that it effected the sale of three Petershams. The elder partner of the firm, however, would allow me only one penny of the charge, and took it upon himself to show in what manner four of the same sized conveniences could be got out of a sheet of foolcap. But it is needless to say that I stood upon the *principle* of the thing. Business is business, and should be done in a business way. There was no *system* whatever in swindling me out of a penny – a clear fraud of fifty per cent. – no *method* in any respect. I left at once the employment of Messrs Cut and Comeagain, and set up in the Eye-Sore line by myself; one of the most lucrative, respectable, and independent of the ordinary occupations.

My strict integrity, economy, and rigorous business habits here again came into play. I found myself driving a flourishing trade, and soon became a marked man upon 'Change'. The truth is, I never dabbled in flashy matters, but jogged on in the good old sober routine of the calling – a calling in which I should, no doubt, have remained to the present hour, but for a little accident which happened to me in the prosecution of one of the usual business operations of the profession. Whenever a rich old hunks, or prodigal heir, or bankrupt corporation, gets into the notion of putting up a palace, there is no such thing in the world as stopping either of them, and this every intelligent person knows. The fact in question is indeed the basis of the Eye-Sore trade. As soon, therefore, as a building project is fairly afoot by one of these parties, we merchants secure a nice corner of the lot in contemplation, or a prime little situation just adjoining or right in front. This done, we wait until the palace is halfway up, and then we pay some tasty architect to run us up an ornamental mud hovel, right against it; or a Down-East or Dutch Pagoda, or a pig-sty, or an ingenious little bit of fancy-work, either Esquimaux, Kickapoo, or Hottentot. Of course, we can't afford to take these structures down under a bonus of five hundred per cent upon the prime cost of our lot and plaster. *Can* we? I ask the question. I ask it of business men. It would be irrational to suppose that we can. And yet there was a rascally corporation which asked me to do this very thing – this *very thing*! I did not reply to their absurd proposition, of course; but I felt it a duty to go that same night and lamp-black the whole of their palace. For this the unreasonable villains clapped me into jail; and the gentlemen of the Eye-Sore trade could not well avoid cutting my connection when I came out.

The Assault and Battery business, into which I was now forced to adventure for a livelihood, was somewhat ill-adapted to the delicate nature of my constitution; but I went to work in it with a good heart, and found my account here, as heretofore, in those stern habits of methodical accuracy which had been thumped into me by that delightful old nurse – I would indeed be the basest of men not to remember her well in my will. By observing, as I say, the strictest system in all my dealings, and keeping a well-regulated set of books, I was enabled to get over many serious difficulties, and in the end to establish myself very decently in the profession. The truth is that few individuals, in any line, did a snugger little business than I. I will just copy a page or so out of my Day-Book; and this will save me the necessity of blowing my own trumpet – a contemptible practice, of which no high-minded man will be guilty. Now, the Day-Book is a thing that don't lie.

January 1. – New Year's day. Met Snap in the street, groggy. Mem. – he'll do. Met Gruff shortly afterwards, blind drunk. Mem. – he'll answer too. Entered both gentlemen in my Ledger, and opened a running account with each.

January 2. – Saw Snap at the Exchange, and went up and trod on his toe. Doubled his fist and knocked me down. Good! – got up again. Some trifling difficulty with Bag, my attorney. I want the damages at a thousand, but he says that, for so simple a knockdown, we can't lay them at more than five hundred. Mem. – must get rid of Bag – no *system* at all.

January 3. – Went to the theatre, to look for Gruff. Saw him sitting in a side box, in the second tier, between a fat lady and a lean one. Quizzed the whole party through an opera-glass, till I saw the fat lady blush and whisper to G. Went round, then, into the box, and put my nose within reach of his hand. Wouldn't pull it – no go. Blew it, and tried again – no go. Sat down then, and winked at the lean lady, when I had the high satisfaction of finding him lift me up by the nape of the neck, and fling me over into the pit. Neck dislocated, and right leg capitally splintered. Went home in high glee, drank a bottle of champagne, and booked the young man for five thousand. Bag says it'll do.

February 15. – Compromised the case of Mr Snap. Amount entered in Journal – fifty cents – which see.

February 16. – Cast by that villain, Gruff, who made me a present of five dollars. Costs of suit, four dollars and twenty-five cents. Net profit – see Journal – seventy-five cents.

Now, here is a clear gain, in a very brief period, of no less than one dollar and twenty-five cents – this is in the mere cases of Snap and Gruff; and I solemnly assure the reader that these extracts are taken at random from my Day-Book.

It's an old saying and a true one, however, that money is nothing in comparison with health. I found the exactions of the profession somewhat too much for my state of body; and discovering at last that I was knocked all out of shape, so that I didn't know very well what to make of the matter, and so that my friends, when they met me in the street, couldn't tell that I was Peter Proffit at all, it occurred to me that the best expedient I could adopt was to alter my line of business. I turned my attention, therefore, to Mud-Dabbling, and continued it for some years.

The worst of this occupation is that too many people take a fancy to it, and the competition is in consequence excessive. Every ignoramus of a fellow who finds that he hasn't brains in sufficient quantity to make his way as a walking advertiser, or an eye-sore-prig, or a salt and batter man, thinks, of course, that he'll answer very well as a dabbler of mud. But there never was entertained a more erroneous idea than that it requires no brains to mud-dabble. Especially, there is nothing to be made in this way without *method*. I did only a retail business myself, but my old habits of *system* carried me swimmingly along. I selected my street-crossing, in the first place, with great deliberation, and I never put down a broom in any part of the town but that. I took care, too, to have a nice little puddle at hand, which I could get at in a minute. By these means I got to be well known as a man to be trusted; and this is one half the battle, let me tell you, in trade. Nobody ever failed to pitch *me* a copper, and got over *my* crossing with a clean pair of pantaloons. And, as my business habits, in this respect, were sufficiently understood, I never met with any attempt at imposition. I wouldn't have put up with it, if I had. Never imposing upon anyone myself, I suffered no one to play the possum with me. The frauds of the banks of course I couldn't help. Their suspension put me to ruinous inconvenience.[2] These, however, are not individuals, but corporations; and corporations, it is very well known, have neither bodies to be kicked, nor souls to be damned.

I was making money at this business when, in an evil moment, I was induced to merge in the Cur-Spattering – a somewhat analogous, but by no means so respectable a profession. My location, to be sure, was an excellent one, being central, and I had capital blacking and brushes. My little dog, too, was quite fat, and up to all varieties of snuff. He had been in the trade a long time, and, I may say, understood it. Our general routine was this: – Pompey, having rolled himself well in the mud, sat upon end at the shop door, until he observed a dandy approaching in bright boots. He then proceeded to meet him, and gave the Wellingtons a rub or two with his wool. Then the dandy swore very much, and looked about for a bootblack. There I was, full in his view, with blacking and brushes. It was only a minute's work, and then came a sixpence. This did moderately well for a time; in fact, I was not avaricious, but my dog was. I allowed him a third of the profit, but he was advised to insist upon half. This I couldn't stand – so we quarreled and parted.

I next tried my hand at the Organ-Grinding for a while, and may say that I made out pretty well. It is a plain, straightforward business, and requires no particular ability. You can get a music-mill for a mere song, and, to put it in order, you have but to open the works, and give them three or four smart raps with a hammer. It improves the tone of the thing, for business purposes, more than you can imagine. This done, you have only to stroll along with the mill on your back, until you see tan-bark in the street, and a knocker wrapped up in buckskin. Then you stop and grind; looking as if you meant to stop and grind till doomsday. Presently a window opens, and somebody pitches you a sixpence, with a request to 'Hush up, and go on', etc. I am aware that some grinders have actually afforded to 'go on' for this sum; but for my part, I found the necessary outlay of capital too great to permit of my 'going on' under a shilling.

At this occupation I did a good deal; but, somehow, I was not quite satisfied, and so finally abandoned it. The truth is, I labored under the disadvantage of having no monkey; and American streets are *so* muddy, and a democratic rabble is *so* obtrusive, and so full of demnition mischievous little boys.

I was now out of employment for some months, but at length succeeded, by dint of great interest, in procuring a situation in the Sham-Post.[3] The duties, here, are simple, and not altogether unprofitable. For example: – very early in the morning I had to make up my packet of sham letters. Upon the inside of each of these I had to scrawl a few lines – on any subject which occurred to me as sufficiently mysterious – signing all the epistles Tom Dobson, or Bobby Tompkins, or anything in that way. Having folded and sealed all, and stamped them with sham postmarks – New Orleans, Bengal, Botany Bay, or any other place a great way off – I set out, forthwith, upon my daily route, as if in a very great hurry. I always called at the big houses, to deliver the letters and receive the postage. Nobody hesitates at paying for a letter, especially for a double one – people are *such* fools – and it was no trouble to get round a corner before there was time to open the epistles. The worst of this profession was that I had to walk so much and so fast; and so frequently to vary my route. Besides, I had serious scruples of conscience. I can't bear to hear innocent individuals abused – and the way the whole town took to cursing Tom Dobson and Bobby Tompkins was really awful to hear. I washed my hands of the matter in disgust.

My eighth and last speculation has been in the Cat-Crowing way. I have found this a most pleasant and lucrative business, and, really, no trouble at all. The country, it is well known, has become infested with cats; so much so of late that a petition for relief, most numerously and respectably signed, was brought before the legislature at its late memorable session. The assembly, at this epoch, was unusually well-informed, and, having passed many other wise and wholesome enactments, it crowned all with the Cat-Act. In its original form, this law offered a premium for *cat-heads* (fourpence apiece), but the Senate succeeded in amending the main clause, so as to substitute the word '*tails*' for 'heads'. This amendment was so obviously proper, that the house concurred in it *nem. con.*[4]

As soon as the Governor had signed the bill, I invested my whole estate in the purchase of Toms and Tabbies. At first, I could only afford to feed them upon mice (which are cheap), but they fulfilled the Scriptual injunction at so marvellous a rate that I at length considered it my best policy to be liberal, and so indulged them in oysters and turtle. Their tails, at a legislative price, now bring me in a good income; for I have discovered a way in which, by means of Macassar oil,[5] I can force three crops in a year. It delights me to find, too, that the animals soon get accustomed to the thing, and would rather have the appendages cut off than otherwise. I consider myself, therefore, a made man, and am bargaining for a country seat on the Hudson.

Why the Little Frenchman
Wears his Hand in a Sling

IT's on my wisiting cards, sure enough (and it's them that's all o' pink satin paper), that inny gintleman that plases may behould the intheristhin words, 'Sir Pathrick O'Grandison, Barronitt, 39 Southampton Row, Russell Square, Parrish o' Bloomsbury'.[1] And shud ye be wantin to diskiver who is the pink of purliteness quite, and the laider of the hot tun in the houl city o' Lonon – why, it's jist mesilf. And, fait, that same is no wonder at all at all (so be plased to stop curlin your nose), for every inch o' the six wakes that I've been a gintleman, and left aff wid the bog-throthing to take up wid the Barronissy, it's Pathrick that's been living like a houly imperor, and gitting the iddication and the graces. Och! and wouldn't it be a blessed thing for your sperrits if ye cud lay your two peepers jist upon Sir Pathrick O'Grandison, Barronitt, when he is all riddy drissed for the hopperer, or stipping into the Brisky for the drive into the Hyde Park. – But it's the illigant big figgur that I ave, for the rason o' which all the ladies fall in love wid me. Isn't it my own swate silf now that'll missure the six fut, and the three inches more nor that, in me stockings, and that am excadingly will-proportioned all over to match? And is it ralelly more than the three fut and a bit that there is, innyhow, of the little ould furrener Frinchman that lives jist over the way, and that's a oggling and a goggling the houl day (and bad luck to him) at the purty widdy Misthress Tracle that's my own nixt-door neighbor (God bliss her) and a most particuller frind and acquaintance? You percave the little spalpeen is summat down in the mouth, and wears his lift hand in a sling; and it's for that same thing, by yur lave, that I'm going to give you the good rason.

The truth of the houl matter is jist simple enough; for the very first day that I com'd from Connaught, and showd my swate little silf in the strait to the widdy, who was looking through the windy, it was a gone case althegither wid the heart o' the purty Misthress Tracle. I percaved it, ye see, all at once, and no mistake, and that's God's thruth. First of all it was up wid the windy in a jiffy, and thin she threw open her two peepers to the itmost, and thin it was a little gould spy-glass that she clapped tight to one o' them, and divil may burn me if it didn't spake to me as plain as a peeper cud spake, and says it, through the spy-glass, 'Och! the tip o' the mornin to ye, Sir Pathrick O'Grandison, Barronitt, mavourneen; and it's a nate gintleman that ye are, sure enough, and it's mesilf and me forten jist that'll be at yur sarvice, dear, inny time o' day at all at all for the asking.' And it's not mesilf ye wud have to be bate in the purliteness; so I made her a bow that wud ha broken yur heart althegither to behould, and thin I winked at her hard wid both eyes, as much as to say, 'Thrue for you, yer a swate little crature, Mistress Tracle, me darlint, and I wish I may be drownthed dead in a bog, if it's not mesilf, Sir Pathrick O'Grandison, Barronitt, that'll make a houl bushel o' love to yur leddyship, in the twinkling o' the eye of a Londonderry purraty.'

And it was the nixt mornin, sure, jist as I was making up me mind whither it wouldn't be the purlite thing to sind a bit o' writin to the widdy by way of a love-litter, when up cum'd the delivery sarvant wid an illigant card, and he tould me that the name on it (for I niver cud rade the copper-plate printin on account of being lift-handed) was all about Mounseer, the Count, A Goose, Look-aisy,[2] Maiter-di-dauns, and that the houl of the divilish lingo was the spalpeeny long name of the little ould-furrener Frinchman as lived over the way.

And jist wid that, in cum'd the little willain himself, and thin he made me a broth of a bow, and thin he said he had ounly taken the liberty of doing me the honor of the giving me a call, and thin he went on to palaver at a great rate, and divil the bit did I comprehind what he wud be afther the tilling me at all at all, excipting and saving that he said 'pully wou, woolly wou,' and tould me, among a bushel o' lies, bad luck to him, that he was mad for the love o' my widdy Misthress Tracle, and that my widdy Misthress Tracle had a puncheon for *him*.

At the hearin of this, ye may swear, though, I was as mad as a grasshopper, but I remimbered that I was Sir Pathrick O' Grandison, Barronitt, and that it wasn't althegither gentaal to lit the anger git the upper hand o' the purliteness, so I made light o' the matter and kipt dark, and got quite sociable wid the little chap, and afther a while what did he do but ask me to go wid him to the widdy's, saying he wud give me the feshionable inthroduction to her leddyship.

'Is it there ye are?' said I thin to mesilf, 'and it's thrue for you, Pathrick, that ye're the fortunnittest mortal in life. We'll soon see now whither it's your swate silf, or whither it's little Mounseer Maiter-di-dauns, that Misthress Tracle is head and ears in the love wid.'

Wid that we wint aff to the widdy's, next door, and ye may well say it was an illigant place; so it was. There was a carpet all over the floor, and in one corner there was a forty-pinny and a jews-harp and the divil knows what ilse, and in another corner was a sofy, the beautifullest thing in all natur, and sitting on the sofy, sure enough, there was the swate little angel, Misthress Tracle.

'The tip o' the morning to ye,' says I, 'Misthress Tracle,' and thin I made sich an illigant obaysance that it wud ha quite althegither bewildered the brain o' ye.

'Wully woo, pully woo, plump in the mud,' says the little furrener Frinchman, 'and sure Misthress Tracle,' says he, that he did, 'isn't this gintleman here jist his riverence Sir Pathrick O'Grandison, Barronitt, and isn't he althegither and entirely the most purticular frind and acquintance that I have in the houl world?'

And wid that the widdy, she gits up from the sofy, and makes the swatest curtchy nor iver was seen; and thin down she sits like an angel; and thin, by the powers, it was that little spalpeen Mounseer Maiter-di-dauns that plumped his silf right down by the right side of her. Och hon! I ixpicted the two eyes o' me wud had cum'd out of my head on the spot, I was so dispirate mad! Howiver, 'Bait who!' says I, after a while. 'Is it there ye are,

Mounseer Maiter-di-dauns?' and so down I plumped on the lift side of her leddyship, to be aven wid the willain. Botheration! it wud ha done your heart good to percave the illigant double wink that I gived her jist thin right in the face wid both eyes.

But the little ould Frinchman he niver beginned to suspect me at all at all, and disperate hard it was he made the love to her leddyship. 'Woully wou,' says he, 'Pully wou,' says he, 'Plump in the mud,' says he.

'That's all to no use, Mounseer Frog, mavourneen,' thinks I; and I talked as hard and as fast as I could all the while, and throth it was mesilf jist that divarted her leddyship complately and intirely, by rason of the illigant conversation that I kipt up wid her all about the dear bogs of Connaught. And by and by she gived me such a swate smile, from one ind of her mouth to the ither, that it made me as bould as a pig, and I jist took hould of the ind of her little finger in the most dilikittest manner in natur, looking at her all the while out o' the whites of my eyes.

And then ounly percave the cuteness of the swate angel, for no sooner did she obsarve that I was afther the squazing of her flipper, than she up wid it in a jiffy, and put it away behind her back, jist as much as to say, 'Now thin, Sir Pathrick O'Grandison, there's a bitther chance for ye, mavourneen, for it's not altogether the gentaal thing to be afther the squazing of my flipper right full in the sight of that little furrener Frinchman, Mounseer Maiter-di-dauns.'

Wid that I giv'd her a big wink jist to say, 'lit Sir Pathrick alone for the likes o' them thricks,' and thin I wint aisy to work, and you'd have died wid the divarsion to behould how cliverly I slipped my right arm betwane the back o' the sofy and the back of her leddyship, and there, sure enough, I found a swate little flipper all awaiting to say, 'the tip o' the mornin to ye, Sir Pathrick O'Grandison, Barronitt.' And wasn't it mesilf, sure, that jist giv'd it the laste little bit of a squaze in the world, all in the way of a commincement, and not to be too rough wid her leddyship? and och, botheration, wasn't it the gentaalest and dilikittest of all the little squazes that I got in return? 'Blood and thunder, Sir Pathrick, mavourneen,' thinks I to myself, 'fait, it's jist the mother's son of you, and nobody else at all at all,

that's the handsomest and the fortunittest young bog-throtter
that ever cum'd out of Connaught!' And wid that I giv'd the
flipper a big squaze, and a big squaze it was, by the powers, that
her leddyship giv'd to me back. But it would ha split the seven sides
of you wid the laffin to behould, jist then all at once, the consated
behaviour of Mounseer Maiter-di-dauns. The likes o' sich a jabber-
ing, and a smirking, and a parly-wouing as he begin'd wid her
leddyship, niver was known before upon arth; and divil may burn
me if it wasn't me own very two peepers that cotch'd him tipping
her the wink out of one eye. Och hon! if it wasn't mesilf thin that
was mad as a Kilkenny[3] cat I shud like to be tould who it was!

'Let me infarm you, Mounseer Maiter-di-dauns,' said I, as
purlite as iver ye seed, 'that it's not the gintaal thing at all at all,
and not for the likes o' you innyhow, to be afther the oggling and
a goggling at her leddyship in that fashion,' and jist wid that
such another squaze as it was I giv'd her flipper, all as much as to
say, 'isn't it Sir Pathrick now, my jewel, that'll be able to the
protecting o' you, my darlint?' and then there cum'd another
squaze back, all by way of the answer. 'Thrue for you, Sir
Pathrick,' it said as plain as iver a squaze said in the world, 'Thrue
for you, Sir Pathrick, mavourneen, and it's a proper nate gintleman ye are – that's God's thruth,' and wid that she opened her
two beautiful peepers till I belaved they wud had com'd out of
her hid althegither and intirely, and she looked first as mad as a
cat at Mounseer Frog, and thin as smiling as all out o' doors at
mesilf.

'Thin,' says he, the willain, 'Och hon! and a wolly wou, pully-
wou,' and thin wid that he shoved up his two shoulders till the
divil the bit of his hid was to be diskivered, and then he let down
the two corners of his purraty-trap,[4] and thin not a haporth more
of the satisfaction could I git out o' the spalpeen.

Belave me, my jewel, it was Sir Pathrick that was unrasonable
mad thin, and the more by token that the Frinchman kept an
wid his winking at the widdy; and the widdy she kipt an wid
the squazing of my flipper, as much as to say, 'At him again, Sir
Pathrick O'Grandison, mavourneen;' so I just ripped out wid a big
oath, and says I, –

'Ye little spalpeeny frog of a bog-throtting son of a bloody-noun!' – and jist thin what d'ye think it was that her leddyship did? Troth, she jumped up from the sofy as if she was bit, and made off through the door, while I turned my head round afther her, in a complete bewilderment and botheration, and followed her wid me two peepers. You percave I had a reason of my own for knowing that she couldn't git down the stares althegither and entirely; for I knew very well that I had hould of her hand, for divil the bit had I iver lit it go. And says I, –

'Isn't it the laste little bit of a mistake in the world that ye've been afther the making, yer leddyship? Come back now, that's a darlint, and I'll give ye yur flipper.' But aff she wint down the stairs like a shot, and then I turned round to the little Frinch furrener. Och hon! if it wasn't his spalpeeny little paw that I had hould of in my own – why thin – thin it wasn't – that's all.

And maybe it wasn't mesilf that jist died then outright wid the laffin, to behould the little chap when he found out that it wasn't the widdy at all at all that he had hould of all the time, but only Sir Pathrick O'Grandison. The ould divil himself niver behild sich a long face as he pet an! As for Sir Pathrick O'Grandison, Barronitt, it wasn't for the likes of his riverance to be afther the minding of a thrifle of a mistake. Ye may jist say, though (for it's God's thruth) that afore I lift hould of the flipper of the spalpeen (which was not till afther her leddyship's futmen had kicked us both down the stairs) I gived it such a nate little broth of a squaze as made it all up into raspberry jam.

'Wouly-wou,' says he, 'pully-wou,' says he – 'Cot tam!'

And that's jist the thruth of the rason why he wears his left hand in a sling.

Never Bet the Devil Your Head

A Tale with a Moral

'Con *tal que las costumbres de un autor,*' says Don Tomas De Las Torres,[1] in the preface to his *Amatory Poems*, '*sean puras y castas, importa muy poco que no sean igualmente severas sus obras*' – meaning, in plain English, that, provided the morals of an author are pure, personally, it signifies nothing what are the morals of his books. We presume that Don Tomas is now in Purgatory for the assertion. It would be a clever thing, too, in the way of poetical justice, to keep him there until his *Amatory Poems* get out of print, or are laid definitely upon the shelf through lack of readers. Every fiction should have a moral;[2] and, what is more to the purpose, the critics have discovered that every fiction *has*. Philip Melancthon, some time ago, wrote a commentary upon the *Batrachomyomachia* and proved that the poet's object was to excite a distaste for sedition. Pierre La Seine, going a step farther, shows that the intention was to recommend to young men temperance in eating and drinking. Just so, too, Jacobus Hugo has satisfied himself that, by Evenus, Homer meant to insinuate John Calvin; by Antinous, Martin Luther; by the Lotophagi, Protestants in general; and, by the Harpies, the Dutch.[3] Our more modern Scholiasts are equally acute. These fellows demonstrate a hidden meaning in *The Antediluvians*,[4] a parable in *Powhatan*,[5] new views in 'Cock Robin', and transcendentalism in 'Hop O' My Thumb'.[6] In short, it has been shown that no man can sit down to write without a very profound design. Thus to authors in general much trouble is spared. A novelist, for example, need have no care of his moral. It is there – that is to say, it is some-where – and the moral and the critics can take care of themselves. When the proper time arrives, all that the gentleman intended, and all that he did not intend, will be brought to light, in the *Dial*,[7] or the *Down-Easter*, together with all that he ought to have intended, and the rest that he clearly meant to intend; – so that it will all come very straight in the end.

There is no just ground, therefore, for the charge brought against me by certain ignoramuses – that I have never written a moral tale, or, in more precise words, a tale with a moral. They are not the critics predestined to bring me out, and *develop* my morals; – that is the secret. By and by the *North American Quarterly Humdrum*[8] will make them ashamed of their stupidity. In the mean time, by way of staying execution, by way of mitigating the accusations against me, I offer the sad history appended; a history about whose obvious moral there can be no question whatever, since he who runs may read it in the large capitals which form the title of the tale. I should have credit for this arrangement: a far wiser one than that of La Fontaine and others, who reserve the impression to be conveyed until the last moment, and thus sneak it in at the fag end of their fables.

Defuncti injuria ne afficiantur was a law of the twelve tables, and *De mortuis nil nisi bonum*[9] is an excellent injunction – even if the dead in question be nothing but dead small beer. It is not my design, therefore, to vituperate my deceased friend, Toby Dammit. He was a sad dog, it is true, and a dog's death it was that he died; but he himself was not to blame for his vices. They grew out of a personal defect in his mother. She did her best in the way of flogging him while an infant; for duties to her well-regulated mind were always pleasures, and babies, like tough steaks, or the modern Greek olive-trees, are invariably the better for beating – but, poor woman! she had the misfortune to be left-handed, and a child flogged left-handedly had better to be left unflogged. The world revolves from right to left. It will not do to whip a baby from left to right. If each blow in the proper direction drives an evil propensity out, it follows that every thump in an opposite one knocks its quota of wickedness in. I was often present at Toby's chastisements, and, even by the way in which he kicked, I could perceive that he was getting worse and worse every day. At last I saw, through the tears in my eyes, that there was no hope of the villain at all, and one day when he had been cuffed until he grew so black in the face that one might have mistaken him for a little African, and no effect had been produced beyond that of making him wriggle himself into a fit, I could stand it no longer, but went down upon my knees forthwith, and, uplifting my voice, made prophecy of his ruin.

The fact is that his precocity in vice was awful. At five months of age, he used to get into such passions that he was unable to articulate. At six months, I caught him gnawing a pack of cards. At seven months, he was in the constant habit of catching and kissing the female babies. At eight months, he peremptorily refused to put his signature to the temperance pledge. Thus he went on increasing in iniquity, month after month, until, at the close of the first year, he not only insisted upon wearing *mustaches*, but had contracted a propensity for cursing and swearing, and for backing his assertions by bets.

Through this latter most ungentlemanly practice, the ruin which I had predicted to Toby Dammit overtook him at last. The fashion had 'grown with his growth and strengthened with his strength', so that, when he came to be a man, he could scarcely utter a sentence without interlarding it with a proposition to gamble. Not that he actually *laid* wagers – no. I will do my friend the justice to say that he would as soon have laid eggs. With him the thing was a mere formula – nothing more. His expressions on this head had no meaning attached to them whatever. They were simple if not altogether innocent expletives – imaginative phrases wherewith to round off a sentence. When he said, 'I'll bet you so and so,' nobody ever thought of taking him up; but still I could not help thinking it my duty to put him down. The habit was an immoral one, and so I told him. It was a vulgar one; this I begged him to believe. It was discountenanced by society; here I said nothing but the truth. It was forbidden by act of Congress; here I had not the slightest intention of telling a lie. I remonstrated – but to no purpose. I demonstrated – in vain. I entreated – he smiled. I implored – he laughed. I preached – he sneered. I threatened – he swore. I kicked him – he called for the police. I pulled his nose – he blew it, and offered to bet the Devil his head that I would not venture to try that experiment again.

Poverty was another vice which the peculiar physical deficiency of Dammit's mother had entailed upon her son. He was detestably poor; and this was the reason, no doubt, that his expletive expressions about betting seldom took a pecuniary turn. I will not be bound to say that I ever heard him make use of such a figure of speech as 'I'll bet you a dollar.' It was usually 'I'll bet you what you please', or 'I'll bet you what you dare', or 'I'll bet you a trifle', or else, more significantly still, '*I'll bet the Devil my head*'.

This latter form seemed to please him best; perhaps because it involved the least risk; for Dammit had become excessively parsimonious. Had anyone taken him up, his head was small, and thus his loss would have been small too. But these are my own reflections, and I am by no means sure that I am right in attributing them to him. At all events, the phrase in question grew daily in favor, notwithstanding the gross impropriety of a man betting his brains like bank-notes; but this was a point which my friend's perversity of disposition would not permit him to comprehend. In the end, he abandoned all other forms of wager, and gave himself up to '*I'll bet the Devil my head*', with a pertinacity and exclusiveness of devotion that displeased not less than it surprised me. I am always displeased by circumstances for which I cannot account. Mysteries force a man to think, and so injure his health. The truth is, there was something in the air with which Mr Dammit was wont to give utterance to his offensive expression – something in his manner of enunciation – which at first interested, and afterwards made me very uneasy – something which, for want of a more definite term at present, I must be permitted to call *queer*; but which Mr Coleridge would have called mystical, Mr Kant pantheistical, Mr Carlyle twistical, and Mr Emerson hyperquizzitistical. I began not to like it at all. Mr Dammit's soul was in a perilous state. I resolved to bring all my eloquence into play to save it. I vowed to serve him as Saint Patrick, in the Irish chronicle, is said to have served the toad, that is to say, 'awaken him to a sense of his situation'. I addressed myself to the task forthwith. Once more I betook myself to remonstrance. Again I collected my energies for a final attempt at expostulation.

When I had made an end of my lecture, Mr Dammit indulged

himself in some very equivocal behavior. For some moments he remained silent, merely looking me inquisitively in the face. But presently he threw his head to one side, and elevated his eyebrows to great extent. Then he spread out the palms of his hands and shrugged up his shoulders. Then he winked with the right eye. Then he repeated the operation with the left. Then he shut them both up very tight. Then he opened them both so very wide that I became seriously alarmed for the consequences. Then, applying his thumb to his nose, he thought proper to make an indescribable movement with the rest of his fingers. Finally, setting his arms akimbo, he condescended to reply.

I can call to mind only the heads of his discourse. He would be obliged to me if I would hold my tongue. He wished none of my advice. He despised all my insinuations. He was old enough to take care of himself. Did I still think him baby Dammit? Did I mean to say anything against his character? Did I intend to insult him? Was I a fool? Was my maternal parent aware, in a word, of my absence from the domiciliary residence? He would put this latter question to me as to a man of veracity, and he would bind himself to abide by my reply. Once more he would demand explicitly if my mother knew that I was out. My confusion, he said, betrayed me, and he would be willing to bet the Devil his head that she did not.

Mr Dammit did not pause for my rejoinder. Turning upon his heel, he left my presence with undignified precipitation. It was well for him that he did so. My feelings had been wounded. Even my anger had been aroused. For once I would have taken him up upon his insulting wager. I would have won for the Arch-Enemy Mr Dammit's little head – for the fact is, my mamma *was* very well aware of my merely temporary absence from home.

But *Khoda shefa midêhed* – Heaven gives relief – as the Mussulmans say when you tread upon their toes. It was in pursuance of my duty that I had been insulted, and I bore the insult like a man. It now seemed to me, however, that I had done all that could be required of me in the case of this miserable individual, and I resolved to trouble him no longer with my counsel, but to leave him to his conscience and himself. But, although I forbore to intrude with my advice, I could not bring myself to give up his society altogether. I even went so far as to humor some of his less reprehensible propensities; and there were times when I found myself lauding his wicked jokes, as epicures do mustard, with tears in my eyes; so profoundly did it grieve me to hear his evil talk.

One fine day, having strolled out together, arm in arm, our route led us in the direction of a river. There was a bridge, and we resolved to cross it. It was roofed over, by way of protection from the weather, and the archway, having but few windows, was thus very uncomfortably dark. As we entered the passage, the contrast between the external glare and the interior gloom struck heavily upon my spirits. Not so upon those of the unhappy Dammit, who offered to bet the Devil his head that I was hipped. He seemed to be in an unusual good-humor. He was excessively lively – so much so that I entertained I know not what of uneasy suspicion. It is not impossible that he was affected with the transcendentals. I am not well enough versed, however, in the diagnosis of this disease to speak with decision upon the point; and unhappily there were none of my friends of the *Dial* present. I suggest the idea, nevertheless, because of a certain species of austere Merry-Andrewism[10] which seemed to beset my poor friend, and caused him to make quite a Tom Fool of himself. Nothing would serve him but wriggling, and skipping about, under and over everything that came in his way; now shouting out, and now lisping out, all manner of odd little and big words, yet preserving the gravest face in the world all the time. I really could not make up my mind whether to kick or to pity him. At length, having passed nearly across the bridge, we approached the termination of the footway, when our progress was impeded by a turnstile of some height. Through this I made my way quietly, pushing it around as usual. But this turn would not serve the turn of Mr Dammit. He insisted upon leaping the stile, and said he could cut a pigeon-wing over it in the air. Now this, conscientiously speaking, I did not think he could do. The best pigeon-winger over all kinds of style was my friend Mr Carlyle, and, as I knew *he* could not do it, I would not believe that it could be done by Toby Dammit. I therefore told him, in so many words, that he was a braggadocio and could not do what he said. For this I had reason to be sorry afterwards; for he straightaway offered to *bet the Devil his head* that he could.

I was about to reply, notwithstanding my previous resolutions, with some remonstrance against his impiety, when I heard, close at my elbow, a slight cough, which sounded very much like the ejaculation '*ahem!*' I started, and looked about me in surprise. My glance at length fell into a nook of the framework of the bridge, and upon the figure of a little lame old gentleman of venerable aspect. Nothing could be more reverend than his whole appearance; for he not only had on a full suit of black, but his shirt was perfectly clean and the collar turned very neatly down over a white cravat, while his hair was parted in front like a girl's. His hands were clasped pensively together over his stomach, and his two eyes were carefully rolled up into the top of his head.[11]

Upon observing him more closely, I perceived that he wore a black silk apron over his small-clothes; and this was a thing which I thought very odd. Before I had time to make any remark, however, upon so singular a circumstance, he interrupted me with a second '*ahem!*'

To this observation I was not immediately prepared to reply. The fact is, remarks of this laconic nature are nearly unanswerable. I have known a *Quarterly Review nonplussed* by the word '*Fudge!*' I am not ashamed to say, therefore, that I turned to Mr Dammit for assistance.

'Dammit,' said I, 'what are you about? don't you hear? the gentleman says "*ahem!*"' I looked sternly at my friend while I thus addressed him; for, to say the truth, I felt particularly puzzled, and when a man is particularly puzzled he must knit his brows and look savage, or else he is pretty sure to look like a fool.

'Dammit,' observed I – although this sounded very much like an oath, than which nothing was farther from my thoughts – 'Dammit,' I suggested, 'the gentleman says "*ahem!*"'

I do not attempt to defend my remark on the score of profundity; I did not think it profound myself; but I have noticed that the effect of our speeches is not always proportionate with their importance in our own eyes; and if I had shot Mr D— through and through with a Paixhan bomb, or knocked him in the head with the *Poets and Poetry of America*,[12] he could hardly have been more discomfited than when I addressed him with those simple words – 'Dammit, what are you about? – don't you hear? – the gentleman says "*ahem!*"'

'You don't say so?' gasped he at length, after turning more colors than a pirate runs up one after the other, when chased by a man-of-war. 'Are you quite sure he said *that*? Well, at all events I am in for it now, and may as well put a bold face upon the matter. Here goes, then – *ahem!*'

At this the little old gentleman seemed pleased – God only knows why. He left his station at the nook of the bridge, limped forward with a gracious air, took Dammit by the hand and shook it cordially, looking all the while straight up in his face with an air of the most unadulterated benignity which it is possible for the mind of man to imagine.

'I am quite sure you will win it, Dammit,' said he, with the frankest of all smiles, 'but we are obliged to have a trial, you know, for the sake of mere form.'

'Ahem!' replied my friend, taking off his coat with a deep sigh, tying a pocket-handkerchief around his waist, and producing an unaccountable alteration in his countenance by twisting up his eyes, and bringing down the corners of his mouth – 'ahem!' And 'ahem', said he again, after a pause; and not another word more than 'ahem' did I ever know him to say after that. 'Aha!' thought I, without expressing myself aloud – 'this is quite a remarkable silence on the part of Toby Dammit, and is no doubt a consequence of his verbosity upon a previous occasion. One extreme induces another. I wonder if he has forgotten the many unanswerable questions which he propounded to me so fluently on the day when I gave him my last lecture? At all events, he is cured of the transcendentals.'

'Ahem!' here replied Toby, just as if he had been reading my thoughts, and looking like a very old sheep in a revery.

The old gentleman now took him by the arm, and led him more into the shade of the bridge, a few paces back from the turnstile. 'My good fellow,' said he, 'I make it a point of conscience to allow you this much run. Wait here, till I take my place by the stile, so that I may see whether you go over it handsomely, and transcendentally, and don't omit any flourishes of the pigeon-wing. A mere form, you know. I will say, "one, two, three, and away". Mind you start at the word "away".' Here he took his position by the stile, paused a moment as if in profound reflection, then *looked up*, and, I thought, smiled very slightly, then tightened the strings of his apron, then took a long look at Dammit, and finally gave the word as agreed upon –

'ONE – TWO – THREE – AND AWAY!'

Punctually at the word 'away', my poor friend set off in a strong gallop. The stile was not very high, like Mr Lord's[13] – nor yet very low, like that of Mr Lord's reviewers – but upon the whole I made sure that he would clear it. And then what if he did not? – ah, that was the question – what if he did not? 'What right,' said I, 'had the old gentleman to make any other gentleman jump? The little old dot-and-carry-one! who is *he*? If he asks *me* to jump, I won't do it, that's flat, and I don't care who *the devil he is*.' The bridge, as I say, was arched and covered in, in a very ridiculous manner, and there was a most uncomfortable echo about it at all times – an echo which I never before so particularly observed as when I uttered the four last words of my remark.

But what I said, or what I thought, or what I heard, occupied only an instant. In less than five seconds from his starting, my poor Toby had taken the leap. I saw him run nimbly, and spring grandly from the floor of the bridge, cutting the most awful flourishes with his legs as he went up. I saw him high in the air, pigeon-winging it to admiration just over the top of the stile; and of course, I thought it an unusually singular thing that he did not *continue* to go over. But the whole leap was the affair of a moment, and, before I had a chance to make any profound reflections, down came Mr Dammit on the flat of his back, on the same side of the stile from which he had started.[14] At the same instant I saw the old gentleman limping off at the top of his speed, having caught and wrapped up in his apron something that fell heavily into it from the darkness of the arch just over the turnstile. At all this I was much astonished; but I had no leisure to think, for Mr Dammit lay particularly still, and I concluded that his feelings had been hurt, and that he stood in need of my assistance. I hurried up to him and found that he had received what might be termed a serious injury. The truth is, he had been deprived of his head, which after a close search I could not find anywhere; so I determined to take him home, and send for the homoeopathists. In the mean time a thought struck me, and I threw open an adjacent window of the bridge; when the sad truth flashed upon me at once. About five feet just above the top of the turnstile, and crossing the arch of the footpath so as to constitute a brace, there extended a flat iron bar, lying with its breadth horizontally, and forming one of a series that served to strengthen the structure throughout its extent. With the edge of this brace it appeared evident that the neck of my unfortunate friend had come precisely in contact.

He did not long survive his terrible loss. The homoeopathists did not give him little enough physic, and what little they did give him he hesitated to take. So in the end he grew worse, and at length died, a lesson to all riotous livers. I bedewed his grave with my tears, worked a *bar* sinister[15] on his family escutcheon, and, for the general expenses of his funeral, sent in my very moderate bill to the transcendentalists. The scoundrels refused to pay it, so I had Mr Dammit dug up at once, and sold him for dog's meat.

The Spectacles

MANY years ago, it was the fashion to ridicule the idea of 'love at first sight'; but those who think, not less than those who feel deeply, have always advocated its existence. Modern discoveries, indeed, in what may be termed ethical magnetism or magnet-aesthetics, render it probable that the most natural and, consequently, the truest and most intense of the human affections are those which arise in the heart as if by electric sympathy – in a word, that the brightest and most enduring of the psychal fetters are those which are riveted by a glance. The confession I am about to make will add another to the already almost innumerable instances of the truth of the position.

My story requires that I should be somewhat minute. I am still a very young man, not yet twenty-two years of age. My name, at present, is a very usual and rather plebeian one – Simpson. I say 'at present'; for it is only lately that I have been so called, having legislatively adopted this surname within the last year, in order to receive a large inheritance left me by a distant male relative, Adolphus Simpson, Esq. The bequest was con-ditioned upon my taking the name of the testator, – the family, not the Christian name. My Christian name is Napoleon Buonaparte – or, more properly, these are my first and middle appellations.

I assumed the name, Simpson, with some reluctance, as in my true patronym, Froissart, I felt a very pardonable pride – believing that I could trace a descent from the immortal author of the *Chronicles*. While on the subject of names, by the by, I may mention a singular coincidence of sound attending the names of some of my immediate predecessors. My father was a

Monsieur Froissart, of Paris. His wife – my mother, whom he married at fifteen – was a Mademoiselle Croissart, eldest daughter of Croissart the banker; whose wife, again, being only sixteen when married, was the eldest daughter of one Victor Voissart. Monsieur Voissart, very singularly, had married a lady of similar name – a Mademoiselle Moissart. She, too, was quite a child when married; and her mother, also, Madame Moissart, was only fourteen when led to the altar. These early marriages are usual in France. Here, however, are Moissart, Voissart, Croissart, and Froissart, all in the direct line of descent. My own name, though, as I say, became Simpson by act of Legislature, and with so much repugnance on my part that at one period I actually hesitated about accepting the legacy with the useless and annoying proviso attached.

As to personal endowments, I am by no means deficient. On the contrary, I believe that I am well made, and possess what nine tenths of the world would call a handsome face. In height I am five feet eleven. My hair is black and curling. My nose is sufficiently good. My eyes are large and gray; and although, in fact, they are weak to a very inconvenient degree, still no defect in this regard would be suspected from their appearance. The weakness, itself, however, has always much annoyed me, and I have resorted to every remedy – short of wearing glasses. Being youthful and good-looking, I naturally dislike these, and have resolutely refused to employ them. I know nothing, indeed, which so disfigures the countenance of a young person, or so impresses every feature with an air of demureness, if not altogether of sanctimoniousness and of age. An eye-glass, on the other hand, has a savor of downright foppery and affectation. I have hitherto managed as well as I could without either. But something too much of these merely personal details, which, after all, are of little importance. I will content myself with saying, in addition, that my temperament is sanguine, rash, ardent, enthusiastic – and that all my life I have been a devoted admirer of the women.

One night last winter, I entered a box at the P— Theatre, in company with a friend, Mr Talbot. It was an opera night, and the bills presented a very rare attraction, so that the house was excessively crowded. We were in time, however, to obtain the front seats which had been reserved for us, and into which, with some little difficulty, we elbowed our way.

For two hours, my companion, who was a musical *fanatico*, gave his undivided attention to the stage; and, in the mean time, I amused myself by observing the audience, which consisted, in chief part, of the very *élite* of the city. Having satisfied myself upon this point, I was about turning my eyes to the *prima donna*, when they were arrested and riveted by a figure in one of the private boxes which had escaped my observation.

If I live a thousand years, I can never forget the intense emotion with which I regarded this figure. It was that of a female, the most exquisite I had ever beheld. The face was so far turned towards the stage that, for some minutes, I could not obtain a view of it – but the form was *divine*; no other word can sufficiently express its magnificent proportion, and even the term 'divine' seems ridiculously feeble as I write it.

The magic of a lovely form in woman, the necromancy of female gracefulness, was always a power which I had found it impossible to resist; but here was grace personified, incarnate, the *beau idéal* of my wildest and most enthusiastic visions. The figure, almost all of which the construction of the box permitted to be seen, was somewhat above the medium height, and nearly approached, without positively reaching, the majestic. Its perfect fullness and *tournure* were delicious. The head, of which only the back was visible, rivalled in outline that of the Greek Psyche, and was rather displayed than concealed by an elegant cap of *gaze aérienne*, which put me in mind of the *ventum textilem*[1] of Apuleius. The right arm hung over the balustrade of the box, and thrilled every nerve of my frame with its exquisite symmetry. Its upper portion was draperied by one of the loose open sleeves now in fashion. This extended but little below the elbow. Beneath it was worn an under one of some frail material, close-fitting, and terminated by a cuff of rich lace which fell gracefully over the top of the hand, revealing only the delicate fingers, upon one of which sparkled a diamond ring, which I at once saw was of extraordinary value. The admirable roundness of the wrist was well set off by a bracelet which encircled it, and which also was ornamented and clasped by a magnificent *aigrette* of jewels –

telling, in words that could not be mistaken, at once of the wealth and fastidious taste of the wearer.

I gazed at this queenly apparition for at least half an hour, as if I had been suddenly converted to stone; and, during this period, I felt the full force and truth of all that has been said or sung concerning 'love at first sight'. My feelings were totally different from any which I had hitherto experienced in the presence of even the most celebrated specimens of female loveliness. An unaccountable, and what I am compelled to consider a magnetic, sympathy of soul for soul seemed to rivet, not only my vision, but my whole powers of thought and feeling upon the admirable object before me. I saw – I felt – I knew that I was deeply, madly, irrevocably in love – and this even before seeing the face of the person beloved. So intense, indeed, was the passion that consumed me, that I really believe it would have received little if any abatement had the features, yet unseen, proved of merely ordinary character; so anomalous is the nature of the only true love – of the love at first sight – and so little really dependent is it upon the external conditions which only seem to create and control it.

While I was thus wrapped in admiration of this lovely vision, a sudden disturbance among the audience caused her to turn her head partially towards me, so that I beheld the entire profile of the face. Its beauty even exceeded my anticipations, and yet there was something about it which disappointed me without my being able to tell exactly what it was. I said 'disappointed', but this is not altogether the word. My sentiments were at once quieted and exalted. They partook less of transport and more of calm enthusiasm – of enthusiastic repose. This state of feeling arose, perhaps, from the Madonna-like and matronly air of the face; and yet I at once understood that it could not have arisen entirely from this. There was something else – some mystery which I could not develop, some expression about the countenance which slightly disturbed me while it greatly heightened my interest. In fact, I was just in that condition of mind which prepares a young and susceptible man for any act of extravagance. Had the lady been alone, I should undoubtedly have entered her box and accosted her at all hazards; but, fortunately, she was attended by two companions – a gentleman, and a strikingly beautiful woman, to all appearance a few years younger than herself.

I revolved in my mind a thousand schemes by which I might obtain, hereafter, an introduction to the elder lady, or, for the present, at all events, a more distinct view of her beauty. I would have removed my position to one nearer her own, but the crowded state of the theatre rendered this impossible; and the stern decrees of Fashion had, of late, imperatively prohibited the use of the opera-glass in a case such as this, even had I been so fortunate as to have one with me – but I had not, and was thus in despair.

At length I bethought me of applying to my companion.

'Talbot,' I said, '*you* have an opera-glass. Let me have it.'

'An opera-glass! – no! – what do you suppose *I* would be doing with an opera-glass?' Here he turned impatiently towards the stage.

'But, Talbot,' I continued, pulling him by the shoulder, 'listen to me, will you? Do you see the stage-box? – there! – no, the next. Did you ever behold as lovely a woman?'

'She is very beautiful, no doubt,' he said.

'I wonder who she can be?'

'Why, in the name of all that is angelic, don't you *know* who she is? "Not to know her, argues yourself unknown."[2] She is the celebrated Madame Lalande[3] – the beauty of the day *par excellence*, and the talk of the whole town. Immensely wealthy, too – a widow – and a great match – has just arrived from Paris.'

'Do you know her?'

'Yes – I have the honor.'

'Will you introduce me?'

'Assuredly – with the greatest pleasure; when shall it be?'

'To-morrow, at one, I will call upon you at B——'s.'

'Very good; and now *do* hold your tongue, *if* you can.'

In this latter respect I was forced to take Talbot's advice; for he remained obstinately deaf to every further question or suggestion, and occupied himself exclusively for the rest of the evening with what was transacting upon the stage.

In the mean time I kept my eyes riveted on Madame Lalande, and at length had the good fortune to obtain a full front view of her face. It was exquisitely lovely; this, of course, my heart had told me before, even had not Talbot fully satisfied me upon the point – but still the unintelligible something disturbed me. I finally concluded that my senses were impressed by a certain air of gravity, sadness, or, still more properly, of weariness, which took something from the youth and freshness of the countenance, only to endow it with a seraphic tenderness and majesty, and thus, of course, to my enthusiastic and romantic temperament, with an interest tenfold.

While I thus feasted my eyes, I perceived at last, to my great trepidation, by an almost imperceptible start on the part of the lady, that she had become suddenly aware of the intensity of my gaze. Still, I was absolutely fascinated, and could not withdraw it, even for an instant. She turned aside her face, and again I saw only the chiselled contour of the back portion of the head. After some minutes, as if urged by curiosity to see if I was still looking, she gradually brought her face again around and again encountered my burning gaze. Her large dark eyes fell instantly, and a deep blush mantled her cheek. But what was my astonishment at perceiving that she not only did not a second time avert her head, but that she actually took from her girdle a double eye-glass – elevated it – adjusted it – and then regarded me through it, intently and deliberately, for the space of several minutes.

Had a thunderbolt fallen at my feet I could not have been more thoroughly astounded – astounded *only* – not offended or disgusted in the slightest degree; although an action so bold in any other woman, would have been likely to offend or disgust. But the whole thing was done with so much quietude, so much nonchalance, so much repose – with so evident an air of the highest breeding, in short – that nothing of mere effrontery was perceptible, and my sole sentiments were those of admiration and surprise.

I observed that, upon her first elevation of the glass, she had seemed satisfied with a momentary inspection of my person, and was withdrawing the instrument, when, as if struck by a second thought, she resumed it, and so continued to regard me with fixed attention for the space of several minutes – for five minutes, at the very least, I am sure.

This action, so remarkable in an American theatre, attracted very general observation, and gave rise to an indefinite movement, or *buzz*, among the audience, which for a moment filled me with confusion, but produced no visible effect upon the countenance of Madame Lalande.

Having satisfied her curiosity – if such it was – she dropped the glass, and quietly gave her attention again to the stage; her profile now being turned toward myself, as before. I continued to watch her unremittingly, although I was fully conscious of my rudeness in so doing. Presently I saw the head slowly and slightly change its position; and soon I became convinced that the lady, while pretending to look at the stage was, in fact, attentively regarding myself. It is needless to say what effect this conduct, on the part of so fascinating a woman, had upon my excitable mind.

Having thus scrutinized me for perhaps a quarter of an hour, the fair object of my passion addressed the gentleman who attended her, and, while she spoke, I saw distinctly, by the glances of both, that the conversation had reference to myself.

Upon its conclusion, Madame Lalande again turned towards the stage, and for a few minutes seemed absorbed in the performances. At the expiration of this period, however, I was thrown into an extremity of agitation by seeing her unfold, for the second time, the eye-glass which hung at her side, fully confront me as before, and, disregarding the renewed buzz of the audience, survey me, from head to foot, with the same miraculous composure which had previously so delighted and confounded my soul.

This extraordinary behavior, by throwing me into a perfect fever of excitement – into an absolute delirium of love – served rather to embolden than to disconcert me. In the mad intensity of my devotion, I forgot everything but the presence and the majestic loveliness of the vision which confronted my gaze. Watching my opportunity, when I thought the audience were fully engaged with the opera, I at length caught the eyes of Madame Lalande, and upon the instant, made a slight but unmistakable bow.

She blushed very deeply – then averted her eyes – then slowly and cautiously looked around, apparently to see if my rash action had been noticed – then leaned over towards the gentleman who sat by her side.

I now felt a burning sense of the impropriety I had committed, and expected nothing less than instant exposure; while a vision of pistols upon the morrow floated rapidly and uncomfortably through my brain. I was greatly and immediately relieved, however, when I saw the lady merely hand the gentleman a play-bill, without speaking; but the reader may form some feeble conception of my astonishment – of my profound amazement – my delirious bewilderment of heart and soul – when, instantly after-wards, having again glanced furtively around, she allowed her bright eyes to settle fully and steadily upon my own, and then, with a faint smile, disclosing a bright line of her pearly teeth, made two distinct, pointed and unequivocal affirmative in-clinations of the head.

It is useless, of course, to dwell upon my joy – upon my transport – upon my illimitable ecstasy of heart. If ever man was mad with excess of happiness, it was myself at that moment. I loved. This was my *first* love – so I felt it to be. It was love supreme – indescribable. It was 'love at first sight'; and at first sight too, it had been appreciated and *returned*.

Yes, returned. How and why should I doubt it for an instant? What other construction could I possibly put upon such conduct, on the part of a lady so beautiful, so wealthy, evi-dently so accomplished, of so high breeding, of so lofty a position in society, in every regard so entirely respectable as I felt assured was Madame Lalande? Yes, she loved me – she returned the enthusiasm of my love, with an enthusiasm as blind – as uncompromising – as uncalculating – as abandoned – and as utterly unbounded as my own! These delicious fancies and reflections, however, were now interrupted by the falling of the drop-curtain. The audience arose; and the usual tumult im-mediately supervened. Quitting Talbot abruptly, I made every effort to force my way into closer proximity with Madame Lalande. Having failed in this, on account of the crowd, I at length gave up the chase and bent my steps homewards; consoling myself for my disappointment, in not having been able to touch even the hem of her robe, by the reflection that I should be introduced by Talbot in due form upon the morrow.

This morrow at last came; that is to say, a day finally dawned upon a long and weary night of impatience; and then the hours until 'one', were snail-paced, dreary and innumerable. But even Stamboul, it is said, shall have an end, and there came an end to this long delay. The clock struck. As the last echo ceased, I stepped into B—'s and inquired for Talbot.

'Out,' said the footman – Talbot's own.

'Out!' I replied, staggering back half a dozen paces – 'let me tell you, my fine fellow, that this thing is thoroughly impossible and impracticable; Mr Talbot is *not* out. What do you mean?'

'Nothing, sir; only Mr Talbot is not in. That's all. He rode over to S—, immediately after breakfast, and left word that he would not be in town again for a week.'

I stood petrified with horror and rage. I endeavored to reply, but my tongue refused its office. At length I turned on my heel, livid with wrath, and inwardly consigning the whole tribe of the Talbots to the innermost regions of Erebus.[4] It was evident that my considerate friend, *il fanatico*, had quite forgotten his appointment with myself – had forgotten it as soon as it was made. At no time was he a very scrupulous man of his word. There was no help for it; so, smothering my vexation as well as I could, I strolled moodily up the street, propounding futile inquiries about Madame Lalande to every male acquaintance I met. By report she was known, I found, to all – to many by sight – but she had been in town only a few weeks, and there were very few, therefore, who claimed her personal acquaintance. These few, being still comparatively strangers, could not, or would not, take the liberty of introducing me through the formality of a morning call. While I stood thus, in despair, conversing with a trio of friends upon the all-absorbing subject of my heart, it so happened that the subject itself passed by.

'As I live, there she is!' cried one.

'Surpassingly beautiful!' exclaimed a second.

'An angel upon earth!' ejaculated a third.

I looked; and in an open cariage which approached up, passing slowly down the street, sat the enchanting vision of the opera, accompanied by the younger lady who had occupied a portion of her box.

'Her companion also wears remarkably well,' said the one of my trio who had spoken first.

'Astonishingly,' said the second; 'still quite a brilliant air; but art will do wonders. Upon my word, she looks better than she did at Paris five years ago. A beautiful woman still; – don't you think so, Froissart? – Simpson, I mean.'

'*Still!*' said I, 'and why shouldn't she be? But compared with her friend she is a rushlight to the evening star – a glow-worm to Antares.'

'Ha! ha! ha! – why, Simpson, you have an astonishing tact at making discoveries – original ones, I mean.' And here we separated, while one of the trio began humming a gay *vaudeville*, of which I caught only the lines –

> 'Ninon, Ninon, Ninon à bas –
> A bas Ninon De L'Enclos!'

During this little scene, however, one thing had served greatly to console me, although it fed the passion by which I was consumed. As the carriage of Madame Lalande rolled by our group, I had observed that she recognized me; and, more than this, she had blessed me, by the most seraphic of all imaginable smiles, with no equivocal mark of the recognition.

As for an introduction, I was obliged to abandon all hope of it, until such time as Talbot should think proper to return from the country. In the mean time I perseveringly frequented every reputable place of public amusement; and, at length, at the theatre where I first saw her, I had the supreme bliss of meeting her, and of exchanging glances with her once again. This did not occur, however, until the lapse of a fortnight. Every day, in the *interim*, I had inquired for Talbot at his hotel, and every day had been thrown into a spasm of wrath by the everlasting 'Not come home yet' of his footman.

Upon the evening in question, therefore, I was in a condition little short of madness. Madame Lalande, I had been told, was a Parisian – had lately arrived from Paris – might she not suddenly return? – return before Talbot came back – and might she not be thus lost to me forever? The thought was too terrible to bear. Since my future happiness was at issue, I resolved to act with a manly decision. In a word, upon the breaking up of the play, I traced the lady to her residence, noted the address, and the next morning sent her a full and elaborate letter, in which I poured out my whole heart.

I spoke boldly, freely – in a word, I spoke with passion. I concealed nothing – nothing even of my weakness. I alluded to the romantic circumstances of our first meeting – even to the glances which had passed between us. I went so far as to say that I felt assured of her love; while I offered this assurance, and my own intensity of devotion, as two excuses for my otherwise unpardonable conduct. As a third, I spoke of my fear that she might quit the city before I could have the opportunity of a formal introduction. I concluded the most wildly enthusiastic epistle ever penned, with a frank declaration of my worldly circumstances – of my affluence – and with an offer of my heart and of my hand.

In an agony of expectation I awaited the reply. After what seemed the lapse of a century it came.

Yes, *actually came*. Romantic as all this may appear, I really received a letter from Madame Lalande – the beautiful, the wealthy, the idolized Madame Lalande. Her eyes – her magnificent eyes – had not belied her noble heart. Like a true Frenchwoman, as she was, she had obeyed the frank dictates of her reason, the generous impulses of her nature – despising the conventional pruderies of the world. She had *not* scorned my proposals. She had *not* sheltered herself in silence. She had *not* returned my letter unopened. She had even sent me, in reply, one penned by her own exquisite fingers. It ran thus:

Monsieur Simpson vill pardonne me for not compose de butefulle tong of his contrée so vell as might. It is only de late dat I am arrive, and not yet ave de opportunité for to – l'étudier.

Vid dis apologie for the manière, I vill now say dat, hélas! – Monsieur Simpson ave guess but de too true. Need I say de more? Hélas! am I not ready speak de too moshe?

EUGÉNIE LALANDE

This noble-spirited note I·kissed a million times, and committed, no doubt, on its account, a thousand other extravagances that have now escaped my memory. Still Talbot *would* not return. Alas! could he have formed even the vaguest idea of the suffering his absence occasioned his friend, would not his sympathizing nature have flown immediately to my relief? Still, however, he came *not*. I wrote. He replied. He was detained by urgent business, but would shortly return. He begged me not to be impatient, to moderate my transports, to read soothing books, to drink nothing stronger than Hock,[5] and to bring the consolations of philosophy to my aid. The fool! if he could not come himself, why, in the name of everything rational, could he not have enclosed me a letter of presentation? I wrote again, entreating him to forward one forthwith. My letter was returned by *that* footman, with the following indorsement in pencil. The scoundrel had joined his master in the country.

Left S— yesterday, for parts unknown – did not say where – or when be back – so thought best to return letter, knowing your handwriting, and as how you is always, more or less, in a hurry.

Yours, sincerely,

STUBBS

After this, it is needless to say, that I devoted to the infernal deities both master and valet; but there was little use in anger, and no consolation at all in complaint.

But I had yet a resource left, in my constitutional audacity. Hitherto it had served me well, and I now resolved to make it avail me to the end. Besides, after the correspondence which had passed between us, what act of mere informality *could* I commit, within bounds, that ought to be regarded as indecorous by Madame Lalande? Since the affair of the letter, I had been in the habit of watching her house, and thus discovered that, about twilight, it was her custom to promenade, attended only by a negro in livery, in a public square overlooked by her windows. Here, amid the luxuriant and shadowing groves, in the gray gloom of a sweet midsummer evening, I observed my opportunity and accosted her.

The better to deceive the servant in attendance, I did this with the assured air of an old and familiar acquaintance. With a presence of mind truly Parisian, she took the cue at once, and, to greet me, held out the most bewitchingly little of hands. The valet at once fell into the rear; and now, with hearts full to overflowing, we discoursed long and unreservedly of our love.

As Madame Lalande spoke English even less fluently than she wrote it, our conversation was necessarily in French. In this sweet tongue, so adapted to passion, I gave loose to the impetuous enthusiasm of my nature, and, with all the eloquence I could command, besought her consent to an immediate marriage.

At this impatience she smiled. She urged the old story of decorum, that bugbear which deters so many from bliss until the opportunity for bliss has forever gone by. I had most imprudently made it known among my friends, she observed, that I desired her acquaintance – thus that I did not possess it – thus, again, there was no possibility of concealing the date of our first knowledge of each other. And then she adverted, with a blush, to the extreme recency of this date. To wed immediately would be improper – would be indecorous – would be *outré*. All this she said with a charming air of *naïveté* which enraptured while it grieved and convinced me. She went even so far as to accuse me, laughingly, of rashness – of imprudence. She bade me remember that I really even knew not who she was – what were her prospects, her connections, her standing in society. She begged me, but with a sigh, to reconsider my proposal, and termed my love an infatuation – a will o' the wisp – a fancy or fantasy of the moment – a baseless and unstable creation rather of the imagination than of the heart. These things she uttered as the shadows of the sweet twilight gathered darkly and more darkly around us; and then, with a gentle pressure of her fairy-like hand, overthrew, in a single sweet instant, all the argumentative fabric she had reared.

I replied as best I could – as only a true lover can. I spoke at length and perseveringly of my devotion, of my passion, of her exceeding beauty, and of my own enthusiastic admiration. In conclusion, I dwelt with a convincing energy upon the perils that encompass the course of love – that course of true love that never did run smooth, and thus deduced the manifest danger of rendering that course unnecessarily long.

This latter argument seemed finally to soften the rigor of her determination. She relented; but there was yet another obstacle, she said, which she felt assured I had not properly considered. This was a delicate point – for a woman to urge, especially so; in mentioning it, she saw that she must make a sacrifice of her feelings; still, for *me*, every sacrifice should be made. She alluded to the topic of *age*. Was I aware – was I fully aware of the discrepancy between us? That the age of the husband should surpass by a few years – even by fifteen or twenty – the age of the wife, was regarded by the world as admissible, and, indeed, as even proper; but she had always entertained the belief that the years of the wife should *never* exceed in number those of the husband. A discrepancy of this unnatural kind gave rise, too frequently, alas! to a life of unhappiness. Now she was aware that my own age did not exceed two and twenty; and I, on the contrary, perhaps, was *not* aware that the years of my Eugénie extended very considerably beyond that sum.

About all this there was a nobility of soul, a dignity of candor, which delighted – which enchanted me – which eternally riveted my chains. I could scarcely restrain the excessive transport which possessed me.

'My sweetest Eugénie,' I cried, 'what is all this about which you are discoursing? Your years surpass in some measure my own. But what then? The customs of the world are so many conventional follies. To those who love as ourselves, in what respect differs a year from an hour? I am twenty-two, you say; granted: indeed you may as well call me, at once, twenty-three. Now you yourself, my dearest Eugénie, can have numbered no more than – can have numbered no more than – no more than – than – than – than –'

Here I paused for an instant, in the expectation that Madame Lalande would interrupt me by supplying her true age. But a Frenchwoman is seldom direct, and has always, by way of answer to an embarrassing query, some little practical reply of her own. In the present instance, Eugénie, who, for a few moments past, had seemed to be searching for something in her bosom, at length let fall upon the grass a miniature, which I immediately picked up and presented to her.

'Keep it!' she said, with one of her most ravishing smiles. 'Keep it for my sake – for the sake of her whom it too flatteringly represents. Besides upon the back of the trinket, you may discover, perhaps, the very information you seem to desire. It is now, to be sure, growing rather dark – but you can examine it at your leisure in the morning. In the mean time, you shall be my escort home to-night. My friends are about holding a little musical *levée*. I can promise you, too, some good singing. We French are not nearly so punctilious as you Americans, and I shall have no difficulty in smuggling you in, in the character of an old acquaintance.'

With this, she took my arm, and I attended her home. The mansion was quite a fine one, and, I believe, furnished in good taste. Of this latter point, however, I am scarcely qualified to judge; for it was just dark as we arrived; and, in American mansions of the better sort, lights seldom, during the heat of summer, make their appearance at this, the most pleasant period of the day. In about an hour after my arrival, to be sure, a single shaded solar lamp was lit in the principal drawing-room; and this apartment, I could thus see, was arranged with unusual good taste and even splendor; but two other rooms of the suite, and in which the company chiefly assembled, remained during the whole evening in a very agreeable shadow. This is a well conceived custom, giving the party at least a choice of light or shade, and one which our friends over the water could not do better than immediately to adopt.

The evening thus spent was unquestionably the most delicious of my life. Madame Lalande had not overrated the musical abilities of her friends; and the singing I here heard I had never heard excelled in any private circle out of Vienna. The instrumental performers were many and of superior talents. The vocalists were chiefly ladies, and no individual sang less than well. At length, upon a peremptory call for 'Madame Lalande', she arose at once, without affectation or demur, from the *chaise longue* upon which she had sat by my side, and, accompanied by one or two gentlemen and her female friend of the opera, repaired to the piano in the main drawing-room. I would have escorted her myself; but felt that, under the circumstances of my introduction to the house, I had better remain unobserved where I was. I was thus deprived of the pleasure of seeing, although not of hearing, her sing.

The impression she produced upon the company seemed electrical; but the effect upon myself was something even more. I know not how adequately to describe it. It arose in part, no doubt, from the sentiment of love with which I was imbued; but chiefly from my conviction of the extreme sensibility of the singer. It is beyond the reach of art to endow either air or recitative with more impassioned *expression* than was hers. Her utterance of the romance in *Otello* – the tone with which she gave the words '*Sul mio sasso*', in the *Capuletti* – is ringing in my memory yet. Her lower tones were absolutely miraculous. Her voice embraced three complete octaves, extending from the contralto D to the D upper soprano, and, though sufficiently powered to have filled the San Carlos,[6] executed, with minutest precision, every difficulty of vocal composition – ascending and descending scales, cadences, or *fiorituri*. In the finale of the *Somnambula*, she brought about a most remarkable effect at the words –

> Ah! non giunge uman pensiero
> Al contento ond' io son piena.

Here, in imitation of Malibran, she modified the original phrase of Bellini, so as to let her voice descend to the tenor G, when, by a rapid transition, she struck the G above the treble stave, springing over an interval of two octaves.

Upon rising from the piano after these miracles of vocal execution, she resumed her seat by my side; when I expressed to her, in terms of the deepest enthusiasm, my delight at her performance. Of my surprise I said nothing, and yet was I most unfeignedly surprised; for a certain feebleness, or a rather a certain tremulous indecision, of voice in ordinary conversation had prepared me to anticipate that, in singing, she would not acquit herself with any remarkable ability.

Our conversation was now long, earnest, uninterrupted, and totally unreserved. She made me relate many of the earlier passages of my life, and listened with breathless attention to every word of the narrative. I concealed nothing – I felt that I had a right to conceal nothing from her confiding affection. Encouraged by her candor upon the delicate point of her age, I entered, with perfect frankness, not only into a detail of my many minor vices, but made full confession of those moral and even of those physical infirmities, the disclosure of which, in demanding so much higher a degree of courage, is so much surer an evidence of love. I touched upon my college indiscretions, upon my extravagances, upon my carousals, upon my debts, upon my flirtations. I even went so far as to speak of a slightly hectic cough with which, at one time, I had been troubled – of a chronic rheumatism – of a twinge of hereditary gout – and, in conclusion, of the disagreeable and inconvenient, but hitherto carefully concealed, weakness of my eyes.

'Upon this latter point,' said Madame Lalande, laughingly, 'you have been surely injudicious in coming to confession; for, without the confession, I take it for granted that no one would have accused you of the crime. By the bye,' she continued, 'have you any recollection' – and here I fancied that a blush, even through the gloom of the apartment, became distinctly visible upon her cheek – 'have you any recollection, *mon cher ami*, of this little ocular assistant which now depends from my neck?'

As she spoke she twirled in her fingers the identical double eye-glass which had so overwhelmed me with confusion at the opera.

'Full well – alas! do I remember it,' I exclaimed, pressing passionately the delicate hand which offered the glasses for my inspection. They formed a complex and magnificent toy, richly chased and filigreed, and gleaming with jewels, which, even in the deficient light, I could not help perceiving were of high value.

'*Eh bien, mon ami*,' she resumed with a certain *empressement* of manner that rather surprised me – '*Eh bien, mon ami*, you have earnestly besought of me a favor which you have been pleased to denominate priceless. You have demanded of me my hand upon the morrow. Should I yield to your entreaties – and, I may add, to the pleadings of my own bosom – would I not be entitled to demand of you a very – a very little boon in return?'

'Name it!' I exclaimed with an energy that had nearly drawn upon us the observation of the company, and restrained by their presence alone from throwing myself impetuously at her feet. 'Name it, my beloved, my Eugénie, my own! – name it! – but alas, it is already yielded ere named.'

'You shall conquer then, *mon ami,*' said she, 'for the sake of the Eugénie whom you love, this little weakness which you have last confessed – this weakness more moral than physical – and which, let me assure you, is so unbecoming the nobility of your real nature – so inconsistent with the candor of your usual character – and which, if permitted farther control, will assuredly involve you, sooner or later, in some very disagreeable scrape. You shall conquer, for my sake, this affectation which leads you, as you yourself acknowledge, to the tacit or implied denial of your infirmity of vision. For this infirmity you virtually deny in refusing to employ the customary means for its relief. You will understand me to say, then, that I wish you to wear spectacles: – ah, hush! – you have already consented to wear them, *for my sake.* You shall accept the little toy which I now hold in my hand, and which, though admirable as an aid to vision, is really of no very immense value as a gem. You perceive that, by a trifling modification thus – or thus – it can be adapted to the eyes in the form of spectacles, or worn in the waistcoat pocket as an eye-glass. It is in the former mode, however, and habitually, that you have already consented to wear it *for my sake.*'

This request – must I confess it? – confused me in no little degree. But the condition with which it was coupled rendered hesitation, of course, a matter altogether out of the question.

'It is done!' I cried, with all the enthusiasm that I could muster at the moment. 'It is done – it is most cheerfully agreed. I sacrifice every feeling for your sake. To-night I wear this dear eye-glass *as* an eye-glass, and upon my heart; but with the earliest dawn of that morning which gives me the pleasure of calling you wife, I will place it upon my – upon my nose – and there wear it ever afterwards, in the less romantic, and less fashionable, but certainly in the more serviceable form which you desire.'

Our conversation now turned upon the details of our arrangements for the morrow. Talbot, I learned from my betrothed, had just arrived in town. I was to see him at once, and procure a carriage. The *soirée* would scarcely break up before two; and by this hour the vehicle was to be at the door; when, in the confusion occasioned by the departure of the company, Madame L. could easily enter it unobserved. We were then to call at the house of a clergyman who would be in waiting; there be married, drop Talbot, and proceed on a short tour to the East; leaving the fashionable world at home to make whatever comments upon the matter it thought best.

Having planned all this, I immediately took leave, and went in search of Talbot, but, on the way, I could not refrain from stepping into a hotel, for the purpose of inspecting the miniature; and this I did by the powerful aid of the glasses. The countenance was a surpassingly beautiful one! Those large luminous eyes! that proud Grecian nose! those dark luxuriant curls! – 'Ah!' said I exultingly to myself, 'this is indeed the speaking image of my beloved!' I turned the reverse, and discovered the words – 'Eugénie Lalande – aged twenty-seven years and seven months.'

I found Talbot at home, and proceeded at once to acquaint him with my good fortune. He professed excessive astonishment, of course, but congratulated me most cordially, and proffered every assistance in his power. In a word, we carried out our arrangement to the letter; and, at two in the morning, just ten minutes after the ceremony, I found myself in a close carriage with Madame Lalande – with Mrs Simpson, I should say – and driving at a great rate out of town, in a direction north-east by north, half-north.

It had been determined for us by Talbot, that, as we were to be up all night, we should make our first stop at C—, a village about twenty miles from the city, and there get an early breakfast and some repose, before proceeding upon our route. At four precisely, therefore, the carriage drew up at the door of the principal inn. I handed my adored wife out, and ordered breakfast forthwith. In the mean time we were shown into a small parlor, and sat down.

It was now nearly if not altogether daylight; and, as I gazed, enraptured, at the angel by my side, the singular idea came, all at once, into my head, that this was really the very first moment since my acquaintance with the celebrated loveliness of Madame Lalande, that I had enjoyed a near inspection of that loveliness by daylight at all.

'And now, *mon ami*,' said she, taking my hand, and so interrupting this train of reflection, 'and now, *mon cher ami*, since we are indissolubly one – since I have yielded to your passionate entreaties, and performed my portion of our agreement – I presume you have not forgotten that you also have a little favor to bestow – a little promise which it is your intention to keep. Ah! – let me see! Let me remember! yes; full easily do I call to mind the precise words of the dear promise you made to Eugénie last night. Listen! You spoke thus: "It is done! – it is most cheerfully agreed! I sacrifice every feeling for your sake. To-night I wear this dear eye-glass *as* an eye-glass, and upon my heart; but with the earliest dawn of that morning which gives me the privilege of calling you wife, I will place it upon my – upon my nose – and there wear it ever afterwards, in the less romantic, and less fashionable, but certainly in the more serviceable form which you desire." These were the exact words, my beloved husband, were they not?'

'They were,' I said; 'you have an excellent memory; and assuredly, my beautiful Eugénie, there is no disposition on my part to evade the performance of the trivial promise they imply. See! Behold! They are becoming – rather – are they not?' And here, having arranged the glasses in the ordinary form of spectacles, I applied them gingerly in their proper position; while Madame Simpson, adjusting her cap, and folding her arms, sat bolt upright in her chair, in a somewhat stiff and prim, and indeed, in a somewhat undignified position.

'Goodness gracious me!' I exclaimed almost at the very instant that the rim of the spectacles had settled upon my nose – '*My!* goodness gracious me! – why, what *can* be the matter with these glasses?' and, taking them quickly off, I wiped them carefully with a silk handkerchief, and adjusted them again.

But if, in the first instance, there had occurred something which occasioned me surprise, in the second, this surprise became elevated into astonishment; and this astonishment was profound – was extreme – indeed, I may say it was horrific. What, in the name of everything hideous, did this mean? Could I believe my eyes? – *could* I? – that was the question. Was that – was that – was that *rouge?* And were those – were those – were those *wrinkles*, upon the visage of Eugénie Lalande? And oh, Jupiter! and every one of the gods and goddesses, little and big! – what – what – what – *what* had become of her teeth? I dashed the spectacles violently to the ground, and, leaping to my feet, stood erect in the middle of the floor, confronting Mrs Simpson, with my arms set akimbo, and grinning and foaming, but, at the same time, utterly speechless and helpless with terror and with rage.

Now I have already said that Madame Eugénie Lalande – that is to say, Simpson – spoke the English language but very little better than she wrote it: and for this reason she very properly never attempted to speak it upon ordinary occasions. But rage will carry a lady to any extreme; and in the present case it carried Mrs Simpson to the very extraordinary extreme of attempting to hold a conversation in a tongue that she did not altogether understand.

'Vell, Monsieur,' said she, after surveying me, in great apparent astonishment, for some moments – 'Vell, Monsieur! – and vat den? – vat de matter now? Is it de dance of de Saint Vitusse dat you ave? If not like me, vat for vy buy de pig in de poke?'

'You wretch!' said I, catching my breath – 'you – you – you villainous old hag!'

'Ag? – ole? – me not so *ver* ole, after all! me not one single day more dan de eighty-doo.'

'Eighty-two!' I ejaculated, staggering to the wall – 'eighty-two hundred thousand baboons! The miniature said twenty-seven years and seven months!'

'To be sure! – dat is so! – ver true! but den de portraite has been take for dese fifty-five year. Ven I go marry my segonde usbande, Monsieur Lalande, at dat time I had de portraite take for my daughter by my first usbande, Monsieur Moissart!'

'Moissart!' said I.

'Yes, Moissart,' said she, mimicking my pronunciation, which, to speak the truth, was none of the best; 'and vat den? Vat *you* know bout de Moissart?'

'Nothing, you old fright! – I know nothing about him at all; only I had an ancestor of that name, once upon a time.'

'Dat name! and vat you ave for say to dat name? 'T is ver *goot* name: and so is Voissart – *dat* is ver goot name too. My daughter, Mademoiselle Moissart, she marry von Monsieur Voissart; and de name is bote *ver* respectaable name.'

'Moissart?' I exclaimed, 'and Voissart! why, what is it you mean?'

"Vat I mean? – I mean Moissart and Voissart; and for de matter of dat, I mean Croissart and Froissart, too, if I only tink proper to mean it. My daughter's daughter, Mademoiselle Voissart, she marry von Monsieur Croissart, and den agin, my daughter's grande-daughter, Mademoiselle Croissart, she marry von Monsieur Froissart; and I suppose you say dat *dat* is not von *ver* respectaable name.'

'Froissart!' said I, beginning to faint, 'why, surely you don't say Moissart, and Voissart, and Croissart, and Froissart?'

'Yes,' she replied, leaning fully back in her chair, and stretching out her lower limbs at great length; 'yes, Moissart, and Voissart, and Croissart, and Froissart. But Monsieur Froissart, he vas von *ver* big vat you call fool – he vas von ver great big donce like yourself – for he lef *la belle France* for come to dis stupide Amérique – and ven he get here he vent and ave von *ver* stupide, von *ver, ver* stupide sonn, so I hear, dough I not yet av ad de plaisir to meet vid him – neither me nor my companion, de Madame Stephanie Lalande. He is name de Napoleon Buonaparte Froissart, and I suppose you say dat *dat*, too, is not von *ver* respectaable name.'

Either the length or the nature of this speech, had the effect of working up Mrs Simpson into a very extraordinary passion indeed; and as she made an end of it, with great labor, she jumped up from her chair like somebody bewitched, dropping upon the floor an entire universe of bustle as she jumped. Once upon her feet, she gnashed her gums, brandished her arms, rolled up her sleeves, shook her fist in my face, and concluded the performance by tearing the cap from her head, and with it an immense wig of the most valuable and beautiful black hair, the whole of which she dashed upon the ground with a yell, and there trampled and danced a fandango upon it, in an absolute ecstasy and agony of rage.

Meantime I sank aghast into the chair which she had vacated. 'Moissart and Voissart!' I repeated, thoughtfully, as she cut one of her pigeon-wings, 'and Croissart and Froissart!' as she completed another – 'Moissart and Voissart and Croissart and Napoleon

Buonaparte Froissart! – why, you ineffable old serpent, that's *me* – that's *me* – d'ye hear? that's *me*' – here I screamed at the top of my voice – 'that's *me-e-e!* I am Napoleon Buonaparte Froissart! and if I haven't married my great-great-grandmother, I wish I may be everlastingly confounded!'

Madame Eugénie Lalande, *quasi* Simpson – formerly Moissart – was, in sober fact, my great-great-grandmother.[7] In her youth she had been beautiful, and even at eighty-two, retained the majestic height, the sculptural contour of head, the fine eyes and the Grecian nose of her girlhood. By the aid of these, of pearl-powder, of rouge, of false hair, false teeth, and false *tournure*, as well as of the most skillful *modistes* of Paris, she contrived to hold a respectable footing among the beauties *un peu passées* of the French metropolis. In this respect, indeed, she might have been regarded as little less than the equal of the celebrated Ninon De L'Enclos.

She was immensely wealthy, and being left, for the second time, a widow without children, she bethought herself of my existence in America, and, for the purpose of making me her heir, paid a visit to the United States, in company with a distant and exceedingly lovely relative of her second husband's – a Madame Stephanie Lalande.

At the opera, my great-great-grandmother's attention was arrested by my notice; and, upon surveying me through her eye-glass, she was struck with a certain family resemblance to herself. Thus interested, and knowing that the heir she sought was actually in the city, she made inquiries of her party respecting me. The gentleman who attended her knew my person, and told her who I was. The information thus obtained induced her to renew her scrutiny; and this scrutiny it was which so emboldened me that I behaved in the absurd manner already detailed. She returned my bow, however, under the impression, that, by some odd accident, I had discovered her identity. When, deceived by my weakness of vision, and the arts of the toilet, in respect to the age and charms of the strange lady, I demanded so enthusiastically of Talbot who she was, he concluded that I meant the younger beauty, as a matter of course, and so informed me, with perfect truth, that she was 'the celebrated widow, Madame Lalande'.

In the street, next morning, my great-great-grandmother encountered Talbot, an old Parisian acquaintance; and the conversation, very naturally, turned upon myself. My deficiencies of vision were then explained; for these were notorious, although I was entirely ignorant of their notoriety; and my good old relative discovered, much to her chagrin, that she had been deceived in supposing me aware of her identity, and that I had been merely making a fool of myself in making open love, in a theatre, to an old woman unknown. By way of punishing me for this imprudence, she concocted with Talbot a plot. He purposely kept out of my way, to avoid giving me the introduction. My street inquiries about 'the lovely widow, Madame Lalande', were supposed to refer to the younger lady, of course; and thus the conversation with the three gentlemen whom I encountered shortly after leaving Talbot's hotel, will be easily explained, as also their allusion to Ninon De L'Enclos. I had no opportunity of seeing Madame Lalande closely during daylight and, at her musical *soirée*, my silly weakness in refusing the aid of glasses effectually prevented me from making a discovery of her age. When 'Madame Lalande' was called upon to sing, the younger lady was intended; and it was she who arose to obey the call; my great-great-grandmother, to further the deception, arising at the same moment, and accompanying her to the piano in the main drawing-room. Had I decided upon escorting her thither, it had been her design to suggest the propriety of my remaining where I was; but my own prudential views rendered this unnecessary. The songs which I so much admired, and which so confirmed my impression of the youth of my mistress, were executed by Madame Stephanie Lalande. The eye-glass was presented by way of adding a reproof to the hoax – a sting to the epigram of the deception. Its presentation afforded an opportunity for the lecture upon affectation with which I was so especially edified. It is almost superfluous to add that the glasses of the instrument, as worn by the old lady, had been exchanged by her for a pair better adapted to my years. They suited me, in fact, to a T.

The clergyman, who merely pretended to tie the fatal knot, was a boon companion of Talbot's, and no priest. He was an excellent 'whip', however; and, having doffed his cassock to put on a greatcoat, he drove the hack which conveyed the 'happy couple' out of town. Talbot took a seat at his side. The two scoundrels were thus 'in at the death', and through a half open window of the back parlor of the inn, amused themselves in grinning at the *dénouement* of the drama. I believe I shall be forced to call them both out.

Nevertheless, I am *not* the husband of my great-great-grandmother; and this is a reflection which affords me infinite relief; but I *am* the husband of Madame Lalande – of Madame Stephanie Lalande – with whom my good old relative, besides making me her sole heir when she dies – if she ever does – has been at the trouble of concocting me a match. In conclusion: I am done forever with *billets doux*, and am never to be met without SPECTACLES.

Diddling Considered as One of
the Exact Sciences

Hey, diddle diddle,
The cat and the fiddle.
Mother Goose

SINCE the world began there have been two Jeremys. The one wrote a Jeremiad about usury, and was called Jeremy Bentham.[1] He has been much admired by Mr John Neal, and was a great man in a small way. The other gave name to the most important of the Exact Sciences, and was a great man in a great way; I may say, indeed, in the very greatest of ways.[2]

Diddling, or the abstract idea conveyed by the verb to diddle, is sufficiently well understood. Yet the fact, the deed, the thing, *diddling*, is somewhat difficult to define. We may get, however, at a tolerably distinct conception of the matter in hand, by defining – not the thing, diddling, in itself – but man, as an animal that diddles. Had Plato but hit upon this, he would have been spared the affront of the picked chicken.

Very pertinently it was demanded of Plato why a picked chicken, which was clearly a 'biped without feathers', was not, according to his own definition, a man? But I am not to be bothered by any similar query. Man is an animal that diddles, and there is *no* animal that diddles *but* man. It will take an entire hen-coop of picked chickens to get over that.

What constitutes the essence, the nare, the principle of diddling is, in fact, peculiar to the class of creatures that wear coats and pantaloons. A crow thieves; a fox cheats; a weasel out-wits; a man diddles. To diddle is his destiny. 'Man was made to mourn,' says the poet. But not so: – he was made to diddle. This is his aim – his object – his *end*. And for this reason when a man's diddled we say he's *done*.

Diddling, rightly considered, is a compound, of which the

ingredients are minuteness, interest, perseverance, ingenuity, audacity, nonchalance, originality, impertinence, and *grin*.

MINUTENESS: – Your diddler is minute. His operations are upon a small scale. His business is retail, for cash or approved paper at sight. Should he ever be tempted into magnificent speculation, he then at once loses his distinctive features, and becomes what we term 'financier'. This latter word conveys the diddling idea in every respect except that of magnitude. A diddler may thus be regarded as a banker *in petto*; a 'financial operation', as a diddle at Brobdingnag.[3] The one is to the other as Homer to 'Flaccus',[4] as a mastodon to a mouse, as the tail of a comet to that of a pig.

INTEREST: – Your diddler is guided by self-interest. He scorns to diddle for the mere *sake* of the diddle. He has an object in view – his pocket – and yours. He regards always the main chance. He looks to Number One. You are Number Two, and must look to yourself.

PERSEVERANCE: – Your diddler perseveres. He is not readily discouraged. Should even the banks break he cares nothing about it. He steadily pursues his end, and

Ut canis a corio nunquam absterrebitur uncto,[5]

so he never lets go of his game.

INGENUITY: – Your diddler is ingenious. he has constructive-ness large. He understands plot. He invents and circumvents. Were he not Alexander, he would be Diogenes. Were he not a diddler, he would be a maker of patent rat-traps or an angler for trout.

AUDACITY: – Your diddler is audacious. He is a bold man. He carries the war into Africa. He conquers all by assault. He would not fear the daggers of the Frey Herren. With a little more prudence Dick Turpin would have made a good diddler; with a trifle less blarney, Daniel O'Connell; with a pound or two more brains Charles the Twelfth.[6]

NONCHALANCE: – Your diddler is nonchalant. He is not at all nervous. He never *had* any nerves. He is never seduced into a flurry. He is never put out – unless put out of doors. He is cool – cool as a cucumber. He is calm – 'calm as a smile from Lady Bury'.[7]

He is easy – easy as an old glove, or the damsels of ancient Baiae.

ORIGINALITY: – Your diddler is original – conscientiously so. His thoughts are his own. He would scorn to employ those of another. A stale trick is his aversion. He would return a purse, I am sure, upon discovering that he had obtained it by an unoriginal diddle.

IMPERTINENCE: – Your diddler is impertinent. He swaggers. He sets his arms akimbo. He thrusts his hands in his trousers' pockets. He sneers in your face. He treads on your corns. He eats your dinner, he drinks your wine, he borrows your money, he pulls your nose, he kicks your poodle, and he kisses your wife.

GRIN: – Your *true* diddler winds up all with a grin. But this nobody sees but himself. He grins when his daily work is done – when his allotted labors are accomplished – at night in his own closet, and altogether for his own private entertainment. He goes home. He locks his door. He divests himself of his clothes. He puts out his candle. He gets into bed. He places his head upon the pillow. All this done, and your diddler *grins*. This is no hypothesis. It is a matter of course. I reason *a priori*, and a diddle would be *no* diddle without a grin.

The origin of the diddle is referable to the infancy of the Human Race. Perhaps the first diddler was Adam. At all events, we can trace the science back to a very remote period of antiquity. The moderns, however, have brought it to a perfection never dreamed of by our thick-headed progenitors. Without pausing to speak of the 'old saws', therefore, I shall content myself with a compendious account of some of the more 'modern instances'.[8]

A very good diddle is this. A housekeeper in want of a sofa, for instance, is seen to go in and out of several cabinet warehouses. At length she arrives at one offering an excellent variety. She is accosted, and invited to enter, by a polite and voluble individual at the door. She finds a sofa well adapted to her views, and, upon inquiring the price, is surprised and delighted to hear a sum named at least twenty per cent lower than her expectations. She hastens to make the purchase, gets a bill and receipt, leaves her address, with a request that the article be sent home as speedily as possible, and retires amid a profusion of bows from the shop-keeper. The night arrives, and no sofa. The next day passes, and still none. A servant is sent to make inquiry about the delay. The whole transaction is denied. No sofa has been sold – no money received – except by the diddler, who played shop-keeper for the nonce.

Our cabinet warehouses are left entirely unattended, and thus afford every facility for a trick of this kind. Visitors enter, look at furniture, and depart unheeded and unseen. Should any one wish to purchase, or to inquire the price of an article, a bell is at hand, and this is considered amply sufficient.

Again, quite a respectable diddle is this. A well-dressed individual enters a shop; makes a purchase to the value of a dollar; finds, much to his vexation, that he has left his pocket-book in another coat pocket; and so says to the shop-keeper –

'My dear sir, never mind! – just oblige me, will you, by sending the bundle home? But stay! I really believe that I have nothing less than a five-dollar bill, even there. However, you can send four dollars in change with the bundle, you know.'

'Very good, sir,' replies the shop-keeper, who entertains at once a lofty opinion of the high-mindedness of his customer. 'I know fellows,' he says to himself, 'who would just have put the goods under their arm, and walked off with a promise to call and pay the dollar as they came by in the afternoon.'

A boy is sent with the parcel and change. On the route, quite accidentally, he is met by the purchaser, who exclaims: –

'Ah! this is my bundle, I see – I thought you had been home with it, long ago. Well, go on! My wife, Mrs Trotter, will give you the five dollars – I left instructions with her to that effect. The change you might as well give to *me* – I shall want some silver for the Post Office. Very good! One, two, is this a good quarter? – three, four – quite right! Say to Mrs Trotter that you met me, and be sure now and do not loiter on the way.'

The boy doesn't loiter at all; but he is a very long time in getting back from his errand, for no lady of the precise name of Mrs Trotter is to be discovered. He consoles himself, however, that he has not been such a fool as to leave the goods without the money, and, re-entering his shop with a self-satisfied air, feels sensibly hurt and indignant when his master asks him what has become of the change.

A very simple diddle, indeed, is this. The captain of a ship, which is about to sail, is presented by an official-looking person with an unusually moderate bill of city charges. Glad to get off so easily, and confused by a hundred duties pressing upon him all at once, he discharges the claim forthwith. In about fifteen minutes, another less reasonable bill is handed him by one who soon makes it evident that the first collector was a diddler, and the original collection a diddle.

And here, too, is a somewhat similar thing. A steamboat is casting loose from the wharf. A traveller, portmanteau in hand, is discovered running towards the wharf at full speed. Suddenly, he makes a dead halt, stoops, and picks up something from the ground in a very agitated manner. It is a pocket-book, and – 'Has any gentleman lost a pocket-book?' he cries. No one can say that he has exactly lost a pocket-book; but a great excitement ensues, when the treasure trove is found to be of value. The boat, however, must not be detained.

'Time and tide wait for no man,' says the captain.

'For God's sake, stay only a few minutes,' says the finder of the book – 'the true claimant will presently appear.'

'Can't wait!' replies the man in authority; 'cast off there, d' ye hear?'

'What *am* I to do?' asks the finder, in great tribulation. 'I am about to leave the country for some years, and I cannot conscientiously retain this large amount in my possession. I beg your pardon, sir' (here he addresses a gentleman on shore), 'but you have the air of an honest man. *Will* you confer upon me the favor of taking charge of this pocket-book – I *know* I can trust you – and of advertising it? The notes, you see, amount to a very considerable sum. The owner will, no doubt, insist upon rewarding you for your trouble –'

'*Me!* – no, *you!* – it was *you* who found the book.'

'Well, if you *must* have it so – I will take a small reward – just to satisfy your scruples. Let me see – why, these notes are all hundreds – bless my soul! a hundred is too much to take – fifty would be quite enough, I am sure –'

'Cast off there!' says the captain.

'But then I have no change for a hundred, and upon the whole *you* had better –'

'Cast off there!' says the captain.

'Never mind!' cries the gentleman on shore, who has been examining his own pocket-book for the last minute or so – 'never mind! *I* can fix it – here is fifty on the Bank of North America – throw me the book.'

And the over-conscientious finder takes the fifty with marked reluctance, and throws the gentleman the book, as desired, while the steamboat fumes and fizzes on her way. In about half an hour after her departure the 'large amount' is seen to be a 'counterfeit presentment', and the whole thing a capital diddle.

A bold diddle is this. A camp-meeting, or something similar, is to be held at a certain spot which is accessible only by means of a free bridge. A diddler stations himself upon this bridge, respectfully informs all passers-by of the new county law, which establishes a toll of one cent for foot passengers, two for horses and donkeys, and so forth, and so forth. Some grumble, but all submit, and the diddler goes home a wealthier man by some fifty or sixty dollars well earned. This taking a toll from a great crowd of people is an excessively troublesome thing.

A neat diddle is this. A friend holds one of the diddler's promises to pay, filled up and signed in due form upon the ordinary blanks printed in red ink. The diddler purchases one or two dozen of these blanks, and every day dips one of them in his soup, makes his dog jump for it, and finally gives it to him as a *bonne bouche*. The note arriving at maturity, the diddler, with the diddler's dog, calls upon the friend, and the promise to pay is made the topic of discussion. The friend produces it from his *écritoire*, and is in the act of reaching it to the diddler, when up jumps the diddler's dog and devours it forthwith. The diddler is not only surprised but vexed and incensed at the absurd behavior of his dog, and expresses his entire readiness to cancel the obligation at any moment when the evidence of the obligation shall be forth-coming.

A very minute diddle is this. A lady is insulted in the street by a diddler's accomplice. The diddler himself flies to her assistance, and, giving his friend a comfortable thrashing, insists upon attending the lady to her own door. He bows, with his hand upon his heart, and most respectfully bids her adieu. She entreats him, as her deliverer, to walk in and be introduced to her big brother and her papa. With a sigh, he declines to do so. 'Is there no way, then, sir,' she murmurs, 'in which I may be permitted to testify my gratitude?'

'Why, yes, madam, there is. Will you be kind enough to lend me a couple of shillings?'

In the first excitement of the moment the lady decides upon fainting outright. Upon second thought, however, she opens her purse-strings and delivers the specie. Now this, I say, is a diddle minute – for one entire moiety of the sum borrowed has to be paid to the gentleman who had the trouble of performing the insult, and who had then to stand still and be thrashed for performing it.

Rather a small, but still a scientific diddle is this. The diddler approaches the bar of a tavern, and demands a couple of twists of tobacco. These are handed to him, when, having slightly examined them, he says: –

'I don't much like this tobacco. Here, take it back, and give me a glass of brandy and water in its place.'

The brandy and water is furnished and imbibed, and the diddler makes his way to the door. But the voice of the tavern-keeper arrests him.

'I believe, sir, you have forgotten to pay for your brandy and water.'

'Pay for my brandy and water! – didn't I give you the tobacco for the brandy and water? What more would you have?'

'But, sir, if you please, I don't remember that you paid for the tobacco.'

'What do you mean by that, you scoundrel? – Didn't I give you back your tobacco? Isn't *that* your tobacco lying *there*? Do you expect me to pay for what I did not take?'

'But, sir,' says the publican, now rather at a loss what to say, 'but, sir –'

'But me no buts, sir,' interrupts the diddler, apparently in very high dudgeon, and slamming the door after him, as he makes his escape. – 'But me no buts, sir, and none of your tricks upon travellers.'

Here again is a very clever diddle, of which the simplicity is not its least recommendation. A purse, or pocket-book, being really lost, the loser inserts in *one* of the daily papers of a large city a fully descriptive advertisement.

Whereupon our diddler copies the *facts* of this advertisement, with a change of heading, of general phraseology, and *address*. The original, for instance, is long and verbose, is headed 'A Pocket-Book Lost!' and requires the treasure, when found, to be left at No. 1 Tom Street. The copy is brief and, being headed with 'Lost' only, indicates No. 2 Dick, or No. 3 Harry Street, as the locality at which the owner may be seen. Moreover, it is inserted in at least five or six of the daily papers of the day, while in point of time it makes its appearance only a few hours after the original. Should it be read by the loser of the purse, he would hardly suspect it to have any reference to his own misfortune. But, of course, the chances are five or six to one that the finder will repair to the address given by the diddler, rather than to that pointed out by the rightful proprietor. The former pays the reward, pockets the treasure, and decamps.

Quite an analogous diddle is this. A lady of *ton* has dropped, somewhere in the street, a diamond ring of very unusual value. For its recovery, she offers some forty or fifty dollars' reward – giving in her advertisement a very minute description of the gem, and of its settings, and declaring that, upon its restoration to No. So and So, in such and such Avenue, the reward will be paid *instanter*, without a single question being asked. During the lady's absence from home, a day or two afterwards, a ring is heard at the door of No. So and So, in such and such Avenue; a servant appears; the lady of the house is asked for and is declared to be out, at which astounding information the visitor expresses the most poignant regret. His business is of importance and concerns the lady herself. In fact, he had the good fortune to find her diamond ring. But perhaps it would be as well that he should call again. 'By no means!' says the servant; and 'By no means!' say the lady's sister and the lady's sister-in-law, who are summoned forthwith. The ring is clamorously identified, the reward is paid, and the finder nearly thrust out of doors. The lady returns, and expresses some little dissatisfaction with her sister and sister-in-law, because they happen to have paid forty or fifty dollars for a facsimile of her diamond ring – a facsimile made out of real pinchbeck and unquestionable paste.

But, as there is really no end to diddling, so there would be none to this essay, were I even to hint at half the variations, or inflections, of which this science is susceptible. I must bring this paper, perforce, to a conclusion, and this I cannot do better than by a summary notice of a very decent but rather elaborate diddle, of which our own city was made the theatre, not very long ago, and which was subsequently repeated with success in other still more verdant localities of the Union. A middle-aged gentleman arrives in town from parts unknown. He is remarkably precise, cautious, staid, and deliberate in his demeanor. His dress is scrupulously neat, but plain, unostentatious. He wears a white cravat, an ample waistcoat, made with an eye to comfort alone; thick-soled cosy-looking shoes, and pantaloons without straps. He has the whole air, in fact, of your well-to-do, sober-sided, exact, and respectable 'man of business', *par excellence* – one of the stern and outwardly hard, internally soft, sort of people that we see in the crack high comedies; fellows whose words are so many bonds, and who are noted for giving away guineas, in charity, with the one hand, while, in the way of mere bargain, they exact the uttermost fraction of a farthing with the other.

He makes much ado before he can get suited with a boarding-house. He dislikes children. He has been accustomed to quiet. His habits are methodical – and then he would prefer getting into a private and respectable small family, piously inclined. Terms, however, are no object; only he must insist upon settling his bill on the first of every month (it is now the second), and begs his landlady, when he finally obtains one to his mind, *not* on any account to forget his instructions upon this point – but to send in a bill, *and* receipt, precisely at ten o'clock on the *first* day of every month, and under no circumstances to put it off to the second.

These arrangements made, our man of business rents an office in a reputable rather than in a fashionable quarter of the town. There is nothing he more despises than pretence. 'Where there is much show,' he says, 'there is seldom anything very solid behind'; an observation which so profoundly impresses his landlady's fancy that she makes a pencil memorandum of it forthwith, in her great family Bible, on the broad margin of the Proverbs of Solomon.

The next step is to advertise, after some such fashion as this, in the principal business sixpennies of this city – the pennies are eschewed as not 'respectable' and as demanding payment for all advertisements in advance. Our man of business holds it as a point of his faith that work should never be paid for until done.

WANTED. – The advertisers, being about to commence extensive business operations in this city, will require the services of three or four intelligent and competent clerks, to whom a liberal salary will be paid. The very best recommendations, not so much for capacity, as for integrity, will be expected. Indeed, as the duties to be performed involve high responsibilities, and large amounts of money must necessarily pass through the hands of those engaged, it is deemed advisable to demand a deposit of fifty dollars from each clerk employed. No person need apply, therefore, who is not prepared to leave this sum in the possession of the advertisers, and who cannot furnish the most satisfactory testimonials of morality. Young gentlemen piously inclined will be preferred. Application should be made between the hours of ten and eleven, a.m., and four and five, p.m., of Messrs

BOGS, HOGS, LOGS, FROGS, & Co.
No 110 Dog Street

By the thirty-first day of the month, this advertisement has brought to the office of Messrs Bogs, Hogs, Logs, Frogs, and Company, some fifteen or twenty young gentlemen piously inclined. But our man of business is in no hurry to conclude a contract with any – no man of business is *ever* precipitate – and it is not until the most rigid catechism, in respect to the piety of each young gentleman's inclination, that his services are engaged and his fifty dollars receipted for, *just* by way of proper precaution, on the part of the respectable firm of Bogs, Hogs, Logs, Frogs, and Company. On the morning of the first day next month, the landlady does *not* present her bill, according to promise; a piece of neglect for which the comfortable head of the house ending in *ogs* would no doubt have chided her severely, could he have been prevailed upon to remain in town a day or two for that purpose.

As it is, the constables have had a sad time of it, running hither and thither, and all they can do is to declare the man of business most emphatically a 'hen knee high' – by which some persons imagine them to imply that, in fact, he is n. e. i. – by which again the very classical phrase *non est inventus*[9] is supposed to be understood. In the mean time the young gentlemen, one and all, are somewhat less piously inclined than before, while the landlady purchases a shilling's worth of the best Indian rubber, and very carefully obliterates the pencil memorandum that some fool has made in her great family Bible, on the broad margin of the Proverbs of Solomon.

The Premature Burial

THERE are certain themes of which the interest is all-absorbing, but which are too entirely horrible for the purposes of legitimate fiction. These the mere romanticist must eschew, if he do not wish to offend or to disgust. They are with propriety handled only when the severity and majesty of truth sanctify and sustain them. We thrill, for example, with the most intense of 'pleasurable pain', over the accounts of the Passage of the Beresina, of the Earthquake at Lisbon, of the Plague at London, of the Massacre of St Bartholomew, or of the stifling of the hundred and twenty-three prisoners in the Black Hole at Calcutta. But, in these accounts, it is the fact – it is the reality – it is the history which excites. As inventions, we should regard them with simple abhorrence.

I have mentioned some few of the more prominent and august calamities on record; but in these it is the extent, not less than the character, of the calamity, which so vividly impresses the fancy. I need not remind the reader that, from the long and weird catalogue of human miseries, I might have selected many individual instances more replete with essential suffering than any of these vast generalities of disaster. The true wretchedness, indeed – the ultimate woe – is particular, not diffuse. That the ghastly extremes of agony are endured by man the unit, and never by man the mass – for this let us thank a merciful God!

To be buried while alive is, beyond question, the most terrific of these extremes which has ever fallen to the lot of mere mortality. That it has frequently, very frequently, so fallen, will scarcely be denied by those who think. The boundaries which divide Life and Death are at best shadowy and vague. Who shall say where the one ends, and where the other begins? We know that there are diseases in which occur total cessations of all the apparent functions of vitality, and yet in which these cessations are merely suspensions, properly so called. They are only temporary pauses in the incomprehensible mechanism. A certain period elapses, and some unseen mysterious principle again sets in motion the magic pinions and the wizard wheels. The silver cord was not forever loosed, nor the golden bowl irreparably broken. But where, meantime, was the soul?

Apart, however, from the inevitable conclusion, *a priori*, that such causes must produce such effects – that the well-known occurrence of such cases of suspended animation must naturally give rise, now and then, to premature interments – apart from this consideration, we have the direct testimony of medical and ordinary experience to prove that a vast number of such interments have actually taken place. I might refer at once, if necessary, to a hundred well-authenticated instances. One of very remarkable character, and of which the circumstances may be fresh in the memory of some of my readers, occurred, not very long ago, in the neighboring city of Baltimore, where it occasioned a painful, intense, and widely extended excitement. The wife of one of the most respectable citizens – a lawyer of eminence and a member of Congress – was seized with a sudden and unaccountable illness, which completely baffled the skill of her physicians. After much suffering, she died, or was supposed to die. No one suspected, indeed, or had reason to suspect, that she was not actually dead. She presented all the ordinary appearances of death. The face assumed the usual pinched and sunken outline. The lips were of the usual marble pallor. The eyes were lustreless. There was no warmth. Pulsation had ceased. For three days the body was preserved unburied, during which it had acquired a stony rigidity. The funeral, in short, was hastened, on account of the rapid advance of what was supposed to be decomposition.

The lady was deposited in her family vault, which, for three subsequent years, was undisturbed. At the expiration of this term, it was opened for the reception of a sarcophagus; – but, alas! how fearful a shock awaited the husband, who, personally, threw open the door. As its portals swung outwardly back, some white apparelled object fell rattling within his arms. It was the skeleton of his wife in her yet unmouldered shroud.

A careful investigation rendered it evident that she had revived within two days after her entombment – that her struggles within the coffin had caused it to fall from a ledge, or shelf, to the floor, where it was so broken as to permit her escape. A lamp which had been accidentally left, full of oil, within the tomb, was found empty; it might have been exhausted, however, by evaporation. On the uppermost of the steps which led down into the dread chamber was a large fragment of the coffin, with which it seemed that she had endeavored to arrest attention, by striking the iron door. While thus occupied, she probably swooned or possibly died, through sheer terror; and, in falling, her shroud became entangled in some iron-work which projected interiorly. Thus she remained, and thus she rotted, erect.

In the year 1810, a case of living inhumation happened in France, attended with circumstances which go far to warrant the assertion that truth is, indeed, stranger than fiction. The heroine of the story was a Mademoiselle Victorine Lafourcade, a young girl of illustrious family, of wealth, and of great personal beauty. Among her numerous suitors was Julien Bossuet, a poor *littérateur*, or journalist, of Paris. His talents and general amiability had recommended him to the notice of the heiress, by whom he seems to have been truly beloved; but her pride of birth decided her, finally, to reject him, and to wed a Monsieur Renelle, a banker, and a diplomatist of some eminence. After marriage, however, this gentleman neglected, and, perhaps, even more positively ill-treated her. Having passed with him some wretched years, she died, – at least her condition so closely resembled death as to deceive every one who saw her. She was buried – not in a vault, but in an ordinary grave in the village of her nativity. Filled with despair, and still inflamed by the memory of a profound attachment, the lover journeys from the capital to the remote province in which the village lies, with the romantic purpose of disinterring the corpse, and possessing himself of its luxuriant tresses. He reaches the grave. At midnight he unearths the coffin, opens it, and is in the act of detaching the hair, when he is arrested by the unclosing of the beloved eyes. In fact, the lady had been buried alive. Vitality had not altogether departed; and she was aroused, by the caresses of her lover, from the lethargy which had been mistaken for death. He bore her frantically to his lodgings in the village. He employed certain powerful restoratives suggested by no little medical learning. In fine, she revived. She recognized her preserver. She remained with him until, by slow degrees, she fully recovered her original health. Her woman's heart was not adamant, and this last lesson of love sufficed to soften it. She bestowed it upon Bossuet. She returned no more to her husband, but, concealing from him her resurrection, fled with her lover to America. Twenty years afterwards, the two returned to France, in the persuasion that time had so greatly altered the lady's appearance that her friends would be unable to recognize her. They were mistaken, however; for, at the first meeting, Monsieur Renelle did actually recognize and make claim to his wife. This claim she resisted; and a judicial tribunal sustained her in her resistance; deciding that the peculiar circumstances, with the long lapse of years, had extinguished, not only equitably, but legally, the authority of the husband.

The *Chirurgical Journal*, of Leipzig – a periodical, of high authority and merit, which some American bookseller would do well to translate and republish – records, in a late number, a very distressing event of the character in question.

An officer of artillery, a man of gigantic stature and of robust health, being thrown from an unmanageable horse, received a very severe contusion upon the head, which rendered him insensible at once; the skull was slightly fractured; but no immediate danger was apprehended. Trepanning was accomplished successfully. He was bled, and many other of the ordinary means of relief were adopted. Gradually, however, he fell into a more and more hopeless state of stupor; and, finally, it was thought that he died.

The weather was warm; and he was buried with indecent haste in one of the public cemeteries. His funeral took place on Thursday. On the Sunday following, the grounds of the cemetery were, as usual, much thronged with visitors; and, about noon, an intense excitement was created by the declaration of a peasant that, while sitting upon the grave of the officer, he had distinctly felt a commotion of the earth, as if occasioned by someone struggling beneath. At first, little attention was paid to the man's asseveration; but his evident terror, and the dogged obstinacy with which he persisted in his story, had at length their natural effect upon the crowd. Spades were hurriedly procured, and the grave, which was shamefully shallow, was in a few minutes so far thrown open that the head of its occupant appeared. He was then, seemingly, dead; but he sat nearly erect within his coffin, the lid of which, in his furious struggles, he had partially uplifted.

He was forthwith conveyed to the nearest hospital, and there pronounced to be still living, although in an asphytic[1] condition. After some hours he revived, recognized individuals of his acquaintance, and, in broken sentences, spoke of his agonies in the grave.

From what he related, it was clear that he must have been conscious of life for more than an hour, while inhumed, before lapsing into insensibility. The grave was carelessly and loosely filled with an exceedingly porous soil; and thus some air was necessarily admitted. He heard the footsteps of the crowd overhead, and endeavored to make himself heard in turn. It was the tumult within the grounds of the cemetery, he said, which appeared to awaken him from a deep sleep – but no sooner was he awake than he became fully aware of the awful horrors of his position.

This patient, it is recorded, was doing well, and seemed to be in a fair way of ultimate recovery, but fell a victim to the quackeries of medical experiment. The galvanic battery was applied; and he suddenly expired in one of those ecstatic paroxysms which occasionally it superinduces.

The mention of the galvanic battery, nevertheless, recalls to my memory a well-known and very extraordinary case in point, where its action proved the means of restoring to animation a young attorney of London, who had been interred for two days. This occurred in 1831, and created, at the time, a very profound sensation wherever it was made the subject of converse.

The patient, Mr Edward Stapleton, had died, apparently, of typhus fever, accompanied with some anomalous symptoms which had excited the curiosity of his medical attendants. Upon his seeming decease, his friends were requested to sanction a *post-mortem* examination, but declined to permit it. As often happens, when such refusals are made, the practitioners resolved to disinter the body and dissect it at leisure, in private. Arrangements were easily effected with some of the numerous corps of body-snatchers with which London abounds; and, upon the third night after the funeral, the supposed corpse was unearthed from a grave eight feet deep, and deposited in the operating chamber of one of the private hospitals.

As incision of some extent had been actually made in the abdomen, when the fresh and undecayed appearance of the subject suggested an application of the battery. One experiment succeeded another, and the customary effects supervened, with nothing to characterize them in any respect, except, upon one or two occasions, a more than ordinary degree of lifelikeness in the convulsive action.[2]

It grew late. The day was about to dawn; and it was thought expedient, at length, to proceed at once to the dissection. A student, however, was especially desirous of testing a theory of his own, and insisted upon applying the battery to one of the pectoral muscles. A rough gash was made, and a wire hastily brought in contact; when the patient, with a hurried but quite unconclusive movement, arose from the table, stepped into the middle of the floor, gazed about him uneasily for a few seconds, and then – spoke. What he said was unintelligible; but words were uttered; the syllabification was distinct. Having spoken, he fell heavily to the floor.

For some moments all were paralyzed with awe – but the urgency of the case soon restored them their presence of mind. It was seen that Mr Stapleton was alive, although in a swoon. Upon exhibition of ether he revived and was rapidly restored to health, and to the society of his friends – from whom, however, all knowledge of his resuscitation was withheld, until a relapse was no longer to be apprehended. Their wonder – their rapturous astonishment – may be conceived.

The most thrilling peculiarity of this incident, nevertheless, is involved in what Mr S. himself asserts. He declares that at no period was he altogether insensible – that, dully and confusedly, he was aware of everything which happened to him, from the moment in which he was pronounced *dead* by his physicians, to that in which he fell swooning to the floor of the hospital. 'I am alive', were the uncomprehended words which, upon recognizing the locality of the dissecting-room, he had endeavored, in his extremity, to utter.

It were an easy matter to multiply such histories as these – but I forbear – for, indeed, we have no need of such to establish the fact that premature interments occur. When we reflect how very rarely, from the nature of the case, we have it in our power to detect them, we must admit that they may *frequently* occur without our cognizance. Scarcely, in truth, is a graveyard ever encroached upon, for any purpose, to any great extent, that skeletons are not found in postures which suggest the most fearful of suspicions.

Fearful indeed the suspicion – but more fearful the doom! It may be asserted, without hesitation, that *no* event is so terribly well adapted to inspire the supremeness of bodily and of mental distress as is burial before death. The unendurable oppression of the lungs – the stifling fumes of the damp earth – the clinging of the death garments – the rigid embrace of the narrow house – the blackness of the absolute Night – the silence like a sea that overwhelms – the unseen but palpable presence of the Conqueror Worm[3] – these things, with thoughts of the air and grass above, with memory of dear friends who would fly to save us if but informed of our fate, and with consciousness that of this fate they can *never* be informed – that our hopeless portion is that of the really dead – these considerations, I say, carry into the heart, which still palpitates, a degree of appalling and intolerable horror from which the most daring imagination must recoil. We know of nothing so agonizing upon Earth; we can dream of nothing half so hideous in the realms of the nethermost Hell. And thus all narratives upon this topic have an interest profound; an interest, nevertheless, which, through the sacred awe of the topic itself, very properly and very peculiarly depends upon our conviction of the *truth* of the matter narrated. What I have now to tell is of my own actual knowledge – of my own positive and personal experience.

For several years I had been subject to attacks of the singular disorder which physicians have agreed to term catalepsy, in default of a more definitive title. Although both the immediate and the predisposing causes, and even the actual diagnosis of this disease, are still mysterious, its obvious and apparent character is sufficiently well understood. Its variations seem to be chiefly of degree. Sometimes the patient lies, for a day only, or even for a shorter period, in a species of exaggerated lethargy. He is senseless and externally motionless; but the pulsation of the heart is still faintly perceptible; some traces of warmth remain; a slight color lingers within the centre of the cheek; and, upon application of a mirror to the lips, we can detect a torpid, unequal, and vacillating action of the lungs. Then again the duration of the trance is for weeks – even for months; while the closest scrutiny and the most rigorous medical tests fail to establish any material distinction between the state of the sufferer and what we conceive of absolute death. Very usually, he is saved from premature interment solely by the knowledge of his friends that he has been previously subject to catalepsy, by the consequent suspicion excited, and, above all, by the non-appearance of decay. The advances of the malady are, luckily, gradual. The first manifestations, although marked, are unequivocal. The fits grow successively more and more distinctive, and endure each for a longer term than the preceding. In this lies the principal security from inhumation. The unfortunate whose *first* attack should be of the extreme character which is occasionally seen would almost inevitably be consigned alive to the tomb.

My own case differed in no important particular from those mentioned in medical books. Sometimes, without any apparent cause, I sank, little by little, into a condition of semi-syncope, or half swoon; and, in this condition, without pain, without ability to stir, or, strictly speaking, to think, but with a dull lethargic consciousness of life and of the presence of those who surrounded my bed, I remained, until the crisis of the disease restored me, suddenly, to perfect sensation. At other times I was quickly and impetuously smitten. I grew sick, and numb, and chilly, and dizzy, and so fell prostrate at once. Then, for weeks, all was void, and black, and silent, and Nothing became the universe. Total annihilation could be no more. From these latter attacks I awoke, however, with a gradation slow in proportion to the suddenness of the seizure. Just as the day dawns to the friendless and houseless beggar who roams the streets throughout the long desolate winter night – just so tardily – just so wearily – just so cheerily came back the light of the Soul to me.

Apart from the tendency to trance, however, my general health appeared to be good; nor could I perceive that it was at all affected by the one prevalent malady – unless, indeed, an idiosyncrasy in my ordinary *sleep* may be looked upon as superinduced. Upon awaking from slumber, I could never gain, at once, thorough possession of my senses, and always remained, for many minutes, in much bewilderment and perplexity; – the mental faculties in general, but the memory in especial, being in a condition of absolute abeyance.

In all that I endured there was no physical suffering, but of moral distress an infinitude. My fancy grew charnel. I talked 'of worms, of tombs and epitaphs'. I was lost in reveries of death, and the idea of premature burial held continual possession of my brain. The ghastly Danger to which I was subjected, haunted me day and night. In the former, the torture of meditation was excessive – in the latter, supreme. When the grim Darkness overspread the Earth, then, with very horror of thought, I shook – shook as the quivering plumes upon the hearse. When Nature could endure wakefulness no longer, it was with a struggle that I consented to sleep – for I shuddered to reflect that, upon awaking, I might find myself the tenant of a grave. And when, finally, I sank into slumber, it was only to rush at once into a world of phantasms, above which, with vast, sable, overshadowing wings, hovered, predominant, the one sepulchral Idea.

From the innumerable images of gloom which oppressed me in dreams, I select for record but a solitary vision. Methought I was immersed in a cataleptic trance of more than usual duration and profundity. Suddenly there came an icy hand upon my forehead, and an impatient, gibbering voice whispered the word 'Arise!' within my ear.

I sat erect. The darkness was total. I could not see the figure of him who had aroused me. I could call to mind neither the period at which I had fallen into the trance, nor the locality in which I then lay. While I remained motionless, and busied in endeavors to collect my thoughts, the cold hand grasped me fiercely by the wrist, shaking it petulantly, while the gibbering voice said again:

'Arise! did I not bid thee arise?'

'And who,' I demanded, 'art thou?'

'I have no name in the regions which I inhabit,' replied the voice, mournfully; 'I was mortal, but am fiend. I was merciless, but am pitiful. Thou dost feel that I shudder. My teeth chatter as I speak, yet it is not with the chilliness of the night – of the night without end. But this hideousness is insufferable. How canst *thou* tranquilly sleep? I cannot rest for the cry of these great agonies. These sights are more than I can bear. Get thee up! Come with me into the outer Night, and let me unfold to thee the graves. Is not this a spectacle of woe? – Behold!'

I looked; and the unseen figure, which still grasped me by the wrist, had caused to be thrown open the graves of all mankind; and from each issued the faint phosphoric radiance of decay; so that I could see into the innermost recesses, and there view the shrouded bodies in their sad and solemn slumbers with the worm. But, alas! the real sleepers were fewer, by many millions than those who slumbered not at all; and there was a feeble struggling; and there was a general sad unrest; and from out the depths of the countless pits there came a melancholy rustling from the garments of the buried. And, of those who seemed tranquilly to repose, I saw that a vast number had changed, in a greater or less degree, the rigid and uneasy position in which they had originally been entombed. And the voice again said to me, as I gazed:

'Is it not – oh, is it *not* a pitiful sight?' But, before I could find words to reply, the figure had ceased to grasp my wrist, the phosphoric lights expired, and the graves were closed with a sudden violence, while from out them arose a tumult of despairing cries, saying again, 'Is it not – oh, God! is it *not* a very pitiful sight?'

Fantasies such as these, presenting themselves at night,

extended their terrific influence far into my waking hours. My nerves became thoroughly unstrung, and I fell a prey to perpetual horror. I hesitated to ride, or to walk, or to indulge in any exercise that would carry me from home. In fact, I no longer dared trust myself out of the immediate presence of those who were aware of my proneness to catalepsy, lest, falling into one of my usual fits, I should be buried before my real condition could be ascertained. I doubted the care, the fidelity, of my dearest friends. I dreaded that, in some trance of more than customary duration, they might be prevailed upon to regard me as irrecoverable. I even went so far as to fear that, as I occasioned much trouble, they might be glad to consider any very protracted attack as sufficient excuse for getting rid of me altogether. It was in vain they endeavored to reassure me by the most solemn promises. I exacted the most sacred oaths, that under no circumstances they would bury me until decomposition had so materially advanced as to render farther preservation impossible. And, even then, my mortal terrors would listen to no reason – would accept no consolation. I entered into a series of elaborate precautions. Among other things, I had the family vault so remodelled as to admit of being readily opened from within.[4] The slightest pressure upon a long lever that extended far into the tomb would cause the iron portals to fly back. There were arrangements also for the free admission of air and light, and convenient receptacles for food and water, within immediate reach of the coffin intended for my reception. This coffin was warmly and softly padded, and was provided with a lid, fashioned upon the principle of the vault-door, with the addition of springs so contrived that the feeblest movement of the body would be sufficient to set it at liberty. Besides all this, there was suspended from the roof of the tomb, a large bell, the rope of which, it was designed, should extend through a hole in the coffin, and so be fastened to one of the hands of the corpse. But, alas! what avails the vigilance against the Destiny of man? Not even these well-contrived securities sufficed to save from the uttermost agonies of living inhumation a wretch to these agonies foredoomed!

There arrived an epoch – as often before there had arrived – in which I found myself emerging from total unconsciousness into the first feeble and indefinite sense of existence. Slowly – with a tortoise gradation – approached the faint gray dawn of the psychal day. A torpid uneasiness. An apathetic endurance of dull pain. No care – no hope – no effort. Then, after a long interval, a ringing in the ears; then, after a lapse still longer, a pricking or tingling sensation in the extremities; then a seemingly eternal period of pleasurable quiescence, during which the awakening feelings are struggling into thought; then a brief resinking into nonentity; then a sudden recovery. At length the slight quivering of an eyelid, and immediately thereupon, an electric shock of a terror, deadly and indefinite, which sends the blood in torrents from the temples to the heart. And now the first positive effort to think. And now the first endeavor to remember. And now a partial and evanescent success. And now the memory has so far regained its dominion, that, in some measure, I am cognizant of my state. I feel that I am not awaking from ordinary sleep. I recollect that I have been subject to catalepsy. And now, at last, as if by the rush of an ocean, my shuddering spirit is overwhelmed by the one grim Danger – by the one spectral and ever-prevalent Idea.

For some minutes after this fancy possessed me, I remained without motion. And why? I could not summon courage to move. I dared not make the effort which was to satisfy me of my fate – and yet there was something at my heart which whispered me *it was sure*. Despair – such as no other species of wretchedness ever calls into being – despair alone urged me, after long irresolution, to uplift the heavy lids of my eyes. I uplifted them. It was dark – all dark. I knew that the fit was over. I knew that the crisis of my disorder had long passed. I knew that I had now fully recovered the use of my visual faculties; and yet it was dark – all dark – the intense and utter raylessness of the Night that endureth for evermore.

I endeavored to shriek; and my lips and my parched tongue moved convulsively together in the attempt – but no voice issued from the cavernous lungs, which, oppressed as if by the weight of some incumbent mountain, gasped and palpitated, with the heart, at every elaborate and struggling inspiration.

The movement of the jaws, in this effort to cry aloud, showed me that they were bound up, as is usual with the dead. I felt, too, that I lay upon some hard substance; and by something similar my sides were, also, closely compressed. So far, I had not ventured to stir any of my limbs – but now I violently threw up my arms, which had been lying at length, with the wrists crossed. They struck a solid wooden substance, which extended above my person at an elevation of not more than six inches from my face. I could no longer doubt that I reposed within a coffin at last.

And now, amid all my infinite miseries, came sweetly the cherub Hope – for I thought of my precautions. I writhed, and made spasmodic exertions to force open the lid: it would not move. I felt my wrists for the bell-rope: it was not to be found. And now the Comforter fled forever, and a still sterner Despair reigned triumphant; for I could not help perceiving the absence of the paddings which I had so carefully prepared – and then, too, there came suddenly to my nostrils the strong peculiar odor of moist earth. The conclusion was irresistible. I was *not* within the vault. I had fallen into a trance while absent from home – while among strangers – when or how I could not remember – and it was they who had buried me as a dog – nailed up in some common coffin – and thrust, deep, deep, and forever, into some ordinary and nameless *grave*.

As this awful conviction forced itself, thus, into the innermost chambers of my soul, I once again struggled to cry aloud. And in this second endeavor I succeeded. A long, wild, and continuous shriek, or yell, of agony, resounded through the realms of the subterrene Night.

'Hillo! hillo, there!' said a gruff voice, in reply.

'What the devil's the matter now?' said a second.

'Get out o' that!' said a third.

'What do you mean by yowling in that ere kind of style, like a cattymount?' said a fourth; and hereupon I was seized and shaken without ceremony, for several minutes, by a junto of very rough-looking individuals. They did not arouse me from my slumber – for I was wide awake when I screamed – but they restored me to the full possession of my memory.

This adventure occurred near Richmond, in Virginia. Accompanied by a friend, I had proceeded, upon a gunning expedition, some miles down the banks of James River. Night approached, and we were overtaken by a storm. The cabin of a small sloop lying at anchor in the stream, and laden with garden mould, afforded us the only available shelter. We made the best of it, and passed the night on board. I slept in one of the only two berths in the vessel – and the berths of a sloop of sixty or seventy tons need scarcely be described. That which I occupied had no bedding of any kind. Its extreme width was eighteen inches. The distance of its bottom from the deck overhead was precisely the same. I found it a matter of exceeding difficulty to squeeze myself in. Nevertheless, I slept soundly; and the whole of my vision – for it was no dream, and no nightmare – arose naturally from the circumstances of my position – from my ordinary bias of thought – and from the difficulty, to which I have alluded, of collecting my senses, and especially of regaining my memory, for a long time after awaking from slumber. The men who shook me were the crew of the sloop, and some labourers engaged to unload it. From the load itself came the earthy smell. The bandage about the jaws was a silk handkerchief in which I had bound up my head, in default of my customary night-cap.

The tortures endured, however, were indubitably quite equal, for the time, to those of actual sepulture. They were fearfully – they were inconceivably hideous; but out of Evil proceeded Good; for their very excess wrought in my spirit an inevitable revulsion. My soul acquired tone – acquired temper. I went abroad. I took vigorous exercise. I breathed the free air of Heaven. I thought upon other subjects than Death. I discarded my medical books. Buchan⁵ I burned. I read no *Night Thoughts*⁶ – no fustian about church-yards – no bugaboo tales, *such as this*. In short, I became a new man, and lived a man's life. From that memorable night, I dismissed forever my charnel apprehensions, and with them vanished the cataleptic disorder of which, perhaps, they had been less the consequence than the cause.

There are moments when, even to the sober eye of Reason, the world of our sad Humanity may assume the semblance of a Hell; but the imagination of man is no Carathis, to explore with impunity its every cavern.⁷ Alas! the grim legion of sepulchral terrors cannot be regarded as altogether fanciful – but, like the Demons in whose company Afrasiab made his voyage down the Oxus, they must sleep, or they will devour us – they must be suffered to slumber, or we perish.

The Angel of the Odd

An Extravaganza

IT was a chilly November afternoon. I had just consummated an unusually hearty dinner, of which the dyspeptic *truffe* formed not the least important item, and was sitting alone in the dining-room, with my feet upon the fender, and at my elbow a small table which I had rolled up to the fire, and upon which were some apologies for dessert, with some miscellaneous bottles of wine, spirit, and liqueur. In the morning I had been reading Glover's *Leonidas*, Wilkie's *Epigoniad*, Lamartine's *Pilgrimage*, Barlow's *Columbiad*, Tuckerman's *Sicily*, and Griswold's *Curiosities*;[1] I am willing to confess, therefore, that I now felt a little stupid. I made an effort to arouse myself by aid of frequent Lafitte, and, all failing, I betook myself to a stray newspaper in despair. Having carefully perused the column of 'houses to let', and the column of 'dogs lost', and then the two columns of 'wives and apprentices run away', I attacked with great resolution the editorial matter, and, reading it from beginning to end without understanding a syllable, conceived the possibility of its being Chinese, and so re-read it from the end to the beginning, but with no more satisfactory result. I was about throwing away, in disgust,

> This folio of four pages, happy work
> Which not even critics criticize,[2]

when I felt my attention somewhat aroused by the paragraph which follows: –

The avenues to death are numerous and strange. A London paper mentions the decease of a person from a singular cause. He was playing at 'puff the dart', which is played with a long needle inserted in some worsted and blown at a target through a tin tube. He placed the needle at the wrong end of the tube, and, drawing his breath strongly to puff the dart forward with force, drew the needle into his throat. It entered the lungs, and in a few days killed him.

Upon seeing this, I fell into a great rage, without exactly knowing why. 'This thing,' I exclaimed, 'is a contemptible falsehood, a poor hoax – the lees of the invention of some pitiable penny-a-liner, of some wretched concocter of accidents in Cocaigne.[3] These fellows, knowing the extravagant gullibility of the age, set their wits to work in the imagination of improbable possibilities – of odd accidents, as they term them; but to a reflecting intellect (like mine),' I added, in parenthesis, putting my forefinger unconsciously to the side of my nose, 'to a contemplative understanding such as I myself possess, it seems evident at once that the marvellous increase of late in these "odd accidents" is by far the oddest accident of all. For my own part, I intend to believe nothing henceforward that has anything of the "singular" about it.'

'Mein Gott, den, vat a vool you bees for dat!' replied one of the most remarkable voices I ever heard. At first I took it for a rumbling in my ears – such as a man sometimes experiences when getting very drunk – but, upon second thought, I considered the sound as more nearly resembling that which proceeds from an empty barrel beaten with a big stick; and, in fact, this I should have concluded it to be, but for the articulation of the syllables and words. I am by no means naturally nervous, and the very few glasses of Lafitte which I had sipped served to embolden me a little, so that I felt nothing of trepidation, but merely uplifted my eyes with a leisurely movement, and looked carefully around the room for the intruder. I could not, however, perceive any one at all.

'Humph!' resumed the voice, as I continued my survey, 'you mos pe so dronk as de pig, den, for not zee me as I zit here at your zide.'

Hereupon I bethought me of looking immediately before my nose, and there, sure enough, confronting me at the table sat a personage nondescript, although not altogether indescribable. His body was a wine-pipe, or a rum-puncheon, or something of that character, and had a truly Falstaffian air. In its nether extremity were inserted two kegs, which seemed to answer all the purposes of legs. For arms there dangled from the upper portion of the carcass two tolerably long bottles, with the necks outward for hands. All the head that I saw the monster possessed of, was one of those Hessian canteens[4] which resemble a large snuff-box with a hole in the middle of the lid. This canteen (with a funnel on its top, like a cavalier cap slouched over the eyes) was set on edge upon the puncheon, with the hole toward myself; and through this hole, which seemed puckered up like the mouth of a very precise old maid, the creature was emitting certain rumbling and grumbling noises which he evidently intended for intelligible talk.

'I zay,' said he, 'you mos pe dronk as de pig, vor zit dare and not zee me zit ere; and I zay, doo, you mos pe pigger vool as de goose, vor to dispelief vat iz print in de print. 'Tiz de troof – dat it iz – eberry vord ob it.'

'Who are you, pray?' said I, with much dignity, although somewhat puzzled; 'how did you get here? and what is it you are talking about?'

'As vor ow I com'd ere,' replied the figure, 'dat iz none of your pizziness; and as vor vat I be talking apout, I be talk apout vat I tink proper; and as vor who I be, vy dat is de very ting I com'd here for to let you zee for yourzelf.'

'You are a drunken vagabond,' said I, 'and I shall ring the bell and order my footman to kick you into the street!'

'He! he! he!' said the fellow, 'hu! hu! hu! dat you can't do.'

'Can't do!' said I, 'what do you mean? – I can't do what?'

'Ring de pell,' he replied, attempting a grin with his little villanous mouth.

Upon this I made an effort to get up, in order to put my threat into execution; but the ruffian just reached across the table very deliberately, and, hitting me a tap on the forehead with the neck of one of the long bottles, knocked me back into the arm-chair from which I had half arisen. I was utterly astounded; and for a moment was quite at a loss what to do. In the mean time, he continued his talk.

'You zee,' said he, 'it iz te bess vor zit still; and now you shall know who I pe. Look at me! zee! I am te *Angel ov te Odd*.'

'And odd enough, too,' I ventured to reply; 'but I was always under the impression that an angel had wings.'

'Te wing!' he cried, highly incensed, 'vat I pe do mit te wing? Mein Gott! do you take me vor a shicken?'

'No – oh no!' I replied, much alarmed, 'you are no chicken – certainly not.'

'Well, den, zit still and pehabe yourself, or I'll rap you again mid me vist. It iz te shicken ab te wing, und te owl ab te wing, und te imp ab te wing, und te head-teuffel ab te wing. Te angel ab *not* te wing, and I am te *Angel ov te Odd*.'

'And your business with me at present is – is –'

'My pizziness!' ejaculated the thing, 'vy, vat a low-bred buppy you mos pe vor to ask a gentleman und an angel about his pizziness!'

This language was rather more than I could bear, even from an angel; so, plucking up courage, I seized a salt-cellar which lay within reach, and hurled it at the head of the intruder. Either he dodged, however, or my aim was inaccurate; for all I accomplished was the demolition of the crystal which protected the dial of the clock upon the mantel-piece. As for the Angel, he evinced his sense of my assault by giving me two or three hard consecutive raps upon the forehead as before. These reduced me at once to submission, and I am almost ashamed to confess that, either through pain or vexation, there came a few tears into my eyes.

'Mein Gott!' said the Angel of the Odd, apparently much softened at my distress; 'mein Gott, te man is eder ferry dronk or ferry zorry. You mos not trink it so strong – you mos put te water in te wine. Here, trink dis, like a goot veller, und don't gry now – don't!'

Hereupon the Angel of the Odd replenished my goblet (which was about a third full of port) with a colorless fluid that he poured from one of his hand bottles. I observed that these bottles had labels about their necks, and that these labels were inscribed 'Kirschwasser'.

The considerate kindness of the Angel mollified me in no little measure; and, aided by the water with which he diluted my port more than once, I at length regained sufficient temper to listen to his very extraordinary discourse. I cannot pretend to recount all that he told me, but I gleaned from what he said that he was the genius who presided over the *contretemps* of mankind, and whose business it was to bring about the *odd accidents* which are continually astonishing the sceptic. Once or twice, upon my venturing to express my total incredulity in respect to his pretensions, he grew very angry indeed, so that at length I considered it the wiser policy to say nothing at all and let him have his own way. He talked on, therefore, at great length, while I merely leaned back in my chair with my eyes shut, and amused myself with munching raisins and filliping the stems about the room. But, by-and-by, the Angel suddenly construed this behavior of mine into contempt. He arose in a terrible passion, slouched his funnel down over his eyes, swore a vast oath, uttered a threat of some character which I did not precisely comprehend, and finally made me a low bow and departed, wishing me, in the language of the archbishop in *Gil Blas*, 'beaucoup de bonheur et un peu plus de bon sens'.[5]

His departure afforded me relief. The very few glasses of Lafitte that I had sipped had the effect of rendering me drowsy, and I felt inclined to take a nap of some fifteen or twenty minutes, as is my custom after dinner. At six I had an appointment of consequence, which it was quite indispensable that I should keep. The policy of insurance for my dwelling-house had expired the day before; and, some dispute having arisen, it was agreed that, at six, I should meet the board of directors of the company and settle the terms of the renewal. Glancing upward at the clock on the mantel-piece (for I felt too drowsy to take out my watch), I had the pleasure to find that I had still twenty-five minutes to spare. It was half-past five; I could easily walk to the insurance office in five minutes; and my usual siestas had never been known to exceed five and twenty. I felt sufficiently safe, therefore, and composed myself to my slumbers forthwith.

Having completed them to my satisfaction, I again looked toward the timepiece and was half inclined to believe in the possibility of odd accidents when I found that, instead of my ordinary fifteen or twenty minutes, I had been dozing only three; for it still wanted seven and twenty of the appointed hour. I betook myself again to my nap, and at length a second time awoke, when, to my utter amazement, it *still* wanted twenty-seven minutes of six. I jumped up to examine the clock, and found that it had ceased running. My watch informed me that it was half-past seven; and, of course, having slept two hours, I was too late for my appointment. 'It will make no difference,' I said, 'I can call at the office in the morning and apologize; in the meantime what can be the matter with the clock?' Upon examining it, I discovered that one of the raisin stems, which I had been filliping about the room during the discourse of the Angel of the Odd, had flown through the fractured crystal, and lodging, singularly enough, in the key-hole, with an end projecting outward, had thus arrested the revolution of the minute-hand.

'Ah!' said I, 'I see how it is. This thing speaks for itself. A natural accident, such as *will* happen now and then!'

I gave the matter no further consideration, and at my usual hour retired to bed. Here, having placed a candle upon a reading-stand at the bed-head, and having made an attempt to peruse some pages of the *Omnipresence of the Deity*,[6] I unfortunately fell asleep in less than twenty seconds, leaving the light burning as it was.

My dreams were terrifically disturbed by visions of the Angel of the Odd. Methought he stood at the foot of the couch, drew aside the curtains, and, in the hollow, detestable tones of a rum puncheon, menaced me with the bitterest vengeance for the contempt with which I had treated him. He concluded a long harangue by taking off his funnel-cap, inserting the tube into my gullet, and thus deluging me with an ocean of Kirschwasser, which he poured in a continuous flood from one of the long-necked bottles that stood him instead of an arm. My agony was at length insufferable, and I awoke just in time to perceive that a rat had run off with the lighted candle from the stand, but *not* in season to prevent his making his escape with it through the hole. Very soon, a strong suffocating odor assailed my nostrils; the house, I clearly perceived, was on fire. In a few minutes the blaze broke forth with violence, and in an incredibly brief period the entire building was wrapped in flames. All egress from my chamber, except through a window, was cut off. The crowd, however, quickly procured and raised a long ladder. By means of this I was descending rapidly, and in apparent safety, when a huge hog, about whose rotund stomach, and indeed about whose whole air and physiognomy, there was something which reminded me of the Angel of the Odd – when this hog, I say, which hitherto had been quietly slumbering in the mud, took it suddenly into his head that his left shoulder needed scratching, and could find no more convenient rubbing-post than that afforded by the foot of the ladder. In an instant I was precipitated, and had the misfortune to fracture my arm.

This accident, with the loss of my insurance and with the more serious loss of my hair, the whole of which had been singed off by the fire, predisposed me to serious impressions, so that, finally, I made up my mind to take a wife. There was a rich widow disconsolate for the loss of her seventh husband, and to her wounded spirit I offered the balm of my vows. She yielded a reluctant consent to my prayers. I knelt at her feet in gratitude and adoration. She blushed and bowed her luxuriant tresses into close contact with those supplied me, temporarily, by Grandjean. I know not how the entanglement took place, but so it was. I arose with a shining pate, wigless; she in disdain and wrath, half buried in alien hair. Thus ended my hopes of the widow by an accident which could not have been anticipated, to be sure, but which the natural sequence of events had brought about.

Without despairing, however, I undertook the siege of a less implacable heart. The fates were again propitious for a brief period; but again a trivial incident interfered. Meeting my betrothed in an avenue thronged with the *élite* of the city, I was hastening to greet her with one of my best-considered bows, when a small particle of some foreign matter, lodging in the corner of my eye, rendered me for the moment completely blind. Before I could recover my sight, the lady of my love had disappeared – irreparably affronted at what she chose to consider my premeditated rudeness in passing her by ungreeted. While I stood bewildered at the suddenness of this accident (which might have happened, nevertheless, to any one under the sun), and while I still continued incapable of sight, I was accosted by the Angel of the Odd, who proffered me his aid with a civility which I had no reason to expect. He examined my disordered eye with much gentleness and skill, informed me that I had a drop in it, and (whatever a 'drop' was) took it out, and afforded me relief.

I now considered it high time to die (since fortune had so determined to persecute me), and accordingly made my way to the nearest river. Here, divesting myself of my clothes (for there is no reason why we cannot die as we were born), I threw myself headlong into the current; the sole witness of my fate being a solitary crow that had been seduced into the eating of brandy-saturated corn, and so had staggered away from his fellows. No sooner had I entered the water than this bird took it into his head to fly away with the most indispensable portion of my apparel. Postponing, therefore, for the present, my suicidal design, I just slipped my nether extremities into the sleeves of my coat, and betook myself to a pursuit of the felon with all the nimbleness which the case required and its circumstances would admit. But my evil destiny attended me still. As I ran at full speed, with my nose up in the atmosphere, and intent only upon the purloiner of my property, I suddenly perceived that my feet rested no longer upon *terra firma*; the fact is, I had thrown myself over a precipice, and should inevitably be dashed to pieces but for my good fortune in grasping the end of a long guide-rope, which depended from a passing balloon.

As soon as I sufficiently recovered my senses to comprehend the terrific predicament in which I stood, or rather hung, I exerted all the power of my lungs to make that predicament known to the aeronaut overhead. But for a long time I exerted myself in vain. Either the fool could not, or the villain would not, perceive me. Meantime the machine rapidly soared, while my strength even more rapidly failed. I was soon upon the point of resigning myself to my fate and dropping quietly into the sea, when my spirits were suddenly revived by hearing a hollow voice from above, which seemed to be lazily humming an opera air. Looking up, I perceived the Angel of the Odd. He was leaning, with his arms folded, over the rim of the car; and with a pipe in his mouth, at which he puffed leisurely, seemed to be upon excellent terms with himself and the universe. I was too much exhausted to speak, so I merely regarded him with an imploring air.

For several minutes, although he looked me full in the face, he said nothing. At length, removing carefully his meerschaum from the right to the left corner of his mouth, he condescended to speak.

'Who pe you,' he asked, 'und what der teuffel you pe do dare?'

To this piece of impudence, cruelty, and affectation, I could reply only by ejaculating the monosyllable 'Help!'

'Elp!' echoed the ruffian – 'not I. Dare iz te pottle – elp yourself, und pe tam'd!'

With these words he let fall a heavy bottle of Kirschwasser, which, dropping precisely upon the crown of my head, caused me to imagine that my brains were entirely knocked out. Impressed with this idea, I was about to relinquish my hold and give up the ghost with a good grace, when I was arrested by the cry of the Angel, who bade me hold on.

'Old on!' he said; 'don't pe in te urry – don't! Will you pe take de odder pottle, or ave you pe got zober yet and come to your zenzes?'

I made haste, hereupon, to nod my head twice – once in the negative, meaning thereby that I would prefer not taking the other bottle at present – and once in the affirmative, intending thus to imply that I *was* sober and *had* positively come to my senses. By these means I somewhat softened the Angel.

'Und you pelief, ten,' he inquired, 'at te last? You pelief, ten, in te possibility of te odd?'

I again nodded my head in assent.

'Und you ave pelief in *me*, te Angel of te Odd?'

I nodded again.

'Und you acknowledge tat you pe te blind dronk und te vool?'

I nodded once more.

'Put your right hand into your left hand preeches pocket, ten, in token ov your vull zubmizzion unto te Angel ov te Odd.'

This thing, for very obvious reasons, I found it quite impossible to do. In the first place, my left arm had been broken in my fall from the ladder, and, therefore, had I let go my hold with the right hand, I must have let go altogether. In the second place, I could have no breeches until I came across the crow. I was therefore obliged, much to my regret, to shake my head in the negative – intending to give the Angel to understand that I found it inconvenient, just at that moment, to comply with his very reasonable demand! No sooner, however, had I ceased shaking my head than –

'Go to der teuffel, ten!' roared the Angel of the Odd.

In pronouncing these words, he drew a sharp knife across the guide-rope by which I was suspended, and, as we then happened to be precisely over my own house (which, during my peregrinations, had been handsomely rebuilt), it so occurred that I tumbled headlong down the ample chimney and alit upon the dining-room hearth.

Upon coming to my senses (for the fall had very thoroughly stunned me), I found it about four o'clock in the morning. I lay outstretched where I had fallen from the balloon. My head grovelled in the ashes of an extinguished fire, while my feet reposed upon the wreck of a small table, overthrown, and amid the fragments of a miscellanous dessert, intermingled with a newspaper, some broken glasses, and shattered bottles, and an empty jug of the Schiedam Kirschwasser. Thus avenged himself the Angel of the Odd.

Thou Art the Man

I WILL now play the Oedipus to the Rattleborough enigma. I will expound to you, as I alone can, the secret of the enginery that effected the Rattleborough miracle – the one, the true, the admitted, the undisputed, the indisputable miracle, which put a definite end to infidelity among the Rattleburghers, and converted to the orthodoxy of the grandames all the carnal-minded[1] who had ventured to be sceptical before.

This event, which I should be sorry to discuss in a tone of unsuitable levity, occurred in the summer of 18—. Mr Barnabas Shuttleworthy, one of the wealthiest and most respectable citizens of the borough, had been missing for several days under circumstances which gave rise to suspicion of foul play. Mr Shuttleworthy had set out from Rattleborough very early one Saturday morning, on horseback, with the avowed intention of proceeding to the city of—, about fifteen miles distant, and of returning the night of the same day. Two hours after his departure, however, his horse returned without him, and without the saddle-bags which had been strapped on his back at starting. The animal was wounded, too, and covered with mud. These circumstances naturally gave rise to much alarm among the friends of the missing man; and when it was found, on Sunday morning, that he had not yet made his appearance, the whole borough arose *en masse* to go and look for his body.

The foremost and most energetic in instituting this search was the bosom friend of Mr Shuttleworthy – a Mr Charles Goodfellow, or, as he was universally called, 'Charley Goodfellow', or 'Old Charley Goodfellow'. Now, whether it is a marvellous coincidence, or whether it is that the name itself has an imperceptible effect upon the character, I have never yet been able to ascertain; but the fact is unquestionable that there never yet was any person named Charles who was not an open, manly, honest, good-natured, and frank-hearted fellow, with a rich, clear voice, that did you good to hear it, and an eye that looked you always straight in the face, as much as to say, 'I have a clear conscience myself; am afraid of no man, am altogether above doing a mean action.' And thus all the hearty, careless, 'walking gentlemen' of the stage are very certain to be called Charles.

Now, 'Old Charley Goodfellow', although he had been in Rattleborough not longer than six months or thereabouts, and although nobody knew anything about him before he came to settle in the neighborhood, had experienced no difficulty in the world in making the acquaintance of all the respectable people in the borough. Not a man of them but would have taken his bare word for a thousand at any moment; and as for the women, there is no saying what they would not have done to oblige him. And all this came of his having been christened Charles, and of his possessing, in consequence, that ingenuous face which is proverbially the very 'best letter of recommendation'.

I have already said, that Mr Shuttleworthy was one of the most respectable men, and, undoubtedly, he was the most wealthy man, in Rattleborough, while 'Old Charley Goodfellow' was upon as intimate terms with him as if he had been his own brother. The two old gentlemen were next-door neighbors, and, although Mr Shuttleworthy seldom, if ever, visited 'Old Charley', and never was known to take a meal in his house, still this did not prevent the two friends from being exceedingly intimate, as I have just observed; for 'Old Charley' never let a day pass without stepping in three or four times to see how his neighbor came on, and very often he would stay to breakfast or tea, and almost always to dinner; and then the amount of wine that was made way with by the two cronies at a sitting, it would really be a difficult thing to ascertain. Old Charley's favorite beverage was Château Margaux, and it appeared to do Mr Shuttleworthy's heart good to see the old fellow swallow it, as he did, quart after quart; so that one day, when the wine was in, and the wit, as a natural consequence, somewhat out, he said to his crony, as he slapped him upon the back – 'I tell you what it is, Old Charley, you are, by all odds, the heartiest old fellow I ever came across in all my born days; and, since you love to guzzle the wine at that fashion, I'll be darned if I don't have to make thee a present of a big box of the Château Margaux. Od rot me,' — (Mr Shuttleworthy had a sad habit of swearing, although he seldom went beyond 'Od rot me', or 'By gosh', or 'By the jolly golly') – 'Od rot me,' says he, 'if I don't send an order to town this very afternoon for a double box of the best that can be got, and I'll make ye a present of it, I will! – ye needn't say a word now – I *will*, I tell ye, and there's an end of it; so look out for it – it will come to hand some of these fine days, precisely when ye are looking for it the least!' I mention this little bit of liberality on the part of Mr Shuttleworthy, just by way of showing you how *very* intimate an understanding existed between the two friends.

Well, on the Sunday morning in question, when it came to be fairly understood that Mr Shuttleworthy had met with foul play, I never saw any one so profoundly affected as 'Old Charley Goodfellow'. When he first heard that the horse had come home without his master, and without his master's saddle-bags, and all bloody from a pistol-shot that had gone clean through and through the poor animal's chest without quite killing him – when he heard all this, he turned as pale as if the missing man had been his own dear brother or father, and shivered and shook all over as if he had had a fit of the ague.

At first, he was too much overpowered with grief to be able to do anything at all, or to decide upon any plan of action; so that for a long time he endeavored to dissuade Mr Shuttleworthy's other friends from making a stir about the matter, thinking it best to wait awhile – say for a week or two, or a month or two – to see if something wouldn't turn up, or if Mr Shuttleworthy wouldn't come in the natural way, and explain his reasons for sending his horse on before. I dare say you have often observed this disposition to temporize, or to procrastinate, in people who are laboring under any very poignant sorrow. Their powers of mind seem to be rendered torpid, so that they have a horror of anything like action, and like nothing in the world so well as to lie quietly in bed and 'nurse their grief', as the old ladies express it – that is to say, ruminate over their trouble.

The people of Rattleborough had, indeed, so high an opinion of the wisdom and discretion of 'Old Charley' that the greater part of them felt disposed to agree with him, and not make a stir in the business 'until something should turn up', as the honest old gentleman worded it; and I believe that, after all, this would have been the general determination, but for the very suspicious interference of Mr Shuttleworthy's nephew, a young man of very dissipated habits, and otherwise of rather bad character. This nephew, whose name was Pennifeather, would listen to nothing like reason in the matter of 'lying quiet', but insisted upon making immediate search for the 'corpse of the murdered man'. This was the expression he employed; and Mr Goodfellow acutely remarked at the time, that it was 'a *singular* expression, to say no more'. This remark of 'Old Charley's', too, had great effect upon the crowd; and one of the party was heard to ask, very impressively, 'how it happened that young Mr Pennifeather was so intimately cognizant of all the circumstances connected with his wealthy uncle's disappearance as to feel authorized to assert, distinctly and unequivocally, that his uncle *was* "a murdered man".' Hereupon some little squibbing and bickering occurred among various members of the crowd, and especially between 'Old Charley' and Mr Pennifeather – although this latter occurrence was, indeed, by no means a novelty, for little good-will had subsisted between the parties for the last three or four months; and matters had even gone so far that Mr Pennifeather had actually knocked down his uncle's friend for some alleged excess of liberty that the latter had taken in the uncle's house, of which the nephew was an inmate. Upon this occasion, 'Old Charley' is said to have behaved with exemplary moderation and Christian charity. He arose from the blow, adjusted his clothes, and made no attempt at retaliation at all – merely muttering a few words about 'taking summary vengeance at the first convenient opportunity', – a natural and very justifiable ebullition of anger, which meant nothing, however, and beyond doubt was no sooner given vent to than forgotten.

However these matters may be (which have no reference to the point now at issue), it is quite certain that the people of Rattleborough, principally through the persuasion of Mr Pennifeather, came at length to the determination of dispersing over the adjacent country in search of the missing Mr Shuttleworthy. I say they came to this determination in the first instance. After it had been fully resolved that a search should be made, it was considered almost a matter of course that the seekers should disperse – that is to say, distribute themselves in parties – for the more thorough examination of the region round about. I forget, however, by what ingenious train of reasoning it was that 'Old Charley' finally convinced the assembly that this was the most injudicious plan that could be pursued. Convince them, however, he did – all except Mr Pennifeather; and, in the end, it was arranged that a search should be instituted, carefully and very thoroughly, by the burghers *en masse*, 'Old Charley' himself leading the way.

As for the matter of that, there could have been no better pioneer than 'Old Charley', whom everybody knew to have the eye of a lynx; but, although he led them into all manner of out-of-the-way holes and corners, by routes that nobody had ever suspected of existing in the neighborhood, and although the search was incessantly kept up day and night for nearly a week, still no trace of Mr Shuttleworthy could be discovered. When I say no trace, however, I must not be understood to speak literally; for trace, to some extent, there certainly was. The poor gentleman had been tracked, by his horse's shoes (which were peculiar), to a spot about three miles to the east of the borough, on the main road leading to the city. Here the track made off into a by-path through a piece of woodland – the path coming out again into the main road, and cutting off about half a mile of the regular distance. Following the shoe-marks down this lane, the party came at length to a pool of stagnant water, half hidden by the brambles to the right of the lane, and opposite this pool all vestige of the track was lost sight of. It appeared, however, that a struggle of some nature had here taken place, and it seemed as if some large and heavy body, much larger and heavier than a man, had been drawn from the by-path to the pool. This latter was carefully dragged twice, but nothing was found; and the party were upon the point of going away, in despair of coming to any result, when Providence suggested to Mr Good-fellow the expediency of draining the water off altogether. This project was received with cheers, and many high compliments to 'Old Charley' upon his sagacity and consideration. As many of the burghers had brought spades with them, supposing that they might possibly be called upon to disinter a corpse, the drain was easily and speedily effected; and no sooner was the bottom visible, than right in the middle of the mud that remained was discovered a black silk velvet waistcoat, which nearly everyone present immediately recognized as the property of Mr Pennifeather. This waistcoat was much torn and stained with blood, and there were several persons among the party who had a distinct remembrance of its having been worn by its owner on the very morning of Mr Shuttleworthy's departure for the city; while there were others, again, ready to testify upon oath, if required, that Mr P. did *not* wear the garment in question at any period during the *remainder* of that memorable day; nor could anyone be found to say that he had seen it upon Mr P.'s person at any period at all subsequent to Mr Shuttleworthy's disappearance.

Matters now wore a very serious aspect for Mr Pennifeather, and it was observed, as an indubitable confirmation of the suspicions which were excited against him, that he grew exceedingly pale, and, when asked what he had to say for himself, was utterly incapable of saying a word. Hereupon, the few friends his riotous mode of living had left him deserted him at once to a man, and were even more clamorous than his ancient and avowed enemies for his instantaneous arrest. But, on the other hand, the magnanimity of Mr Goodfellow shone forth with only the more brilliant lustre through contrast. He made a warm and intensely eloquent defence of Mr Pennifeather, in which he alluded more than once to his own sincere forgiveness of that wild young gentleman – 'the heir of the worthy Mr Shuttleworthy', – for the insult which he (the young gentleman) had, no doubt in the heat of passion, thought proper to put upon him (Mr Goodfellow). 'He forgave him for it,' he said, 'from the very bottom of his heart; and for himself (Mr Goodfellow), so far from pushing the suspicious circumstances to extremity, which, he was sorry to say, really *had* arisen against Mr Pennifeather, he (Mr Goodfellow) would make every exertion in his power, would employ all the little eloquence in his possession to – to – to – soften down, as much as he could conscientiously do so, the worst features of this really exceedingly perplexing piece of business.'

Mr Goodfellow went on for some half-hour longer in this strain, very much to the credit both of his head and of his heart; but your warm-hearted people are seldom apposite in their observations – they run into all sorts of blunders, *contretemps*, and *mal-à-proposisms*, in the hot-headedness of their zeal to serve a friend – thus, often with the kindest of intentions in the world, doing infinitely more to prejudice his cause than to advance it.

So, in the present instance, it turned out with all the eloquence of 'Old Charley'; for, although he labored earnestly in behalf of the suspected, yet it so happened, somehow or other, that every syllable he uttered of which the direct but unwitting tendency was not to exalt the speaker in the good opinion of his audience, had the effect of deepening the suspicion already attached to the individual whose cause he pleaded, and of arousing against him the fury of the mob.

One of the most unaccountable errors committed by the orator was his allusion to the suspected as 'the heir of the worthy old gentleman, Mr Shuttleworthy'. The people had really never thought of this before. They had only remembered certain threats of disinheritance uttered a year or two previously by the uncle (who had no living relative except the nephew); and they had, therefore, always looked upon this disinheritance as a matter that was settled – so single-minded a race of beings were the Rattleburghers; but the remark of 'Old Charley' brought them at once to a consideration of this point, and thus gave them to see the possibility of the threats having been nothing *more* than a threat. And straightway, hereupon, arose the natural question of *cui bono?*[2] – a question that tended even more than the waistcoat to fasten the terrible crime upon the young man. And here, lest I be misunderstood, permit me to digress for one moment merely to observe that the exceedingly brief and simple Latin phrase, which I have employed, is invariably mistranslated and misconceived. *'Cui bono'*, in all the crack novels and elsewhere, – in those of Mrs Gore,[3] for example (the author of *Cecil*), a lady who quotes all tongues from the Chaldaean to Chickasaw, and is helped to her learning, 'as needed', upon a systematic plan,

by Mr Beckford, – in *all* the crack novels, I say, from those of
Bulwer and Dickens to those of Turnapenny and Ainsworth, the
two little Latin words *cui bono* are rendered 'to what purpose', or
(as if *quo bono*), 'to what good'. Their true meaning, nevertheless,
is 'for whose advantage'. *Cui*, to whom; *bono*, is it for a benefit. It
is a purely legal phrase, and applicable precisely in cases such as
we have now under consideration, where the probability of the
doer of a deed hinges upon the probability of the benefit accruing
to this individual or to that from the deed's accomplishment. Now,
in the present instance, the question *cui bono* very pointedly
implicated Mr Pennifeather. His uncle had threatened him, after
making a will in his favor, with disinheritance. But the threat had
not been actually kept; the original will, it appeared, had not been
altered. *Had* it been altered, the only supposable motive for murder
on the part of the suspected would have been the ordinary one of
revenge; and even this would have been counteracted by the hope
of reinstation into the good graces of the uncle. But the will being
unaltered, while the threat to alter remained suspended over the
nephew's head, there appears at once the very strongest possible
inducement of the atrocity: and so concluded, very sagaciously,
the worthy citizens of the borough of Rattle.

Mr Pennifeather was, accordingly, arrested upon the spot, and
the crowd, after some farther search, proceeded homewards,
having him in custody. On the route, however, another circumstance occurred tending to confirm the suspicion entertained. Mr
Goodfellow, whose zeal led him to be always a little in advance
of the party, was seen suddenly to run forward a few paces,
stoop, and then apparently to pick up some small object from
the grass. Having quickly examined it, he was observed, too, to
make a sort of half attempt at concealing it in his coat pocket;
but this action was noticed, as I say, and consequently prevented,
when the object picked up was found to be a Spanish knife which
a dozen persons at once recognized as belonging to Mr Pennifeather. Moreover, his initials were engraved upon the handle.
The blade of this knife was open and bloody.

No doubt now remained of the guilt of the nephew, and
immediately upon reaching Rattleborough he was taken before a
magistrate for examination.

Here matters again took a most favorable turn. The prisoner, being questioned as to his whereabouts on the morning of Mr Shuttleworthy's disappearance, had absolutely the audacity to acknowledge that on that very morning he had been out with his rifle deer-stalking, in the immediate neighborhood of the pool where the blood-stained waistcoat had been discovered through the sagacity of Mr Goodfellow.

This latter now came forward, and, with tears in his eyes, asked permission to be examined. He said that a stern sense of the duty he owed his Maker, not less than his fellow-men, would permit him no longer to remain silent. Hitherto, the sincerest affection for the young man (notwithstanding the latter's ill-treatment of himself, Mr Goodfellow) had induced him to make every hypothesis which imagination could suggest, by way of endeavoring to account for what appeared suspicious in the circumstances that told so seriously against Mr Pennifeather; but these circumstances were now altogether *too* convincing – *too* damning; he would hesitate no longer – he would tell all he knew, although his heart (Mr Goodfellow's) should absolutely burst asunder in the effort. He then went on to state that, on the afternoon of the day previous to Mr Shuttleworthy's departure for the city, that worthy old gentleman had mentioned to his nephew, in *his* hearing (Mr Goodfellow's), that his object in going to town on the morrow was to make a deposit of an unusually large sum of money in the Farmers' and Mechanics' Bank, and that then and there the said Mr Shuttleworthy had distinctly avowed to the said nephew his irrevocable determination of rescinding the will originally made, and of cutting him off with a shilling. He (the witness) now solemnly called upon the accused to state whether what he (the witness) had just stated was or was not the truth in every substantial particular. Much to the astonishment of every one present, Mr Pennifeather frankly admitted that *it was*.

The magistrate now considered it his duty to send a couple of constables to search the chamber of the accused in the house of his uncle. From this search they almost immediately returned with the well-known steel-bound, russet leather pocket-book which the old gentleman had been in the habit of carrying for years. Its valuable contents, however, had been abstracted, and the magistrate in vain endeavored to extort from the prisoner the use which had been made of them, or the place of their conceal-ment. Indeed, he obstinately denied all knowledge of the matter. The constables, also, discovered, between the bed and sacking of the unhappy man, a shirt and neck-handkerchief both marked with the initials of his name, and both hideously besmeared with the blood of the victim.

At this juncture, it was announced that the horse of the mur-dered man had just expired in the stable from the effects of the wound he had received, and it was proposed by Mr Goodfellow that a *post mortem* examination of the beast should be immediately made, with the view, if possible, of discovering the ball. This was accordingly done; and, as if to demonstrate beyond a question the guilt of the accused, Mr Goodfellow, after considerable searching in the cavity of the chest, was enabled to detect and to pull forth a bullet of very extraordinary size, which, upon trial, was found to be exactly adapted to the bore of Mr Pennifeather's rifle, while it was far too large for that of any other person in the borough or its vicinity. To render the matter even surer yet, however, this bullet was discovered to have a flaw or seam at right angles to the usual suture; and upon examination, this seam corresponded precisely with an accidental ridge or elevation in a pair of moulds acknowledged by the accused himself to be his own property. Upon the finding of this bullet, the examining magistrate refused to listen to any farther testimony, and immediately committed the prisoner for trial – declining resolutely to take any bail in the case, although against this severity Mr Goodfellow very warmly remon-strated, and offered to become surety in whatever amount might be required. This generosity on the part of 'Old Charley' was only in accordance with the whole tenor of his amiable and chivalrous conduct during the entire period of his sojourn in the borough of Rattle. In the present instance, the worthy man was so entirely carried away by the excessive warmth of his sympathy that he seemed to have quite forgotten, when he offered to go bail for his young friend, that he himself (Mr Goodfellow) did not possess a single dollar's worth of property upon the face of the earth.

The result of the committal may be readily foreseen. Mr Penni-feather, amid the loud execrations of all Rattleborough, was brought to trial at the next criminal sessions, when the chain of circumstantial evidence (strengthened as it was by some additional damning facts, which Mr Goodfellow's sensitive conscientiousness forbade him to withhold from the court) was considered so unbroken, and so thoroughly conclusive, that the jury, without leaving their seats, returned an immediate verdict of *'Guilty of murder in the first degree'*. Soon afterwards the unhappy wretch received sentence of death, and was remanded to the county jail to await the inexorable vengeance of the law.

In the meantime, the noble behavior of 'Old Charley Goodfellow' had doubly endeared him to the honest citizens of the borough. He became ten times a greater favorite than ever; and, as a natural result of the hospitality with which he was treated, he relaxed, as it were, perforce, the extremely parsimonious habits which his poverty had hitherto impelled him to observe, and very frequently had little *réunions* at his own house, when wit and jollity reigned supreme – dampened a little, of course, by the occasional remembrance of the untoward and melancholy fate which impended over the nephew of the late lamented bosom friend of the generous host.

One fine day, this magnanimous old gentleman was agreeably surprised at the receipt of the following letter:—

Charles Goodfellow, Esq., Rattleborough

From H. F. B. & Co.
Chât.Mar.A – No. 1 – 6 doz. bottles ($\frac{1}{2}$ Gross)

CHARLES GOODFELLOW, ESQUIRE –

Dear Sir – In conformity with an order transmitted to our firm about two months since by our esteemed correspondent, Mr Barnabas Shuttleworthy, we have the honor of forwarding this morning, to your address, a double box of Château Margaux, of the antelope brand, violet seal. Box numbered and marked as per margin.

> We remain, sir,
> Your most ob'nt ser'ts,
> HOGGS, FROGS, BOGS, & CO.

City of—, June 21st, 18—

P.S. – The box will reach you, by wagon, on the day after your receipt of this letter. Our respects to Mr Shuttleworthy.

H. F. B. & Co.

The fact is that Mr Goodfellow had, since the death of Mr Shuttleworthy, given over all expectation of ever receiving the promised Château Margaux; and he, therefore, looked upon it *now* as a sort of especial dispensation of Providence in his behalf. He was highly delighted, of course, and, in the exuberance of his joy, invited a large party of friends to a *petit souper* on the morrow, for the purpose of broaching the good old Mr Shuttleworthy's present. Not that he said anything about 'the good old Mr Shuttleworthy' when he issued the invitations. The fact is, he thought much and concluded to say nothing at all. He did not mention it to any one – if I remember aright – that he had received a *present* of Château Margaux. He merely asked his friends to come and help him drink some of a remarkably fine quality and rich flavor, that he had ordered up from the city a couple of months ago, and of which he would be in the receipt upon the morrow. I have often puzzled myself to imagine *why* it was that 'Old Charley' came to the conclusion to say nothing about having received the wine from his old friend, but I could never precisely understand his reason for the silence, although he had some excellent and very magnanimous reason, no doubt.

The morrow at length arrived, and with it a very large and highly respectable company at Mr Goodfellow's house. Indeed, half the borough was there – I myself among the number – but, much to the vexation of the host, the Château Margaux did not arrive until a late hour, and when the sumptuous supper supplied by 'Old Charley' had been done very ample justice by the guests. It came at length, however, – a monstrously big box of it there was, too, – and as the whole party were in excessively good humor, it was decided, *nem. con.*,⁴ that it should be lifted upon the table and its contents disembowelled forthwith.

No sooner said than done. I lent a helping hand; and, in a trice, we had the box upon the table, in the midst of all the bottles and glasses, not a few of which were demolished in the scuffle. 'Old Charley', who was pretty much intoxicated, and excessively red in the face, now took a seat, with an air of mock dignity, at the head of the board, and thumped furiously upon it with a decanter, calling upon the company to keep order 'during the ceremony of disinterring the treasure'.

After some vociferation, quiet was at length fully restored, and, as very often happens in similar cases, a profound and remarkable silence ensued. Being then requested to force open the lid, I complied, of course, 'with an infinite deal of pleasure'. I inserted a chisel, and giving it a few slight taps with a hammer, the top of the box flew suddenly and violently off, and, at the same instant, there sprang up into a sitting position, directly facing the host, the bruised, bloody and nearly putrid corpse of the murdered Mr Shuttleworthy himself. It gazed for a few moments, fixedly and sorrowfully, with its decaying and lack-lustre eyes, full into the countenance of Mr Goodfellow; uttered slowly, but clearly and impressively, the words – 'Thou art the man!' and then, falling over the side of the chest as if thoroughly satisfied, stretched out its limbs quiveringly upon the table.

The scene that ensued is altogether beyond description. The rush for the doors and windows was terrific, and many of the most robust men in the room fainted outright through sheer horror. But after the first wild, shrieking burst of affright, all eyes were directed to Mr Goodfellow. If I live a thousand years, I can never forget the more than mortal agony which was depicted in that ghastly face of his, so lately rubicund with triumph and wine. For several minutes, he sat rigidly as a statue of marble; his eyes seeming, in the intense vacancy of their gaze, to be turned inwards and absorbed in the contemplation of his own miserable, murderous soul. At length, their expression appeared to flash suddenly out into the external world, when, with a quick leap, he sprang from his chair, and falling heavily with his head and shoulders upon the table, and in contact with the corpse, poured out rapidly and vehemently a detailed confession of the hideous crime for which Mr Pennifeather was then imprisoned and doomed to die.

What he recounted was in substance this: – He followed his victim to the vicinity of the pool; there shot his horse with a pistol; despatched the rider with its butt end; possessed himself of the pocket-book; and, supposing the horse dead, dragged it with great labor to the brambles by the pond. Upon his own beast he slung the corpse of Mr Shuttleworthy, and thus bore it to a secure place of concealment a long distance off through the woods.

The waistcoat, the knife, the pocket-book and bullet, had been placed by himself where found, with the view of avenging himself upon Mr Pennifeather. He had also contrived the discovery of the stained handkerchief and shirt.

Towards the end of the blood-chilling recital, the words of the guilty wretch faltered and grew hollow. When the record was finally exhausted, he arose, staggered backwards from the table, and fell – *dead.*[5]

The means by which this happily timed confession was extorted, although efficient, were simple indeed. Mr Goodfellow's excess of frankness had disgusted me, and excited my suspicions from the first. I was present when Mr Pennifeather had struck him, and the fiendish expression which then arose upon his countenance, although momentarily, assured me that his threat of vengeance would, if possible, be rigidly fulfilled. I was thus prepared to view the manoeuvring of 'Old Charley' in a very different light from that in which it was regarded by the good citizens of Rattleborough. I saw at once that all the criminating discoveries arose, either directly, or indirectly, from himself. But the fact which clearly opened my eyes to the true state of the case was the affair of the bullet, *found* by Mr G. in the carcass of the horse. *I* had not forgotten, although the Rattleburghers had, that there was a hole where the ball had entered the horse, and another where it *went out*. If it were found in the animal then, after having made its exit, I saw clearly that it must have been deposited by the person who found it. The bloody shirt and handkerchief confirmed the idea suggested by the bullet; for the blood upon examination proved to be capital claret, and no more. When I came to think of these things, and also of the late increase of liberality and expenditure on the part of Mr Goodfellow, I entertained a suspicion which was none the less strong because I kept it altogether to myself.

In the mean time, I instituted a rigorous private search for the corpse of Mr Shuttleworthy, and, for good reasons, searched in quarters as divergent as possible from those to which Mr Goodfellow conducted his party. The result was that, after some days, I came across an old dry well, the mouth of which was nearly hidden by brambles; and here, at the bottom, I discovered what I sought.

Now it so happened that I had overheard the colloquy between the two cronies, when Mr Goodfellow had contrived to cajole his host into the promise of a box of Château Margaux. Upon this hint I acted. I procured a stiff piece of whalebone, thrust it down the throat of the corpse, and deposited the latter in an old wine box – taking care so to double the body up as to double the whalebone with it. In this manner I had to press forcibly upon the lid to keep it down while I secured it with nails; and I anticipated, of course, that as soon as these latter were removed, the top would fly *off* and the body *up*.

Having thus arranged the box, I marked, numbered, and addressed it as already told; and then, writing a letter in the name of the wine merchants with whom Mr Shuttleworthy dealt, I gave instruction to my servant to wheel the box to Mr Goodfellow's door, in a barrow, at a given signal from myself. For the words which I intended the corpse to speak, I confidently depended upon my ventriloquial abilities; for their effect, I counted upon the conscience of the murderous wretch.

I believe there is nothing more to be explained. Mr Pennifeather was released upon the spot, inherited the fortune of his uncle, profited by the lessons of experience, turned over a new leaf, and led happily ever afterwards a new life.

The System of Doctor Tarr
and Professor Fether

DURING the autumn of 18—, while on a tour through the extreme southern provinces of France, my route led me within a few miles of a certain *Maison de Santé*, or private Mad-House, about which I had heard much, in Paris, from my medical friends. As I had never visited a place of the kind, I thought the opportunity too good to be lost; and so proposed to my travelling companion (a gentleman with whom I had made casual acquaintance a few days before) that we should turn aside, for an hour or so, and look through the establishment. To this he objected – pleading haste, in the first place, and, in the second, a very usual horror at the sight of a lunatic. He begged me, however, not to let any mere courtesy towards himself interfere with the gratification of my curiosity, and said that he would ride on leisurely, so that I might overtake him during the day, or, at all events, during the next. As he bade me good-bye, I bethought me that there might be some difficulty in obtaining access to the premises, and mentioned my fears on this point. He replied that, in fact, unless I had personal knowledge of the superintendent, Monsieur Maillard, or some credential in the way of a letter, a difficulty might be found to exist, as the regulations of these private mad-houses were more rigid than the public hospital laws. For himself, he added, he had some years since made the acquaintance of Maillard, and would so far assist me as to ride up to the door and introduce me; although his feelings on the subject of lunacy would not permit of his entering the house.

I thanked him, and, turning from the main-road, we entered a grass-grown by-path which, in half an hour, nearly lost itself in a dense forest clothing the base of a mountain. Through this dank and gloomy wood we rode some two miles, when the *Maison de Santé* came in view. It was a fantastic *château*, much dilapidated, and indeed scarcely tenantable through age and neglect. Its aspect inspired me with absolute dread, and, checking my horse, I half resolved to turn back. I soon, however, grew ashamed of my weakness, and proceeded.

As we rode up to the gateway, I perceived it slightly open, and the visage of a man peering through. In an instant afterward, this man came forth, accosted my companion by name, shook him cordially by the hand, and begged him to alight. It was Monsieur Maillard himself. He was a portly, fine-looking gentleman of the old school, with a polished manner and a certain air of gravity, dignity, and authority which was very impressive.

My friend, having presented me, mentioned my desire to inspect the establishment, and received Monsieur Maillard's assurance that he would show me all attention, now took leave, and I saw him no more.

When he had gone, the superintendent ushered me into a small and exceedingly neat parlor containing, among other indications of refined taste, many books, drawings, pots of flowers, and musical instruments. A cheerful fire blazed upon the hearth. At a piano, singing an aria from Bellini, sat a young and very beautiful woman who, at my entrance, paused in her song and received me with graceful courtesy. Her voice was low, and her whole manner subdued. I thought, too, that I perceived the traces of sorrow in her countenance, which was excessively, although to my taste not unpleasingly, pale. She was attired in deep mourning, and excited in my bosom a feeling of mingled respect, interest, and admiration.

I had heard, at Paris, that the institution of Monsieur Maillard was managed upon what is vulgarly termed the 'system of soothing'; that all punishments were avoided; that even confinement was seldom resorted to; that the patients, while secretly watched, were left much apparent liberty, and that most of them were permitted to roam about the house and grounds, in the ordinary apparel of persons in right mind.

Keeping these impressions in view, I was cautious in what I said before the young lady; for I could not be sure that she was sane; and, in fact, there was a certain restless brilliancy about her eyes which half led me to imagine she was not. I confined my remarks, therefore, to general topics, and to such as I thought would not be displeasing or exciting even to a lunatic. She replied in a perfectly rational manner to all that I said; and even her original observations were marked with the soundest good sense; but a long acquaintance with the metaphysics of mania had taught me to put no faith in such evidence of sanity, and I continued to practise, throughout the interview, the caution with which I commenced it.

Presently a smart footman in livery brought in a tray with fruit, wine, and other refreshments, of which I partook, the lady soon afterwards leaving the room. As she departed I turned my eyes in an inquiring manner towards my host.

'No,' he said, 'oh, no – a member of my family – my niece, and a most accomplished woman.'

'I beg a thousand pardons for the suspicion,' I replied, 'but of course you will know how to excuse me. The excellent adminis-tration of your affairs here is well understood in Paris, and I thought it just possible, you know –'

'Yes, yes – say no more – or rather it is myself who should thank you for the commendable prudence you have displayed. We seldom find so much of forethought in young men; and, more than once, some unhappy *contretemps* has occurred in conse-quence of thoughtlessness on the part of our visitors. While my former system was in operation, and my patients were per-mitted the privilege of roaming to and fro at will, they were often aroused to a dangerous frenzy by injudicious persons who called to inspect the house. Hence I was obliged to enforce a rigid system of exclusion; and none obtained access to the premises upon whose discretion I could not rely.'

'While your *former* system was in operation!' I said, repeating his words – 'do I understand you, then, to say that the "soothing system" of which I have heard so much is no longer in force?'

'It is now,' he replied, 'several weeks since we have concluded to renounce it forever.'

'Indeed! you astonish me!'

'We found it, sir,' he said, with a sigh, 'absolutely necessary to return to the old usages. The *danger* of the soothing system was, at all times, appalling; and its advantages have been much over-rated. I believe, sir, that in this house it has been given a fair trial, if ever in any. We did everything that rational humanity could suggest. I am sorry that you could not have paid us a visit at an earlier period, that you might have judged for yourself. But I presume you are conversant with the soothing practice – with its details.'

'Not altogether. What I have heard has been at third or fourth hand.'

'I may state the system then, in general terms, as one in which the patients were *ménagés*, humored. We contradicted *no* fancies which entered the brains of the mad. On the contrary, we not only indulged but encouraged them; and many of our most permanent cures have been thus effected. There is no argument which so touches the feeble reason of the madman as the *reductio ad absurdum*. We have had men, for example, who fancied themselves chickens. The cure was, to insist upon the thing as a fact – to accuse the patient of stupidity is not sufficiently per-ceiving it to be a fact – and thus to refuse him any other diet for a week than that which properly appertains to a chicken. In this manner a little corn and gravel were made to perform wonders.'

'But was this species of acquiescence all?'

'By no means. We put much faith in amusements of a simple kind, such as music, dancing, gymnastic exercises generally, cards, certain classes of books, and so forth. We affected to treat each individual as if for some ordinary physical disorder; and the word "lunacy" was never employed. A great point was to set each lunatic to guard the actions of all the others. To repose confidence in the understanding or discretion of a madman is to gain him body and soul. In this way we were enabled to dispense with an expensive body of keepers.'

'And you had no punishments of any kind?'

'None.'

'And you never confined your patients?'

'Very rarely. Now and then, the malady of some individual growing to a crisis, or taking a sudden turn of fury, we conveyed him to a secret cell, lest his disorder should infect the rest, and there kept him until we could dismiss him to his friends – for with the raging maniac we have nothing to do. He is usually removed to the public hospitals.'

'And you have now changed all this – and you think for the better?'

'Decidedly. The system had its disadvantages, and even its dangers. It is now, happily, exploded throughout all the *Maisons de Santé*[1] of France.'

'I am very much surprised,' I said, 'at what you tell me; for I made sure that, at this moment, no other method of treatment for mania existed in any portion of the country.'

'You are young yet, my friend,' replied my host, 'but the time will arrive when you will learn to judge for yourself of what is going on in the world, without trusting to the gossip of others. Believe nothing you hear, and only one half that you see. Now, about our *Maisons de Santé*, it is clear that some ignoramus has misled you. After dinner, however, when you have sufficiently recovered from the fatigue of your ride, I will be happy to take you over the house, and introduce you to a system which, in my opinion, and in that of every one who has witnessed its operation, is incomparably the most effectual as yet devised.'

'Your own?' I inquired – 'one of your own invention?'

'I am proud,' he replied, 'to acknowledge that it is – at least in some measure.'

In this manner I conversed with Monsieur Maillard for an hour or two, during which he showed me the gardens and conservatories of the place.

'I cannot let you see my patients,' he said, 'just at present. To a sensitive mind there is always more or less of the shocking in such exhibitions; and I do not wish to spoil your appetite for dinner. We will dine. I can give you some veal *à la Ste Ménehould*, with cauliflowers in *velouté* sauce – after that a glass of Clos Vougeot – then your nerves will be sufficiently steadied.'

At six, dinner was announced; and my host conducted me into a large *salle à manger*, where a very numerous company were assembled – twenty-five or thirty in all. They were, apparently, people of rank – certainly of high breeding – although their

habiliments, I thought, were extravagantly rich, partaking somewhat too much of the ostentatious finery of the *vile cour*. I noticed
that at least two-thirds of these guests were ladies; and some of
the latter were by no means accoutred in what a Parisian would
consider good taste at the present day. Many females, for example,
whose age could not have been less than seventy, were bedecked
with a profusion of jewelry, such as rings, bracelets, and ear-rings,
and wore their bosoms and arms shamefully bare. I observed, too,
that very few of the dresses were well made – or, at least, that very
few of them fitted the wearers. In looking about, I discovered the
interesting girl to whom Monsieur Maillard had presented me in
the little parlor; but my surprise was great to see her wearing a
hoop and farthingale, with high-heeled shoes, and a dirty cap of
Brussels lace, so much too large for her that it gave her face a
ridiculously diminutive expression. When I had first seen her, she
was attired, most becomingly, in deep mourning.[2] There was an
air of oddity, in short, about the dress of the whole party, which,
at first, caused me to recur to my original idea of the 'soothing
system', and to fancy that Monsieur Maillard had been willing to
deceive me until after dinner, that I might experience no uncomfortable feelings during the repast, at finding myself dining
with lunatics; but I remembered having been informed, in Paris,
that the southern provincialists were a peculiarly eccentric people,
with a vast number of antiquated notions; and then, too, upon
conversing with several members of the company, my apprehensions were immediately and fully dispelled.

The dining-room, itself, although perhaps sufficiently comfortable, and of good dimensions, had nothing too much of
elegance about it. For example, the floor was uncarpeted; in
France, however, a carpet is frequently dispensed with. The
windows, too, were without curtains; the shutters, being shut,
were securely fastened with iron bars, applied diagonally, after
the fashion of our ordinary shop-shutters. The apartment, I
observed, formed, in itself, a wing of the *château*, and thus the
windows were on three sides of the parallelogram; the door being
at the other. There were no less than ten windows in all.

The table was superbly set out. It was loaded with plate, and
more than loaded with delicacies. The profusion was absolutely

barbaric. There were meats enough to have feasted the Anakim. Never, in all my life, had I witnessed so lavish, so wasteful an expenditure of the good things of life. There seemed very little taste, however, in the arrangements; and my eyes, accustomed to quiet lights, were sadly offended by the prodigious glare of a multitude of wax candles, which, in silver candelabra, were deposited upon the table, and all about the room, wherever it was possible to find a place. There were several active servants in attendance; and, upon a large table, at the farther end of the apartment, were seated seven or eight people with fiddles, fifes, trombones, and a drum. These fellows annoyed me very much, at intervals, during the repast, by an infinite variety of noises, which were intended for music, and which appeared to afford much entertainment to all present, with the exception of myself.

Upon the whole, I could not help thinking that there was much of the *bizarre* about everything I saw – but then the world is made up of all kinds of persons, with all modes of thought, and all sorts of conventional customs. I had travelled so much as to be quite an adept in the *nil admirari*; so I took my seat very coolly at the right hand of my host, and, having an excellent appetite, did justice to the good cheer set before me.

The conversation, in the mean time, was spirited and general. The ladies, as usual, talked a great deal. I soon found that nearly all the company were well educated; and my host was a world of good-humored anecdote in himself. He seemed quite willing to speak of his position as superintendent of a *Maison de Santé*; and, indeed, the topic of lunacy was, much to my surprise, a favorite one with all present. A great many amusing stories were told, having reference to the *whims* of the patients.

'We had a fellow here once,' said a fat little gentleman, who sat at my right – 'a fellow that fancied himself a tea-pot; and, by the way, is it not especially singular how often this particular crotchet has entered the brain of the lunatic? There is scarcely an insane asylum in France which cannot supply a human tea-pot. *Our* gentleman was a Britannia-ware tea-pot, and was careful to polish himself every morning with buckskin and whiting.'

'And then,' said a tall man, just opposite, 'we had here, not long ago, a person who had taken it into his head that he was a donkey – which, allegorically speaking, you will say, was quite true. He was a troublesome patient; and we had much ado to keep him within bounds. For a long time he would eat nothing but thistles; but of this idea we soon cured him by insisting upon his eating nothing else. Then he was perpetually kicking out his heels – so – so –'

'Mr De Kock! I will thank you to behave yourself!' here interrupted an old lady, who sat next to the speaker. 'Please keep your feet to yourself! You have spoiled my brocade! Is it necessary, pray, to illustrate a remark in so practical a style? Our friend, here, can surely comprehend you without all this. Upon my word, you are nearly as great a donkey as the poor unfortunate imagined himself. Your acting is very natural, as I live.'

'*Mille pardons! Mamzelle!*' replied Monsieur De Kock, thus addressed – 'a thousand pardons! I had no intention of offending Mamzelle Laplace – Monsieur De Kock will do himself the honor of taking wine with you.'

Here Monsieur De Kock bowed low, kissed his hand with much ceremony, and took wine with Mamzelle Laplace.

'Allow me, *mon ami*,' now said Monsieur Maillard, addressing myself, 'allow me to send you a morsel of this veal *à la Ste Ménehould* – you will find it particularly fine.'

At this instant three sturdy waiters had just succeeded in depositing safely upon the table an enormous dish, or trencher, containing what I supposed to be the '*monstrum, horrendum, informe, ingens, cui lumen ademptum*'.[3] A closer scrutiny assured me, however, that it was only a small calf roasted whole, and set upon its knees, with an apple in its mouth, as is the English fashion of dressing a hare.

'Thank you, no,' I replied; 'to say the truth, I am not particularly partial to veal *à la Ste* – what is it? – for I do not find that it altogether agrees with me. I will change my plate, however, and try some of the rabbit.'

There were several side dishes on the table, containing what appeared to be the ordinary French rabbit – a very delicious *morceau*, which I can recommend.

'Pierre,' cried the host, 'change this gentleman's plate, and give him a side-piece of this rabbit *au-chat*.'

'This what?' said I.

'This rabbit *au-chat*.'

'Why, thank you – upon second thoughts, no. I will just help myself to some of the ham.'

There is no knowing what one eats, thought I to myself, at the tables of these people of the province. I will have none of their rabbit *au-chat* – and, for the matter of that, none of their *cat-au-rabbit* either.

'And then,' said a cadaverous-looking personage, near the foot of the table, taking up the thread of the conversation where it had been broken off – 'and then, among other oddities, we had a patient, once upon a time, who very pertinaciously maintained himself to be a Cordova cheese, and went about, with a knife in his hand, soliciting his friends to try a small slice from the middle of his leg.'

'He was a great fool, beyond doubt,' interposed someone, 'but not to be compared with a certain individual whom we all know, with the exception of this strange gentleman. I mean the man who took himself for a bottle of champagne, and always went off with a pop and a fizz, in this fashion.'

Here the speaker, very rudely, as I thought, put his right thumb in his left cheek, withdrew it with a sound resembling the popping of a cork, and then, by a dexterous movement of the tongue upon the teeth, created a sharp hissing and fizzing, which lasted for several minutes, in imitation of the frothing of champagne. This behavior, I saw plainly, was not very pleasing to Monsieur Maillard; but that gentleman said nothing, and the conversation was resumed by a very lean little man in a big wig.

'And then there was an ignoramus,' said he, 'who mistook himself for a frog; which, by the way, he resembled in no little degree. I wish you could have seen him, sir,' – here the speaker addressed myself – 'it would have done your heart good to see the natural airs that he put on. Sir, if that man was *not* a frog, I can only observe that it is a pity he was not. His croak thus – o-o-o-o-gh – o-o-o-o-gh! was the finest note in the world – B flat; and when he put his elbows upon the table thus – after taking a glass or two of wine – and distended his mouth, thus, and rolled up his eyes, thus, and winked them with excessive rapidity, thus, why, then, sir, I take it upon myself to say, positively, that you would have been lost in admiration of the genius of the man.'

'I have no doubt of it,' I said.

'And then,' said somebody else, 'then there was Petit Gaillard, who thought himself a pinch of snuff, and was truly distressed because he could not take himself between his own finger and thumb.'

'And then there was Jules Desoulières, who was a very singular genius, indeed, and went mad with the idea that he was a pumpkin. He persecuted the cook to make him up into pies – a thing which the cook indignantly refused to do. For my part, I am by no means sure that a pumpkin pie *à la Desoulières*, would not have been very capital eating, indeed!'

'You astonish me!' said I; and I looked inquisitively at Monsieur Maillard.

'Ha! ha! ha!' said that gentleman – 'he! he! he! – hi! hi! hi! – ho! ho! ho! – hu! hu! hu! – very good indeed! You must not be astonished, *mon ami*: our friend here is a wit – a *drôle* – you must not understand him to the letter.'

'And then,' said some other one of the party, 'then there was Bouffon Le Grand – another extraordinary personage in his way. He grew deranged through love, and fancied himself possessed of two heads. One of these he maintained to be the head of Cicero; the other he imagined a composite one, being Demosthenes from the top of the forehead to the mouth, and Lord Brougham from the mouth to the chin.[4] It is not impossible that he was wrong; but he would have convinced you of his being in the right; for he was a man of great eloquence. He had an absolute passion for oratory, and could not refrain from display. For example, he used to leap upon the dinner-table thus, and – and –'

Here a friend, at the side of the speaker, put a hand upon his shoulder, and whispered a few words in his ear; upon which he ceased talking with great suddenness, and sank back within his chair.

'And then,' said the friend who had whispered, 'there was Boullard, the teetotum. I call him the teetotum, because, in fact, he was seized with the droll, but not altogether irrational crotchet, that he had been converted into a teetotum. You would have roared with laughter to see him spin. He would turn round upon one heel by the hour, in this manner – so –'

Here the friend whom he had just interrupted by a whisper performed an exactly similar office for himself.

'But then,' cried an old lady, at the top of her voice, 'your Monsieur Boullard was a madman, and a very silly madman at best; for who, allow me to ask you, ever heard of a human teetotum? The thing is absurd. Madame Joyeuse was a more sensible person, as you know. She had a crotchet, but it was instinct with common sense, and gave pleasure to all who had the honor of her acquaintance. She found, upon mature delibera-tion, that, by some accident, she had been turned into a chicken-cock; but, as such, she behaved with propriety. She flapped her wings with prodigious effect – so – so – so – and, as for her crow, it was delicious! Cock-a-doodle-doo! – cock-a-doodle-doo – cock-a-doodle-de-doo-doo-dooo-do-o-o-o-o-o-o!'[5]

'Madame Joyeuse, I will thank you to behave yourself!' here interrupted our host, very angrily. 'You can either conduct your-self as a lady should do, or you can quit the table forthwith – take your choice.'

The lady (whom I was much astonished to hear addressed as Madame Joyeuse, after the description of Madame Joyeuse she had just given) blushed up to the eyebrows, and seemed exceedingly abashed at the reproof. She hung down her head, and said not a syllable in reply. But another and younger lady resumed the theme. It was my beautiful girl of the little parlor!

'Oh, Madame Joyeuse *was* a fool!' she exclaimed; 'but there was really much sound sense, after all, in the opinion of Eugénie Salsafette. She was a very beautiful and painfully modest young lady, who thought the ordinary mode of habiliment indecent, and wished to dress herself, always, by getting outside, instead of inside of her clothes. It is a thing very easily done, after all. You have only to do so – and then so – so – so – and then so – so – so – and then –'

'*Mon Dieu!* Mamzelle Salsafette!' here cried a dozen voices at once. 'What *are* you about? – forbear! – that is sufficient! – we see very plainly how it is done! – hold! hold!' and several persons were already leaping from their seats to withhold Mamzelle Salsafette from putting herself upon a par with the Medicean Venus, when the point was very effectually and suddenly accomplished by a series of loud screams, or yells, from some portion of the main body of the *château*.

My nerves were very much affected, indeed, by these yells; but the rest of the company I really pitied. I never saw any set of reasonable people so thoroughly frightened in my life. They all grew as pale as so many corpses, and, shrinking within their seats, sat quivering and gibbering with terror, and listening for a repetition of the sound. It came again – louder and seemingly nearer – and then a third time *very* loud, and then a fourth time with a vigor evidently diminished. At this apparent dying away of the noise, the spirits of the company were immediately regained, and all was life and anecdote as before. I now ventured to inquire the cause of the disturbance.

'A mere *bagatelle*,' said Monsieur Maillard. 'We are used to these things, and care really very little about them. The lunatics, every now and then, get up a howl in concert; one starting another, as is sometimes the case with a bevy of dogs at night. It occasionally happens, however, that the *concerto* yells are succeeded by a simultaneous effort at breaking loose; when, of course, some little danger is to be apprehended.'

'And how many have you in charge?'

'At present, we have not more than ten, altogether.'

'Principally females, I presume?'

'Oh, no – every one of them men, and stout fellows, too, I can tell you.'

'Indeed! I have always understood that the majority of lunatics were of the gentler sex.'

'It is generally so, but not always. Some time ago, there were about twenty-seven patients here, and of that number no less than eighteen were women; but lately matters have changed very much, as you see.'

'Yes – have changed very much, as you see,' here interrupted the gentleman who had broken the shins of Mamzelle Laplace.

'Yes – have changed very much as you see!' chimed in the whole company at once.

'Hold your tongues, every one of you!' said my host, in a great rage. Whereupon the whole company maintained a dead silence for nearly a minute. As for one lady, she obeyed Monsieur Maillard to the letter, and thrusting out her tongue, which was an excessively long one, held it very resignedly, with both hands, until the end of the entertainment.

'And this gentlewoman,' said I, to Monsieur Maillard, bending over and addressing him in a whisper – 'this good lady who has just spoken, and who gives us the cock-a-doodle-de-doo – she, I presume, is harmless – quite harmless, eh?'

'Harmless!' ejaculated he, in unfeigned surprise, 'why – why what *can* you mean?'

'Only slightly touched?' said I, touching my head. 'I take it for granted that she is not particularly – not dangerously affected, eh?'

'*Mon Dieu!* what *is* it you imagine? This lady, my particular old friend, Madame Joyeuse, is as absolutely sane as myself. She has her little eccentricities, to be sure – but then, you know, all old women – all *very* old women are more or less eccentric!'

'To be sure,' said I – 'to be sure – and then the rest of these ladies and gentlemen –'

'Are my friends and keepers,' interrupted Monsieur Maillard, drawing himself up with *hauteur* – 'my very good friends and assistants.'

'What! all of them?' I asked – 'the women and all?'

'Assuredly,' he said – 'we could not do at all without the women; they are the best lunatic nurses in the world; they have a way of their own, you know; their bright eyes have a marvellous effect, – something like the fascination of the snake, you know.'

'To be sure,' said I – 'to be sure! They behave a little odd, eh? – they are a little *queer*, eh? – don't you think so?'

'Odd! – queer! – why, do you really think so? We are not very prudish, to be sure, here in the South – do pretty much as we please – enjoy life, and all that sort of thing, you know –'

'To be sure,' said I – 'to be sure.'

'And then, perhaps, this Clos Vougeot is a little heady, you know – a little *strong* – you understand, eh?'

'To be sure,' said I – 'to be sure. By the bye, monsieur, did

I understand you to say that the system you have adopted in place of the celebrated soothing system, was one of very vigorous severity?'

'By no means. Our confinement is necessarily close; but the treatment – the medical treatment, I mean – is rather agreeable to the patients than otherwise.'

'And the new system is one of your own invention?'

'Not altogether. Some portions of it are referable to Professor Tarr, of whom you have, necessarily, heard; and, again, there are modifications in my plan which I am happy to acknowledge as belonging of right to the celebrated Fether, with whom, if I mistake not, you have the honor of an intimate acquaintance.'

'I am quite ashamed to confess,' I replied, 'that I have never even heard the name of either gentleman before.'

'Good Heavens!' ejaculated my host, drawing back his chair abruptly, and uplifting his hands. 'I surely do not hear you aright! You did not intend to say, eh? that you had never *heard* either of the learned Doctor Tarr, or of the celebrated Professor Fether?'

'I am forced to acknowledge my ignorance,' I replied; 'but the truth should be held inviolate above all things. Nevertheless, I feel humbled to the dust, not to be acquainted with the works of these, no doubt, extraordinary men. I will seek out their writings forthwith, and peruse them with deliberate care. Monsieur Maillard, you have really – I must confess it – you have *really* – made me ashamed of myself!'

And this was the fact.

'Say no more my good young friend,' he said kindly, pressing my hand – 'join me now in a glass of Sauterne.'

We drank. The company followed our example, without stint. They chatted – they jested – they laughed – they perpetrated a thousand absurdities; the fiddles shrieked – the drum row-de-dowed – the trombones bellowed like so many brazen bulls of Phalaris[6] – and the whole scene, growing gradually worse and worse, as the wines gained the ascendency, became at length a sort of Pandemonium *in petto*. In the mean time, Monsieur Maillard and myself, with some bottles of Sauterne and Vougeot between us, continued our conversation at the top of the voice. A word spoken in an ordinary key stood no more chance of being heard than the voice of a fish from the bottom of Niagara Falls.

'And, sir,' said I, screaming in his ear, 'you mentioned something before dinner, about the danger incurred in the old system of soothing. How is that?'

'Yes,' he replied, 'there was, occasionally, very great danger, indeed. There is no accounting for the caprices of madmen; and, in my opinion, as well as in that of Doctor Tarr and Professor Fether, it is *never* safe to permit them to run at large unattended. A lunatic may be "soothed", as it is called, for a time, but, in the end, he is very apt to become obstreperous. His cunning, too, is proverbial, and great. If he has a project in view, he conceals his design with a marvellous wisdom; and the dexterity with which he counterfeits sanity presents, to the metaphysician, one of the most singular problems in the study of mind. When a madman appears *thoroughly* sane, indeed, it is high time to put him in a strait-jacket.'

'But the *danger*, my dear sir, of which you were speaking – in your own experience – during your control of this house – have you had practical reason to think liberty hazardous, in the case of a lunatic?'

'Here? – in my own experience? – why, I may say, yes. For example: no *very* long while ago, a singular circumstance occurred in this very house. The "soothing system", you know, was then in operation, and the patients were at large. They behaved remarkably well – especially so – any one of sense might have known that some devilish scheme was brewing from that particular fact, that the fellows behaved so *remarkably* well. And, sure enough, one fine morning the keepers found themselves pinioned hand and foot, and thrown into the cells, where they were attended, as if *they* were the lunatics, by the lunatics themselves, who had usurped the offices of the keepers.'

'You don't tell me so! I never heard of anything so absurd in my life!'

'Fact – it all came to pass by means of a stupid fellow – a lunatic – who, by some means, had taken it into his head that he had invented a better system of government than any ever heard of before – of lunatic government, I mean. He wished to give his invention a trial, I suppose – and so he persuaded the rest of the patients to join him in a conspiracy for the overthrow of the reigning powers!'

'And he really succeeded?'

'No doubt of it. The keepers and kept were soon made to exchange places. Not that exactly either – for the madmen had been free, but the keepers were shut up in cells forthwith, and treated, I am sorry to say, in a very cavalier manner.'

'But I presume a counter revolution was soon effected. This condition of things could not have long existed. The country people in the neighborhood – visitors coming to see the establishment – would have given the alarm.'

'There you are out. The head rebel was too cunning for that. He admitted no visitors at all – with the exception, one day, of a very stupid-looking young gentleman of whom he had no reason to be afraid. He let him in to see the place – just by way of variety – to have a little fun with him. As soon as he had gammoned him sufficiently, he let him out, and sent him about his business.'

'And how long, then, did the madmen reign?'

'Oh, a very long time, indeed – a month certainly – how much longer I can't precisely say. In the mean time, the lunatics had a jolly season of it – that you may swear. They doffed their own shabby clothes, and made free with the family wardrobe and jewels. The cellars of the *château* were well stocked with wine; and these madmen are just the devils that know how to drink it. They lived well, I can tell you.'

'And the treatment – what was the particular species of treatment which the leader of the rebels put into operation?'

'Why, as for that, a madman is not necessarily a fool, as I have already observed; and it is my honest opinion that his treatment was a much better treatment than that which it superseded. It was a very capital system indeed – simple – neat – no trouble at all – in fact, it was delicious – it was –'

Here my host's observations were cut short by another series of yells, of the same character as those which had previously disconcerted us. This time, however, they seemed to proceed from persons rapidly approaching.

'Gracious Heavens!' I ejaculated – 'the lunatics have most un-doubtedly broken loose.'

'I very much fear it is so,' replied Monsieur Maillard, now becoming excessively pale. He had scarcely finished the sentence, before loud shouts and imprecations were heard beneath the windows; and, immediately afterward, it became evident that some persons outside were endeavoring to gain entrance into the room. The door was beaten with what appeared to be a sledge-hammer, and the shutters were wrenched and shaken with prodigious violence.

A scene of the most terrible confusion ensued. Monsieur Maillard, to my excessive astonishment, threw himself under the sideboard. I had expected more resolution at his hands. The members of the orchestra, who, for the last fifteen minutes, had been seemingly too much intoxicated to do duty, now sprang all at once to their feet and to their instruments, and, scrambling upon their table, broke out, with one accord, into 'Yankee Doodle', which they performed, if not exactly in tune, at least with an energy superhuman, during the whole of the uproar.

Meantime, upon the main dining-table, among the bottles and glasses, leaped the gentleman who with such difficulty had been restrained from leaping there before. As soon as he fairly settled himself, he commenced an oration, which, no doubt, was a very capital one, if it could only have been heard. At the same moment, the man with the teetotum predilections set himself to spinning around the apartment, with immense energy, and with arms outstretched at right angles with his body; so that he had all the air of a teetotum in fact, and knocked everybody down that happened to get in his way. And now, too, hearing an incredible popping and fizzing of champagne, I discovered at length, that it proceeded from the person who performed the bottle of that delicate drink during dinner. And then, again, the frog-man croaked away as if the salvation of his soul depended upon every note that he uttered. And, in the midst of all this, the continuous braying of a donkey arose over all. As for my old friend, Madame Joyeuse, I really could have wept for the poor lady, she appeared so terribly perplexed. All she did, however, was to stand up in a corner by the fireplace, and sing out incessantly, at the top of her voice, 'Cock-a-doodle-de-dooooooh!'

And now came the climax – the catastrophe of the drama. As no resistance, beyond whooping and yelling and cock-a-doodle-ing, was offered to the encroachments of the party without, the ten windows were very speedily, and almost simultaneously, broken in. But I shall never forget the emotions of wonder and horror with which I gazed, when, leaping through these windows, and down among us *pêle-mêle*, fighting, stamping, scratching, and howling, there rushed a perfect army of what I took to be chimpanzees, ourang-outangs, or big black baboons of the Cape of Good Hope.

I received a terrible beating – after which I rolled under a sofa and lay still. After lying there some fifteen minutes, however, during which time I listened with all my ears to what was going on in the room, I came to some satisfactory *dénouement* of this tragedy. Monsieur Maillard, it appeared, in giving me the account of the lunatic who had excited his fellows to rebellion, had been merely relating his own exploits. This gentleman had, indeed, some two or three years before, been the superintendent of the establishment; but grew crazy himself, and so became a patient. This fact was unknown to the travelling companion who introduced me. The keepers, ten in number, having been suddenly overpowered, were first well tarred, then carefully feathered, and then shut up in underground cells. They had been so imprisoned for more than a month, during which period Monsieur Maillard had generously allowed them not only the tar and feathers (which constituted his 'system') but some bread and abundance of water. The latter was pumped on them daily. At length, one, escaping through a sewer, gave freedom to all the rest.

The 'soothing system', with important modifications, has been resumed at the *château*; yet I cannot help agreeing with Monsieur Maillard that his own 'treatment' was a very capital one of its kind. As he justly observed, it was 'simple – neat – and gave no trouble at all – not the least'.

I have only to add that, although I have searched every library in Europe for the works of Doctor Tarr and Professor Fether, I have, up to the present day, utterly failed in my endeavors at procuring an edition.

Mellonta Tauta

On Board Balloon *Skylark*, April 1, 2848

Now, my dear friend – now, for your sins, you are to suffer the infliction of a long gossiping letter. I tell you distinctly that I am going to punish you for all your impertinences by being as tedious, as discursive, as incoherent and as unsatisfactory as possible. Besides, here I am, cooped up in a dirty balloon, with some one or two hundred of the *canaille*, all bound on a pleasure excursion (what a funny idea some people have of pleasure!), and I have no prospect of touching *terra firma* for a month at least. Nobody to talk to. Nothing to do. When one has nothing to do, then is the time to correspond with one's friends. You perceive, then, why it is that I write you this letter – it is on account of my ennui and your sins.

Get ready your spectacles and make up your mind to be annoyed. I mean to write at you every day during this odious voyage.

Heigho! when will any *Invention* visit the human pericranium? Are we forever to be doomed to the thousand inconveniences of the balloon? Will nobody contrive a more expeditious mode of progress? This jog-trot movement, to my thinking, is little less than positive torture. Upon my word we have not made more than a hundred miles the hour since leaving home! The very birds beat us – at least some of them. I assure you that I do not exaggerate at all. Our motion, no doubt, seems slower than it actually is; this on account of our having no objects about us by which to estimate our velocity, and on account of our going with the wind. To be sure, whenever we meet a balloon we have a chance of perceiving our rate, and then, I admit, things do not appear so very bad. Accustomed as I am to this mode of travelling, I cannot get over a kind of giddiness whenever a balloon passes us in a current directly overhead. It always seems to me like an immense bird of prey about to pounce upon us and carry us off in its claws. One went over us this morning about sunrise, and so nearly overhead that its drag-rope actually brushed the net-work suspending our car, and caused us very serious apprehension. Our captain said that, if the material of the bag had been the trumpery varnished 'silk' of five hundred or a thousand years ago, we should inevitably have been damaged. This silk, as he explained it to me, was a fabric composed of the entrails of a species of earth-worm. The worm was carefully fed on mulberries – a kind of fruit resembling a watermelon – and, when sufficiently fat, was crushed in a mill. The paste thus arising was called *papyrus* in its primary state, and went through a variety of processes until it finally became 'silk'. Singular to relate, it was once much admired as a article of female dress! Balloons were also very generally constructed from it. A better kind of material, it appears, was subsequently found in the down surrounding the seed-vessels of a plant vulgarly called *euphorbium*, and at that time botanically termed milk-weed. This latter kind of silk was designated as silk-buckingham,[1] on account of its superior durability, and was usually prepared for use by being varnished with a solution of gum caoutchouc – a substance which in some respects must have resembled the *gutta-percha* now in common use. This caoutchouc was occasionally called India rubber or rubber of whist, and was no doubt one of the numerous *fungi*. Never tell me again that I am not at heart an antiquarian.

Talking of drag-ropes – our own, it seems, has this moment knocked a man overboard from one of the small magnetic propellers that swarm in ocean below us, a boat of about six thousand tons and, from all accounts, shamefully crowded. These diminutive barks should be prohibited from carrying more than a definite number of passengers. The man, of course, was not permitted to get on board again, and was soon out of sight, he and his life-preserver. I rejoice, my dear friend, that we live in an age so enlightened that no such a thing as an individual is supposed to exist. It is the mass for which the true Humanity cares. By the bye, talking of Humanity, do you know that our immortal Wiggins is not so original, in his views of the Social Condition and so forth, as his contemporaries are inclined to suppose? Pundit assures me that the same ideas were put, nearly in the same way, about a thousand years ago, by an Irish philosopher called Furrier,[2] on account of his keeping a retail shop for cat peltries and other furs. Pundit *knows*, you know; there can be no mistake about it. How very wonderfully do we see verified every day the profound observation of the Hindoo Aries Tottle (as quoted by Pundit) – 'Thus must we say that, not once or twice, or a few times, but with almost infinite repetitions, the same opinions come round in a circle among men.'

April 2. – Spoke to-day the magnetic cutter in charge of the middle section of floating telegraph wires. I learn that when this species of telegraph was first put into operation by Horse, it was considered quite impossible to convey the wires over sea; but now we are at a loss to comprehend where the difficulty lay! So wags the world. *Tempora mutantur* – excuse me for quoting the Etruscan. What *would* we do without the Atalantic telegraph? (Pundit says Atlantic was the ancient adjective.) We lay to, a few minutes, to ask the cutter some questions, and learned, among other glorious news, that civil war is raging in Africia, while the plague is doing its good work beautifully both in Yurope and Ayesher. Is it not truly remarkable that, before the magnificent light shed upon philosophy by Humanity, the world was accustomed to regard War and Pestilence as calamities? Do you know that prayers were actually offered up in the ancient temples to the end that these *evils* (!) might not be visited upon mankind? Is it not really difficult to comprehend upon what principle of interest our forefathers acted? Were they so blind as not to perceive that the destruction of a myriad of individuals is only so much positive advantage to the mass!

April 3. – It is really a very fine amusement to ascend the rope-ladder leading to the summit of the balloon-bag and then survey the surrounding world. From the car below, you know, the prospect is not so comprehensive – you can see little vertically. But seated here (where I write this) in the luxuriously cushioned open piazza of the summit, one can see everything that is going

on in all directions. Just now, there is quite a crowd of balloons
in sight, and they present a very animated appearance, while
the air is resonant with the hum of so many millions of human
voices. I have heard it asserted that when Yellow or (as Pundit
will have it) Violet,[3] who is supposed to have been the first aeronaut, maintained the practicability of traversing the atmosphere
in all directions, by merely ascending or descending until a
favorable current was attained, he was scarcely hearkened to
at all by his contemporaries, who looked upon him as merely
an ingenious sort of madman, because the philosophers (?) of
the day declared the thing impossible. Really now it does seem
to me *quite* unaccountable how anything so obviously feasible
could have escaped the sagacity of the ancient savants. But in
all ages the great obstacles to advancement in art have been
opposed by the so-called men of science. To be sure, *our* men
of science are not quite so bigoted as those of old: – oh, I have
something *so* queer to tell you on this topic. Do you know that
it is not more than a thousand years ago since the metaphysicians
consented to relieve the people of the singular fancy that there
existed but *two possible roads for the attainment of Truth!* Believe
it if you can! It appears that long, long ago, in the night of
Time, there lived a Turkish philosopher (or Hindoo possibly) called
Aries Tottle. This person introduced, or at all events propagated,
what was termed the deductive or *a priori* mode of investigation.
He started with what he maintained to be *axioms* or 'self-evident
truths', and thence proceeded 'logically' to results. His greatest
disciples were one Neuclid and one Cant. Well, Aries Tottle
flourished supreme until the advent of one Hog, surnamed the
'Ettrick Shepherd', who preached an entirely different system,
which he called *a posteriori* or *in*ductive. His plan referred
altogether to Sensation. He proceeded by observing, analysing,
and classifying facts – *instantiae naturae*, as they were affectedly
called – into general laws. Aries Tottle's mode, in a word, was
based on *noumena*; Hog's, on *phenomena*. Well, so great was the
admiration excited by this latter system that, at its first introduction, Aries Tottle fell into disrepute; but finally he recovered
ground and was permitted to divide the realm of Truth with
his more modern rival. The savants maintained that the Aristo-

telian and Baconian roads were the sole possible avenues to knowledge. 'Baconian', you must know, was an adjective invented
as equivalent to Hogian and more euphonious and dignified.

Now, my dear friend, I do assure you most positively that I
represent this matter fairly, on the soundest authority; and you
can easily understand how a notion so absurd on its very face
must have operated to retard the progress of all true knowledge,
which makes its advances almost invariably by intuitive bounds.
The ancient idea confined investigation to *crawling*; and for
hundreds of years so great was the infatuation, about Hog
especially, that a virtual end was put to all thinking properly
so called. No man dared utter a truth to which he felt himself
indebted to his *Soul* alone. It mattered not whether the truth
was even *demonstrably* a truth, for the bullet-headed savants of
the time regarded only *the road* by which he had attained it.
They would not even *look* at the end. 'Let us see the means,'
they cried, 'the means!' If, upon investigation of the means, it
was found to come neither under the category Aries (that is
to say Ram) nor under the category Hog, why then the savants
went no farther, but pronounced the 'theorist' a fool, and would
have nothing to do with him or his truth.

Now, it cannot be maintained, even, that by the crawling
system the greatest amount of truth would be attained in any
long series of ages, for the repression of *imagination* was an evil
not to be compensated for by any superior *certainty* in the ancient
modes of investigation. The error of these Jurmains, these Vrinch,
these Inglitch, and these Amriccans (the latter, by the way, were
our own immediate progenitors) was an error quite analogous
with that of the wiseacre who fancies that he must necessarily
see an object the better the more closely he holds it to his eyes.
These people blinded themselves by details. When they proceeded
Hoggishly, their 'facts' were by no means always facts; a matter
of little consequence had it not been for assuming that they *were*
facts and must be facts because they appeared to be such. When
they proceeded on the path of the Ram, their course was scarcely
as straight as a ram's horn, for they *never had* an axiom which
was an axiom at all. They must have been very blind not to
see this, even in their own day; for even in their own day many

of the long 'established' axioms had been rejected. For example –'*Ex nihilo, nihil fit*'; 'a body cannot act where it is not'; 'there cannot exist antipodes'; 'darkness cannot come out of light'; all these, and a dozen other similar propositions, formerly admitted without hesitation as axioms, were, even at the period of which I speak, seen to be untenable. How absurd in these people, then, to persist in putting faith in 'axioms' as immutable bases of Truth! But even out of the mouths of their soundest reasoners it is easy to demonstrate the futility, the impalpability of their axioms in general. Who *was* the soundest of their logicians? Let me see! I will go and ask Pundit and be back in a minute ... Ah, here we have it! Here is a book written nearly a thousand years ago and lately translated from the Inglitch – which, by the way. appears to have been the rudiment of the Amriccan. Pundit says it is decidedly the cleverest ancient work on its topic, Logic. The author (who was much thought of in his day) was one Miller, or Mill;[4] and we find it recorded of him, as a point of some importance, that he had a mill-horse called Bentham. But let us glance at the treatise.

Ah! – 'Ability or inability to conceive,' says Mr Mill, very properly, 'is in no case to be received as a criterion of axiomatic truth.' What *modern* in his senses would ever think of disputing this truism? The only wonder with us must be how it happened that Mr Mill conceived it necessary even to hint at anything so obvious. So far good – but let us turn over another page. What have we here? – 'Contradictories cannot both be true – that is, cannot co-exist in nature.' Here Mr Mill means, for example, that a tree must be either a tree or not a tree; that it cannot be at the same time a tree and not a tree. Very well; but I ask him *why*. His reply is this, and never pretends to be anything else than this – 'Because it is impossible to conceive that contradictories can both be true.' But this is no answer at all, by his own showing; for has he not just admitted as a truism that 'ability or inability to conceive is *in no case* to be received as a criterion of axiomatic truth'?

Now I do not complain of these ancients so much because their logic is, by their own showing, utterly baseless, worthless, and fantastic altogether, as because of their pompous and imbecile proscription of all *other* roads of Truth, of all *other* means for its attainment than the two preposterous paths – the one of creeping and the one of crawling – to which they have dared to confine the Soul that loves nothing so well as to *soar*.

By the bye, my dear friend, do you not think it would have puzzled these ancient dogmaticians to have determined by *which* of their two roads it was that the most important and most sublime of *all* their truths was, in effect, attained? I mean the truth of Gravitation. Newton owed it to Kepler. Kepler admitted that his three laws were *guessed at*: these three laws of all laws which led the great Inglitch mathematician to his principle, the basis of all physical principle, to go behind which we must enter the Kingdom of Metaphysics. Kepler guessed, that is to say *imagined*. He was essentially a 'theorist', that word now of so much sanctity, formerly an epithet of contempt. Would it not have puzzled these old moles, too, to have explained by which of the two 'roads' a cryptographist unriddles a cryptograph of more than usual secrecy, or by which of the two roads Champollion directed mankind to those enduring and almost innumerable truths which resulted from his deciphering the Hieroglyphics?

One word more on this topic and I will be done boring you. Is it not passing strange that, with their eternal prating about *roads* to Truth, these bigoted people missed what we now so clearly perceive to be the great highway – that of Consistency? Does it not seem singular how they should have failed to deduce from the works of God the vital fact that a perfect consistency *must* be an absolute truth! How plain has been our progress since the late announcement of this proposition! Investigation has been taken out of the hands of the ground-moles and given, as a task, to the true and only true thinkers, the men of ardent imagination. These latter theorize. Can you not fancy the shout of scorn with which my words would be received by our progenitors were it possible for them to be now looking over my shoulder? These men, I say, *theorize*; and their theories are simply corrected, reduced, systematized – cleared, little by little, of their dross of inconsistency – until finally a perfect consistency stands apparent which even the most stolid admit, because it *is* a consistency, to be an absolute and an unquestionable *truth*.

April 4. – The new gas is doing wonders, in conjunction with the new improvement with gutta-percha. How very safe, commodious, manageable, and in every respect convenient are our modern balloons! Here is an immense one approaching us at the rate of at least a hundred and fifty miles an hour. It seems to be crowded with people – perhaps there are three or four hundred passengers – and yet it soars to an elevation of nearly a mile, looking down upon poor us with sovereign contempt. Still a hundred or even two hundred miles an hour is slow travelling, after all. Do you remember our flight on the railroad across the Kanadaw continent? – fully three hundred miles the hour – *that* was travelling. Nothing to be seen, though; nothing to be done but flirt, feast, and dance in the magnificent saloons. Do you remember what an odd sensation was experienced when, by chance, we caught a glimpse of external objects while the cars were in full flight? Everything seemed unique – in one mass. For my part, I cannot say but that I preferred the travelling by the slow train of a hundred miles the hour. Here we were permitted to have glass windows, even to have them open, and something like a distinct view of the country was attainable ... Pundit says that *the route* for the great Kanadaw railroad must have been in some measure marked out about nine hundred years ago! In fact, he goes so far as to assert that actual traces of a road are still discernible, traces referable to a period quite as remote as that mentioned. The track, it appears, was *double* only; ours, you know, has twelve paths; and three or four new ones are in preparation. The ancient rails were very slight, and placed so close together as to be, according to modern notions, quite frivolous, if not dangerous in the extreme. The present width of track – fifty feet – is considered, indeed, scarcely secure enough. For my part, I make no doubt that a track of some sort *must* have existed in very remote times, as Pundit asserts; for nothing can be clearer to my mind than that, at some period – not less than seven centuries ago, certainly – the Northern and Southern Kanadaw continents were *united*; the Kanawdians, then, would have been driven by necessity, to a great railroad across the continent.

April 5. – I am almost devoured by ennui. Pundit is the only conversible person on board; and he, poor soul! can speak of nothing but antiquities. He has been occupied all the day in the attempt to convince me that the ancient Amriccans *governed themselves*! – did ever anybody hear of such an absurdity? – that they existed in a sort of every-man-for-himself confederacy, after the fashion of the 'prairie dogs' that we read of in fable. He says that they started with the queerest idea conceivable, viz.: that all men are born free and equal – this in the very teeth of the laws of *gradation* so visibly impressed upon all things both in the moral and physical universe. Every man 'voted', as they called it – that is to say, meddled with public affairs – until, at length, it was discovered that what is everybody's business is nobody's, and that the 'republic' (so the absurd thing was called) was without a government at all. It is related, however, that the first circumstance which disturbed, very particularly, the self-complacency of the philosophers who constructed this 'Republic', was the startling discovery that universal suffrage gave opportunity for fraudulent schemes, by means of which any desired number of votes might at any time be polled, without the possibility of prevention or even detection, by any party which should be merely villanous enough not to be ashamed of the fraud. A little reflection upon this discovery sufficed to render evident the consequences, which were that rascality *must* predominate, in a word, that a republican government *could* never be anything but a rascally one. While the philosophers, however, were busied in blushing at their stupidity in not having foreseen these inevitable evils, and intent upon the invention of new theories, the matter was put to an abrupt issue by a fellow of the name of 'Mob',[5] who took everything into his own hands and set up a despotism, in comparison with which those of the fabulous Zeros and Hellofagabaluses were respectable and delectable. This 'Mob' (a foreigner, by the bye) is said to have been the most odious of all men that ever encumbered the earth. He was a giant in stature – insolent, rapacious, filthy; had the gall of a bullock with the heart of an hyena and the brains of a peacock. He died, at length, by dint of his own energies, which exhausted him. Nevertheless, he had his uses, as everything has, however vile, and taught mankind a lesson which to this day it is in no danger of forgetting – never to run directly contrary to the natural analogies. As for Republicanism, no analogy could be found for it upon the face of the earth, unless we except the case of the 'prairie dogs', an exception which seems to demonstrate, if anything, that democracy is a very admirable form of government – for dogs.

April 6. – Last night had a fine view of Alpha Lyrae, whose disk, through our captain's spy-glass, subtends an angle of half a degree, looking very much as our sun does to the naked eye on a misty day. Alpha Lyrae, although so *very* much larger than our sun, by the bye, resembles him closely as regards its spots, its atmosphere, and in many other particulars. It is only within the last century, Pundit tells me, that the binary relation existing between these two orbs began even to be suspected. The evident motion of our system in the heavens was (strange to say!) referred to an orbit about a prodigious star in the centre of the galaxy. About this star, or at all events about a centre of gravity common to all the globes of the Milky Way and supposed to be near Alcyone in the Pleiades, every one of these globes was declared to be revolving, our own performing the circuit in a period of 117,000,000 of years! *We*, with our present lights, our vast telescopic improvements, and so forth, of course find it difficult to comprehend *the ground* of an idea such as this. Its first propagator was one Mudler.[6] He was led, we must presume, to this wild hypothesis by mere analogy in the first instance; but, this being the case, he should have at least adhered to analogy in its development. A great central orb *was*, in fact, suggested; so far Mudler was consistent. This central orb, however, dynamically, should have been greater than all its surrounding orbs taken together. The question might then have been asked – 'Why do we not see it?' *we*, especially, who occupy the mid region of the cluster, the very locality *near* which, at least, must be situated this inconceivable central sun. The astronomer, perhaps, at this point took refuge in the suggestion of non-luminosity; and here analogy was suddenly let fall. But, even admitting the central orb non-luminous, how did he manage to explain its failure to be rendered visible by the incalculable host of glorious suns glaring in all directions about it? No doubt what he finally maintained was merely a centre of gravity common to all the revolving orbs; but here again analogy must have been let fall. Our system revolves, it is true, about a common centre of gravity, but it does this in connection with and in consequence of a material sun whose mass more than counterbalances the rest of the system. The mathematical circle is a curve composed of an infinity of straight lines; but this idea of the circle – this idea of it which, in regard to all earthly geometry, we consider as merely the mathematical, in contradistinction from the practical, idea – is, in sober fact, the *practical* conception which alone we have any right to entertain in respect to those Titanic circles with which we have to deal, at least in fancy, when we suppose our system, with its fellows, revolving about a point in the centre of the galaxy. Let the most vigorous of human imaginations but attempt to take a single step towards the comprehension of a circuit so unutterable! It would scarcely be paradoxical to say that a flash of lightning itself, travelling *forever* upon the circumference of this inconceivable circle, would still *forever* be travelling in a straight line. That the path of our sun along such a circumference – that the direction of our system in such an orbit – would, to any human perception, deviate in the slightest degree from a straight line even in a million of years, is a proposition not to be entertained; and yet these ancient astronomers were absolutely cajoled, it appears, into believing that a decisive curvature had become apparent during the brief period of their astronomical history – during the mere point – during the utter nothingness of two or three thousand years! How incomprehensible that considerations such as this did not at once indicate to them the true state of affairs, that of the binary revolution of our sun and Alpha Lyrae around a common centre of gravity!

April 7. – Continued last night our astronomical amusements. Had a fine view of the five Nepturian asteroids, and watched with much interest the putting up of a huge impost on a couple of lintels in the new temple at Daphnis in the moon. It was amusing to think that creatures so diminutive as the lunarians, and bearing so little resemblance to humanity, yet evinced a mechanical ingenuity so much superior to our own. One finds it difficult, too, to conceive the vast masses, which these people handle so easily, to be as light as our reason tell us they actually are.

April 8. – Eureka! Pundit is in his glory. A balloon from Kanadaw spoke us to-day and threw on board several late papers; they contain some exceedingly curious information relative to Kanawdian or rather Amriccan antiquities. You know, I presume, that laborers have for some months been employed in preparing the ground for a new fountain at Paradise,[7] the emperor's principal pleasure garden. Paradise, it appears, has been, *literally* speaking an island time out of mind – that is to say, its northern boundary was always (as far back as any records extend) a rivulet, or rather a very narrow arm of the sea. This arm was gradually widened until it attained its present breadth – a mile. The whole length of the island is nine miles; the breadth varies materially. The entire area (so Pundit says) was, about eight hundred years ago, densely packed with houses, some of them twenty stories high; land (for some most unaccountable reason) being considered as especially precious just in this vicinity. The disastrous earthquake, however, of the year 2050, so totally uprooted and overwhelmed the town (for it was almost too large to be called a village) that the most indefatigable of our antiquarians have never yet been able to obtain from the site any sufficient data (in the shape of coins, medals, or inscriptions) wherewith to build up even the ghost of a theory concerning the manners, customs, etc., etc., etc., of the aboriginal inhabitants. Nearly all that we have hitherto known of them is, that they were a portion of the Knickerbocker[8] tribe of savages infesting the continent at its first discovery by Recorder Riker, a knight of the Golden Fleece. They were by no means uncivilized, however, but cultivated various arts and even sciences after a fashion of their own. It is related of them that they were acute in many respects, but were oddly afflicted with a monomania for building what, in the ancient Amriccan, was denominated 'churches' – a kind of pagoda instituted for the worship of two idols that went by the names of Wealth and Fashion. In the end, it is said, the island became, nine tenths of it, church. The women, too, it appears, were oddly deformed by a natural protuberance of the region just below the small of the back – although, most unaccountably, this deformity was looked upon altogether in the light of a beauty. One or two pictures of these singular women have, in fact, been miraculously preserved. They look very odd, *very* – like something between a turkey-cock and a dromedary.

Well, these few details are nearly all that have descended to us respecting the ancient Knickerbockers. It seems, however, that while digging in the centre of the emperor's garden (which, you know, covers the whole island), some of the workmen unearthed a cubical and evidently chiselled block of granite, weighing several hundred pounds. It was in good preservation, having received, apparently, little injury from the convulsion which entombed it. On one of its surfaces was a marble slab with (only think of it!) *an inscription – a legible inscription.* Pundit is in ecstasies. Upon detaching the slab, a cavity appeared, containing a leaden box filled with various coins, a long scroll of names, several documents which appear to resemble newspapers, with other matters of intense interest to the antiquarian! There can be no doubt that all these are genuine Amriccan relics belonging to the tribe called Knickerbocker. The papers thrown on board our balloon are filled with facsimiles of the coins, MSS., typography, etc., etc. I copy for your amusement the Knickerbocker inscription on the marble slab:–

THIS CORNER-STONE OF A MONUMENT TO THE
MEMORY OF
GEORGE WASHINGTON
WAS LAID WITH APPROPRIATE CEREMONIES ON THE
19TH DAY OF OCTOBER, 1847,
THE ANNIVERSARY OF THE SURRENDER OF
LORD CORNWALLIS
TO GENERAL WASHINGTON AT YORKTOWN,
A.D. 1781,
UNDER THE AUSPICES OF THE
WASHINGTON MONUMENT ASSOCIATION OF THE
CITY OF NEW YORK.[9]

This, as I give it, is a *verbatim* translation done by Pundit himself, so there *can* be no mistake about it. From the few words thus preserved we glean several important items of knowledge, not the least interesting of which is the fact that a thousand years ago *actual* monuments had fallen into disuse – as was all very proper – the people contenting themselves, as we do now, with a mere indication of the design to erect a monument at some future time; a corner-stone being cautiously laid by itself 'solitary and alone' (excuse me for quoting the great Amriccan poet Benton) as a guarantee of the magnanimous *intention.* We ascertain, too, very distinctly, from this admirable inscription, the how, as well as the where and the what, of the great surrender in question. As to the *where*, it was Yorktown (wherever that was), and as to the *what*, it was General Cornwallis (no doubt some wealthy dealer in corn). *He* was surrendered. The inscription commemorates the surrender of – what? – why, 'of Lord Cornwallis'. The only question is what could the savages wish him surrendered for. But when we remember that these savages were undoubtedly cannibals, we are led to the conclusion that they intended him for sausage. As to the *how* of the surrender, no language can be more explicit. Lord Cornwallis was surrendered (for sausage) 'under the auspices of the Washington Monument Association', no doubt a charitable institution for the depositing of corner-stones. – But, Heaven, bless me! what is the matter? Ah, I see – the balloon has collapsed, and we shall have a tumble into the sea. I have, therefore, only time enough to add that, from a hasty inspection of the facsimiles of newspapers, etc., etc., I find that *the* great men in those days among the Amriccans were one John, a smith, and one Zacchary, a tailor.[10]

Good-bye, until I see you again. Whether you ever get this letter or not is a point of little importance, as I write altogether for my own amusement. I shall cork the MS. up in a bottle however, and throw it into the sea.

Yours everlastingly,

PUNDITA

X-ing a Paragrab

As it is well known that the 'wise men' came 'from the East',[1] and as Mr Touch-and-go[2] Bullet-head came from the East, it follows that Mr Bullet-head was a wise man; and if collateral proof of the matter be needed, here we have it – Mr B— was an editor. Irascibility was his sole foible; for in fact the obstinacy of which men accused him was anything but his foible, since he justly considered it his forte. It was his strong point – his virtue; and it would have required all the logic of a Brownson[3] to convince him that it was 'anything else'.

I have shown that Touch-and-go Bullet-head was a wise man; and the only occasion on which he did not prove infallible was when, abandoning that legitimate home for all wise men, the East, he migrated to the city of Alexander-the-Great-o-nopolis, or some place of a similar title, out West.

I must do him the justice to say, however, that when he made up his mind finally to settle in that town it was under the impression that no newspaper, and consequently no editor, existed in that particular section of the country. In establishing the *Tea-Pot*, he expected to have the field all to himself. I feel confident he never would have dreamed of taking up his residence in Alexander-the-Great-o-nopolis had he been aware that in Alexander-the-Great-o-nopolis there lived a gentleman named John Smith (if I rightly remember), who, for many years, had there quietly grown fat in editing and publishing the *Alexander-the-Great-o-nopolis Gazette*. It was solely, therefore, on account of having been misinformed, that Mr Bullet-head found himself in Alex – suppose we call it Nopolis,[4] 'for short' – but, as he *did* find himself there, he determined to keep up his character for obst— for firmness, and remain. So remain he did; and he did more; he unpacked his press, type, etc., etc., rented an office exactly opposite to that of the *Gazette*, and, on the third morning after his arrival, issued the first number of the *Alexan* – that is to say, of the *Nopolis Tea-Pot*: – as nearly as I can recollect, this was the name of the new paper.

The leading article, I must admit, was brilliant, not to say severe. It was especially bitter about things in general – and as for the editor of the *Gazette*, he was torn all to pieces in particular. Some of Bullet-head's remarks were really so fiery that I have always, since that time, been forced to look upon John Smith, who is still alive, in the light of a salamander.[5] I cannot pretend to give *all* the *Tea-Pot*'s paragraphs *verbatim*, but one of them ran thus:–

Oh, yes! – Oh, we perceive! Oh, no doubt! The editor over the way is a genius – Oh my! Oh, goodness, gracious! – What *is* this world coming to? *O tempora! O Moses!*[6]

A philippic, at once so caustic and so classical, alighted like a bombshell among the hitherto peaceful citizens of Nopolis. Groups of excited individuals gathered at the corners of the streets. Everyone awaited, with heartfelt anxiety, the reply of the dignified Smith. Next morning it appeared, as follows:

We quote from the *Tea-Pot* of yesterday the subjoined paragraph: – '*Oh*, yes! – *Oh*, we perceive! *Oh*, no doubt! *Oh*, my! *Oh*, goodness! *O tempora! O Moses!*' Why, the fellow is all *O!* That accounts for his reasoning in a circle, and explains why there is neither beginning nor end to him, nor to anything that he says. We really do not believe the vagabond can write a word that hasn't an o in it. Wonder if this *O*-ing is a habit of his? By the bye, he came away from Down-East in a great hurry. Wonder if he *O*'s as much there as he does here? '*O!* it is pitiful.'

The indignation of Mr Bullet-head at these scandalous insinuations I shall not attempt to describe. On the eel-skinning principle, however, he did not seem to be so much incensed at the attack upon his integrity as one might have imagined. It was the sneer at his *style* that drove him to desperation. What! – he, Touch-and-go Bullet-head! – not able to write a word without an o in it! He would soon let the jackanapes see that he was mistaken. Yes! he would let him see how *much* he was mistaken, the puppy!

He, Touch-and-go Bullet-head, of Frogpondium,[7] would let Mr John Smith perceive that he, Bullet-head, could indite, if it so pleased him, a whole paragraph – ay! a whole article – in which that contemptible vowel should not once – not even *once* – make its appearance. But no; – that would be yielding a point to the said John Smith. *He*, Bullet-head, would make *no* alteration in his style, to suit the caprices of any Mr Smith in Christendom. Perish so vile a thought! The *O* forever! He would persist in the *O*. He would be as *O*-wy as *O*-wy could be.

Burning with the chivalry of this determination, the great Touch-and-go, in the next *Tea-Pot*, came out merely with this simple but resolute paragraph in reference to this unhappy affair:–

The editor of the *Tea-Pot* has the *honor* of advising the editor of the *Gazette* that he (the *Tea-Pot*) will take an opportunity in to-morrow morning's paper of convincing him (the *Gazette*) that he (the *Tea-Pot*) both can and will be *his own master*, as regards style; – he (the *Tea-Pot*) intending to show him (the *Gazette*) the supreme, and indeed the withering, contempt with which the criticism of him (the *Gazette*) inspires the independent bosom of him (the *Tea-Pot*), by composing for the especial gratification (?) of him (the *Gazette*) a leading article, of some extent, in which the beautiful vowel – the emblem of Eternity, yet so offensive to the hyper-exquisite delicacy of him (the *Gazette*) – shall most certainly *not be avoided* by his (the *Gazette*'s) most obedient, humble servant, the *Tea-Pot*. 'So much for Buckingham.'[8]

In fulfilment of the awful threat thus darkly intimated rather than decidedly enunciated, the great Bullet-head, turning a deaf ear to all entreaties for 'copy', and simply requesting his foreman to 'go to the d—l', when he (the foreman) assured him (the *Tea-Pot*) that it was high time to 'go to press'; turning a deaf ear to everything, I say, the great Bullet-head sat up until day-break, consuming the midnight oil, and absorbed in the composition of the really unparalleled paragraph which follows:–

So ho, John! how now? Told you so, you know. Don't crow, another time, before you're out of the woods! Does your mother *know* you're out? Oh, no, no! – so go home at once, now, John, to your odious old woods of Concord![9] Go home to your woods, old owl, – go! You won't? Oh, poh, poh, John, don't do so! You've *got* to go, you know! So go at once, and don't go slow; for nobody owns you here, you know. Oh, John, John, if you *don't* go you're no *homo* – no! You're only a fowl, an owl; a cow, a sow; a doll, a poll; a poor, old, good-for-nothing-to-

nobody, log, dog, hog, or frog, come out of a Concord bog. Cool, now
– cool! *Do* be cool, you fool! None of your crowing, old cock! Don't frown
so – don't! Don't hollo, nor howl, nor growl, nor bow-wow-wow! Good
Lord, John, how you *do* look! Told you so, you know – but stop rolling
your goose of an old poll about so, and go and drown your sorrows
in a bowl!

Exhausted, very naturally, by so stupendous an effort, the great
Touch-and-go could attend to nothing farther that night. Firmly,
composedly, yet with an air of conscious power, he handed
his MS. to the devil in waiting, and then, walking leisurely home,
retired with ineffable dignity to bed.

Meantime the devil, to whom the copy was intrusted, ran up-
stairs to his 'case', in an unutterable hurry and forthwith made
a commencement at 'setting' the MS. 'up'.

In the first place, of course, – as the opening word was 'So',
– he made a plunge into the capital-*S* hole and came out in
triumph with a capital-*S*. Elated by this success, he immediately
threw himself upon the little-*o* box with a blindfold impetuosity
– but who shall describe his horror when his fingers came up
without the anticipated letter in their clutch? who shall paint
his astonishment and rage at perceiving, as he rubbed his
knuckles, that he had been only thumping them, to no purpose,
against the bottom of an *empty* box. Not a single little-*o* was
in the little-*o* hole; and, glancing fearfully at the capital-*O* parti-
tion, he found *that*, to his extreme terror, in a precisely similar
predicament. Awe-stricken, his first impulse was to rush to the
foreman.

'Sir!' said he, gasping for breath, 'I can't never set up nothing
without no *o*'s.'

'*What* do you mean by that?' growled the foreman, who was
in a very ill-humor at being kept up so late.

'Why, sir, there beant an *o* in the office, neither a big un
nor a little un!'

'What – what the d—l has become of all that were in the
case?'

'*I* don't know, sir,' said the boy, 'but one of them ere *Gazette*
devils is bin prowling bout here all night, and I spect *he's* gone
and cabbaged em every one.'

'Dod rot him! I haven't a doubt of it,' replied the foreman, getting purple with rage – 'but I tell you what you do, Bob, that's a good boy – you go over the first chance you get and hook every one of their *i*'s and (d—n them!) their izzards.'

'Jist so,' replied Bob, with a wink and a frown – '*I'll* be in to em, *I'll* let em know a thing or two; but in de mean time, that ere paragrab? *Mus* go in to-night, you know – else there'll be the d—l to pay, and –'

'And not a *bit* of pitch hot,' interrupted the foreman, with a deep sigh and an emphasis on the 'bit'. 'Is it a *very* long paragraph, Bob?'

'Shouldn't call it a *wery* long paragrab,' said Bob.

'Ah, well, then! do the best you can with it! we *must* get to press,' said the foreman, who was over head and ears in work; 'just stick in some other letter for *o*, nobody's going to read the fellow's trash, anyhow.'

'*Wery* well,' replied Bob, 'here goes it!' and off he hurried to his case; muttering as he went – 'Considdeble vell, them ere expressions, perticcler for a man as doesen't swar. So I's to gouge out all their eyes, eh? and d—n all their gizzards! Vell! this here's the chap as is jist able *for* to do it.' The fact is that, although Bob was but twelve years old and four feet high, he was equal to any amount of fight, in a small way.

The exigency here described is by no means of rare occurrence in printing-offices; and I cannot tell how to account for it, but the fact is indisputable, that when the exigency does occur, it almost always happens that *x* is adopted as a substitute for the letter deficient. The true reason, perhaps, is that *x* is rather the most superabundant letter in the cases, or at least *was* so, in old times, long enough to render the substitution in question an habitual thing with printers. As for Bob, he would have considered it heretical to employ any other character, in a case of this kind, than the *x* to which he had been accustomed.

'I *shell* have to *x* this ere paragrab,' said he to himself, as he read it over in astonishment, 'but it's jest about the awfulest *o*-wy paragrab I ever *did* see': so *x* it he did, unflinchingly, and to press it went *x*-ed.

Next morning the population of Nopolis were taken all

aback by reading, in the *Tea-Pot* the following extraordinary leader:–

Sx hx, Jxhn! hxw nxw! Txld yxu sx, yxu knxw. Dxn't crxw, anxther time, befxre yxu're xut xf the wxxds! Dxes yxur mxther *knxw* yxu're xut? Xh, nx, nx! sx gx hxme at xnce, nxw, Jxhn, tx yxur xdixus xld wxxds xf Cxncxrd! Gx hxme tx yxur wxxds, xld xwl, – gx! Yxu wxn't? Xh, pxh, pxh, Jxhn, dxn't dx sx! Yxu've *gxt* tx gx, yxu knxw! sx gx at xnce, and dxn't gx slxw; fxr nxbxdy xwns yxu here, yxu knxw. Xh, Jxhn, Jxhn, if yxu *dxn't* gx yxu're nx *hxmx* – nx! Yxu're xnly a fxwl, an xwl; a cxw, a sxw; a dxll, a pxll; a pxxr xld gxxd-fxr-nxthing-tx-nxbxdy lxg, dxg, hxg, xr frxg, cxme xut xf a Cxncxrd bxg. Cxxl, nxw – cxxl! Dx be cxxl, yxu fxxl! Nxne xf yxur crxwing, xld cxck! Dxn't frxwn sx – dxn't! Dxn't hxllx, nxr hxwl, nxr grxwl, nxr bxw-wxw-wxw! Gxxd Lxrd, Jxhn, hxw yxu *dx* lxxk! Txld yxu sx, yxu knxw, but stxp rxlling yxur gxxse xf an xld pxll abxut sx, and gx and drxwn yxur sxrrxws in a bxwl!

The uproar occasioned by this mystical and cabalistical article is not to be conceived. The first definite idea entertained by the populace was that some diabolical treason lay concealed in the hieroglyphics; and there was a general rush to Bullet-head's residence, for the purpose of riding him on a rail; but that gentleman was nowhere to be found. He had vanished, no one could tell how; and not even the ghost of him has ever been seen since.

Unable to discover its legitimate object, the popular fury at length subsided; leaving behind it, by way of sediment, quite a medley of opinion about this unhappy affair.

One gentleman thought the whole an X-ellent joke.

Another said that, indeed, Bullet-head had shown much X-uberance of fancy.

A third admitted him X-entric, but no more.

A fourth could only suppose it the Yankee's design to X-press, in a general way, his X-asperation.

'Say, rather, to set an X-ample to posterity,' suggested a fifth.

That Bullet-head had been driven to an extremity was clear to all; and in fact, since *that* editor could not be found, there was some talk about lynching the other one.

The more common conclusion, however, was that the affair was, simply, X-traordinary and in-X-plicable. Even the town mathematician confessed that he could make nothing of so dark a problem. X, everybody knew, was an unknown quantity; but in this case (as he properly observed) there was an unknown quantity of X.

The opinion of Bob, the devil (who kept dark 'about his having X-ed the paragrab'), did not meet with so much attention as I think it deserved, although it was very openly and very fearlessly expressed. He said that, for his part, he had no doubt about the matter at all; that it was a clear case that Mr Bullet-head never *could* be persvaded fur to drink like other folks, but vas *con*tinually a-svigging o' that ere blessed XXX ale,[10] and, as a naiteral consekvence, it just puffed him up savage, and made him X (cross) in the X-treme.

Notes

THE following annotations are intended as a general guide for the reader who is unfamiliar with Poe's topical allusions and literary references – many of which were, even in the author's own lifetime, somewhat arcane. To annotate all of them would create a cumbersome apparatus that could only interfere with the comic flow of individual pieces, and I have therefore tried to keep the commentaries as brief as possible. Sabine Büssing was of invaluable help to me in researching the material which follows.

Lionizing

The story was published in the *Southern Literary Messenger* in May 1835, later in *Tales of the Grotesque and Arabesque* (1840). On 15 March 1845 it appeared in the *Broadway Journal*. Rufus W. Griswold's edition of Poe's *Works* (1850) provides the version printed here.

1. (p. 25) The motto is misquoted from Bishop Joseph Hall's *Satires* (1597), II, iii, 19–20: 'Genus and Species long since barefoote went/ Upon their ten-toes in wilde wonderment.'
2. (p. 25) 'Junius' was the author of a famous series of political letters in the London *Public Advertiser*, 1769–1772.
3. (p. 25) The Man in the Iron Mask was a political prisoner in France, well known to readers of romance.
4. (p. 25) Nosology is actually the science of diseases; nosology as the science of noses is, of course, a pun.
5. (p. 26) Casparus Bartholinus, a Scandinavian scholar and physician, published *De olfactus organo* in 1679 and *De respiratione animalium* in 1700, two works about noses.
6. (p. 26) Poe lists the most important British literary reviews of his day.
7. (p. 27) In Poe's time London's Jermyn Street was known for the distinguished men who had lodgings there.

8. (p. 27) 'Her Majesty' replaces 'His Majesty' for the first version and appears in those versions published after the accession of Queen Victoria on the death of William IV, 20 June 1837.

9. (p. 27) The Prince of Wales was added in 1845; no one had the title from 1820 when George IV became king until 1842 when Albert Edward, later Edward VII, received the title at less than two years of age.

10. (p. 27) A corresponding passage can be found in Benjamin Disraeli's *Vivian Grey*, book I, chapter 6: '"Father! I wish to make myself master of the latter platonists. I want Plotinus, and Porphyry, and Iamblichus, and Syrianus, and Maximus Tyrios, and Proclus, and Hierocles, and Sallustius, and Damascius."' These philosophers flourished between 150 B.C. and A.D. 485.

11. (p. 27) All the perfectionists, save Richard Price, are well known. The latter was an English moralist and preacher (1723–1791).

12. (p. 28) Homoeomery is the doctrine that elementary substances are composed of parts each similar to the whole.

13. (p. 28) Eusebius, Bishop of Nicomedia, died in 342. Arius, founder of Arianism, thought Christ less than the Father, something condemned at the Council of Nice (Nicaea in Bithynia) in 325, when the Nicene Creed was framed. Puseyism is a reference to Edward Bouverie Pusey (1800–1882), who led the high-church party of Anglicans.

14. (p. 28) The standard English forms of the Greek terms are 'homoousian' (of the same essence) and 'homoiousian' (of like essence); they refer to arguments about the question as to whether Christ has the same or merely a similar nature to that of the Father.

15. (p. 28) The Rocher de Cancale is a great rock in Brittany, which gave its name to a Parisian restaurant.

16. (p. 28) All of the lost Greek books (except those of Homer Junior) are mentioned in 'Some Ancient Greek Authors' in the *Southern Literary Messenger*, April 1836. The article is signed 'P.' and has been assigned to Poe.

17. (p. 29) Almack's balls were held in the Assembly Rooms in King Street, St James's; until 1781 the proprietor of these rooms was William Almack.

18. (p. 30) Chalk Farm was a well-known duelling place near Regent's Park.

Loss of Breath

The first form of this story, entitled 'A Decided Loss', was one of the five tales Poe submitted for the contest announced by the *Philadelphia Saturday Courier* in June 1831. Poe revised the story completely, until only the framework was left, and expanded it into 'Loss of Breath' in 1833 for his *Tales of the Folio Club*. This modified text was first published in the *Southern Literary Messenger* in September 1835, and in *Tales of the*

Grotesque and Arabesque in 1840. In a letter to J. P. Kennedy, 11 February 1836, Poe calls his tale a satire 'of the extravagancies of Blackwood', which it is indeed. 'A Decided Loss' was only intended to ridicule *Blackwood's Edinburgh Magazine* (founded 1817) and is partly based on Adalbert von Chamisso's *Peter Schlemihl* (1814) and several chapters of Voltaire's *Candide* (1759), where Dr Pangloss, unskillfully hanged, revives when a surgeon begins to dissect his body.

1. (p. 31) The motto is the opening ('Oh! breathe not his name') of the *Irish Melodies* of Thomas Moore (1779–1852).
2. (p. 31) The course of the story shows that Poe may have in mind another famous siege, that of Jericho, a city that could not resist the power of sound.
3. (p. 32) J. J. Rousseau (1712–1778), *Julie, ou la Nouvelle Héloïse*, part II, letter iii, paragraph 2: 'The road of the passions has led me to true philosophy.'
4. (p. 32) Cf. 'How to Write a *Blackwood* Article': Poe makes Blackwood explain that the proper tone of a story must be 'made up of everything deep, great, odd, piquant, pertinent, and pretty'. A 'deep, odd tone' is an ambiguous term, as it refers to mode of expression and pitch as well, as clearly illustrated in 'Loss of Breath'.
5. (p. 32) The word 'breath' must be taken symbolically; a god inspires his creatures with his breath, for instance, so that one can put 'breath' and 'spirit' on the same level.
6. (p. 33) See William Godwin, *Mandeville* (1817), vol. III, iii, paragraph 8.
7. (p. 33) Anaxagoras actually said there must be blackness in snow which turned into dark water; Pierre Bayle in his *Dictionnaire* (1696) accused him of saying that snow was black, a misinterpretation which has often been repeated.
8. (p. 34) *Metamora* by John Augustus Stone (1800–1834) was first performed in New York, later in Philadelphia (22 January 1830).
9. (p. 35) Phalaris, tyrant of Agrigentum (about 510 B.C.), had a hollow brazen bull into which an offender was put, and a fire lit beneath. The victim's cries simulated the roarings of a bull.
10. (p. 37) Angélique Catalani (1782–1849) was a celebrated opera singer.
11. (p. 37) Herodotus refers to the Persian Magian, who lost his ears for a serious offense under Cyrus; he later usurped the throne after the murder of Cyrus' elder son Smerdis by order of his brother Cambyses.
12. (p. 38) The philosophers are said to have been called cynics, from the Greek word for dog, because of their sneering, aggressive behavior.
13. (p. 38) Cf. 'How to Write a *Blackwood* Article': Blackwood's advice is, 'Should you ever be drowned or hung, be sure and make a note of your sensations.'
14. (p. 38) Horace Smith in *Zillah* (1828), III, 40, has Mark Antony say,

'as to toping ... I have had long ... practice, and I have ... written a treatise upon drunkenness'.

15. (p. 38) *Pinxit* means 'he painted'. 'The Flaying of Marsyas' is the subject of a painting by Raphael.

16. (p. 38) Cf. 'How to Write a *Blackwood* Article'. One of *Blackwood's* favorite topics is 'The Dead Alive', the 'record of a gentleman's sensations when entombed before the breath was out of his body'.

17. (p. 38) The verse is not from John Marston's *Malcontent*, but from his *Antonio and Mellida*, part I, act III, scene ii.

18. (p. 39) The poetry of George Crabbe is probably mentioned because crabs are said to move backwards only.

19. (p. 39) During a war against the gods, the Giants tried to pile Mount Pelion on Mount Ossa to reach the summit of Olympus (Homer, *Odyssey*, XI, 315; Virgil, *Georgics*, I, 281).

20. (p. 40) *South on the Bones* is the title of American reprints of *A Short Description of the Bones* (1825) by John Flint South, M.D.

21. (p. 43) The Greek inscription was *to prostekonti theo*, which means 'to the proper divinity'. The record comes from Diogenes Laertius, *Lives*, I, 'Epimenides', 3.

King Pest

'King Pest' was first published in the *Southern Literary Messenger* in September 1835. It is Poe's profoundest and gloomiest comic tale, a brilliant combination of wit and horror. The peregrinations of the two protagonists are nothing more than the march of their destinies. In this respect the archetype of seafaring stands for life and its vicissitudes; the nautical imagery which permeates the whole story thus has a high symbolic value. One can assume that one of Poe's reasons for composing this tale was the necessity to cope with certain incidents of his own life. In his time great parts of the Eastern coast of the United States were regularly plagued by the yellow fever. Some of his relatives died of this disease. The sick were often isolated on islands, where they died together with physicians and nurses. The nickname of the plague, 'Yellow Jack', proves how common this experience was in those days.

1. (p. 44) The motto is from *Gorboduc*, a play by Thomas Norton and Thomas Sackville (first printed in 1565). Its subtitle is 'Ferrex and Porrex', and it has been much discussed as 'the earliest English tragedy in blank verse'.

2. (p. 44) The pest ravaged England several times during the reign of Edward III (1327–1377).

3. (p. 45) Ben Nevis is the highest mountain in Great Britain.

4. (p. 46) The 'plague' which is mentioned here can also mean a human plague; the indication of time may as well refer to the Hundred Years' War between England and France. Though this war took place exclusively on the European continent, it meant a plague to the English

subjects, for new recruits were drafted semi-annually, and only the rich were able to ransom themselves from the service in France.

5. (p. 46) The fact that it is *the king* who is responsible for the barriers which separate the pestilential area from that of the healthy people is reminiscent of the story 'The Masque of the Red Death', where Prince Prospero makes a similar division.

6. (p. 47) This is another variety of the human plague. In their fear, people do not notice that their fellows are the ones to profit by the disease and its consequences.

7. (p. 48) The undertaker's shop is indeed a suitable dais-chamber for King Pest. That the most exquisite wines can be found here suggests that death was frequently a good source of revenue. The sailors have thus come from the tap-house of the living to the 'tap-house' of the dead.

8. (p. 49) King Pest's symptoms of disease are those of the yellow fever. The Royal Family are all allegorical figures standing for death; they form a whole panopticon of representatives of the most common diseases in Poe's time – galloping consumption, dropsy, gout, paralysis, and dipsomania.

9. (p. 53) The term 'metropolis' appears first on p. 46 in connection with King Edward's domain. Just as the two kings in this story comprise counterparts, their territories have different centers, though that of King Pest might better be called 'necropolis'.

10. (p. 53) Davy Jones is a seaman's name for 'the fiend who presides over all the evil spirits of the deep' (Tobias Smollet, *Peregrine Pickle*, 1751).

11. (p. 53) Black Strap is inferior thick port.

12. (p. 54) For the 'law of the Medes and the Persians which altereth not' see Esther 1:19, Daniel 6:8, and other passages in the Bible.

13. (p. 55) Hurlygurly is a street organ, or the person who plays one.

A Tale of Jerusalem

The story was first published in the *Southern Literary Messenger* in April 1836. It is a remarkable satire on bigotry, and though its climax shows no great originality, the subject of ridicule is cleverly expressed. Many details in the description of the city are taken from the novel *Zillah, a Tale of Jerusalem* by Horatio Smith.

1. (p. 57) The Latin phrase translates, 'He let his uncut gray hair hang down over his stern forehead.'

2. (p. 57) Thammuz is the tenth month of the Hebrew year; the tenth day does not seem to be significant. The year of the world 3941 was 65–64 B.C.

3. (p. 57) *Zillah*, I, 44: 'Three Gizbarin, or sub-collectors of the offerings'.

4. (p. 57) Adonai is translated 'Lord'.

5. (p. 58) The Great Pyramid of Cheops is over 480 feet high. Indications

of place are very important in this story. From their high stronghold the Jews look down, both literally and symbolically, upon the besiegers.

6. (p. 58) Joshua 15:7, 'the going up to Adummim', the steep road from the plain of Jericho to the hilly country around Jerusalem.

7. (p. 59) By playing freely with a whole catalogue of gods and idols Poe makes every kind of bigotry ridiculous. The Romans despise the Jewish 'idolaters'; the god mentioned by them as 'a true god', however, is Phoebus (Apollo), a Greek divinity.

8. (p. 59) *El Elohim* (cognate with Arabic Allah) means 'the gods'.

9. (p. 59) The first seven gods in the list are mentioned in II Kings 17:30–31. Nergal was a god of the men of Cuth. Ashimah was a god of the men of Hameth. Nibhaz and Tartak were gods of the Arvites. To Adrammelech and Anammelech the Sepharvites burned their children. Succoth-benoth was worshipped at Babylon. Dagon was a sea divinity of the Philistines. Belial is regarded as a deity in *Paradise Lost*. Baal-perith was worshipped by the Israelites in Shechem after Gideon's death; Baal-peor was a god of the Moabites. Baal-zebub, the 'Lord of the Flies', is mentioned in II Kings 1:2 ff. as a god of Ekron. The monotheistic Pharisees seem suspiciously well informed about the idols that their forefathers and their neighbors adored.

10. (p. 60) The twelve jewels of the pectoral of the High Priest are listed in Exodus 28:15 ff.

11. (p. 60) In *Zillah*, III, 51, at a feast given by Mark Antony, a wild boar is brought in and the heroine's father exclaims, 'El Elohim! – it is the unutterable flesh.'

How to Write a *Blackwood* Article

This story, as well as 'A Predicament', which has the function of a tale within a tale, was first published in the Baltimore *American Museum* in November 1838. In 1840 it was re-edited for *Tales of the Grotesque and Arabesque*. On 12 July 1845, it appeared in the *Broadway Journal*. As the title already indicates, the story is a satire on one of Poe's contemporary writers and editors, but it contains self-criticism as well. Even as a boy Poe was almost certainly familiar with *Blackwood's Edinburgh Magazine* (founded 1817), as his foster father dealt, among other things, in imported books and periodicals.

1. (p. 61) The motto is taken from a speech ascribed to Dr Johnson's ghost in *Rejected Addresses: or The New Theatrum Poetarum* by James and Horace Smith (1812), and asserts that 'a swelling opening is too often succeeded by an insignificant conclusion'.

2. (p. 61) Zenobia inherited the throne of Palmyra from her husband in A.D. 269 or 268. She was said to be a woman of great beauty and supreme intelligence, who could ride, hunt, lead troops and discuss philosophy as well as any man.

62) Henry Peter Brougham (1778–1868) was a contributor to the

Edinburgh Review, founder of the Society for the Diffusion of Useful Knowledge in 1825, and Lord Chancellor of England from 1830 to 1834.

4. (p. 62) Poe makes fun of those authoresses in his time who did not work in order to satisfy an intellectual or financial need, but out of boredom or silly caprice.

5. (p. 63) *The Times* and the *Examiner* are London newspapers.

6. (p. 64) The story outlined comes from 'The Buried Alive', published in *Blackwood's*, October 1821, and is used in Poe's 'Premature Burial' as well.

7. (p. 64) *Confessions of an English Opium Eater* by Thomas De Quincey appeared in the *London Magazine* in 1821, and as a book in 1822.

8. (p. 64) 'The Involuntary Experimentalist' is about a man repairing a boiler which began to be heated, and appeared in *Blackwood's*, October 1837.

9. (p. 64) *Passages from the Diary of a Late Physician* by Samuel Warren began as a serial for *Blackwood's* in August 1830.

10. (p. 64) 'The Man in the Bell' (*Blackwood's*, November 1821) probably influenced 'The Devil in the Belfry' and the last stanza of 'The Bells' by Poe.

11. (p. 66) The 'Critique of Pure Reason' (1781) and 'Metaphysical Foundations of Natural Science' (1786) by Immanuel Kant.

12. (p. 66) The *Dial* (1840–1844) was the chief organ of the Transcendentalists; the editors were, in succession, Margaret Fuller and Ralph Waldo Emerson.

13. (p. 66) *Poems* (1842) by William Ellery Channing was reviewed by Poe in 1843. The lines actually run, 'Thou meetest a common man,/ With a delusive show of *can*!'

14. (p. 67) The Chinese novel *Ju-Kiao-Li or The Two Fair Cousins* was published in London in 1827.

15. (p. 68) Voltaire's tragedy *Zaïre* is referred to here.

16. (p. 68) The Spanish verses, which have been ascribed to the Valenian Escrivá, are quoted by Cervantes in *Don Quixote*, II, 38.

17. (p. 68) In the preface to his translation of Ariosto's *Orlando Furioso*, John Hoole traces the couplet to faulty recollection of lines in Berni's version of Bojardo's *Orlando Innamorato*.

18. (p. 68) The German lines are not from Schiller, but from Goethe's ballad 'Das Veilchen'.

19. (p. 69) The Greek line is from the *Monosticha* of Menander preserved by Aulus Gellius, but Francis Bacon ascribed it to Demosthenes.

Article for *Blackwood*: A Predicament

1. (p. 71) The motto is from Milton's *Comus*, line 277.

2. (p. 71) Edina is Edinburgh.

3. (p. 78) The original title, 'A Scythe of Time', clearly indicates the

symbolic aspect of the tale. Psyche's predicament is not only the symbol of Man exposed to his eternal enemy, Time, but also an example of how a human being can behave in a crucial situation. Psyche is a fool, and like Toby Dammit (who bet the Devil his head) she deserves to be decapitated. The protagonist of Poe's later story 'The Pit and the Pendulum', who is in a similarly hopeless situation, escapes because he is capable of *thought*, the key term of that tale, and Man's only help in the struggle with his fate.

The Devil in the Belfry

The story was first printed in the Philadelphia *Saturday Chronicle* on 8 May 1839. It also appeared in *Tales of the Grotesque and Arabesque* (1840) and in the *Broadway Journal* (1845). 'The Devil in the Belfry' is a bizarre satire on the bourgeois life-style and contains numerous political allusions as well. The idea of 'revolution' with its double meaning – the political movement and the movements of the hands of a clock – determines the whole plot.

1. (p. 81) Vondervotteimittiss means, of course, 'Wonder what time it is.'
2. (p. 83) At close examination the borough of Vondervotteimittiss is situated on the very face of a clock. Sixty houses form a perfect circle around the belfry, which contains the mechanism that keeps the community going.

The Man that was Used Up

First published in *Burton's Gentleman's Magazine* when Poe was editor, the tale was slightly revised for publication in *Tales of the Grotesque and Arabesque, the Prose Romances of Edgar A. Poe*, and the *Broadway Journal*. In the subtitle Poe may have been playing on the 'Tippecanoe and Tyler Too' slogan of the 1840 presidential election, when General Harrison's victory over Tecumseh at Tippecanoe (1811) was celebrated as part of the coon-skin and log-cabin ethos with which the Whigs sought to remake their fading national image into that of the party of the people.

1. (p.90) The epigraph, from Corneille's *Le Cid*, translates,
   'Weep, weep, my eyes, and dissolve in water!
   The better half of my life has placed the other in the tomb.'

The Business Man

The story first appeared in *Burton's Gentleman's Magazine* in February 1840. It was re-edited by the *Broadway Journal* (2 August 1845).

Peter Pendulum, the hero of the original version of the story, may have taken his name from a character invented by Joseph Dennie (whose sketches were published in the *Farmer's Museum* of Walpole, New Hampshire, about 1795). At any rate, it had a further meaning to Poe. 'Peter

Pendulum' is on the one hand the slurred pronunciation of 'Pit and Pendulum' (1843), and on the other hand an indication of the fickleness and inconstancy of the hero, whose later name, Peter Proffit, emphasizes another trait of character. The story must be seen in close relation to 'Diddling'. The only difference between the narrator and a typical diddler consists in the fact that nearly all of the eight modes of business presented here are perfectly legal. Proffit is the embodiment of a modern American, a 'Yankee hero', who does not shrink from humiliation or physical and mental inflictions while following the holy course of his career.

1. (p. 102) At close examination each of the eight endeavors includes a proverb or idiom – an example of Poe's predilection for puns and riddles. In this case the hero is all 'tailormade'.
2. (p. 106) Proffit's trouble with banks alludes to the frequent suspensions of banks during the Jackson and Van Buren administrations. Poe himself had to defer his plans for the *Penn Magazine* and accept a position offered him at *Graham's* because of the bank suspensions.
3. (p. 107) The Sham-Post incident does not appear in the first version and was probably suggested by a story in the *Saturday Evening Post* (12 November 1842) about fraudulent letter-carriers whose messages proved to be a hoax.
4. (p. 108) *Nem[ine] con[tradicente]* means 'without opposition'.
5. (p. 108) Macassar oil was a popular hair tonic.

Why the Little Frenchman Wears his Hand in a Sling

The story first appeared in an unlocated periodical between 1837 and 1839. The first located publication is that in the *Tales of the Grotesque and Arabesque* (1840). On 6 September 1845 it was printed in the *Broadway Journal*.

1. (p. 109) The Baronet's London address is that of a house in which John Allan lived with his family for a time. The landlord was a Frenchman, whose sister's school Edgar Poe attended as a boy.
2. (p. 110) The dancing master Luchesi probably refers to a Baltimore character, the music-master Frederick Lucchesi, of whom John H. Hewitt wrote in *Shadows on the Wall* (1877).
3. (p. 113) Two Kilkenny cats in Irish legend fought with each other until only their tails were left.
4. (p. 113) The purraty-trap is the trap for 'praties' (potatoes); here, of course, it means 'mouth'.

Never Bet the Devil Your Head

The story was first published in *Graham's Magazine* in September 1841. It is a biting satire on some of Poe's contemporary writers, especially the Transcendentalists. Poe was particularly angered by their insistence that every work of art must have a moral. The hero of the tale is an obvious caricature of Poe's literary opponents, and the plot serves well for interweaving vicious remarks and puns; moreover, it is an allegorical paraphrase of the Transcendentalists' own philosophical efforts.

1. (p. 115) The sentence is taken from *Cuentos en verso castellano* by Tomás Hermenegildo de las Torres (Zaragoza, 1828).
2. (p. 115) Cf. Poe's 'Poetic Principle': 'Every poem, it is said, should inculcate a moral; and by this moral is the poetical merit of the work to be adjudged.' The so-called 'Didactic' 'accomplished more in the corruption of our Poetical Literature than all its other enemies combined'. To Poe's mind vice must only be condemned if it interferes with the beauty of a work of art.
3. (p. 115) Philip Melancthon's commentary appeared in an edition of the pseudo-Homeric *Batrachomyomachia* (on the Battle of the Frogs and Mice; Paris, 1542). Pierre La Seine wrote *Homeri Nepenthes, seu, de abolendo luctu* (Lyons, 1624). Jacobus Hugo thought that Homer under divine influence prophesied the development of Christianity in his account of the Trojan War, hence the awkward analogies. The ideas of the former writers are presented correctly by Poe.
4. (p. 115) *The Antediluvians, or The World Destroyed*, a narrative poem in ten books (London, 1839; Philadelphia, 1840), was by Dr James McHenry.
5. (p. 115) Seba Smith's *Powhatan: A Metrical Romance* was reviewed by Poe in *Graham's* (July 1841).
6. (p. 115) Both the nursery rhyme and the fairy tale have been part of English children's literature since the early eighteenth century.
7. (p. 116) The *Dial*, founded in 1840, was the organ of the Transcendentalists, including Emerson and Margaret Fuller.
8. (p. 116) Poe has in mind the *North American Review*, which together with the *Dial* is more openly attacked in his review of *Twice-Told Tales*: 'Let him [Hawthorne] mend his pen, get a bottle of visible ink, come out from the Old Manse, cut Mr Alcott, hang (if possible) the editor of the *Dial*, and throw out of the window to the pigs all his odd numbers of the *North American Review*.'
9. (p. 116) The sentences translate, 'Let the dead suffer no injury', and 'Nothing but good of the dead'.
10. (p. 120) Both Merry Andrew and Tom Fool are buffoons.
11. (p. 121) The devil has, just as in Poe's 'Bon-Bon', the outward appearance of a clergyman.
12. (p. 121) Poe refers to R. W. Griswold's *Poets and Poetry of America*, a royal octavo of over 400 pages, often called 'The Big Book'. The first edition appeared in 1842.
13. (p. 123) Poe reviewed William W. Lord's *Poems* in the *Broadway Journal*, 24 May 1845.
14. (p. 123) Like the Transcendentalists, Toby Dammit cannot cross the

barrier without losing his head. The former ones also try in vain to
reach the 'other side' of experience and make no progress at all.

15. (p. 124) A 'bar sinister' is a sign of illegitimacy in heraldry.

The Spectacles

The story was first printed in the *Philadelphia Saturday Courier* on 24
June and 1 and 8 July 1843. Rufus Griswold's edition provides the final
text. The tale is a clever and original travesty of the life of Ninon de
l'Enclos (1615–1705), who was, like the fictitious lady, of French
nationality and a celebrated beauty even in old age. At seventy she still
had several lovers, but was as highly regarded for her wit and intellect.
With the Marquis of Gersai she had a son, who was never told of his
real mother. When she was over sixty, he was introduced to her *salon*
and fell in love with his own mother. She hesitated too long to tell him
about his origin, and the young man committed suicide out of lover's
grief. Ninon de l'Enclos regularly corresponded with several people and
revealed her philosophical theories to them. One fundamental feature
of her doctrines was the clear distinction between love and friendship.
Love was nothing but an illusion of the senses for her, though a pleasant
occupation, whereas friendship meant an intellectual bond based on
mutual esteem.

1. (p. 127) *Ventum textilem* may be translated 'woven air'.
2. (p. 129) *Paradise Lost*, IV, 830 ('Not to know me argues yourself
   unknown') is slightly misquoted.
3. (p. 129) The Lalande is from the celebrated opera singer, Mme
   Henriette Clementine Lalande (1797–1867). She appears in *Memoirs
   and Letters of Madame Malibran* by the Countess de Merlin (Philadelphia,
   1840). Poe reviewed the book in *Burton's*.
4. (p. 133) Erebus is Hades.
5. (p. 136) Hock is a common term for Rhine wine.
6. (p. 140) San Carlo is the opera house at Naples.
7. (p. 147) Cf. Poe's letter to his friends F. W. Thomas and Jesse E. Dow,
   16 March 1843: 'I never saw a man ... more surprised to see another.
   He ... would as soon have thought of seeing his great-great-great-
   grandmother.'

Diddling Considered as One of the Exact Sciences

'Diddling' appeared in the *Philadelphia Saturday Courier* on 14 October
1843, and in the *Broadway Journal* in September 1845.

1. (p. 150) Poe's correspondent John Neal became a friend of the
   utilitarian Jeremy Bentham during his stay in England (1824–1827).
2. (p. 150) In the first version Poe used the name of Jeremy Diddler,
   the main character of James Kenney's *Raising the Wind*.

3. (p. 151) Brobdingnag is the land of giants in Swift's *Gulliver's Travels*.
4. (p. 151) 'Flaccus' was the pen-name of Thomas Ward (1807–1873), whose *Passaic* (1842) was reviewed by Poe in *Graham's*.
5. (p. 151) The Latin phrase translates, 'As a dog is never driven from a greasy hide' (Horace, *Satires*).
6. (p. 151) In 202 B.C. Scipio defeated Hannibal by carrying the war into Africa (Livy, XXIX, 26). Dick Turpin (1706–1739) was an English highwayman who became the hero of several legendary romances. Daniel O'Connell (1775–1847) was an Irish patriot and an ardent abolitionist. Charles XII, King of Sweden from 1697 to 1718, was known as a reckless fighter.
7. (p. 151) Lady Charlotte Susan Maria Bury (1775–1861) was an English novelist and diarist.
8. (p. 152) Cf. *As You Like It*, II, vii, 156: 'Full of wise saws and modern instances'.
9. (p. 160) *Non est inventus* means 'He is not to be found.'

The Premature Burial

The tale was printed in the *Philadelphia Dollar Newspaper* on 31 July 1844, and in the *Broadway Journal* on 14 June 1845. In June 1849 it appeared in the *Southern Literary Messenger*. The Griswold edition (1850) provides the final text.

1. (p. 165) 'Asphytic' is an adjective derived from asphyxia, which means 'a suspension of life, with all the appearance of death'.
2. (p. 166) Galvanic batteries also appear in 'Some Words with a Mummy' and 'Loss of Breath'.
3. (p. 167) The expression 'Conqueror Worm', which originally comes from Spencer Wallace Cone's *Proud Ladye* (New York, 1840), is used by Poe as the title of the poem first printed in *Graham's* (1843), later inserted in 'Ligeia'.
4. (p. 171) Life-preserving coffins were indeed manufactured in America and throughout Europe in Poe's lifetime.
5. (p. 174) William Buchan (1729–1805) wrote *Domestic Medicine; or The Family Physician*, first published in 1769 and highly regarded for many decades thereafter.
6. (p. 174) Dr Edward Young's *Night Thoughts, of Death, Time, and Immortality* (1742), a poem of the Graveyard School, was still very popular in Poe's time.
7. (p. 174) Two sentences in Horace Binney Wallace's *Stanley* (1838) are combined here: '... with all the ardor of desperation; he sounded passion to its depths, and raked the bottom of the gulf of sin; he explored, with the indomitable spirit of Carathis, every chamber and cavern of the earthly hell of bad delights.'

The Angel of the Odd

The story was first published in the *Columbian Magazine* in October 1844. It may be regarded as an attack on Blackwood and other writers who became famous for their accounts of horrible (and impossible) incidents. Poe seeks to instil in his readers a certain scepticism and, as the Angel calls it, a 'dispelief vat iz print in de print'.

1. (p. 176) Poe considered all of these works, which appeared between 1737 and 1844, as dull and somnolent.
2. (p. 176) The lines are from Cowper's *Task*, IV, 50–51.
3. (p. 177) Cocaigne is a humorous name for London, the home of the Cockneys.
4. (p. 178) A Hessian canteen is made of tinned iron, has a cylindrical body ($7\frac{3}{4}$ inches high and $5\frac{1}{4}$ wide) and a spout one inch high centered in the top.
5. (p. 180) The French translates, 'plenty of happiness and a little more good sense'. The original words of the archbishop in Le Sage's *Gil Blas* run 'toutes sortes de prospérité avec un peu de goût'.
6. (p. 181) Robert Montgomery's *Omnipresence of the Deity* (London, 1828) is famed for its dullness.

Thou Art the Man

This excellent parody of a detective story was published in *Godey's Lady's Book* in November 1844 and in Griswold's edition (1850). The latter text is printed here.

1. (p. 186) Cf. Romans 8:6, 'For to be carnally minded is death.'
2. (p. 192) *Cui bono* is from Cicero's oration *Pro Roscio Amerino*, XXX, 84. Poe explains the term correctly here.
3. (p. 192) Catherine Gore (1799–1861) published *Cecil* in 1841.
4. (p. 197) *Nem. con.* means 'without opposition'.
5. (p. 199) Popular superstition alleged that at the beginning of a plague the first victim buried was responsible for the victims to follow. The corpse was thought to sit *upright* in the coffin and gnaw at its shroud; until the meal was finished, others would die.

The System of Doctor Tarr and Professor Fether

The story was first published in *Graham's Magazine* in November 1845. The later publication in Griswold's edition (1850) is the basis of the text printed here. 'The System of Doctor Tarr and Professor Fether' is an ingenious combination of several topics of ridicule. Above all, one must regard it as a brilliant political satire, whose lasting message is veiled by the extravagant framework of the plot. On the surface the setting refers to a novel kind of medical treatment much in discussion in Poe's time. Poe himself was well informed about the so-called 'soothing system'. Dr Pliny Earle, a personal acquaintance of Poe's, had served as resident physician at the asylums of Frankford, Pennsylvania, and Bloomingdale, New York, where this treatment had been introduced. Instead of using chains and strait-jackets, the new system was based on mutual confidence and respect. An ardent advocate of this 'Moral Treatment' was Charles Dickens, and Poe's story must partly be understood as a direct parody of Dickens's idealistic conception. Beneath the surface, however, one can clearly perceive the idea of 'revolution' which is expressed in the actions of keepers and patients. Harold Beaver (*The Science Fiction of Edgar Allan Poe*, Penguin, 1976) suggests a parallel to the slavery system in the South of the United States. Indeed, the tarring and feathering in the story bears resemblance to the lynching of Negroes and Abolitionists in the Southern states. There is, however, much clearer reference to the French Revolution. An important source for the tale may have been the life of Marquis de Sade, which Poe certainly knew of to some extent. The Marquis, who became an inconvenient critic of the Revolution, was interned in the lunatic asylum of Charenton, where he was allowed to direct theater performances with the mad people as actors. Here he could openly express the ideas he was imprisoned for, in a world where everything was turned topsy-turvy.

1. (p. 205) *Maison de Santé* is a very ironical expression; only outsiders and madmen use the term.
2. (p. 206) Poe's allusions to Napoleon extend to Maillard's family. His sister has a monomania which manifests itself in the constant desire to strip in public. Her frivolity can be found in two of Napoleon's sisters – Elisa, who used to perform in pink tights on certain notorious Parisian stages (Emil Ludwig, *Napoleon*, Berlin, 1931), and Pauline, who created a great scandal when she allowed the sculptor Canova to immortalize her in the nude. As the 'Venus of Medici' is mentioned here, the latter source is more probable. The mourning-weeds are a hint at Pauline's widowhood after the death of General Leclerc.
3. (p. 208) The phrase translates, 'a monster fearful and hideous, vast and eyeless', and refers to Polyphemus (Virgil, *Aeneid* III, 658).
4. (p. 210) Lord Brougham, Lord Chancellor (1830–1834), one of the founders of the *Edinburgh Review* and of the University of London, was frequently attacked by Poe.
5. (p. 211) The old woman is of course France, symbolized by the Gallic cock.
6. (p. 214) Phalaris was a tyrant of Agrigentum in Sicily (*c.* 550 B.C.) who burnt his victims alive in a brazen bull.

Mellonta Tauta

'Mellonta Tauta' was first published in *Godey's Lady's Book* in February 1849. Prefixed to the original publication was the following letter:

Notes

Poe's vision of the future does not correspond with the spirit of Enlightenment which permeates other prophecies made in his time. Poe neither believed in an untroubled technical progress nor in a just and humane future society. The title phrase ('These things are in the future') is from the *Antigone* of Sophocles, line 1334.

1. (p. 220) The silk is named after James Silk Buckingham, an Egyptologist, who, while ascending the Nile to Nubia in 1813, narrowly escaped death by exposure in the desert.
2. (p. 221) Charles Fourier (1772–1837), a French social philosopher, argued that industrial communities must be reorganized as a *phalanx* (an economic commune of 1,620 people) living in a so-called phalanstery or community center.
3. (p. 222) This is a pun on Jean Pierre Blanchard, reputed inventor of the parachute. He took part in the first oversea voyage by air, crossing the English Channel by balloon (1785).
4. (p. 224) John Stuart Mill's *A System of Logic* (1843) is alluded to here.
5. (p. 227) 'Mob' is also referred to in 'Some Words with a Mummy' and 'The Thousand-and-Second Tale of Scheherazade'. This figure is the expression of Poe's great contempt for democracy and 'Man the mass'.
6. (p. 228) Johann Heinrich von Mädler (1794–1874).
7. (p. 230) 'Paradise' refers to Manhattan, which is 12¼ miles broad at its widest point, and bounded by the Hudson River, New York Bay, East River, and Harlem River.
8. (p. 230) Dietrich Knickerbocker was Washington Irving's pseudonym for his burlesque *History of New York* (1809).
9. (p. 231) The proponents of a 'suitable' monument had been trying to raise funds for this project since the beginning of a subscription list in 1843. The proposed location was Hamilton Square. Accompanied by elaborate ceremonies, a corner-stone was laid, but agreement was never reached on the design of the monument.
10. (p. 232) Zacchary Taylor, twelfth President of the United States, had been recently elected.

X-ing a Paragrab

'X-ing a Paragrab' was first printed in the *Flag of Our Union* (Boston) on 12 May 1849. In the same year it appeared in the Boston *Spanish Galleon*.

1. (p. 233) The wise men from the East are mentioned in the second chapter of St Matthew. Here the East means of course New England.
2. (p. 233) Touchandgo appears as a personal name in Thomas Love Peacock's *Crotchet Castle* (1831).
3. (p. 233) The reference is to the argument in Orestes Augustus Brownson's novel *Charles Elwood, or The Infidel Converted* (1840).
4. (p. 233) Nopolis means 'no city'.
5. (p. 234) The expressions 'fiery' and 'salamander' appear as well in *Twice-Told Tales*: ' "It becometh not a divine to be of a fiery and salamandrine spirit." ' The quotation by Lord Coke is used to illustrate Poe's contempt for 'the cultivated old clergymen of the *North American Review*', who, in his opinion, fear nothing more than 'being moved', never move themselves.
6. (p. 234) The commonplace runs, of course, *O tempora, o mores* (from Cicero's first oration against Catiline).
7. (p. 235) Frogpondium was Poe's name for Boston. The Frog Pond is still a feature of Boston Common.
8. (p. 235) The quotation is from Shakespeare's *Richard III*, act IV, scene iv: 'Off with his head. So much for Buckingham.'
9. (p. 235) Concord, Massachusetts, was the home of Emerson, Alcott, and other Transcendentalists.
10. (p. 239) Ale marked XXX is of excellent quality.